riding the
dolphin

riding the dolphin

Amanda Thomas

A NOVEL

A PETER WEED BOOK
Beaufort Books Publishers
New York

Copyright © 1987 by Amanda Thomas

Library of Congress Cataloging-in-Publication Data

Thomas, Amanda.
  Riding the dolphin.

  "A Peter Weed book."
  I. Title.
PS3570.H54R5   1987   813'.54   87–1049
ISBN 0–8253–0427–X

Published in the United States by Beaufort Books Publishers, New York.

Designed by Irving Perkins Associates

Printed in the U.S.A.   /   First Edition

10   9   8   7   6   5   4   3   2   1

riding the
dolphin

In all probability it's October. Mid October. I guess it could possibly be September. Or November even. I don't know. All I know is today I am starting a journey of ten thousand thousand miles and I'm not packed yet. That crucial point—*I have not started to pack*—I scrawl in my journal in large loopy letters without proper endings. M says I wrote better when I was in fifth grade. I am now 24 (going on 16, D says), which would put me in about the nineteenth grade if it worked that way, which it doesn't. Not that much in life is logical, which is logical, yes no?

Paula comes in and stands there. "I've got something for you," she says. A little something, she actually says. Underplays everything, that's my sister for you. When I don't reach out for it, whatever it is, to tell the truth it doesn't look that great, she puts it beside me on the bed, the little something, wrapped in paper with upside down umbrellas, which I realize many light years later is left over from one of her bridal showers. Paula is 22. Paula is getting married. Not me. I wouldn't consider it.

Paula likes to save gift wrap, smooth out the creases, and peel off the slicks of Scotch tape. She's frugal, Paula is, like M in a way. The world could be falling apart, the ultimate MX spurting out of its silo toward Siberia or Santa Barbara or wherever and they would still save the rubber band from the morning paper just in case. Talk about weird!

Paula is dressed for work—long black skirt, white linen jacket, mouse-colored stockings, sling pumps, bridge toll dollar at the ready. Miss Ritzy Titzy Glitzy. She has smooth honey-colored hair and a smooth honey-colored job at Dean Witter selling deferred something.

Gratification maybe. She puts a hand on my head, at least I think it's a hand she puts. "Bam," I say. I am still thinking nuclear.

She'll call me, first chance she gets. I probably don't know my number yet, but she'll get it from the folks. Paula has one of those fragile high-intensity necks, you can see everything going on, throb, throb.

She waits, her non-impact aerobics shoes in a vari-colored string bag in one hand, her little skinny-thigh yogurt in a baggie in the other.

"Did you put raisins in?"

"In where?"

Where would she think? "In your left shoe, in your Nike."

She looks pained, which she often does when I speak.

"Just kidding." Which I am. I am being, for me, very agreeable. Kindly. "In the yogurt," I say for utmost clarity.

She frowns, appearing to consider the matter seriously, like she's Ralph Nader or Spinoza or somebody. "No, not this time," she says.

"What kind is it anyway?"

"Peach."

"Peach." I repeat it. I don't know why, I guess I just feel like talking.

We'll go to a movie or something, she says. Over the weekend maybe.

Yah sure, Paula. It would be a piece of cake to do CPR on Paula— when she's keyed up there's this flutter in her neck tells you right off where the pulse is.

"What are you looking at?"

"Nothing. You can sit down if you want." I consider moving my foot but don't.

"No, I've got to buzz," she says, but she stands there for three hot intolerable seconds. The yellow plastic tail of the wall cat clock we got with Blue Chip stamps when I was in fourth grade swipes right, left, right. I close my eyes. See you, kiddo, she says.

M shows up, stands in the doorway. I'm getting popular in my old age. You should really eat something, she says, you should have you a good breakfast. She has on a necklace I once gave her—one of those metal circlets you see African women wearing. But on her it doesn't look right, it doesn't lay flat. I don't think I ever saw her with it on before.

D appears in the doorway behind her. What's coming off, an earthquake drill?

You should have something in your stomach, he says, which he always says. He thinks something in the stomach will weight you down, keep you from soaring.

"What are you doing home?" I say. "What's he doing here?" They look at each other. I mean, how many does it take to run me over there? The whole PLO?

The phone is ringing. Chirping, actually. They have one of those made-in-Hong-Kong jobs that sounds like a bird. Ten bucks at Phone Mart. But it isn't a bird. It's M's friend Ceci, Ceci Hazeltine Schroeder. She used to be just Cecile Hazeltine way back there. But Mr. Hazeltine dropped dead on the tenth green at Pebble Beach and she dropped the *le* off of Cecile and married Mr. Schroeder who she went to to financial plan what to do with Mr. Hazeltine's insurance with. (There's an extra *with* in there somewhere but let's not sweat it.) M thinks it was Fate, what with the yellow pages loaded to the eyeballs with financial planners, meaning what made her go out of her way to sign up with Leland Schroeder in El Cerrito on a rainy day? I can tell it's Ceci by M's tone. Ceci is the only one M ever talks to, really talks to.

She won't eat, M says, and she isn't packed. This really winkles me off. It's not that I *won't* eat. It's just that I haven't happened to eat. Or pack. I debate about putting on my jellies or my thongs— I'm not into decisions—and going downstairs. Shit—there's only one pearly pink jelly to be found. So I clop around for a while in my thongs with the rainbow on the platform part and a blue grosgrain caret between the toes. Then I hit the kitchen and fix myself two peanut butter with butter sandwiches and an ingot of German chocolate cake. When we were little, Paula and I would make it a point to always leave the littlest smidgin on the plate. This time I take it all. My grand final finale. She's eating, M says in a whisper. I cart everything out to the patio and dig my heels into the plastic slats of the chaise, which is something I like to do, it keeps you slotted in. I finish off with a Granny Smith apple and a guzzle of milk from the carton.

While I'm out there trying to decide whose granny Granny Smith is or was as well as other considerations, such as will I barf or not, they decide to pack me. I hear their voices conferring softly. They'll wrap my cameras in the Hudson Bay blanket. They won't take any of the pill bottles without caps.

"It's time," D says nervously when I come back. His hair is splashed with gray and it's wavy like wet sand. "It's getting to be time," he says. I can hear the washer chugging fervently in the utility room.

"You want to start off with everything clean," M says.

Apparently we were both thinking *washer*. We used to do that a lot, think the same stuff. Now we don't any more.

What she is actually saying, she is actually saying two different things. She wants things clean all right, so she will not be incorrectly judged by the denizens of where I'm going. But *to start off with* carries its own seeds of prophecy: things will not stay clean; I will not keep them clean, I will become dirty, but by then it will be out of her hands and clear to all that she is helpless, without blame in the matter. Half of life is stepping over puddles of guilt, or landing in them (that's the other half).

Their big soft brown nylon suitcase is open in the middle of my room with its elastic destination petals flapping, LAX, SF, HON, MAN, and the absurd bow of lilac yarn that makes it instantly recognizable thumping down the baggage carousel, a refugee from a parade of why-did-you-ruin-it family vacations.

Paula's little something occupies five inches in the lower right-hand corner. If they were not there hovercrafting over every move

I make or don't make, I might shake it, just to see if it rattles or gurgles or thunks.

I see they have also packed my pills, Mellaril and Kenadrin. They sound like Shakespearean characters or visitors from a strange planet, which they kind of are. Kenadrin counteracts the Mellaril which presumably counteracts me.

And sheets, the old stained ones, the camp sheets, not the seven-flower jobs from Neiman's that M puts on the guest bed when Jake, Paula's about-to-be, stays over. He's a municipal bond broker and part owner of a family business in Brazil so naturally the folks think he's one hot tamale, and he and Paula have all this cutesy common stock business in common.

Churning in the porthole froth of the washer are the last-minute dredgings from under my bed—bikini peelings, a stray sock, my Kauai the Garden Island T-shirt—a cleansing rite of M's. They will not make it in their pilgrimage through the sultry wasteland of the dryer before I start mine. To Camelot. That's what it's called, no shit, Camelot House, Cam House, C House.

M looks in. I can tell she would really like the sheets out from under me, so they can begin their journey to the linen closet, smoothly layered there like so many silent prayer books. Not being a yanker, she settles for waiting it out.

Ceci calls again. We're getting there, M says. She had a sandwich. "Two" I say, but as usual nobody hears me. And you were right, Ceci, she had the cake. The German chocolate one from Cocolat.

Let's hear it for Ceci. Let's not.

I hate this crappy room—it's somebody's medieval idea—they should go ahead and put it in a time capsule. How to turn out a flounce. White French provincial furniture brushed with fairy tale gold and plastic tops that nothing can mar, not even tears. Every fucking thing matches every other fucking thing—the desk, the hutch, the canopy bed, the dresser, the mirror. So why not me? Why don't I match every other fucking kid that learned to masturbate French provincial style?

One of the bureau drawers is skewed, off its track. Something's wedged back there, I forget what, maybe a leg warmer, and the other ones are open with stuff spewing out. I can't wait to see the last of this.

I curl up on my bed, on *the* bed, knees drawn up in my isolette, warmed by brash patches of sun planting itself wherever it chooses, on a breast, a thigh. My right elbow is probably on fire. I should really check. Instead I sleep. When I wake up the washer is becalmed and D is disconnecting my record player. He wraps the cord around the black oysters of a headphone. "Don't you think you better think about getting dressed?" He starts to put the Timex alarm in the suitcase. It's an hour off he says, three o'clock when it's really two. I tell him not to worry, it's three o'clock somewhere and it'll be okay locally once we go off daylight savings again. "This is the first week in October, Mary Alice," he says. Apparently it *is* October. Just as I suspected.

D looks sad that it's October. "We don't go off daylight saving till the end of the month," he says. It's like he expects an argument. "Okay, okay, okay," I say, I won't fight it, whatever makes them happy.

The suitcase by now contains an epithalamium of underwear I have never seen before, well, never been in anyway. Paula also has a new batch, but hers is from Wedding Belles, couture lingerie custom monogrammed. M's idea as regards moi is that I should have a bunch of fresh-start stuff. You like the double cotton crotch? the saleslady at Little Daisy said. That's a good question, I said, which it was, except nobody ever comes right out and says something's a bad question so therefore saying it's a good question is not all that much of a compliment, right? Do you know, does she like the double cotton crotch? the saleslady finally asked M. I left for a smoke.

I reach down and dabble a hand in. Apparently I like a double cotton crotch. Protectopussy? I think I might even have said that, back there when they were squeezing the bejesus out of M's MasterCard in the machine at Little Daisy.

"Look out now." D zips the suitcase, stands it by the door. One of the little pseudopods the thing stands on has come off and it sits lopsided. I dredge a pompommed footie out of my tennis shoe and ram my toes in, leaving the laces flapping. Hey, bright blue stars on the side, I never noticed that before. Maybe because I don't play tennis, although I suppose if I played tennis I would be watching the ball, only knowing me, I wouldn't be. That makes sense, doesn't it? It computes, that's what Paula says. She has all these clever sayings.

My left foot steps on my right foot's laces, which grounds me. Clearly M wants to tie them, but she can't, doesn't. It would be the world's simplest thing, so satisfying to her, to just reach down there and tie them, but she knows she's not supposed to. She is wearing dark glasses. She does that with situations involving me, the dark-glasses daughter, when she thinks she's vulnerable.

I watch D load my patchwork bunny hop sleeping sack with the squared-off bottom which you are supposed to sit and read in only I never did. It looks funny fluffed there in the back window of the station wagon. "Will you be able to see all right?" M says to D, who grunts. She's carrying a barbecued chicken in a foil-lined bag and a box of cookies she made to help ace me in with my peer group at Cam House.

The right front fender of the Volvo is crumpled, accusing, beginning to spot rust.

"Why didn't you go and get it fixed?"

"We have to get three bids," D says.

"Triple A is sending the adjuster out Monday," M says. "Mr. Hanson," she adds.

It seems a long time ago I had my recorded conversation with Mr. Hanson in which I explained every little thing. How I came to this crossing with Bank of America on the corner. The south corner? Mr. Hanson said. I don't know about that, I said. B. of A. was on your right was it when you went to make your turn onto the frontage road? I tried to explain it didn't matter where B. of A. was. It was the truck that mattered, the truck with slanted sides of glass that trapped the sun. A Chevy, Mr. Hanson inserted into the middle of our bleeping conversation. From Continental Glass and Sash in Oakland. I explained patiently about the refracted light, the ray beams that siphoned out my thoughts, splintered them into bright rainbow shards there on the pavement. And about walking through the crunch in my white sandals, getting a cut on my little toe, a bright berry of blood. What was the weather condition? I don't know, average, I said, but it was my left foot. I remember saying that to aid in the investigation. The brakes didn't work? Mr. Hanson interrupted. Is that what it came down to? They went out on you? I don't know. You don't know? No, see, I didn't try them that particular time, there was all this light. You were blinded by the sun, Mr. Hanson said heartily, he made it sound like a myth, but then Triple A went and canceled our insurance anyway. Schmucks.

"Okay, hop in," D is saying, as if I was, were, some kind of rabbit.

But I can't stand the hot stale Volvo breath.

"Wait, I've got to take a picture."

They look at each other. They're always looking at each other.

"Don't you think you have enough pictures?" D says.

"No, I don't think." I am busy rooting out the cameras from the Hudson Bay blanket. I take pictures of myself like other people weigh themselves, to see if I've changed. I have two cameras, a Nikon 3 and a Polaroid 600SE. I keep the Polaroid prefocused to where if I sit in what I call the King Kong chair, the wicker one with the flared back, and I put the camera on the bamboo table with the glass top in the sun porch, all I have to do is hold the 20-foot air release bulb to trip the shutter.

In a couple of minutes this face I hardly recognize but am eagerly waiting for swims up out of the wet Polaroidal blur—dark questioning eyes, they're the focal point, thick black brows. Well all right! When people talk about beauty, you don't too often hear mention of eyebrows, which to my way of thinking can be your

most important feature. Eyebrows give definition, substance to a
face, they oversee everything. And they convey stuff—surprise, a
question, doubt. How many breasts which people make such a big
deal of have you seen do that? Any of it? Paula's eyebrows are little
plucked croquet wickets, whereas mine are full, responsive. I can
even raise one—the left—without the other. I can cock, knit,
furrow . . .

"Mary Alice!"

Okay, okay. . . . Straight utilitarian nose shaped like a sail, half
smile, framed by a dark eddy of freshly uncombed hair. Hair like
those Chinese rice sticks that swell up in hot grease. Yesterday's
eyes were flat, day before that's, dreamy. The nose is the same, an
is-now-and-ever-shall-be doxology of a nose, the brows—

He's coming in. "Come on, let's go," D says. "It's time." High
time, he usually says, whatever that is. A high old time. I smile.

I go back upstairs, look around for stuff I've missed, gather up
an armload of crud—my journal, my would-have-been prom dress,
yes? no, yes. A dime from the floor, the orange corduroy wedge
pillow M thinks is too dirty to bring but I don't. Think, agree,
concur, assent.

I run my hand along the welt of the pillow till I find the little
hole I know is there, the one I poked with a cuticle stick. I push
back a little cotton. This pillow is stuffed with me, my tears, my
frayed thoughts pounded into it like a pepper steak, my head's spot.

"All set now?"

I can't leave it. "Si, señor."

"Does she want you to take that?" He says *she* in this embarrassed
way—they quit calling each other Mom and Dad a million years
ago, like they abdicated or something.

"It's okay," I say.

I flop down in back of the station wagon, which I might as well,
they being a bear on me smoking in the car. We slide out of the
driveway in our edgy hierarchy, M giving her artful dodger advice—
Careful, I think the Bixbys are going to pull out—D saying Do

you want to drive, Francine? Do you want to drive the car? It's rhetorical, but M doesn't catch on. No, Glenn, I don't want to drive the car, I just don't want us to have an accident. They're really cranked up. Not me. I am calm as the door handle or ricotta or dead birds.

My bottom teeth are roped together by coconut strands from the German chocolate cake. It's a mildly interesting sensation. D twiddles the radio. A commercial for the Hartz two-in-one flea collar. Kills fleas and ticks while it glows in the dark and protects your pet from oncoming headlights. Kills fleas and ticks if they get hit by a car, D says. No one laughs so he says ha ha.

M starts pointing out the sights along the Nimitz Freeway, providing stimulation. Chrysanthemums! Will you look at that mass of mums!

No thanks.

"And candytuft," she says later. "See there, that white patch?" But I'm not seeing there, I'm flipping the lid of the ashtray. "Do you think we should stop for something? Stop for a treat?" she says. "Glenn?"

"I don't know. Ask her," he says.

"Do you want anything, Mary Alice? Do you want some ice cream?"

I'm thinking. I'm full up to here with peanut butter, cake, etsoforth, but on the one hand ice cream is ice cream. On the other hand, I don't want to bite on their bait, but then on the other other hand, there is the consideration that any pit stop is a delaying action, not that I want to delay, it's just another factor to dwell on. All this stuff to be netted out, it begins to weigh on me, they know I don't like decisions.

"I guess she doesn't," D says. "We'd better just keep moving, get her installed, get it over and done with."

"I don't care," I say. "Makes-a-no-matta me."

"She says she doesn't care," M says.

"I heard her."

A cement truck with shamrocks on the side passes us. Leprechauns on board?

"Well maybe we should," M says. "It might be nice."

"Suit yourself, but make up your mind before we have to pick up the MacArthur Freeway."

Back and forth. And they call me immature!

"Let's stop at Baskin Robbins on Rockridge," M says. "It can't hurt anything."

A mother and toddler in a supermarket basket are sharing a cone, which is unsanitary, you could catch things from babies, roseola, a runny nose.

"They have fresh peach," M says.

"Or jamaica almond fudge," D says.

"Jamoca," M says.

"She used to like that."

They apparently think my taste buds, being part of my head, are also impaired.

"I'll have coffee on the bottom and blueberry praline on top."

"We're all out of the blueberry praline," the girl says. I may well have gone to high school with her. Maybe not. She looks like somebody anybody might well have gone to high school with, long straight ash-blond hair, rimless glasses that would have flashed light if I hadn't backed off in time, an eager-to-please smile.

"It says blueberry praline up there."

"Yes, but they're all out of the blueberry praline," D says. "You heard her say they're out of that particular flavor."

"We have blueberry cheesecake," the girl says.

"You want blueberry cheesecake?" D says.

The girl looks at me, glitters her glasses at me. I wander off, light a cigarette. Thirty-One Flavors does false advertising, they could be sued. Taken to court. Given 39 licks. I smile.

"They're out of blueberry praline," D says, summing up. "Give her the blueberry cheesecake." He's really pushing it. He sounds exasperated. Who's he mad at? Me? Her? The girl who is running her metal scoop around the edges of a vat swirled with chocolate, mounding the shavings back in the center? Maybe he's mad at Baskin. Or Robbins.

"She might rather have the rum raisin," M says. "Would you like the rum raisin? Or how about marshmallow pistachio delight?"

The girl dips the scoop in water and waits. I pluck a Mudslide from the Special Occasions counter that also has a cake with a green football on it. Mudslides are crappo chocolate cookies glued together with chocolate butter cream, almond paste, and vanilla ice cream. They're not all that bad.

"That do ya?" D says in his steady provider voice.

"Sure," I say. "It fixes everything."

"I could no more eat that much chocolate," M says.

We sit in a row, three crows in black ice cream chairs with broad paddle arms. Someone has carved Gina on mine, but my name is Tiffani now. It was Mary Alice once, but I changed over. At the time I was planning to move to Terre Haute, Indiana, but I never got around to it. A name like Tiffani, you have to have a place that matches up to base your life on.

"Paula says we should give some thought to investing in Dreyer's Grand Ice Cream," D says. "It's over the counter." He waits for a reaction, gives up.

I can tell M has got the pain she gets between her eyes from eating cold stuff. She closes her eyes, makes a fist around a Kleenex she's clutching, waits for it to pass. She is missing her right earring. What she does, she takes it off to talk on the phone and forgets. I forget things too, but I don't talk on the phone all that much.

"Your chin," D whispers at me like I have AIDS or something. "You're dripping." M gets more napkins. She looks at my chin. Her mind goes on WIPE, but she resists temptation. I am watching the mama with the kid in the shopping cart, one bite apiece, rocky road it looks like, nobody cheating, and then when they're done, she cleans it with her spit while the kid tries to dodge. "Oh

HARRISONBURG
MANUFACTURING DIVISION
PRODUCT IDENTIFICATION

BEAUFORT BOOKS   JOB NO: 45400

RIDING THE DOLPHIN   ·   NEW TITLE

JIM OPPY   JUDITH WELLING
****
785   5 1/2 X 8 1/4   336 PAGES

BODY STOCK: 384 PPI CR/WT SEBAGO

COPY TYPE: REPRO
****

JACKETS   FURN

****
BIND STYLE   PATENT-BOUND
****
SAMPLES SELECTED BY:

DATE:

7-24-87

youuuuuu!" she says, and I wish she was talking to me, that I was that baby.

I don't want the rest of my Mudslide, which was billed as the world's richest ice cream cookie and is the world's shittiest.

"We better get going," D says.

"Let her finish," M says.

"Maybe she doesn't want to. She's just messing with it."

We pass a sign that says WELCOME TO WEST HAMILTON, pop. 6021.

"Six thousand twenty-one people," M says. "Golly."

"Six thousand twenty-two now," D says. I knew he would say that.

Camelot House is in West Hamilton, which is near Walnut Creek, which is near Concord, which is not that far from Oakland, which is forget it.

"Well, folks, here we is," D says, jovial as a department store Santa Claus. We have previously driven by C House, squinted up at it and remarked—some of us—on its presumed advantages. I did the squinting and M, D, and Paula the remarking. Near the bus line. In an okay district. Not that far away as the crow flies. (Just who's this crow? I said.) But to date we have not been inside.

It's old. Two storey. Clapboard. Peeling paint. Victorian was how Miriam Myers from the West Hamilton Community Mental Health Center (WHCMHC), known in the trade as Wookmook, described it. With consumers à la myself, she also refers to it as a Group Home.

The front lawn is plowed up. The concrete steps are cracked. There's a piece of pipe that serves as a rusted iron railing. A purple bra is hooked to an upstairs window, drying I suppose, or maybe it's the Cam House flag.

In front a kitten is chasing a leaf. "Look at him go, Tiffani!" M says enthusiastically. "Did you see that kitten?" Little pansy face I expect her to say, but she does the unexpected and doesn't. She's looking at the house next door, at the two little kids sitting on the porch. "Izzat your kitty?" M asks. "We can't—" the little boy says. "We're not supposed to talk to those ones in the nut house," the little girl says. "C'mon, Justin." M looks stricken. "Thanks a bunch," I say. They go inside.

Miriam-Mental-Health-Myers is supposed to be there to show us around, orientate us is how she put it, but I don't see her. I sight through the open end of the pipe like it's a telescope, making a cameo of the front door, which D is now knocking on. I give a few trial huffs to see if the pipe echoes. "Just look at you, you've got a big circle around your eye," M says. She hands me a Kleenex as Miriam Myers advances on us, distorted through the beveled glass pane by the front door. Short and widespread until she fumbles the bolt, opens the door, and assumes her normal proportions. Which is still short and widespread.

"I've left the car in the driveway," D says.

"That's fine, no problem," Miriam Myers says. She smiles a no-problem smile.

"That's rust," M is saying, "we didn't give her a black eye."

"Mind if we start getting her unloaded?"

"Sure, go ahead," Miriam Myers says. "Her room is on the second floor, the one on the end. I'll get Tiffani checked out on the kitchen."

M and D start carrying boxes. "This is your space in the refrigerator, Tiffani." Miriam Myers moves an ivory rectangle of tofu from my space. I am calm as tofu, that's another thing I am calm as. I'm watching M to see if she is going to drop one of my speakers. "Are you with me, Tiffani?" I come back to the business at hand. There are two lemon halves that look mentally ill. The refrigerator blithers back on, as though it's self-conscious being looked at. It's one of the old kind, rounded, with its motor or something squatting on top, ice scalloped over pipes and a freezer door that doesn't seem to want to shut all the way. You probably couldn't keep ice cream.

"There's a Quik Stop on the corner and then there's a Safeway

three blocks over in the shopping center, okay?" Safeway, everything
you want in a store and a little bit more. Why would you want
more than you want? This is an interesting philosophical question
which some corporate gadfly should pose at the annual shareholders'
meeting. I start to explain this to Miriam Myers but she isn't there
any more. Nobody is. I'm left standing like an arctic explorer in
this bleak white place.

I start up the stairs. They creak. I stop. The whole place has a
saturated old-house smell, a cassoulet of grass, urine, mildew, cab-
bage, cats, cigarettes, tears, sex, or maybe it's just coriander. I'm
not too sure what sex smells like, but I think it's like coriander.
The Chinese use a lot of coriander. China has sixty billion people.
You figure it out.

We are all standing on the stairs. I wonder if there is a load limit
like on the San Mateo Bridge. "Coming?" D says. He's clutching
the patchwork bed sack under one arm and my Nikon in the other
hand.

"That's called a crazy quilt," I say.

Miriam Myers half smiles, looks at M.

The stairs have that variegated go-ahead-spill-anything carpet,
raveling away from black tacks at the edges. If you step down hard
dust swirls around your shoes. M wants to say don't do that, I can
tell.

Our procession gets going. We pass an open door, a bed with
the soles of bare daytime feet sticking out of the covers. There being
generally no hair on the soles of the feet, unless maybe you're a
werewolf, I can't tell the sex of the owner.

"Don't they all do something during the day?" M asks Miriam
Myers in what I think is called a stage whisper. "Doesn't everybody
have to do something? Have an activity?"

"Right. It's a house rule, they have to have a structured activity
from 9 to 3, but sometimes somebody just needs a quiet day to get
things sorted out."

"This it?" D says, planting a box so it keeps the door from swinging shut. "This is really something, a corner room, Mary Alice. Cross ventilation."

"Just what I always wanted."

It suffers from battered room syndrome, a montage of peeling wallpaper—roses on top of fans on top of painted-over stars—a gouge in the plaster, a ceiling bulb on a chain, a leak in the shape of a starfish, pits in the wall where stuff was hung, where it still hangs in pale phantom blocks, some silver thumbtacks, a portable cardboard closet with a little gold ring you put your finger in to slide the door. I put my finger in but it doesn't slide.

"Must be something in the track," D says. "We'll free it up for you in half a shake."

A wood-grained formica bureau, bright metal pulls in the shape of tildes, and a mirror that has leaked black amoebas around the edges. The mercury eaten away by decades of desperate reflection? Then there's the bed. It has a bookcase headboard that must have come from a different size bed, so that taken together they form a T. Roll it and pat it and mark it with T, and put it in the oven for Tiffani and me.

God I'm tired. I throw myself stomach first on the mattress, which has a gully down the middle like the Colorado River. A naked mattress is a very gruesome thing, I don't care where you are. This one is stained out of its mind. "Why don't you get up and we'll go ahead and put fresh sheets on," M says urgently.

"It's been fumigated," Miriam Myers says.

"Fumigated?" M says weakly. It's a buzz word that spirals round us like a bee. "Was there someone . . . did the person . . . ?" she can't get her question out. She probably can't even isolate it, pluck it out of the confusion. AIDS? Herpes? Hepatitis? The Black Death? Fleas? "Get up," she says.

"It's okay," I say.

"Quite a place," D says.

This strikes me as funny so I laugh.

Miriam Myers and M are talking. "And that one. How long has

he been here?" M points to Feet across the hall. How does she know it's a he? The big toe probably. It's large, like on a male lobster.

"I can't tell you exactly. A year and a half maybe. I came to WHCMHC it'll be a year in January and Geoffrey was here then," Miriam Myers says.

"Well how long do most of them stay, would you say?" and it comes to me for the first time, I'm one of *them*. I don't live with M and D and Paula any more.

"It's really impossible to say," Miriam Myers is saying. "You just can't hardly generalize, it's all so much on the individual. People move through the system at their own pace, some this is just the thing to get them going."

M says something about a genuine opportunity.

There are five people in the house at the present time, Miriam Myers says, two men and three women, including Tiffani. All of them, like Tiffani here, have made the decision to come to C House.

Decision? Can you make decisions if you don't have choices? I was invited to leave home. It just isn't working out, Mary Alice, was the phraseology. You need to be more on your own, we won't be around forever, gas like that.

Cam House is run by its residents, Miriam Myers explains. Matters affecting the house are decided by democratic vote. There are house meetings every Wednesday with staff present, but there is no in-house staff person because the residents of C House are functioning at that high of a level.

The bare feet across the hall haven't moved, never mind how high a level their owner is cracking along at. I am tired of inhaling mattress and I turn my head to one side.

"Don't you want to help your dad bring in your things?" Miriam Myers says.

"It's okay, he can do it," I say.

"Well, I'll let you get settled," Miriam Myers says. "If you need anything, or have any questions I'll be at Serendipity House over in Emeryville the rest of the day."

D has planted the brown suitcase in the middle of the floor just the way he did at home. At their place, I should say. I mean, I've been booted out, never mind the purple prose about Growth and Independence. It's fucksville. "You wouldn't stay here," I say to M, who has retreated behind her dark glasses.

"It'll look different when you get settled, get your things stashed around."

"You want me to go ahead and hook up your record player for you?" D says.

"Why don't you?" M says.

"Why don't you just let her say if she wants it," D says. "Instead of all the time answering for her, goddamit."

Usually this means that in a minute they'll be fighting, not fighting exactly, just pelting each other with small gray squabble, like pieces of shit in the monkey house. But not today, in deference to The Big Move.

"You can even see the U.C. campanile sticking up there in the distance," M says.

"Lucky me," I say.

"I told you she has her a nice view. Let's open the window, get her some fresh air in here." D bats the window up with the heel of his palm, "There." He wipes his hand with a handkerchief.

I would very much like to take a nap.

"Where's the bathroom?" M says. "We don't even know where the bathroom is, she didn't think to show us the bathroom."

"You want to see your bathroom?" D says.

"No, I want to take a nap, you can if you want. Anyway it's not my bathroom."

"Well, I guess it's communal, you're right there, to a certain extent. It's everybody's, you'll have to pitch in and do your share to keep it up," D says. "Come on, Francine, she can unpack at her leisure and we can get the suitcase back another time." He's getting antsy.

M and I look at each other. "Don't you want to find the bathroom?" It's like she's pleading or something. My first day at kindergarten I screamed when M left, lay on the cork floor and kicked my new Stride Rite feet. Just go quickly, Miss Sanderson said, but even then M didn't know enough not to keep looking back.

"Just so you'll know where it is," M is saying.

"Okay," I say finally. I sit up, shake my head, ream out an ear.

It's two doors down, is where it is. Everything in it is white or aspiring white—high gloss wood-paneled walls with prominent grooves and dark places where the paint didn't get to, hexagonal dirt-grimed floor tiles, a high punched-out ceiling, a window held open by a chain, a big tub on legs, a stopper with a chain that has bled rust. I don't know it at the time but this room will play a decisive role in my life.

"That tub must be a hundred years old," M is saying. "If it's a day." A preposterous comment which is, however, accepted without challenge by the functional world. "Don't you think it's probably a hundred years old, Glenn?"

"Couldn't be the original fixtures," D says. "I doubt very much, I seriously doubt it's the original fixtures." He's probing the inside of the toilet tank for a date.

"Wouldn't an antique dealer give his eye teeth to get ahold of that though?" M says. "It's a knockout."

"Maybe that's an antique dealer, the one in bed with the feet," I say. "The tub bowled him over, knocked him out."

"Got it, 1926," D says, "that's about right." He puts the top back on the tank.

Along the counter below the medicine chest amber pill bottles are lined up. M picks up one. "Don't!" I say. She puts it back. It's like for a microsecond she's the child.

A blue velour robe is hanging inside out on a hook on the back of the bathroom door. "Magnin's, it's from Magnin's," M says. She flushes, knowing it's an idiotic comment.

"Come on," D says, "it's time." But they just stand there, we just stand there, all three of us. What am I doing in the john with my two parents? It's obscene, it's practically incest, three-way incest. "I have to use it," I say, "the facilities."

"Awright," D says. He claps a hand on my shoulder. "See you round." This time they leave.

It's good in a way because nobody ever says goodbye in a bathroom. Have you heard of anyone saying goodbye in the bathroom? I lock the door behind them. Once I hear their feet on the stairs I come out. I stand to the side of the window with the great view and the U.C. campanile sticking up. I don't want them to know I'm looking at them. Their hands are barely touching, like clumsy adolescents. They stop halfway down the broken cement steps. M pulls away and looks back up—I knew it!—shading her hidden dark-glasses eyes, but she can't possibly see me. If I called to her, she might come back, but I don't. She might not anyway.

The kitten again. It rubs against her legs like it's thanking her for another day, like she personally gave him October the whatever, kibbled it up just for him. She scoops him up, holds that boneless fluff till it nestles against her. "It shouldn't be so close to the street," M says. She looks apprehensively at the house next door.

"Put it down, Francine, it knows what it's doing," D says.

Yah, I want to yell, it'll take care of itself! but I don't want them to know I'm even up there where they left me. There's really nothing between us any more. I lean my chin on my arm on the sill with the upside down dead flies. That's when I see the face in the dormer window of the house next door. It's behind a white lace curtain and it's watching me. A woman's face. It's a hundred percent not friendly.

I give a little wave.

The face retreats, but a hand still holds the curtain. It gives me an anxious twinge. Maybe I should take my Mellaril.

I look across the hall. "Feet?" I say very softly—Miriam Myers said his name but I forget what she said. "Listen, Feet . . . " I say, keeping to my doorway so I can retreat if necessary. No answer. I was planning to tell Feet about the face in the window but it's no use.

I wonder if M is crying. She wears dark glasses when she thinks she might. There's a leaden lump in the middle of me, a chocolate Mudslide depression.

I lie down. They give you this brochure that explains C House, it's there on the blue desk beside the bed.

Camelot House is set up to accommodate a special population of young adults with some degree of mental dysfunction, who do not require on-site supervision and who are thought to be capable of responding to the challenge of a democratically run Group Home in the community.

Three hots and a cot it's called. I fan myself with the brochure. Once you're in the system you become a special population. That's right up there with goals. You've got to have goals or you've got to call what you *do* have goals, that's the scam. There's a silhouette on the back of a some-degree dysfunctional man and woman in jeans striding man and womanfully up a hill that is supposedly life.

The typical C House resident is 25.2 years old, became ill in late adolescence, and was diagnosed between ages 18 and 25. Most but not all residents are on anti-psychotic or neuroleptic medications and all must be seen on a regular basis by a licensed therapist.

Then come the house rules, a minimum of house rules, it says. Residents may not smoke in the bedrooms. Residents must participate in household chores with rotating assignments. Residents must attend weekly house meetings. No controlled substances other than those prescribed by physicians are permitted. No sexual relations between house members, no overnight guests.

I check for the face in the window. It isn't there. I toss the brochure back on the blue desk where I found it. One of the things they don't bother saying is that Cam House is somebody else's idea for you, which they then endeavor by some emotional ventriloquism to make seem your idea, your Decision.

At this time, or point in time as they say, I eat the cookies M made for everybody. Be sure to share them with Everybody. They're the good old camp cookies all right, the ones she used to send to

Paula and I when we went to Arturo Morales' tennis camp in Carmel Valley that was supposed to equip you for gracious serves in Suburbia. The cookies are mainly cinnamon stars but thank God there are a few butter pecan mixed in. The way you make the butter pecan, you roll them into marbles and then squash them down with a glass and put tine marks with the back of a fork. I was the smasher and Paula did the fork number. I eat them till I feel yucky (which is what I used to do at camp too) and an ant starts crawling on me, patroling for crumbs.

I decide to open Paula's present. Something on a cord that says Audubon Society. I put it around my neck, tweet like an oriole, and wait for the birds.

Nothing.

Okay, fuck you.

Maybe it's an Audubon rape whistle. You sound the alarm and all those types with Life Lists who scrunch around in waders start rescuing you. Or stand there with their binoculars leering, I don't know. I adjust my whistle for the wood warbler and give a good blast.

Suddenly there's another face in the people-next-door's window. A man's. He waggles a threatening finger at me. I put the whistle away and close the shade.

I plug in the old black and white TV from the den they let me have. Niente. I guess it needs an aerial, but I leave it on anyway. It's something there humming, trying to get through to me, letting the light of its featureless countenance shine on me.

It's getting dark. The vibes are piss poor. Come on, I say to myself, let's not get all paranoid. It's only a face in the window. Two faces.

ii It's night. Dark grungy dirty-teeth long-toenails away-from-home nightmare night. I must have slept some. A moment ago I was riding a dolphin. Somebody, something—M? D? the figures in the window next door?—hoisted me onto its slick dime-gray back. Dolphins are friendly, they say, trying to trick me. You'll see, they say. No, not yet, don't let go, I'm not ready! But I'm launched, skimming the waves behind the dolphin's bold knowing eye, desperately clutching its mane (not the right word) trying to tame it, they say you can. They have a sureshot sonar system, they can read your emotional state just like that. Hang in there, Mary Alice! D shouts, but we're going under, brine chafing my lips, stinging invisible wounds. I'm dizzy with a lungful of banked out-of-place air. Breathe deeply, Mary Alice, M says. Rusted nails of plundered ships tear at me, rip tides, bony old-women fingers of white coral. Glinting tropical fish swirl by like dancers at a ball I don't know the music to. Stop! Please! I drum the side of the dolphin, a percussion steady as the beat of a hard rock heart. He hears me! We're headed up. We are communicating, the dolphin and I, aiming for the top, breaking the surface, and suddenly I'm there wet and cold and alone and I see the covers have slid off again.

I lie on my stomach clutching my pillow like it's a somebody. From across the hall a sound between a moan and a yawn, a mawn. Good mawnin', y'all.

I decide to check out the bathroom. There's something spooky about a brightly lit night bathroom. I study the pill bottles, the ones I wouldn't let M touch, it being none of her business.

Geoffrey—that was what Miriam Myers said—Geoffrey Crenshaw. Sounds like a melon. Maybe he's a fruit. Thorazine, 500 milligrams, 1 capsule at bedtime, Dr. Berlin. The top is off and I peer in at the orange torpedoes, the Jedi that blitz in and blast out the hallucinations, the voices. Everybody I've ever known who's been on Thorazine has been in rough shape, really fogged upstairs.

I decide not to put my Mellaril into the lineup. It's quality stuff, the best. I don't want to cast my lot with the crazies, no way. I'm schizo-affective, which is top of the line, just ask any qualified shrink. I've never been hospitalized and I don't hear voices. Oh, sometimes whole scenes that aren't technically real life float through my mind, but that's how it must be for people like George Lucas and Woody Allen, right? Or sometimes I'll be in a room and I think people are talking about me and that gets me going so I'm nervous as a clam, and then chances are I find out they aren't paying me any mind whatsoever and then that gets me depressed, which makes me more wired, which is how come shrinks drive Cadillac Sevilles and 380 SL Mercedeses. (I once asked Dr. Madsen what kind of car he had and all he said was why did I want to know? Which means it's at least a Jag, right? or he would have said.)

Warren Sommerfeld, lithium, 300 milligrams, 1 capsule 3 times daily. Got to be manic depressive. They're so elitest, it's sickening. What they claim to have is mood swings and not thought disorders like us lower-echelon weirdies. Well, if you took all the mood swingers and strung them end to end (not that they would let you, as a group they're very uncooperative) you'd have total havoc, believe me, monkey island, that's what you'd have, the last of the human race as we know it. It'd make all-out nuclear war look like the Pickle Family circus—no exaggeration.

Carla Janus, another lithium. Bipolar, that's the con word they use for themselves. Bipolar instead of manic depressive. Sounds like you have a mere electrical foul-up. People think manic means happy because it's at the other end from depression, but this is a crock, I'm here to tell you. What they really are is driven. They claim lithium is nothing more than a salt, whereas stuff like Mellaril they refer to as anti-psychotic meds. Better not pull that on me, Warren Sommerfeld, and what's her name? Carla Janus, because I'll shoot right back—Mellaril is one of your most highly respected sought-after major tranquilizers. That's how much you know. And it doesn't make people thirsty like lithium. All it does is, it makes your skin a little shiny. I look at mine in the mirror. One eye is still ringed with rust from the pipe like I'm part raccoon. What I might say, very dignified and matter-of-factually, is that Mellaril is a neuroleptic, folks, excepting that sounds like somebody who screws dead people and then steals their money.

There's one bottle left. Please, God, don't let it be Mellaril. I just don't want it to be Mellaril, I don't know why, but I don't. Lynne D. Palshaw, Navane. Good! Thank you, Heavenly Father. Thank you, Dr. . . . who is it? . . . Miller, Dr. Miller. Forty milligrams. At bedtime. Lynne D. Palshaw, I'd guess you are most likely common ordinary schizophrenic residual, meaning chronic, but *residual* is how they drop your hot-air balloon off in a gentler meadow.

This is a game. I'm really getting into it. Like reading a P. D. James and trying to figure who done it. You look at the meds and you figure the diagnosis. Meds is a funny word, ingroupy. If you were taking say Bactrim for prostate (like D) or estrogen for menopause (like M) you don't call them meds, you see what I'm saying? Can you see a saying? Well I can.

So. Looks like I'm the only one on Mellaril. Good. It's the best. Dr. Madsen says he personally likes to work with Mellaril, so it's got to be the best, right?

Whatever you come up with these little pills are supposed to deal with. If you're into anxiety, they de-angst you, zip it away like a depilatory. If you can't concentrate they go in and get your head back from lunch. If you—

"Whaddya doin' in there hogging it. Open the fucking door!"

I'm hearing voices. I'm also hearing violent pounding on the door. Okay, okay. I stuff the cotton back in the lithium (which is like trying to cram a sleeping bag back in its case)—awright awright!—hunt for the top to the Navane, shove the pills back on the shelf. "The name's Tiffani," I say as I open the door on this gross-me-out fat farm chick who is wearing jeans with what looks like a piece of clothesline for a belt and a black T-shirt with a button that says WHO KNOWS? WHO CARES? WHY BOTHER?

"Hi, I take Mellaril," I say conversationally. "I'm Tiffani."

"I gotta upchuck," she says. She claps a hand with gnawed fingernails over her mouth.

"Certainly," I say. I want to make a good impression. So that's how I meet Lindy Palshaw if you could call it meeting.

I start prowling around the house like a Bengal tiger. All the tigers you hear about are Bengal. There must be a Bengal Tiger Advisory Board, a lobby somewhere.

This must be the lobby, the front room. It's bizarre. Half a dozen stalagmites from another world, monster creatures with long necks and leathery skin, feathered heads and furry bodies, spiny squat munchkins with one eye. I can't figure out if I'm dreaming. I step back and there's a yowl. A Bengal tiger? I put my hand over my heart. Oh, it's the kitten. I stepped on his tail. Sorry, Charlie.

Then I see Geoffrey, although I don't at the time know it's Geoffrey. You should never see Geoffrey for the first time in the middle of the night if you can help it. Nobody should. He's totally pale, ghostlike, and he wears this tan nightshirt and a knitted cap and his eyes are definitely strange, sort of backlit. It's like special effects, an eerie Star Wars blue like the tip of flames. Plus he smells like old daisy stems.

I point to the creepie crawlies behind us. "What's all that?"

"My people," Geoffrey says, like he's the King of Siam, if Siam still has a king.

"For sure," I say carefully, but I don't turn around. Later I learn that Geoffrey makes these oddball George Lucasy creatures in Day Care. Mini sculptures. It's his way of communicating. He's not a word person and also they want you to turn out a certain amount of stuff in Day Care, to produce. It's a microcosm of our industrial society.

Geoffrey is holding the kitten. "Cathouse," he says. "Cathouse sleeps with me."

"That's neat, that's really neat," I say. "I didn't mean to step on him. See, I didn't know he was there, had no way of—" But Geoffrey is no longer there or Cathouse either. I'm left with only these nubbin people and I think maybe it was all an apparition.

I edge my way into the kitchen, looking behind me. I open the refrigerator. A pound of ground chuck and the tofu on the shelf marked Warren. Half a Sara Lee berry pie in a foil tin on the Lindy shelf, together with a gigantic chocolate chip cookie with bite inlets, a package of Mrs. Fields' extra creamy fudge marked *Don't touch! this means you!!!* and a pudding that has started to brown out around the edges and come away from the sides. V-8 juice and carrot salad, Carla. A half-eaten can of cat food, Geoffrey.

I check the bottom shelf. Just where's my barbecued chicken from Safeway? Fled the coop? Except for two pointy little wings. So it didn't fly anywhere. Upstairs the toilet is flushing. You see where I'm headed, conclusionwise? It's probably her that helped herself to my chicken. In a brilliant retaliatory strike, I whack off a slab of fudge.

I decide to ring up M and D. First I have to find two dimes. There's the one I picked up from the floor—must be another one somewhere, yup. They've got a pay phone in the hall, just like at J. Paul Getty's, although he wouldn't have hung out in a place like this.

It's 4 A.M. but I doubt M and D are asleep anyway. They're probably tossing and turning. Can you toss without turning? It's one of those expressions it wouldn't surprise me if nobody thought about till right now.

They get it on the first ring. There's a minute there when I don't say anything, when the sound of M's voice—hello? hello?—clogs me up.

"I can't stay here," I say eventually. "My chicken's gone. It's sick." I cover my mouth and more or less whisper.

Pause. "Your chicken's sick?" M says in a careful voice. I hear her hiss to D that it's me, to get on the extension. "I just got that chicken today—now I guess it's yesterday—it was perfectly fresh, I just don't see how there could have been anything—"

"No, the situation, the situation. They've got monsters all over the living room, that's why she didn't show us the living room."

"Have you taken your Mellaril?" M says. "She's had one of her nightmares," she says to D.

"Has she taken her meds?" There's an echo because he's on the extension.

"Yes," I say, "sure," which is untrue, but irrelevant. "No, I haven't. You never believe me. Had a nightmare. And they eat cat food. Plus my chicken. And the cookies. All the cookies are gone."

"It doesn't mean *you* have to eat cat food," D says after a pause. He really is a dork.

"How is everything?" M says. "Everything else?"

"Terrible. You wouldn't stay here. Like I said, my food's all gone. There's this girl and I think she's upstairs throwing up my chicken. I know she is, and then there's this guy in a beanie who has monsters with feathers on them."

"She's hallucinating, Glenn."

"No, I'm telling you. His people he calls them. You can come on over and see for yourself if you don't believe me."

"We can't—"

"I want to come home," I say. I don't plan to say it, it just pops out. "Another thing, there's a face in the window next door that just stands there spying. It's bad vibes, I know it is, I can feel it, you know how I feel those things."

"You have to—"

"I know what you're going to say, give it time. How much time do you want me to give people who steal chicken and keep monsters and eat cat food?"

"The cat food is probably just for that cat, the kitten," D says. "Once it's open, they put it in the refrigerator, that's all."

I flash on it, it probably *is* for the cat, he's right for once. "It's not for the kitten," I say. "I know it isn't. I can prove it if you guys come over."

"Why don't you just go on back to bed and—"

"And what? I haven't been to bed—"

"And have some granola in the morning."

". . . so I can't go back to it." We are talking at the same time.

"Maybe we should think about taking her over the bananas she forgot," M says.

"Yah, I want you guys to come over. I want the bananas, I mean. I need the potassium. I'm hungry."

"No," D says. "She has money. She has granola. She knows where the store is."

"Okay, if you don't care that your daughter eats cat food," I say. I hang up assertively.

I stand there by the phone to see if they call back. M will want to. They'll be arguing. Leave her alone, D will say. Give her a chance to adjust. I hate him.

The phone gurgles my dimes, exulting. I pick up the receiver. Nothing, only the dial tone, except that noise the phone made was M wanting to call, M with her hand on the phone. I know things like that.

A few Fridays later I am sitting on one of those long front seats that go the way the bus does on my way to see Dr. Madsen. Across from me is this girl about 12 in a school jumper. She's got a little gold cross on. Catholic, I guess. Her hair is combed straight down and she has this white plastic barrette in the shape of a bow and white knee socks she keeps pulling up and a tam with a thing you hang it by, although I've never actually seen a tam hanging. She has amber eyes and a shy quiet look to her. She also has a dynamo kid brother with a Pac Man lunch pail who keeps roaring up and down the aisle, bumping into elbows.

"You sit you down now, Donny, I mean it," she says, shaking her mother-of-the-future head.

"You can't win," a woman in the next seat says, smiling at the girl. "Not when they're that age and all boy."

Does this mean you can win if they're not that age and only part boy? I don't necessarily buy that, I start to say, but the girl is talking.

"He gets me so mad. He's not supposed to do that." She tugs

up her half socks again in this classy style she has, pulling them by the top ribbing and then adjusting them all the way down as though she wants to make sure the legs are still there inside.

"I went to a parochial school too," the woman is saying. "One thing I'll sure say for uniforms, you never ever have to think what to put on in the morning, your thinking's all done for you."

"That's what my mom says," the girl says, "but sometimes I get fed up with them." She is pushing in her barrette, running it up the flagpole of hair, but she stops to grab at her brother.

"Donny," I say, "you go sit down like she says." He doesn't. The girl looks at me, doesn't say anything, but it's kind of a none-of-your-business look.

"Don't worry, honey," the woman in the next seat says. Not to me, to the girl. You can see how she admires her. It bugs me the way people don't communicate, whole bus loads of them, the way they back off, won't have anything to do with you.

The girl sifts a leaf from her hair, squinting at it. I wouldn't mind if I was to have a daughter like her. I suppose if I had one she'd have blown-out hair like myself. But I'd start right in training it in the hospital before I ever took her home. I'd get me some Wella Balsam Instant Conditioner right when I went into labor. And every month I'd take her in to Dr. Madsen for a check-up. Never mind the pediatrician, they just give shots, they're just mechanics. I'd dress her in Mexican baby clothes, they're the best—cotton with all those little pleats—and she'd hold Dr. Madsen's finger. Psychiatrists aren't supposed to touch, but with her it'd be different. He'd show me how to bring her up so she wouldn't be schizo-affective or infantilized (except when she was an infant, of course). We'd be close but separate. I'd never ever pry. I'd get her a diary with a lock and key. And she'd find her identity early. By six months max. People would marvel at how mature she was. Her name would be Mara Laurielle.

What a crock. She won't happen. Not in a million light years. When I look up I see that the girl with the brother and the amber eyes is gone and I am three stops beyond where I should have got off, which means I have to run to make it for my appointment.

Dr. Madsen's wearing a blue rep tie, so I know the session's going to be a downer and I'm right. It's like with photography—you go to blues and purples, they're cold colors, whereas highly saturated warm colors with yellows in them give a joyous mood, so it is said. I can always tell from the tie Dr. Madsen has on how it will be, it practically never fails.

He wants to know how things are going. How is the peer group? I shrug in such a manner as to convey I am giving it every chance but it's your basic shit pit. Geoffrey sleeps all the time except when he's feeding Cathouse. Either that or he goes to Day Care and comes back with these outer space creatures. Currently it's a set of galactic chessmen. Lindy steals my food and pigs out all the time, you have to nail everything down and when she isn't eating, she's bad-mouthing. Warren is a hypochondriac. He has this Vespa he's all the time tinkering with when he isn't tinkering with Carla who Lindy says is the next thing to a prostitute. (I hope Dr. Madsen doesn't ask me what the next thing is because I don't know.)

So what do you do? he says finally.

Go to *Out of Africa*.

Again? How many times does that make?

Six.

You must know it by heart. . . . What else?

Stay in my room and play my Billy Joel.

And?

And there's this one next door, this bitchy woman who hates me, she hates all of us, she starts in yelling and carrying on. It's too loud, she says.

Is it?

Not for me.

If it is for her, should you think about toning it down a little?

No. That's not it anyway. She has it in for them, for us, for C House. Like the kids aren't supposed to even talk to us. If we're just standing around outside, she calls the kids in. What she is, she's really into spying on us. Warren says she's been like that ever since they moved in. I mean, man, it's like real bad vibes.

Anything else? he says, looking at his clock while pretending not to be looking at his clock.

I think about the kids next door, how one day they're out there peeking through the fence and I sneaked up and put my eye there and they ran shrieking into the house. "She's after us, one of 'em is!"

Yah, there is one thing. . . . Could a baby, a kid, come up with this thing that's wrong with me?

He pauses—which he practically never does—he's fast on the trigger, the way I used to be—and then he says very softly, "Some people think so."

I don't care for him hesitating like that and then speaking gentle as a lullaby. *Some people think so.* This really gets to me, like it's a sentence for my unborn children, like I'd been nuclear radiated and my genes are all barbecued. How about you, Dr. Madsen? never mind some people, what do *you* think? I want to shake an answer out of him, but instead I sit very quiet with my hands dead in my lap for once.

It's shitty, I say finally.

What is?

Everything. It's not fair.

By which I mean, but don't say, you, Dr. Madsen, and M and D and Paula and Jake and Warren and Carla and Lindy and Geoffrey and Miriam Myers and the one next door who has it in for us, have I forgotten anybody? The kitten. And me, I guess, even especially me. I just wish I was bipolar. I probably am bipolar and he just hasn't noticed. Nobody is tuned in to me.

Nobody ever said the world is fair, he says.

He shoves the Kleenex box toward me. Probably lots of people have said the world is fair. With it going on as long as it has, somebody's got to have said it. He can be an unbelievable asshole. He always is when he wears those blue regimental striped ties. So that's the story.

■ ■ ■
▮▮▮ It's November. It's Wednesday. It's house meeting. (See,
▮▮▮ I know.)

Miriam Myers sits facing us, clipboard in hand, her back to the
fireplace, which is crammed with the embers of the week—crumpled
cigarette packages, sleek Wonderbread bags the *Chronicle* came in
on several rainy days, the previous week's chores chart in Carla's
spidery green handwriting, a flyer about half-price drapery and carpet
cleaning that was slotted into the door handle by some mysterious
hand.

"So how much time are you people going to devote to this?" she
says. We are to think of her as a Facilitator.

Warren is jiggling his knees. We are about to vote whether he
has to keep his Vespa on the other side of C House. The people
next door, the Ryans, have been pissing and moaning about the
noise level. That's what they call it—the noise level—why can't
they just go ahead and say noise?

Warren objects on the grounds he can't keep an eye on his scooter
there, it isn't secure, it isn't insured, so fuck the Ryans.

Miriam Myers explains in essence that we can't fuck the Ryans
without fucking ourselves in the process. An A therefore B kind of
thing. She has this way she exhales, hissing like a train getting ready
to do something, the way a train in a station does. You think time
is running out on you and you should run for it, get out of the way,
anything. *The* paramount issue is maintaining good community relations is what she actually says. Without that C House wouldn't
continue to exist, she says. Everybody get that?

"Paramount my ass," Lindy mumbles, spitting a seed. True, her
ass *is* paramount, as is her stomach. She is, as usual, compulsively

feeding her face, tossing in handfuls of Cheez-its, sunflower seeds, trail mix, trying to swallow fast enough to keep the floor, to "filibluster" as Warren says. "See, they just want to stick it to us. Any little thing, a candy wrapper even, and they're right there climbing all over our case." She fishes out a seed from between her teeth with her little finger, looks at it, feeds it back into the system. There's a lot of waste motion there.

"They just want to hassle us over, that's all," Warren says. He is six feet with dark scraggly sideburns like graph lines on a chart, the kind of person people ask directions from. He looks as though he should know things. He does, but not things like directions. Sometimes he'll tell people anyway just to be nice.

"All in favor of the change in parking area . . . ?" Miriam Myers says quickly before Lindy has a chance to start in again.

Everybody just naturally waits for Carla. She's just washed her hair, which is running down in little drizzlets. She squeezes the ends, observing the run-off before she votes. Turns out she's in favor, so Lindy is in favor. I'm basically not in favor, but I'm a little afraid of Carla so I'm in favor. Carla, I don't know just how to say it, Carla's potent. People want to be on her side. It's a mixture of admiration and fear that she'll blow you away if you aren't. She never thinks the same thing for long so you never know where you're at because she doesn't know where she's at. Her mind is always chasing its own tail. Like she can convince you of one thing in the morning and the complete opposite by night, it kind of strings you out sometimes.

Geoffrey as usual is riding his own monorail, above and beyond it all. He's sitting at the card table with the ailing leg, moving his outer space chessmen around. Geoffrey doesn't play chess, he plays chessmen. His kings and queens and bishops move any old way, which is probably the way kings and queens and bishops actually conduct themselves if you believe the *National Enquirer*.

"Geoffrey? Get with it!" Carla pokes him with a metallic toe. "You're in favor, nerdball." Geoffrey's black knight with a rooster head and a silver helmet votes yes yes yes, which really ought to make it illegal.

"Okay, we deep six that one," Carla says. "Next?" She has a dazzle to her, like an artist's palette—iridescent green eye shadow the color of flies' backs, long pearly white nails, a tempest of wavy chestnut hair that she adds red highlights to, bright spots of ruby blush and chipping-off silver sparkles on her toes (that's what I meant when I said metallic toe), and she sits with her legs apart the way bitchy models do, like they're daring somebody to hop on.

"Opposed?" Miriam Myers says, going doggedly on like a doggy with a degree in parliamentary procedure.

Warren is opposed and mumbling. He should really abstain, it being his Vespa screwing the works.

"Fucking Nazis," Warren says. He's kind of moody.

Moving right along, C Housers, the subject is our old friend trash bags. Do we want to go with the extra strength 2 ply 3 mil bags which don't puncture as opposed to the 1.5 mil ones that do but cost less? Do we want to go for money or mess? Miriam Myers seems to be asking. Do we have a motion? is what she actually says. (Dr. Madsen says it's important to hear what people are really saying. This assumes they're really saying anything, which I for one don't. Assume they are, I mean.)

"Do we have a second? Any discussion?"

"Well, see," Lindy says, and everybody groans, except Miriam Myers. She is probably programmed not to, it's most likely a no-groan class these psychiatric social worker types have to take. "What I think is we should get the 3 ply Cart All ones not the 2 whatever it is Glad ones."

"You just want the coupon you get with them," Carla says. "So you can go an' convert it to pizza."

Lindy: "You're a flaming asshole!"

Carla: "You suck."

Carla is the type of person who always has the last word.

Miriam Myers calls for the vote. Her voice has a gavel in it. We vote on every little thing. We are a final gasp of the democratic process, the illusion of infinite choice. Everybody except Lindy sides with Carla. Lindy sulks and shovels in a handful of shiny fish-shaped crackers. Lindy (whose name comes from her first name Lynne, plus her middle initial D) thinks she has a special dispensation to fuck up her life.

Warren, looking at him, you wouldn't believe there's a problem, but then you come to find out there are all these things he's scared shitless of. He's always going out to look for a job—tomorrow, but then his voices tell him something bad will happen if he does. But he looks so good Wookmook keeps putting him on panels and task forces as the Consumer Rep. *Consumer, client,* they're all cover-ups like shoe white—everybody knows the blue grime, the sad looking part is right there not quite below the surface. Anyway, last week Warren got a buttermilk pancake breakfast with his choice of sausage or bacon just for sitting there looking like he looks while staff told a panel of realtors how we need places in the community.

"Are you with us, Tiffani?" Miriam Myers is saying. "Tiffani!"

"What? What are we voting on now?"

"No, I was just asking how you people feel about Thanksgiving coming up."

"Let it roll," Carla says. "Who gives a rat's ass?"

I give an appreciative little laugh. So does Lindy, but mine was first.

"Like six kinds of shit," Warren says. He's still p.o'd over being aced on the Vespa vote.

"Don't any of you have any warm memories of Thanksgiving?" Miriam Myers says. "I sure do. We'd all of us get bundled up to here. Scarves, we'd have scarves and earmuffs and we'd pile into my cousin Mickey's van and off we'd go to the Penn State game and then we'd come home after, all the cousins, and have wassail by the fire."

Silence. We all sit there like people in a small town watching the train go by. I mean I have memories but I'd sure never admit to them in this group. I'm like that. I read *The Color Purple* and right away I start in talking like that girl, like Celie, I'm like that, no voice of my own.

"Relatives arriving?" Miriam Myers perseveres. "The house full of good smells?"

"Not with my relatives," Warren says, which cracks me up. I really fall out, laughing till my nose runs and I start coughing. Four packs of Viceroys a day will do it to you, low tar and nic to the contrary. What Warren should be is a stand-up comedian, which as a matter of fact is one of the things he's considering, but the closest he'll probably come is the mike at Taco Bell, ordering, clowning, reordering—lemme changa the chimichanga—things like that, but Warren is wasted there. They just look at him, huh? I crack up again thinking about the time he ordered flautas—

"When Tiffani has control of herself," Miriam Myers says—she has rope sandals that look to be about a size 7½ and would therefore fit me except I don't like wedgies—"we can go on." She doesn't address me directly. Instead she talks to my illness, something out there, separate from me, the real Tiffani, whose laughter and tears stay in neat little cassettes waiting to be played at the appropriate times. This approach is supposedly very therapeutic. Oh sure, once I start in laughing, sometimes I just keep on, after the joke has gone ahead and volatilized, but that's because it stays in my system longer.

"Well, see, Thanksgiving's a bummer," Lindy is saying, "basically a bummer, man." She has the sleeves of her sweater pulled down over her hands, it's a habit she has, stretching the sleeves. "So you go to your family's, okay? You don't even think about it, you just go. You're on automatic pilot. Then if you don't want to eat just when *they* want to eat . . . . " Lindy pauses to root around for her jar of dry roasted cashews.

"That's because you're all the time stuffing your face," Carla says.

"That's better than what you're all the time stuffing, herpes head," Lindy says, looking at Miriam Myers for confirmation. Or protection.

"Watch it, scumbag," Carla hisses.

"Okay, forget it," Lindy says.

"Listen, guys, why don't we have everybody here?" I say off the top of my head, which is where a lot of the world's cruddiest ideas come from. Not the deranged ones. They emanate from lower central, the limbic area it's called. Which sounds like cheese and who knows. "Have them here at C House and us decide when we eat." I find I am sweating through my double cotton crotch, since I'm usually not into the making suggestions gig. I expect it to go like last year's calendar, but are you ready for this? Instead right off there's all this yak, yak, Miriam Myers saying let's explore Tiffani's idea, let's look at it and then people saying Who would get the dinner? How would we pay for it? Out of the General Fund or what? Maybe they could bring stuff, we could assign them. No way! Then it wouldn't be ours. What would we have? Turkey? We'd have to have turkey, asshole! Who are you calling asshole? Are you trying to bait me? It's bedlam in Bedlam and all out of my innocent little question. I sit there gnawing on my right little finger nail, which is really long. I have trouble cutting it, being right-handed and it really starts bothering me sometimes.

What about cranberry? Lindy is saying. (Is it cranberry or cramberry? I consider myself very literate but I don't go around boggling myself down with run-of-the-mill detail anybody could know.) How about cran/mberry shrub? I say, muddling the n/m. Shrub? Lindy says. Yah, for dessert, I say, it's like sherbert. That'd kill two birds with one stone. Kill birds? What birds? Lindy says. It's getting slightly wild.

Geoffrey is now on the floor, his head in his hands. He dislikes all mention of violence, especially as regards animals. Carla rubs Geoffrey's neck with her foot. This looks interesting. I wonder if there's great customer demand for it. Possibly in Japan.

"We have to vote," I say, it being my idea under consideration. I'm on this big mega trip, I admit it. "Let's just go ahead and take the vote."

Lindy suddenly says, if we do it, we have to have little pearl onions.

Little pearl onions! Carla says. Why? *Why* is generally a good suggestion torpedoer. It's simple, sudden, aggressive, and generally hard to field.

Because my mother always has little pearl onions, that's why, Lindy sputters. I doubt she'd even come if we didn't have little pearl onions.

Up yours, Carla says, this is our place. I think she really means up Lindy's mother's, there's a name for that kind of figure of speech, euphemism or something.

By now Lindy is embarrassed to have a pearl onion mother.

We vote, Lindy seconding her own resolution, which Miriam Myers doubts is legal and the onions squeak by. Lindy says, okay, what she'll do, she'll personally make the white sauce, her white sauce never ever lumps up on her because she knows to add the milk a little at a time, but if it was to, she'd run it back through the strainer.

White sauce? Carla says turning red. What's this white sauce horseshit? This makes me think of creamed horseradish, which is called free association. It's a frequently used term.

Carla takes back her illegal vote.

I take back my vote too. I'm not excited about onions anyway and it's imperative to have Carla on your team or you on hers, I mean.

Why cream sauce? Warren says, hitting his knees together, just tell me why! The reasoning, I'm slow, just lay it out for me.

Because that's what you do with little pearl onions, Lindy shouts, that's their natural medium.

Carla says fuck that noise, we have to vote again because of the sauce thing.

Are you people sure you can handle this? Miriam Myers keeps saying. Have you considered the stress? This question seems sensible, right? but isn't. We are not really heavy in the consider area. We shoot more from the hip, like Congress. This may be because we are unglued or again because we are as normal as you or I and too glued. The whole field needs a lot of research and the funds aren't available.

By midnight and about a zillion cigarette butts, it's all set. How about that? *We* are getting the Thanksgiving dinner. At our house. And inviting *them*. And it's basically Yours Truly's idea. For once something I came up with actually flew, was embraced by everybody, even Carla, Queen of Camelot. George Shultz couldn't have brought this one off. Not to mention the Pope himself, which has nothing to do with him being Polish.

The screen door which hangs up on the porch light twangs shut in two syllables, and we listen to Miriam Myers' battery grinding away in the driveway. Eventually her Subaru grunts and she takes off.

There's a full moon and we all go outside to check on the garden, see what we can count on for Thanksgiving. There's garlic, chives, and crab grass. We sit on the back steps, passing around a joint, singing old Beatles songs. "Hey Jude," "Sergeant Pepper," all B.S., meaning Before Schizophrenia, when the world was mellower. We even belt out some choruses of "Tzena Tzena." This is a Jewish song Miriam Myers tried to teach everybody when we went to Angel Island to count deer for the U.S. Forest Service for 50 cents an hour, those cheap bastards. Not the deer. I don't mean them.

We're swaying from side to side, arms linked, even Geoffrey, it's kind of mystical. We pretend, or I do anyway that we're kibbutzim, which is those big settlements they keep building on the West Bank to stick it to the Arabs. We're about at the millionth *b'mosheva-a-a-a* when the bedroom window in the house next door goes up like a guillotine. I know, I know, guillotines go down, but the noise was exactly like a guillotine when it beheads and decapitates you.

It's Mrs. Ryan—Bernadette's her name—saying if you don't I will. Then he goes, Art Ryan goes, "Hey, you over there! Just knock it off!" Geoffrey starts to whimper. Lindy is shut down for once in her life. "Or I call the police. We've got two kids trying to sleep over here, you realize what time it is, goddamit?"

"Up yours," Carla says in an aside. Warren is whiter than moonlight. If you even say police to him you might about as well say acid rain. He gets really wiggy. "Get in the house, get in!" he yells at everybody, even Carla, who he never yells at.

"Some of us have to get up and work for a living," Ryan shouts after us, emboldened by our retreat. "Even if you don't." He is silhouetted in the window wearing one of those Japanese things with the fanned-out sleeves. "You people dim or something?" He gives a savage tug to the sash of his kimono before Warren starts pulling the blinds, which I help him do. I kind of like Warren.

"They're trying to get us," he says, gasping like he just ran the Bay to Breakers. "We're being watched. It's El fucking Salvador, man."

"Calm down, baby, you're just hyper," Carla says.

It's true. You can just feel this sudden dark energy flowing through Warren. Carla goes over to him, rubs her chin on his shoulder, runs her pearly nails along his arm like a grater.

"Okay, I'm overreacting, I can't help it."

He has his hand inside her jeans till the point where you can't tell what's his hand and what's her hip bone. I mean, I certainly don't give a tomboy's tit what anybody does, I'm a very liberated person, but it's where they do it and how, you know what I mean? It's absolutely nothing to me, I mind my own business, it just drives me up the wall is all, when people are farts.

Lindy is demolishing a pepperoni the size of a pony's penis. A big pony. And Warren has his face in Carla's hair.

"Fatso!" I scream at Lindy. I'm trying to save her from herself, that's all the fuck the reason I'm yelling.

Her eyes narrow ominously. "Listen, Dr. Miller thinks I'm looking real good. He says I'm his favorite patient."

"Oh sure, I bet. That's so far off the wall!"

"Then why are you turning purple in the face then?" she says.

"Any shrink who knows his ass would never ever say that and if they did, they wouldn't be any good," I say, which puts her in a double bind. (Who wants to be the favorite of some squirrelly theraquack?)

They are all looking at me—Lindy from behind her pepperoni, which she is holding like a microphone, Warren and Carla from the stairs which they seem to be on the way up. "You seem to have forgotten whose idea Thanksgiving is," I shout after them.

"If it wasn't for you and your big ideas, we wouldn't have *them* after us again," Lindy says.

"That Bernadette woman, she's the devil," Warren says. "You can see it in her face. She's out to destroy us." He thinks like that sometimes.

"Well, I'll be your repair service," Carla says. "Come on, it's R and R time."

Shit.

iv Looking back on it, the Great Thanksgiving Toilet Paper Crunch (GTTPC—in the System initials are everything) was the beginning of the train that was to hit Camelot House like a Gothic laser. But that's getting ahead of myself. I do that. Let's start in the morning. The spores of my idea are germinating all around.

I awake to "Bringing in the Sheaves." The music could be from the radio. Or it could be one of Carla's Mormon Tabernacle Choir records. Doesn't seem to fit, does it? But hold on. Carla was a Mormon before she was a Moonie, which was before she was whatever she is now. Or maybe after, I'm not exactly into exact dates, I'm no oral historian or anything like that, although I heard Jake say it's an up and coming field.

All I know for sure is she's been all these things—she even has a kid somewhere—Doreen Nicole—or says she has. Same diff. You are what you think you are, you have what you think you have, although I am by no means a Christian Scientist. The fact is, everybody in C House is an incredible bull shitter excepting Geoffrey who isn't capable and myself who am that rare thing, a very honest person. So honest you could run me through the eye of a needle like a camel. I am more your basic bel canto embellisher as opposed to your hard-core lying asshole. It's an important distinction and one I take pride in and justifiably so.

My problem, which I keep on telling Dr. Madsen till I'm blue in the face (although I've never actually been blue in the face), is if people ask me, there's not one single solitary thing I can say I've ever been. Not a Moonie or a Mormon or a partial prostitute even. This stems from the fact I bonkered out right after high school—

actually it began at Commencement—and never worked a day in my life except a couple of days at Wendy's and a different week at Chuck E. Cheese Pizza Time Theatre once. I got fired just because I happened to land an anchovy in this kid's peach melba. He thought it was a worm or something, some dead yucksville thing. He was obviously a rotten little turd. Wendy's, I don't know, I just plain walked out because their customers there are like you wouldn't believe. You bring them their burger with avocado and salsa and they'll tell you they ordered a stuffed baked potato with cheese and green onions and your super won't back you up. Plus you have to pay for your meals you eat there. What I'm really saying is, if you haven't been something, you plain old haven't been anything. You haven't happened, you're a non-event, was how Warren once put it to me, which was totally uncalled for.

I see that I still have a low opinion of myself. I check this every morning like some people check their tongue color. Some day I'll wake up and say, Tiffani Gilchrist, I'm glad to make your acquaintance, I'm glad I am you. But not today, definitely not today. Today my toenails are so long they turn under at the ends like Howard Hughes'. Possibly also the Pilgrims. I should have cut them. It was on my yesterday's list, but I went and lost it. Not *went* and lost—stayed put and lost, which is even worse. If anybody was to ask me for a working definition of schizophrenia, I'd say it's a losing illness—you lose everything, your money, keys, friends, self-respect, shoes, matches, marbles, forms, pencils, money (I said that already), bathing suit tops, next-appointment cards, telephone numbers. Nail scissors, of course, they're among the first to go. The world is whizzing by and you have this feeling you could get on if only you could find what you needed to take with you in time, but forget it. You're a shelled pea, rolling around, displaced.

Since I sleep in my jeans, I save myself the trouble of getting dressed. I save time and energy. PG&E loves me. I am like the firemen all ready to slide down a pole with their Dalmatians. I smile, thinking of Dalmatians sliding down a pole, putting out one tentative

paw and then—*tchoong!* I laugh silently, just the smile and the mus-
cles in my diaphragm shaking a little. Carla waves a hand in front
of my face. "Hey, wake it up. Let's get on the stick, okay? You're
on cleanup so let's get the ass in gear."

I sog up some granola, checking first to be sure it is my box with
the T on it and not Carla's. She has a flaming shit fit if you take
so much as a teaspoon of her stuff, which I believe to be your typical
disruptive manic depressive. Dr. Madsen says no, she's just upset
because I raided her grub again, that's what he says, grub. I thrash
my granola with a red-handled spoon, which through some physical
principle going back to Newton splashes milk over the kitchen floor.

"Clean up your slobby mess!" Warren yells. He is peering into
the cavity of the turkey with the silver flashlight from his Vespa
kit and yanking out slimy stuff that looks like voodooed kidneys
which he then has trouble getting off his fingers. He is strung way
out with company coming, including someone called Randy with
whom Carla is currently very tight. Her mother couldn't make it
from Nevada and Dorie, her kid, is going to Disneyland with her
foster family, and so Carla invited Randy.

That's the trouble, we are all kind of hyper, I admit it. Carla
flings a couple of my old lists at me, which I leave around like bird
droppings. Cigarettes one says. Well actually they both say cigarettes
but one says cigarettes and john, whatever that means. "Here, here's
another one," Carla says. Cigarettes again.

I keep trying to imagine what M and D and Paula will make of
Carla. And Warren, Lindy, and Geoffrey and vice versa. Let's face
it, this is an important occasion of which I am the originating brain,
the Doctor Who.

Warren throws a yellow sponge at me. "What mess, Warren?"
I say reasonably. "I fail to see any slobby mess."

"The milk."

"Oh *that* milk. Don't be picky. I'll get it when I'm done eating."
Warren looks menacing and I wipe the milk up with my sleeve,
which will now begin to smell sour just about the time everybody

starts coming, but you can't let it throw you. I make it a point to never fight before nine in the morning, it is part of a creed I am developing in an on-going effort to find my identity, which I possibly don't have any of. "What time is it anyway?"

"Look at the clock, for God's sake," Warren says. Snarls would be more like it. Teeth bared, voice shaky—the whole gum ball. Maybe this tough guy approach of his will make me more self-reliant, but I doubt it. Dr. Madsen says I have to get so I'm not always asking people for stuff—dimes to phone with, cigarettes, the time, reassurance, toothpaste, that sort of thing.

I stand there leaning down with my hands on my knees, trying to decide where to begin. I have problems in this general area, like everybody, only a little more severe. Beginnings are curious things. It's hard to know where to start, like with a spool of thread. You pick and pick looking for the loose end and maybe finally you give up and give the spool a good gouge with the scissors and that gives you something to unravel all right but pretty soon it breaks off and you have another end. Or another beginning. Which is why I'm not that into sewing.

"So what's the story?" Warren says. "Are we moving right along?"

"I'm on my way to the Promised Land," I say. I start to step on a roach, but Warren yells "Don't!" He thinks somebody Up There keeps count and when you get to your body weight in smashed bugs, Something comes down and squashes you.

To be very honest, the front room, the living room, doesn't look all that great. In fact it's on the depressing side, though not as much so as cleaning it would be. It's a trade-off, like everything in life. Don't get me wrong, the place is decorated to the nines, which is less than a perfect ten, but still way up there. We have a wide assortment of artifacts made by various C House residents, past and present, in various craft and therapy programs. Like we have 21 man-in-the-moon ashtrays Lindy made in Rehab, 16 mugs, 4 hand-tooled leather phone book covers with Aztec suns, creator unknown, 19 creature monsters Geoffrey had fired in his Day Care program which Warren says he plans someday to take to George Lucas as Geoffrey's agent, lots of luck, and 24 macramé plant hangers with tricky knots and blue and orange beads, although I have to admit half the plants are dead and the rest never found their identity either.

"Hey you guys, we're almost out of toilet paper," Lindy yells. "Not more than one sitting's worth." She makes it sound like a Cunard Line cruise.

"Tell me about it!" Carla groans. "Who needs this one?"

The problem is simple—the stores are all closed on Thanksgiving. How come we ran out anyway? Who was supposed to be on top of it? Let's look at the Chores Chart posted on the kitchen door. It says Sanka and john supplies, Tiffani. "That's not my handwriting," I say. "There's forgery all over the place, just look at the Hitler diaries."

"Oh sure, you lying cunt," Lindy says righteously. I ignore her completely. I'm aloof, dignified, like someone waiting for his dog to do its business.

"Knock it off," Carla says. "Do we have Kleenex?"

"Yes, but it's used," Lindy says.

"Forget it. Okay, the deal is the guests have first call to the bathroom, to what's left. Got it, gang?" Carla says.

"Don't we even get to vote?" I say.

"I just did," Carla says. "Now get the front room shaped up."

I yank the vacuum to the end of its leash trying to reach the davenport and it unplugs itself, leaving Carla shouting at me even after the vacuum quits.

"And don't go forgetting the mess under the table."

God am I tired of being bossed around. This is independent living? I'll take San Quentin.

We have a scratchy brick-colored davenport that seems to harbor a certain number of fleas, meaning an uncertain number of fleas. I remove a banana peel from the center cushion, being reasonably fastidious. In front of the davenport is an old blue footlocker we use for a coffee table (Warren retrieved it from a dumpster). And we have a color TV on a cart donated by someone's mother and a 1930's radio, a walnut console with a tiny dial that turns orange when it's on. It looks like an old man in an overcoat hunkered down in a corner. The room has wall lights in the shape of candles with black wrought iron petals and a heavy old lamp with a mixing bowl globe.

I stack the man-in-the-moon ashtrays on top of the piano that came with the place, which used to be a manse. There's still a rectangular iron stand in the front yard that once held a wooden plaque that said Home of the Pastor of Immanuel Baptist Church. Something like that. When the place was sold and Mental Health took it over, they removed the sign, which is still in the broom closet, but the frame they left, as it was sunk in concrete.

As for the piano, it has chipped keys and a permanently depressed E that you have to pry up with a fingernail if you want to play anything and two keys at the far right that are jammed where a penny fell in. Occasionally Lindy'll knuckle out "Chopsticks" as she goes by or Cathouse will land on the keys and crash out chords.

Warren's metallic red motorcycle helmet with decorative white flames is up there, and an empty bag of Stella D'Oro anise toast which is undoubtedly Lindy's. There is absolutely no reason why I have to go and dust all that crud when it isn't even mine. "It's not fair," I say to Warren's helmet.

"I agree, baby," this deep mellow voice comes back at me. I jump. (Did I forget my meds?)

"Tiffani, this is Randy, Mister Randy McNamara Forbes," Carla says, mocking, flirtsy, looking up at him. There I am standing there like a wimp and a half with this feather duster in hand and there he is, something unbelievable. Randy McNamara Forbes is black, high gloss black. His skin has a radiance, it's like he has switched-on strobe lights inside, there's a pulse to him, a beat. He's wearing a wine velvet jacket, a black cummerbund, tight black pants, a ruffled shirt, and a skinny maroon bow tie. Before I know what's happened he takes my hand and kisses it. I study my hand when I get it back. "Hi," I think I say. A tiny yellow feather from the duster floats onto his shoulder. Carla blows it off.

Carla herself is the layered look like the Grand Canyon, polyester snakeskin dress and slung over that this fringed shawl and coming from underneath these opaque white stockings with clever little arrows up the side. The dress is so tight on her that the snakes seem to wiggle in where you wouldn't expect to find them, except maybe in Biblical times. It's super low cut so you can see to Inner Mongolia. Carla is thin—all her features are blades, her nose, her chin, even the tendon that comes up from the heel if you can rightly call that a feature. Built for speed, Warren says. Sure it's a feature, why not?

"What the cross-eyed Christ are you staring at?" Carla says.

She has a dusting of gold sprinkles on her right temple. "Nothing," I say, "nothing." It's scary when Carla turns on you. I can see she's very nervous and I'm willing to bet she hasn't taken her lithium.

Warren is glowering in the background. "That Buick of yours is quite a smokehouse, man," he says. "A real polluter."

"Needs a ring job," Randy says lightly. "Like I'd like to give you," he whispers to Carla, I don't know whether Warren heard.

"Goddam shitbelcher," Warren says, looking at Randy as though he's what belches shit, so I guess maybe he did hear. In any case, there's a tension in the atmosphere, like *Psycho III* or downtown Beirut.

Warren deposits a string bag of onions on the piano bench. He goes, "Okay, Carla, you were going to fix these last night, right? but instead you just happened to be out catting around, slurping up Dos Equis at the Juarez, right?" The last *right* is kind of ground out.

"Hey, wait a minute, man," Randy says. "I feel like we're getting a lot of anger from you."

"Yah," I say. Did Randy mean me too? I move in closer, trying to decide whose side I'm on.

"So lay it back, friend," Randy goes. He's every bit as scary as Carla.

So I'm going, "Yah," I go, "take it easy, Warren. This is Thanksgiving."

Warren totally ignores me. "I have just one question I'd like to put to you, if you'll permit me."

"Depends what it is," Randy says. He may be a little paranoid, I don't know. He's standing in back of Carla, his arms casually looped over her shoulders the way people sometimes knot sweater sleeves.

"Not overly personal in nature," Warren is saying. "I could submit it to you in writing first, Mr. Forbes." Calling him Mr. Forbes like that is a big insult, anybody who's anybody at all we call by their first names. "What I would like to know is, I'd just like to ask Carla, do you intend on peeling the motherfucking onions you signed up to peel or not?"

Carla's ready for him. "I'll peel you, sleazebag!" she says, she's pretty high strung, and she lets fly with this fuselage of onions, I think that's the word, one at a time like she's skipping stones. Warren ducks. One grazes his shoulder, one he catches, one bowls over two of Geoffrey's creatures from outer space. At this point she starts pitching overhand.

"You wanta maim me for life?" Warren says. "Is that what you want? Like a hockey puck right in the ying yangs?"

I hightail it into the kitchen, no point in standing around waiting to be onioned by the super powers. "No!" I scream. Lindy is in there eating the stuffed olives and chestnuts out of the turkey dressing. "Hey, you guys, come here quick!" Lindy cuts out, thunders upstairs like a herd of elk.

The dressing is totally one hundred percent gutted. An enamel pan of voted-on stuffed olives and chestnut dressing minus the stuffed olives and chestnuts. No, I find one chestnut hunk she missed. "You missed one, Lindy honey," Carla says in a dreamy way, plopping it into Randy's mouth. Warren slams the bread knife into the knife block so hard the tip jams.

"Yah, Lindy, you missed one," I say. The whole discovery kind of puts me back in the picture, front and center, if you know what I mean, while getting everyone's mind off onions, which is excellent unintentional strategy.

I turn in time to see a man with an elongated face like a raindrop looking in the Dutch door at us. "Howard Crenshaw," he says, "Geoffrey's father. Hi there."

"Oh wow." I don't know what I expected Geoffrey's father to be like. I had heard he was a professor somewhere but even so I didn't think he'd be tall and distinguished looking. He's holding candy, a Whitman's Sampler (I can't tell if it's milk chocolate or dark) which he hands me—for the cooks, he says.

I feel momentarily proud, standing there holding the box, and I wish for a minute we were a family, Warren and me, say, in our own place and I would be standing on the porch telling people where to park and receiving bounty (fortunately it's milk chocolate) instead of in the kitchen with the cooks and the chestnutless chestnut dressing. Wait a minute, did he say cooks or kooks? He must have said cooks. They're pronounced a little different, I think. I say them over in my head, cooks, kooks, cooks—

"Tell him to come in, don't just stand there," Carla says.

Mr. Crenshaw tells us to go ahead and call him Howard, which we would have in all probability anyway since we run an informal operation.

Howard asks after Geoffrey, how's he doing? Is he talking more now? For some reason he addresses his questions to Randy.

"No point in asking him anything," Warren says, "he doesn't belong here." Howard says, "I see," but he doesn't look like he does. "He's coming along," Warren says to Howard, which is the original tall tale from Timberland, but never mind.

Geoffrey shows up eventually, wearing his stocking cap, which he kind of always does. "Still wearing your hat inside, son?" his father says. "Well, that's A-okay. If it wasn't for eccentrics, the world would never make any progress." Howard looks around at the rest of us, Randy too, kind of embarrassed like he wants it known we're all in this thing together, all except Geoffrey. Like we all of us know you don't wear stocking caps in the house, but we'll sure go along with the gag, won't we?

It makes me feel good, conspiratorial even, for about a second, a split second, till I reflect that I know that look. I've seen it with M and D. Take the time when I was sitting on the curb in front of the Curran Theatre on Geary after *The Gin Game* and this man in an Eagle Security Service uniform came up and said was I all right? And they said oh my yes, it's just a habit she's got herself into, don't you know? And then there's this expression on their faces like Howard's that's pain and apology and exasperation. Get up, they said right after they made it sound to the Eagle man like it's okay, get up, they said, it's inappropriate to sit on the curb like a little kid when you're a grown woman.

Or the time at Alpha Beta when I decided to look in the vegetable mirror while M was shopping. This manager guy came over. He'd had a complaint from a customer he said to M, not quite looking at her, to the effect that there was this girl standing there swaying back and forth by the leeks, staring in the mirror and smiling. Was she maybe on something? And M said, no, it's okay, my goodness no, he needn't worry about anything like that, it's just something she likes to do, a habit, you know, perfectly harmless, but she'd take me with her while she finished up. But we left instead. I walked on ahead knowing she was looking at me that way, sending a depth charge into my back, through the myelin sheath along the neurons to my brain: something is wrong with Tiffani—past the straightened fortune-costing unbrushed teeth out in a wobbly unstable blue smoke ring—don't hold us responsible, world, we tried.

"None of us, none of the rest of us wear hats in the house," I say. Why did I? Sometimes I am just not a good person.

"I'm sure you don't," Howard says.

I start pacing, up and down, zip zip, which is a thing I do, which makes me more nervous. You never catch up with yourself that way. I go out and sit on the porch to wait for the family. See, I don't know what I'm part of—*them* (I look out toward the street), or *them* in there. I don't even know if I want them to like each other.

M and D will think Howard's okay and the screw-up over the john won't matter. I already told M that Carla got herpes during the Democratic Convention, so there's absolutely no way they'll use the facilities at Camelot House, none. What they'll probably do, they'll stop off going and coming at the Shell station a couple of blocks away. They have a Shell credit card, not that it makes any difference.

I try and picture Paula, how she'll look. If I can see her ahead of time it sometimes helps. Like they have this treatment where kids with cancer try to picture just how the drugs are bombarding the malignant cells, and it seems to help, the visualization. Holistic medicine it's called, there's a place in Tiburon does it. One way or another you have to be crazy to have children. That being the case, no wonder children are crazy. It's genetic in both directions.

I smoke a bunch of cigarettes, which means I'll most likely be out by dinner. Mooch mooch. I close my eyes and I see Paula wearing her white linen jacket, which D likes because it reminds him of dental hygienists, which he always wanted one of us to be, and her straight rust skirt with the mother-of-pearl buttons down the side. I put her in black flats. Once when M was in the hospital with a kidney stone I dressed Paula for a birthday party. I went through the whole closet, all her little stuff on the pole D installed half way down so we could reach and I picked out her navy jumper with the yellow daisy on the pocket. I combed and combed her hair—hold still, you hafta hold still—till it was straight as a door frame, bangs on top, so fine you could blow on them and see them lift, long on the sides. We even have a picture. She was like one of those Florence Eiseman kids that never get dirty or bunged up or pushed out of shape, that's Scotchgarded all their life. Have a good time, honey,

I said just like a regular mother. And if Cheryl Ann gets another Sesame Street record, she can take it back, just don't let her take the cellophane off. . . . I was really tracking back then.

Paula has ballet shoes like the ones we used to have. Maybe she'll wear the ballet shoes. She has little feet. Paula has little everything, except she's a big pain in the ass.

What arrives is not, however, Paula. It's somebody in a blue Camaro who slows down, peers up at the house, squinting. Turns out it's Lindy's mom from Visalia. Plump as a duck but nothing like Lindy-size. She's wearing a two-piece knit suit, green with silver threads. She looks like an adult cheerleader with a charm bracelet— little gold heads of people clinking on her wrists.

"Is this 481 Princeton? You happen to know?"

"Yes, ma'am," I say. "I happen to know."

She hesitates, uncertain. Well is it? she seems to say, but doesn't. "You wouldn't happen to know if Lynne Palshaw lives here, would you, dear?" she says finally, addressing me properly.

"Yes, as a matter of fact," I say. "I would."

"Well, does she?" This time she goes ahead and says it, with an embarrassed tag end of a laugh. People are odd. They rarely cease to amaze me.

"That's her room up there," I say, polite as a teacher at open house. I point to the garret room, where a lavender bra is still drying on the rail. By now it's probably stiff. "She puts her stuff on the gable but you're not supposed to, it's against the regs." (She may have heard garbage about me, things I do, so it doesn't hurt to get a few licks in.) "You can go on in if you want."

"Thank you, dear."

She clutches her purse tightly and squeezes past. (I have my cigarettes and ashtray spread out on the top step.) She has freckles and tinges of red to her hair. She is sort of rusted out, you might say. Red rusty, dead dusty, bed busty, led lusty, med musty. I've talked to Tiffani about taking her meds, Dr. Madsen said to M and D the day he told them I had the Big S. Think of schizophrenia as civil war, he said smoothly. It was familiar terrain to him.

But aren't there any tests you can do on her to be sure? Absolutely a hundred percent sure, D said.

Blood tests he means, X rays, M said.

Spinal taps, D said. Whatever.

Yuck me out, I said. Forget it.

What you have to realize, Dr. Madsen said, is there's no one test that's in and of itself diagnostic. We have to look to the symptoms, the behavior. A few patients have abnormal CAT scans. Another group you might find some irregularity in the EEG's, especially those with no family history of the disease.

Like us, M said. There's nobody on either side.

Which is the case with 50 percent of all schizophrenics, Dr. Madsen said.

Well, there was your Uncle Lorne, he was a queer duck, a loner, D said. Never married, lived at home with his parakeets.

Well if we're getting into that, what about your cousin Fiona? Took I don't know how many trips to the dump to shovel out ten years of debris when she finally went.

That was a different case altogether. We're getting off the track, D said.

What you have to keep in mind is that a third of all those diagnosed get better, become functional, Dr. Madsen said.

I have another cigarette and start in coughing, which I do when I smoke too much, which I always do, smoke too much. But I'm probably going to quit, once I get the willpower built up. That's definite. Everything in its season—lung cancer too, I suppose. It's part of nature's grand design.

I'm sitting there in this old armchair we keep on the porch with my legs draped over the side when I realize they aren't coming. *They* aren't coming to my Thanksgiving dinner that I had the idea for. Everybody else is here. Lindy's mother, Geoffrey's father, Carla's

Randy. Warren is from New Jersey, which is why he doesn't have anybody. He got this letter saying how they really wished they could make it, maybe some other year. Meanwhile they might be able to figure somebody to drive the old Fiat out, which had just had a good going over if Warren had use for it, provided he would go ahead and get his English as a Second Language Teaching Credential, which shouldn't be that hard after all the time he spent bumming around Mexico presumably absorbing Spanish at a great rate. Warren read the letter aloud, folded it up carefully. Ay caramba, he said— it's true he doesn't have that good of an accent.

That's New Jersey, but my people are right here in Orinda, and I have nobody. It was my idea to have everybody and I have nobody. The four of them, M and D and Paula and Jake, have taken off for the seventeen-course dinner at the Claremont Hotel, which was discussed and abandoned last year. It just might be too difficult, M said, under the circumstances. Those being myself. Why can't we just ask her if she wants to, Paula said, if she's willing to get dressed up and everything? Right this minute they are sitting there having Campari and sodas or Rob Roys, Jake likes Rob Roys. Tears start streaming down. Sometimes they really get me going, I get so mad at them. That's when I see the Volvo.

She's actually in jeans, my sister Paula, the dresser, is in jeans.

"Howdy doody," she waves.

"Is that how you dress for a formal Thanksgiving dinner?" I say, sniffing back my desertion tears.

"Well look at you, kiddo."

It's true I myself am in jeans, but the hostess shouldn't be overdressed, quote unquote M. Still Paula is flustered, which pleases me. Well, sort of. It doesn't displease me, let me put it that way. But I must work not to be immature. This is on my list, a priority item. I'm older but I don't call her kiddo. It's demeaning.

M and I kiss and D says where do I put this? They have brought six jars of Sonoma Farms Gift Pack separated by shredded waxy green Easter basket grass. Zucchini relish. Marmalade.

"It's lime marmalade," Paula says. "You liked it last time."
"I did?"

They have also brought a lug if that's what it's called (that's what D calls it) of Golden Delicious apples. I take one. I'm starving. Maybe it's a peck, although nobody knows what pecks are.

"You should wash them first," M says. "You'll ruin your dinner," D says. "You don't know what kind of spray they used," Paula says. The usual bazooka fire. I chomp away, ruining my health, my appetite, their dispositions, and feeling little-twerpy again, a kiddo. M tucks a box of toilet seat covers under my arm. You might want to put this away, she says, embarrassed. And I'm going I don't know what kind of joint you think this is as we go up the steps.

People start saying their first names. Sheila, that's Lindy's mother. Francine, that's M, Glenn, that's D, Randy, that's Randy. I read somewhere where Einstein had a son who was schizophrenic and I wonder if Einstein ever went to Thanksgiving dinner and somebody said, Hey gang, this is Al. The comical humor of this is not lost on me, so I start laughing.

"Stay with it now, Mary Alice," D says. There's the warning in his voice, a blend of fear and squelch. Squear, felch. I keep on laughing.

"Lindy, if you could point me the way to the bathroom, dear," Sheila says.

"Do you really have to?" Lindy says, "because—"

"Well after the ride and all," Sheila says with a nervous little laugh.

"It's all right," Carla says, "show her."

I slink back to the potatoes I'm supposed to mash. They are cowering in the pot. I quit laughing. I should have told D my name's Tiffani now, not Mary Alice, remember? I should have said this is our house. I should have said get lost. What's currently lost is the potato masher. I should have said you're lucky to be invited at all considering how you've ske-rewed me up. You must have. I started out extra normal. A smiley baby in the pictures. One of Smiley's people. And I had friends—remember Karen Flax? There wasn't anything much wrong with her. She came over all the time till they moved to Modesto. Was it my fault she moved to Modesto? . . . What am I trying to do? Drain the potatoes. No, find the colander, that comes first. I won a yo-yo contest in junior high, that took concentration, and I was The First Shepherd's Wife in the Christmas tableau at the firehouse. The base of the fire extinguisher looks like it could mash potatoes in a pinch. . . . I got second prize for Sunset over Lahaina in the Senior Foto Fair. I did a lot of stuff. Right now I am trying to hold the potatoes back, but the steam blinds me. I would have made the Commencement speech even, if certain things hadn't happened. I was a person back then.

The potatoes have fallen into the sink. Lindy was signed up to peel them, but she didn't and now when I go to peel them cooked they break up on me and fall off into the sink, so much gray slush. I go to ask M what to do. She and Lindy's mom are yakking away.

"I can't help but think of all those Sunday mornings when they were little and we were all in the big bed together—Mary Alice always wanted to be in the middle—and you couldn't believe anything like this could ever happen."

"Oh right, I know what you mean."

"You run into somebody who knew the family back then and they'll say I saw Mary Alice the other day and then like as not, they'll just wait for you to say something, to comment."

"Or they say is there anything they can do to help. To my way of thinking, Lindy's trouble all stems from her metabolism she has, her weight problem. I've tried absolutely everything with her— diets, you wouldn't believe! Atkins, Cambridge, Pritikin, Beverly Hills, the Jean Harris one who got murdered, the Cooper Institute in Texas, you may have heard of it, they're very highly . . . "

A Big Game growl comes up from the belly of the crowd on the TV.

" . . . a real heartbreaker," M is saying, "no question about it."

I storm back into the kitchen, kick the door shut. Screw the potatoes. Carla tells me to get the bird out of the oven. I yank it out, but it's in one of those dumb disposable foil jobs and it buckles on me, shooting hot grease all over the floor and into my shoe.

"Ayeee!" I howl. "My foot!"

"Shit!" Carla screeches.

There's a momentary silence in the living room. "If you need any help out there . . ." M carols, "you've got lots of volunteers."

"No, it's okay," Carla coos. She's glopping sweet potatoes into scalloped orange cups Warren did with his Swiss army knife, glaring at them like they're an encounter group. Some are lopsided and drop down all of a sudden where he couldn't make the scallops meet.

"Here, take these," Carla says. "And don't go dropping them either." I glide cross country, snow plow from the stove to the doorway, leaving a track of melted grease.

"When the psychiatrist first said schizophrenic, I hit her," Lindy's mother is saying.

(Which is more loyal than M and D would ever be. They think they're so controlled.)

"You actually hit him?" M says. "What did he do then?"

"Her. It was a her. Dr. Ernestine Geller. She was supposedly the best in Lassen County. At the time. Well, she just looked, I would say she looked stunned for a minute. I thought she might go ahead and have me booked, have me arrested for assault and battery, something like that, but then she just said, don't shoot the messenger, it doesn't do any good to shoot the messenger. She was wearing a gray blouse with little tucks here and shell earrings, funny what you remember."

"I always thought I had a charmed life, in a minor way, you know," M speaking. "Till this."

"Well, at least you don't have just the one," Sheila says, looking at Paula, who is flipping through an old *Newsweek*.

I slam down the sweet potatoes in orange cups.

"Is it upstairs?" Howard says, "the . . . "

"Well, it is but—" I say. "We already, that is Lindy's mom . . . "

"It's okay," Carla says. "We'll chance it."

Howard gives her a puzzled look, not unlike Geoffrey's.

"It's a crap shoot," Warren says.

"Turn on the hall light for him," Carla says.

Carla lights the candle in the Chianti bottle.

"I think they want us now," Randy says.

People start milling around. I stand there looking at the erupting skirts of cheerleaders on Channel 4. I always wanted to be one of those. One of the cheerleaders—Hot Peppers they were called at Foothill J.C. where I went briefly, very briefly—does three cartwheels in a row. "Isn't she a doll?" M says, racking up another useful comment.

I went to the tryouts once, they let people watch, and the ones who made it through the finals leap in the air—yahoo! One of them leaped so high you'd of thought it was the Resurrection or something. Everybody laughed, and the ex Hot Peppers who had coached them one on one—I might well have made it if I'd found me somebody to train with night and day the way they do—they come out onto the field and give a rose apiece and then it's said they all go off to the Little Switzerland on the pike and have fondue. There's this table all set up for 18, 9 old Hot Peppers and 9 pledges. I waited in the stadium till they all left. Whatcha doin', holdin' up the fence? Eric Noon said. I didn't answer. When I finally left it was dark and I had diamonds on my palms from where I'd been holding on to the chain link fence. That night I sat in the student union drinking coffee and chewing on the wooden stirrers till they started stacking chairs on tables, which got me confused. Paula claims she never wanted to be a pom pom girl, but I think there's a dominant female cheerleader gene, just like there's a horseback riding one that comes to the fore about age 14. She just doesn't know herself that well, not being in therapy.

"Come on, we're all waiting for you, Mary Alice," D says.

"Don't wait on her, just go ahead." M.

"No, I think she should sit down with the rest of us." D.

There's room at the isthmus end (we had to add the ironing board and two bar stools to make the table long enough) but M and D are there so I plop down beside Geoffrey on the hassock, which makes a gruesome noise. Also, Geoffrey's chin is barely over the edge because nobody can find the phone book to build him up, all we have is the phone book covers.

"Any book will do," Howard says.

Carla goes, "See, we don't have any books."

"No books? I can't imagine a house without books," Howard says. "We'll have to see what we can do about that, what do you say to that, Geoff?" Howard gives Geoffrey's head a pat, a twist actually as though he's trying to screw it on straight. "This fellow here was named for Geoffrey Chaucer, spelled the same way even. What kind of books do you people think you'd like to have?"

Nobody says anything. It's kind of a stilted silence. I think of silence, which is just air—basically oxygen, nitrogen, and carbon dioxide—there on stilts stumping from chair to chair till it gets to me. I smile. D gives me a look.

"Checkbooks," I say.

"No, Tiffani," M says. "He means to read." I mean, Jesus!

"How about you, young lady?" Howard is saying to Carla, whose name he seems to have forgotten. "What do you like in the way of reading matter?"

"I don't know, I lost my glasses," Carla says. "In New Mexico."

"Oh, what part of New Mexico was that?" M says.

"I don't know, I wasn't driving."

"Because we were to Mesilla State Park in '81," M says. She is looking at the slaw Carla fixed like it's a pile of gonorrhea.

"They say Santa Fe's really come along," D says, looking at Carla as though she's the living proof. Everybody looks at Carla, even million-year-old fathers.

"Why don't we just eat the fuckin' dinner, okay?" Carla says, sort of embarrassed but gracious nonetheless.

Warren stands up, his temple vein throbbing. "I want to propose a toast," he says holding out his glass of Perrier. "To the young woman in our midst who I understand is forsaking all others on the sixth of January." He is looking at Carla but talking about Paula, who blushes. (Her skin is very fine and she colors easily.)

"Well, I'll sure second that," Sheila says as though we were taking a vote. "Especially these days. Anybody who does it the old-fashioned way."

"It's going to be really low profile," Paula says. "No attendants or anything." She doen't look at me.

"I'm the no attendant," I say. I do my best to keep things going, the life of the party (or maybe it's the death of the party, I don't know). She's a kick, Ceci Schroeder used to say, that one is. She's just too much. I'm supposed to be the wedding photographer, which is better anyway.

Cathouse jumps onto the table. Carla bats him off, beat it.

"It's neat they let you have pets here," Paula says.

"What do you mean *they*? This is our house," I say, suddenly scalded by fury. (Actually if the truth be known, Wookmook doesn't allow pets.)

The lights flicker out momentarily, which they do sometimes when the refrigerator cycles.

"What's the matter, you got cheap electricity around here?" D says.

"What do you mean, cheap electricity, Glenn?" Warren says scowling.

"Oh he's just making a joke," M says hastily. "Tell him it was a joke, Glenn. You mustn't mind him, he's a great kidder."

"Our electricity is just like everybody else's," Warren says hotly. D looks nonplussed.

"Of course it is," Sheila says, "only better if anything." She's holding onto her breasts as though she thinks they might fly across the table, given a sudden power surge.

Dinner is over. Geoffrey is whimpering and wiggling. He turns to Carla. She shakes her head no. Lindy goes upstairs to upchuck her three cranberry shrubs. Sheila says what do you say we all pitch in and get the dishes done? M says so they won't be left with this mess, she wouldn't feel right about it. Geoffrey goes out in the yard, leaving the door open behind him. I try to write a metaphysical seventeenth-century Thanksgiving-type poem combining the spangled light that drips from the water glasses onto the table with the crenelated anus of Cathouse. It isn't Alfred North Tennyson, but beats doing the dishes. In my poem I refer to Cathouse as a Manx, which rhymes with thanks, but he isn't really. He isn't anything. I tell people we have us a genuine Manx cat because I want for us to have something special.

I find it hard to concentrate. Sheila is blithering on about how she even considered the business where they go in there and take a tuck in the intestine, shorten it and M is saying she'd think a long time before she'd go that route, try anything drastic like that and everybody is urging Paula to put on an apron. It's not the kind of environment in which sonnets are born.

Suddenly the knocker on the front door starts clanging. I have an instantaneous funny feeling it's bad news. I know things like that, being considerably in tune with what's coming down at any given time.

"I'm getting it," I say.

It's Bernadette Ryan, the one from next door. In a rose jogging suit with a white stripe up her thighs and her fists knotted.

"He's out back exposing himself," she says, spitting the words out in little foggy thrusts that shoot past me into the house.

"Who?" I say. "Exposing whatself?" I turn and look back at them, at everybody.

"You tell me," Rose Jogging Suit hisses. "One of you. I don't know any of you people's names." She is trying to see inside. "The short one with the beanie."

"Geoffrey?" I say. I have already inwardly said Geoffrey.

"Geoffrey who? I want his full name."

Right off I see what's happened. It doesn't take an Apple computer to figure out. It's all related to the scarcity of toilet paper and to Carla saying the bathroom is For Guests Only, meaning number two-wise, and nobody thinking to explain slowly, go over and over it the way you have to with Geoffrey in words of one syllable or less just what is meant by that phrase. You can use the bathroom *for certain things* we should have said, those being as follows.

"So what's the deal? Are you going to tell me his name or are you just going to stand there?" Rose Jogging says.

"I bet anything I know what's happened," I say.

"I'm telling you what happened, I just witnessed it."

"Yah, but he's not exposing himself, Geoffrey's not, no way."

"I'd just like to know what you call it then. He's got his dinger out—"

"He's peeing, that's all there is to it, it's that simple. He may have been exposed, but he wasn't exposing himself. It's all a misunderstanding. You don't know Geoffrey—"

"Geoffrey who?"

"Like we do, he's the original Mr. Shy."

"Shy! You call that shy?" she's shouting now. "Tell that one to the police."

I'm shaking, I don't know why. Well, of course I do. "Wait here," I say. I leave the door ajar. "Don't come in." They're all just standing there in a group. They know something afoot's at hand.

I can't go to Warren, not with her talking police. Carla? No—she'd come on like Mean Joe Green, take on this witch bitch, tear into her, chew her into chowder and spit her out like spaghetti through a nutcracker. Like what? through a what? That's stupid, but my mind is stressed.

"Maybe I can be of help," Howard says. I would rather it was D. Howard comes out on the porch. So be it.

This one, Bernadette, looks him over, head to toe—cord sport jacket with leather elbow patches, sideburns, brogues (I just wish they didn't have those little tassels). He looks somewhat Gregory Peckish. I hope she notices the notched lapels and the foulard I think it's called pocket handkerchief, especially the handkerchief. I will try to work it into the conversation.

"Maybe I can get somewhere with you," she says. "It sure doesn't do any good trying to reason with the likes of them."

"Could I please borrow your handkerchief, Howard?"

"Why don't you go on inside, Tiffani," Howard says smooth as vaseline yogurt, "finish up what you're doing and let me handle this."

"Well here's the thing, I've got to give you the straight scoop so you understand what really—"

"Not now, Tiffani," Howard says. "First I want to satisfy this lady's concerns if I can."

Lady? Howard is easing me in, closing the door rather rudely behind me.

Warren goes, "Why didn't you call us? This is our house, our situation to deal with. You make it seem like we're all little punks or something." I am flanked by hostility, the air is polluted with it.

"It's not my fault, he wanted to handle it himself. Howard did. Go ahead, go on out there, nobody's stopping you," I say but Warren is deflating—you can almost see it happen, the shoulders, the slump, the depression that rinses through him, empties him out, crumples him.

Geoffrey comes in the back door, zipping his fly and humming an old Pointer Sisters song.

Howard is back, mopping his forehead with his pocket hand-kerchief, which won't look sharp any more if he puts it back. He goes up to Geoffrey. "Son—" Howard says. "You and I have to have a talk."

Geoffrey smiles.

"I know you don't want to let all these good people down," Howard says. "Godammit!"

"He's not," I blurt out. "You don't understand, he just had to—"

"Hush," D who doesn't know anything, doesn't comprehend the situation says, and M puts a hand on my shoulder. Paula keeps putting her hair behind her ears so her face is in parentheses.

Geoffrey starts talking urgently on the phone, only there isn't a phone. "Except in Nebraska. Just tell them to wait. The Alliance is intact."

"What kind of rubbish is that?" Howard says. He starts in shaking Geoffrey. "You're not talking on the phone, the phone's over there, look where I'm pointing, okay? There in the hall, that's where the phone is, but you're not even looking at it."

I go, "It's just his messages he gets, his message center."

"It's his voices he hears," Warren says.

"No he doesn't," Howard says. "Anybody here hear any extra voices? If you do, let me know. . . . See there, nobody hears voices. Because there aren't any." He's shaking Geoffrey. A kind of gurgle comes from him that vibrates with the shaking but he keeps the phantom receiver to his ear.

"Why can't you just be normal, okay? That's all I ask. You could be a gas station attendant, Christ, I don't care, sell belts on the corner at Fisherman's Wharf, anything, if you'd just be normal," Howard says, tears streaming down. He just totally loses self control of himself.

In a minute it's over. Howard walks out, eight, nine, ten heavy steps and Geoffrey goes back to his conversation. "We are being attacked," he says, "from Krypton Two." (I remember thinking—he's right.)

We all stand there silent. It's like that moment after the cop stops you and before he comes around front with his ticket book. Sheila sighs. She says she wants for us to break up "on a happy note." We should all gather around the piano and sing a song together. "Wait," I say. I flick up the E for her.

Sheila pumps the pedals, looking down at her espadrille feet, and then she does this stylish business of starting before she really starts with chords that you can tell are about to be John Jacob Jingleheimer Schmidt, but aren't quite yet. Lindy chimes in too soon. "Hold it, darlin', " Sheila says. Lindy backs off, heads for the kitchen, and Sheila beckons Paula to take Lindy's place on the piano bench, completely ignoring me who fixed her up with a playable E. By the time we hit *His name is my name too* we hear the refrigerator door.

Finally they're leaving, which is today's award-winning idea. Paula is working her thumbs in the pockets of her down coat, which she's done ever since she was a little girl when she gets nervous, diddle her fingers so her pockets wiggle like packets of night crawlers.

"Hey, Spook," she says—that's what I used to be known as, in the family, in the dim dead days beyond recall, just one of the names—"I really dug your potatoes."

"They weren't mine."

"They weren't? I thought you said you were doing the potatoes for everybody."

"That was the white ones. You ate the yams in Warren's orange cups."

"Well, I didn't even see the white ones."

I am really too tired for this conversation, it takes too much energy. You have to spell out everything to Paula. "They fell in the sink."

"Oh." She isn't sure whether to laugh. Me either, but I do. Light is shining through her agate earlobes. I wish for a minute she was staying over and we could flop on the bed like we used to—it'd be a gas—so whadid you think? whadid you really think?—have one of those private conversations that even M felt left out of. I'd do one of my imitations, maybe Sheila playing the piano like it's Carnegie Hall, fingers prancing, head bobbing, gold charms clacking the keys. I used to get Paula going till her nose ran and she held her ribs and begged me to quit. What's so funny up there? M'd say. But that was a million years ago, give or take a few.

Lindy won't come down to say goodbye. She's locked herself in the bathroom. Sheila blows a kiss up the stairwell, which is obviously for the benefit of those below since how would Lindy who is locked in the bathroom know, right?

"She's put so much into this day, Lindy has, she's just probably all tuckered out," M says. (Five pounds is about what she's put into it, I think but decide not to say.)

"They can't take too much excitement," D says.

"Oh, I think the laurels go to Tiffani here, she stuck it out," Sheila says. She sprays when she talks.

"Put up with the old folks," D says.

Paula and I give each other an old-fashioned what-nerds-they-are look.

"Listen, you could probably stay, you could spend the night if you wanted to," I say to Paula, but she says she can't and I explain we really don't have room anyway.

They go down the steps clumsily in a group, M, D, Sheila, holding Paula's elbow. Like people who don't know each other but are about to climb out of a rocking boat.

"Better get a coat," Randy says to Carla.

"She needs to stay in tonight," Warren says. "We have to get squared away, have a special house meeting about what's happened."

" 'Fraid we gotta be in the Haight by seven, man," Randy says.

Carla slings her long Shaker knit cardigan with the fox collar over her shoulders and they step out into the night without a backward glance.

We have the Special House Meeting, all right. Warren and me in his room. We are sitting on the floor around ten-thirty Thanksgiving night and he is on a big Carla trip.

"Over and over, same old shit."

"Yah, same shitty old shit," I say. I'm trying to calm him, see.

"She just trashes herself. She'll get stabilized and then zap, she goes out and does it again. If it isn't that fucker Forbes, it's that slimy Indian with the spice store in Berkeley and the bamboo flute. She wants to make it with a bamboo flute, be my guest."

"Oh right," I say. I kind of giggle. Some of the time I giggle just because I giggle, it's a nervous habit or something, but this time it's because I picture old Carla with this bamboo flute installed guess where and this Rajneesh type playing a raga on it. The Kamasutra Rag. It could be a great photo mural. Maybe even double exposed, which you can do with the Nikon, just press the rewind button and advance the film wind lever, that way the shutter will cock but the film won't move and you have this double image, outrageous! But I suppose you could never exhibit it or anything except maybe in Copenhagen, which is a million miles from India, which is ironical.

Warren is watching me giggle. Actually I'm also shivering, it being drafty on the floor.

"Here," he says. He flings a velour robe at me—the one that was in the john the day I moved in. He gets it from his closet.

"Thanks. This Carla's?"

"No, it's Dianne Feinstein's."

Me wearing Dianne Feinstein's bathrobe? Wow! Ladies and gentlemen—Mayor Tiffani Gilchrist.

"Really? It's Dianne Feinstein's? No, don't lie, Warren. It's Carla's. How'd you get it?"

"How do you think I got it? Use your imagination. Go ahead, put it on, you've got goose pimples."

I start to step into the robe but it's awkward. What I should have done was slip it on over my head, lift up my arms, and let it fall gracefully like rain instead of this hop on one foot business like a first grader. Once I get into it, I close my eyes and grope my way over to the mirror on Warren's bureau. I open my eyes. I look about as seductive as Mother Teresa. What it needs is Carla's volcanic free-fall hair, vertical instead of horizontal like mine. And she has this way of fingering her bangs, a sensuous way of fooling with it. Or them. I guess you can't have just one bang, they're like kudos.

"Can you?" I say.

"Can you what?"

"Have just one bang?" I try dragging a strand across my forehead but it flicks in my eye, which begins to water.

"Sure," Warren says. "Happens every day." He comes over.

I'm glad he's taking my query seriously. He starts rubbing his thumb on the inside of my elbow where it's soft. I wonder if I should do that back to be polite. "See, my hair's frizzed out of its mind, it doesn't want to—"

"Don't talk, Tiffani," Warren says.

"Don't talk?"

He's kissing me. "Relax," he says.

"That's a totally dumbass thing to say," I say, spitting out his tongue, "like telling a worrier not to worry."

"Shh!" He's holding me so tight it's like CPR only different. I start to say that but when I open my mouth, he's in it.

Warren is unzipping the robe I just went to the trouble of getting into, but the zipper gets stuck. "There's probably a thread there somewhere," I say looking down cross-eyed. Warren leads me by the zipper pull over to the light.

"There, you're getting it, try from underneath, there. No?"

He works the zipper delicately, like a surgeon, which is one of the things he's considering being. But the zipper doesn't budge. He gives a ferocious yank, which works fine. There's something to be said for the whole macho thing. Magnum force.

Warren is taking off his stuff, zing, zing, zing, crossing his arms and walking his T-shirt up and over, stepping out of his skivvies. D calls them skivvies. There must be another word that's more of a today terminology. I look down at the floor.

"I always leave my socks on," he says. "I hope you don't mind."

"Oh no, sure. I always seem to be attracted to people who leave their socks on, you know what I mean? In sync with them, it's something in me." His socks are black, worn thin at the heel. I will buy him beautiful new fuzzy white ones, crew socks with green bands around the top like Jake's. Absorbent with Biogard. I stand there smiling and freezing, freezing and smiling, Carla's robe puddled at my feet. I try to think what Carla would do under the circumstances. Probably ask for fifty bucks.

"Can I have a cigarette?" (I think there was even one in the pocket of Carla's robe.)

"Come on, *please,* Tiffani."

This may be a Group Home and all, but I'll have to hand it to Warren, he has manners, he can be very polite. "Yah sure," I say. Yah sure what?

I start peeling off my jeans and stop. Maybe I should start at the top. Maybe it looks too forward this way—also I'm not sure if I have on distinguished high-grade bikinis. If I happen to have on my old lavender ones that say Tuesday when this is Thanksgiving and therefore Thursday, will Warren think it's because I'm schizo-affective?

Warren kisses my knee.

"Did you have any of the drumstick?" I say. He stops doing the knee thing.

"What do you want me to do, Tiffani? Get down and beg? That's what that bitch makes me do."

"She is bitchy, Warren. Everybody says Carla's bitchy, not just you, it's definitely not you." Shit! it's my Tuesday underwear. "It must be Belgium," I say conversationally.

Warren goes "What?"

I stand there with my hands crossed across my double strength crotch like a statue I saw once. It had stone blank eyes and a half smile and those crossed hands. I remember thinking it was funny, the smile and the hands.

Warren is on the bed, holding out his arms. His front teeth toe in a little bit, I never noticed that before. "Please, Tiffani. . . ."

I inch closer without stepping out of my bikinis although I guess that's probably coming, though you never know, Dr. Madsen says I shouldn't go jumping to conclusions about every little thing.

"Warren, when Howard said that about not letting all the good people down, did he mean us or the people next door?"

"Jesus, Tiffani, not now, okay? Hurry!"

Things start going on all over the place. Relax, he says again. (I thought we'd had it out on that one.) He's pushing my head down. Take it all in, he says. People love to tell me what to do. Jesus, he says. He's turning into glue.

Everything seems to subside. I remove a small kinked hair from my tongue and keep it delicately poised on my fingertip. I will press it in a book like M's wildflowers, keep it forever.

Warren wraps me in the robe, which he must do with Carla whom I resemble in many ways. "Was it okay?" I whisper, but Warren is snoring small whistles, or whistling small snores, I can't totally tell. I just wish he wouldn't do that. I wish he would stay awake and talk to me. I put my finger under his nose until it warms from his carbon monoxide or methane or whatever. I think maybe the sound will alter with the finger like an oboe or some such wind instrument, but it doesn't, though they say dogs can hear all kinds of stuff we can't. However, we only have a cat.

I go over and check myself in the mirror, which is held by two cobra-shaped side pieces. Warren has a bumper strip across the bottom that says I BRAKE FOR HALLUCINATIONS. I can't say I look all that different.

Some day I will write up my experiences. An article for Cosmo— "I Was Used But It Was Useful." Never mind some day, by the time Warren wakes up, I may have it done. I will put it right under his nose, the pages, on my rolled-up jeans we made into a pillow for me. God, woman, he will say, probably toying with my hair, I didn't know you could write like that—it's Vonnegut, Krantz, Brautigan, McKuen, and Harlequin Whoever, the whole nine yards. Dynamite stuff.

Dynamite? Maybe I will get the Nobel Prize or something. SAS to Sweden, Land of the Midnight Sun. I'll take M and D as my guests. We'll have Swedish pancakes with lingonberries. D will pig out on herring and he'll sing My Name Is Yon Yonson, I come from Visconsin, belch belch. God is he gross!

I come by my talent naturally. M once sold Hallmark a bereavement verse in which her peace rhymed with never cease or it might have been surcease, I forget. We—they—have 50 of them in a drawer somewhere with purple parchment hyacinths on the front and M's verse inside.

What I need is an outline. See, I may have occasional disconnected thought, inappropriate behavior, and impaired judgment, but I'm not totally up the Columbia. I know why things happen all right.

Warren was pissed with Carla, that was for openers. Then I don't know what exactly. I guess I felt sorry for Warren in a way. And in a way attracted to him, plus I was ready to take childhood and dump it out a seven-storey window. I mean with me it wasn't desire exactly, it was more the zipper I was concentrating on. I may not be a fully sexual being at this particular point, but I now feel I have potential in that segment of the human com—

The door is flung open. Carla! Yikes. Warren's snore snorts to a stop. Carla snaps on the overhead light, which is a naked bulb, as they say, and Warren bolts up. Meaning sits bolt upright. I don't understand the grammar in "bolt upright."

"You came back!" Warren says, rubbing his eyes like it's a miracle or something. The Second Coming. Actually it's more like the soaps.

"What's *she* doing in *that*?" Carla has one hand on a hip. (Some people cock eyebrows, Carla cocks a hip. It's a matter of personal assertiveness styles.)

"Look, Carla, no big hoo-hah, the kid was cold," Warren says.

"I could have told you that," Carla says to Warren and they kind of laugh. I can't stand when people are in league, like Warren and Carla or M and D or Paula and Jake.

Carla's going, "Take it off, dingbat," which is not the way you address a sexually active mature adult.

If I accede to what appears to be popular demand and take it off, I won't have anything on. So I can't take it off. I cinch the sash tighter and look from her to Warren, Warren to her.

"In all fairness—" I say.

"Like you've got 10 seconds," Carla says.

"You better give it to her, kid," Warren says.

Carla is looking at me like I'm a Libyan beetle. I can't believe it, what's coming down here. She is snapping her fingers, indicating count down, click, click.

I unzip the fucking robe, meaning the post-fucking robe, throw it at her, take off running. I set a record for the two-yard dash into my room.

It's twelve oh four. Thanksgiving has come and gone. It took off from us, slid away. Warren tried to use Paula to get at Carla because of Randy, but I was the only one it bothered. M and Sheila loved each other's miserable company. Geoffrey will probably never pee again. I shouldn't have let Howard get in the act when Bernadette showed up, that was immature. I shouldn't have got it on with Warren, if that's what I did. That was mature, but didn't get me anywhere. Now they're over there laughing in the cold scabby night. Am I the joke?

I light one of Warren's cigarettes. He finally gave me three. Three. That seems to represent his self-image of me. My Tuesday pants are over there humiliating me. I may never get them back.

The face is in the window again like Doom itself. Or is it? I'm beginning to think it's always there. But I feel too planetary to get up and check.

V Next day is Friday, the day after Thanksgiving. It's always a Friday, right? I get to Dr. Madsen's half an hour early. I can't wait to tell him, that may well be the best part of the whole Warren deal. What I'm going to say, I have it all planned, I'm going to tell him I am now a private in the sexual revolution. PFC T. Gilchrist. I've considered all different approaches and this is the one I favor. It'll make his day. He'll say he's proud of me. He's always on my case about how I am refusing to deal with my sexuality. I hate to think what that phrase is worth to him, at $95 per 50 minute hour, if he says it three times a session at 10 seconds each, it's costing, oh I don't know, you'd need Charlie Chaplin with his IBM and all the widgets. In the past when Dr. Madsen gets off on his sexuality roll, I've pointed out that it's other people who refuse to deal with my sexuality, not me, and then he jabbers about defense mechanisms and something he calls projective smoke screen which I asked Warren to ask Dr. Frick, his therapist, about and Dr. Frick told Warren to tell me to ask Dr. Madsen to explain it. I really think what it was was that Dr. Madsen is too deep for Dr. Frick. Warren is into Transactional Analysis and he's happy because he just discovered in T.A. that he was scripted for joylessness and he thinks he's on the edge of a breakthrough. I forgot to ask him whether it's to or from joylessness.

"It'll be just a bit, he's running a little late," Kimmie, the receptionist with braces says. I asked her once how much they set her back, but she wouldn't tell me. Plenty was all she said. She's reclusive. She shouldn't withdraw like that. If you wanted to talk to Dr. Madsen about why you hold back, would he give you a rate? I said. Oh I don't know, she said, blushing and kind of laughing.

I study the fluorescent lights with what looks like ice cube dividers over them. I count the squares for something to do even though I know by now there are 28. Finally! He comes for me. Swing low sweet chariot. Maroon tie, white seagulls?

Easy does it. I go into Thanksgiving first. I explain how I jinned up the whole concept and how I came to Geoffrey's defense and how I tried to reason reasonably with the one from next door who has a thing about us. Dr. Madsen says great, I am beginning to identify with the house, I no longer find it threatening, I am beginning to develop a sense of belonging, an emerging sense of self. He rockets right along, but my mind is elsewhere.

Dr. Madsen is looking at me.

I look at Dr. Madsen. It's one on one. And then I blurt it all out in one raggle taggle razzle dazzle spurt. A little like Warren's ejaculation. I even forget the stuff about the sexual revolution, but I put in the part about the zipper. Dr. Madsen takes my bulletin in stride, as they say. I didn't expect a standing ovation, but he could at least react, not just sit there like a barrel of blunt.

How do I feel about it he wants to know. (Of course you never know what he really wants to know. If anything.)

Great. Really terrific. Like the northern lights, I say. (I am still thinking Nobel.)

Dr. Madsen waits. That's his specialty. He's a great waiter. I guess I better come up with more stuff. I sit there clicking my nails, considering.

"It was like. . . ." God, what should it be like? I try to think back to *Princess Daisy,* but then he might possibly have read that too. "He held me after, rubbed my back and everything, and then we fell asleep like we were riding the Vespa, me curled against his back with my arms around his waist . . . that's the way Paula told me she and Jake sleep." I add that last in case he didn't think it sounded right on, that nobody did that. "I'm not totally sure how it all got going, but Warren said it was like with Carla. Only better maybe even. . . ." I kind of trail off. I don't want it to sound like disinformation. "I forget just how he put it."

Pause.

This one belongs to him. It's his turn, his move, I'm exhausted. "So are you going to try it again?"

This really pisses me off. They're absolutely never satisfied! And also what's this *try it*? Like it didn't happen. I go, "Why? Aren't you proud of me? Do I have to keep proving stuff? Or what?" Dr. Madsen has on his navy blazer which he looks great in. He dresses for the occasion (unlike Dr. Frick who wears jeans). Like he's going out to dinner. "Do you ever eat at Seven Lanterns?"

He says no, he's not that crazy about Szechuan. I don't personally think in his chosen profession he should bandy around the word crazy that way. I picture *crazy* taking off like one of those wind-up balsa airplanes kids have that blitz around your head and get you eventually. I look up. Dr. Madsen is saying he's heard there's often an hour wait for a table at Seven Lanterns. I kind of like it when we just talk people to people. But then he's back to S.O.P. He says he thinks it's good that I am opening up to experience on a number of levels, beginning to feel things, but he'd like me to get it through my head that I'm not Carla. Or Paula. Or anybody else. (Mrs. Madsen?) I smile. He smiles.

He goes on. I'm Tiffani Gilchrist, and what I've got to do is figure out who that is, find my own identity. Same old jazz. What does he think I've been doing? Well, he can go fuck himself, thereby finding *his* own identity.

"Okay," I say. "Sure thing, "I'll work on it."

"Attagirl," he says. Meaning I hit the right button. All in all it was not a bad session, which I could tell anyway from the tie.

On the way home I stop off at Caffe Roma for a double mocha cappuccino. Paolo, the waiter, is a buddy of mine. He comes on to me although he has a wife and bambinos coming out the kazoo.

He swirls the foamed milk in a P for Paolo—he's kind of an artist in his own right, whatever that means—and dusts my mocha with chocolate from an aluminum flour shaker.

"Tiffani, you are knowing that lady, Meesus Ryan?" Behind Paolo are bottles of viscous Orgeat syrup that put me in mind of my episode with Warren. "She is live near to you, Meesus Ryan, no?"

"How about another hit with the chocolate?" I say. "Ryan?" I wrinkle up my nose which has some foam on it. "*Ryan?* No. . . ." Paolo reaches over, blots the foam with a paper napkin, leans back, and sketches her figure in the air, rolling his eyes.

"Oh her. I don't personally think she's that great. The people next door, they're named Ryan, yah. Nerd City."

"Well, Paolo is not wanting to freak out Tiffani, it's not Paolo's affair, but . . ." he twists the ends of an amaretto paper.

He's acting dicey. "C'mon, spit it out, man."

Paolo looks around, holds back a hunk of my hair like it's a curtain and says in my ear, "She is come in, see?"

"Si," I say, moving out of range of his anisy breath.

"And she is not sit, so right away it's a beeg special deal, right? And then Paolo he see she's a got all these Zurox copies in her hand. She say she's a out collecting the signatures. She's a go around with what you call it? a paper? A petition paper which is get C House ca-bam!" He slams the basket that holds the espresso grounds against the yellow plastic slop can and holds it up for me to see. "All gone, justa like C House."

I stop mid-guzzle. A paper? A petition? To shut down C House? The foam on the cappuccino suddenly tastes like liquid chalk. My hackles go up. What are hackles? Are they like dander? Which is like dandruff? "Just what do you mean, Paolo, C House gone?"

"Is not what Paolo means, Paolo not the bad guy. What she is say is like so. This place, this Camelot House, he is operating without a permit, that's what she say." Paolo folds a gray piece of towel into a neat little package and sets it to catch the drip from the Vesuvio.

"So?"

"So all is take is for Meesus Ryan she is get for herself enough of the neighbors which is include businesses too. Say tutti we all sign this piece of the paper she has, then the pezzi grossi they take over and arrivederci, so long paesano." Paolo draw his finger across his throat.

"That scumbag bitch! What's she got against us? We never did anything to her! She just likes to hear herself squawk, you should hear what she calls *him* when he forgets to take out the garbage."

"Okay, okay, don't aska me," Paolo says. "What does Paolo know?" He taps three fingers on his lips. "What she is say, she is say it's much noisy like you wouldn't believe and pazzo happenings and everything lika that. . . . Look, don't get hot on your collar, Paolo is only tell you what she is tell me, okay?"

I am pacing like I do, from the cassata in its glass dome to the pan forte that Lindy once broke a tooth on. "Listen, Paolo, you didn't sign anything? You wouldn't?"

"Me? Naw. Paolo never sign nothing. Paolo he is not even having a green card yet. Paolo say to her to come back when the Chief is here, see? Paolo doesn't need more beeg trouble in his life, right?" Every time he says Paolo he points at the third snap on his Hawaiian shirt.

I scoop out my bottom foam with a finger. I don't trust people who talk about themselves like they weren't themselves.

"What you are looking me for?" Paolo says. "Paolo's here to swear you, he didn't do absolutely nothing, assolutamente niente."

I barrel into the house and collect everybody in the living room. Power! I know something they don't. I'm personally of course depressed by the shit-sucking turn of events, but exhilarated at turning up something newsworthy.

"You guys, we're probably gonna get thrown out a here." I'm breathing hard. "Out of C House." I give them what Paolo said, faster than Channel 2 news, the bottom-line gist.

It's like a grenade, an attack on the embassy. I watch their confusion, forgetting for the moment it's mine too. Where'll everybody go? Where?

Geoffrey slept in an Amana side-by-side freezer carton under the 580 Overpass in San Mateo until an out-reach worker found him. The County had this patch of beds in Glenlake which is an L facility but then they found out Geoffrey was cheeking his meds and they threw him out.

With Lindy she tried six different "treatment modalities" in 18 months before she came to C House, such that she refuses to take the tape off her Tide, she just keeps on bumming my Bold.

Carla is always a fingernail ahead of the law. She kept getting picked up on a 5150, mentally disturbed. What she'd do, she'd wait till the Jolson Lincoln Mercury dealership on Walnut closed and then she'd slip under the chain and sleep in this metallic gray Mark II. Sometimes she'd take people there, sometimes it was just her. Or what she'd do, she'd reach over the top of the cubicles in bus station johns and snatch purses from their hooks while people were busy peeing, it gave you a 10-second lead, she said. New definition of pissing your money away.

Warren says the places he lived, you had to take drugs to survive the drug scene. He's held together by a mortar of pessimism. Everything that goes wrong, all tragedy has been weakened, pre-defused by having taken place already in his imagination. Unless, of course, he's in his manic phase.

Camelot is part of a chain of moves, moving on, continental drift. Strange nightmare-saturated beds that belong to the System. That's C House, if you're lucky. If not, an icy unlit cave called All Alone. Of course, with me it's entirely different because of M and D out there. My safety net.

"We've got to call Miriam Myers," Carla is saying. "Like it or not, Miriam's got to be wired in." I wish it was me that had said that.

Friday is my day to have dinner at home, at the folks' place, I mean. Ex-home, which is almost like exhume. I can't stand the thought of moving back there, getting buried alive under all that *don't this, don't that* tonnage, but what can you do?

What I do is I sit on the curb, waiting to be picked up. It's misting. I can hear the fog horns lowing on the Bay. I pretend it's Genesis (I was very religious the first half of my sophomore year). God has just created the world, breathed a sigh of relief. (In the beginning was a sigh of relief. That wouldn't be a cliche, it being the first one ever.) The fog is God's phlegmy breath. He's made a few people on spec—prototype models. And he's satisfied. Why, I'm not sure. So I'm sitting there on a rock, sedentary on a sedimentary rock, that's not bad, and M comes out of the mist—"Tiffani!" and finds me. She's happier than I've ever seen her. And young. She has flowers in her arms like in a picture around the time I was born—a bouquet Ceci Schroeder sent to welcome us home from the hospital. She comes upon me and she can't believe it at first—another perfect creature—she's not alone in the world—and there's none of that poke-jab-gouge stuff between us. She doesn't say why do you just sit staring in the mirror that way? why do you all the time take pictures of yourself? ring the doorbell a zillion times? sleep in your clothes? put them on backwards? laugh into space? slurp your food? sit on the curb? beg cigarettes? lose your key? squander your money? hang your head? pull out your hair? smoke that weird way? bite your nails? cough? stare? shamble? pace? pant? stand too close? why? She can say all that with her eyes, the line of her mouth. It's embedded in private history, our stones of Venice. But in my vision she's just excited to see me, ME. She holds out her arms—an earth mother, all joy and bosoms, not a guilt-ridden gray-haired muddle.

I used to spend a lot of time looking at my baby pictures. There's this one underexposed and everything taken in the hospital, Alta Bates, where I was born. M is beaming. Why are you looking like that? I used to ask. Because of you, she'd answer. Last year I was doing it again—looking at the pictures—and I asked her again.

Why are you looking like that? She hesitated. I thought she wasn't going to reply. I kind of held my breath. But then she said it, "Because of you," except she had tears in her eyes like she wasn't even answering what I asked.

I reach over and pick some neato daisies, the purple African kind, from the patch by the curb. I twirl the stems between my palms. I might even give M a bouquet.

A window goes up. "We'd appreciate if you didn't go picking our flowers," Bernadette Ryan says. "That don't belong to you."

"Sure thing." I stick them back in the dirt, which is surprisingly warm.

Mrs. Ryan shakes her head like she doesn't believe I'm putting her shitty little flowers back.

M shows up. I get in.

"How's everything?"

"Let's go," I say. "Terrible. Let's just get out of here, Bernadette's freaking out over a few dumb daisies that happened to get picked."

"You shouldn't go picking the flowers. How many times do I have to tell you?"

"Forever," I say, which ends the conversation. Something always does.

I was planning on telling her about the petition, sharing input with her, but piss on it. I sit as far away as possible, leaning against the door, smoking a butt from the ashtray from my last week's visit—if D is there I can't smoke in the car. She reaches across me and pushes down the door lock. We mustn't lose our treasure on the MacArthur Freeway. I stare at her, not blinking or anything. She knows I'm looking at her, but she doesn't formally acknowledge. She doesn't like it when I stare. I drop my head. She doesn't like that either. Why do you hang your head like a donkey? Once in a children's zoo I studied a little donkey as old as time, as the centuries, standing in a brazen grove of children who didn't appreciate him. They thought he was comical even. They hee hawed around him, around us, hee haw, hee haw. He looked at them grayly, one dis-

dainful eye at a time. They kept him there with the minor beasts,
the afro'd sheep, the frisking goats, so dumb they chomp on flowered
dresses, the turtles with linoleum patterns. He definitely shouldn't
be there. I tried to get him to come on out through the metal stile
they, whoever built the children's zoo, thought he was too dumb
to operate. I'm going now, and you can come if you want, I said
to him. All you have to do is push, see, it isn't that hard, but he
didn't budge. C'mon, you. I gave him a last chance, a nudge. I'm
part of that donkey, our heads are the same, but he didn't see it.
Creatures are used to staying where they are used to staying.

I look at M.

We glide into the carport. They live in a condo now, called—
are you ready for this?—Sparrow Glen. M probably thinks this is
Fate too, Glen for Glenn, D's name, I don't know. All I know is
a month after I moved out, that is to say, a month after they moved
me out, they went and sold the house on Poplar Canyon. Paula
moved in with Jake and M and D cleaned out the rampant past, all
the stacks of banana yellow *Geographic*s in the attic that were supposed
to help with homework, my doll house with lights that worked,
Paula's lilac tutu, the snail head with the buckram feelers we fought
over, my size 4 soccer boots, the cage for my hamster Ringo, the
pith helmet from my Isak Dinesen phase, the two halves of the
ceramic professor book ends. I could go ahead and give you a list
that long. They never should have sold that place, they had no right.
As long as the past was there, intact, there was always the chance
you could go back, find out what went wrong, straighten it out,
pick up the dropped stitch.

"Come on, Tiffani," M is holding the door open. The Volvo is
there in the carport so I know D's home. *There,* I mean. I avoid a
crotch sniffing dog, probably a Doberman, step over a fat orange
hose that connects a 50 hp Steamex Supersonic Rug Cleaning truck
to the condo upstairs with a heavy insistent *whoosh.* The side door
of the truck is open and I peer in at the brushes and plastic bottles.
Pet Odor Off, Chem Dry, Color Brightener, Duraclean.

"What would you rather we had tonight? Red snapper with sesame oil or Nancy Reagan's Down Home Chicken?" M says. It's a bribe. She doesn't want me there looking in the truck. We go in.

She is back to her charades. We are playing Normal Daughter Has Come Home for Normal Dinner. She is even putting on Normal Apron. "So what'll it be?"

I don't answer for a long time as it happens. I'm thinking about everything.

"Tiffani honey?" There's a kind of concession to hopelessness to it.

"Duraclean," I say. She looks pained, more pained than usual so I say I don't care, which I don't. Actually I decide to go ahead and make myself a tomato sandwich. I slap on the mayo thick as a quilt. "Whoa Tillie, take it easy there," D says.

"He just doesn't want you to have all that oil, it's not good for you," M says.

"She's got it on her sleeve there," D says.

Eventually we sit at the table, which is the same one we always had, Duncan Phyfe, whoever he was. I think about the petition, about not sitting at a table, not having a table to sit at, I mean. It's scary, where am I supposed to live, guys? I see myself sleeping in the old J. C. Penney building on Market, shuffling along toward Skid Row with my aluminum camp stuff—a cup within a sauce pan within a skillet within a wing nut—I used to have to help Paula work hers.

"You're not eating," M says.

"She's just picking," D says.

"Try her on some snapper."

"Did you throw out my canteen?"

"Your what?" D says. He's studying the salt shaker to see if the holes are plugged again.

"You know, my canteen. When you cleaned out the attic. With my initials in nail polish on the bottom, the one I took to camp."

"You wouldn't believe the stuff she hauled out of there," D says.

"We got the middle size dumpster and she had to send back for the big one."

"But what about my canteen? What about the canteen?"

"What's the matter, you figuring on going back to camp?"

"That reminds me. Glenn, did I tell you that that Minot girl who was at camp when Paula was died of leukemia? Lisa Marie. Twenty-two the paper said."

D tsk tsks.

"There's worse things, things that go on and on."

"Like me?"

"No, like that Collins boy where he just disappeared off the face of the earth and they don't know, they don't know what to think, they just have to wait and see."

It still seems like they're talking about me. I wish I knew, did they mean me? In which case I'd never come back, never ever bother them again.

"I'm not going back to that crappy camp. I'm too old." I stand up the little white slabs of snapper and fence in my carrots. "I'm really kind of considering I might come back to live here." M and D exchange looks. "I could help with the housework. I'm better with chores now." I start picking up grains of rice that have splattered around my plate on the pads of my fingers. "Just for a while. Okay?"

I don't bother looking at them.

"Is something the matter, Tiffani?" M says. "You're not getting on with the people at C House, is that it?"

"No, that's not it."

"Because it's normal, people have their little differences," M says, as usual not hearing me.

"They may close C House, they're probly going to. The people next door are circulating a petition to get us out."

"I knew there was something," M says.

"So I hafta come home. Of course I don't want to, but there it is."

I look from one to the other.

"There's no room at the inn," D says. It's one of his expressions. "Anyway, it's only a petition. Probably doesn't mean a hoot except you guys need to clean up your act. Besides, we're jam packed, up to the gills, with all the stuff she won't part with from Poplar Canyon." He used to call it Popular Canyon when Paula was home, before she moved out.

"We're getting old, set in our ways," M is saying. "You need to be with young people. Your own age."

"Out there having fun," D says.

"Yah, sure," I say. I exhale from my mouth, which for some reason they have always found irritating. "There's the den," I say.

"The den's the den."

"I know the den's the den," I say.

"It doesn't even have a closet," M says.

"That's no big deal, I could just keep my stuff in the record cabinet. Now that you're more into cassettes."

"It just gets harder if we let it go on now," D says. "Till everybody's too old to make changes."

It's like it's a conversation they have rehearsed even though we haven't officially had it before.

"When you're old and really out of it, you might even want me here, to look after you, you can't tell."

"Old age is certainly creeping up, you're right there, Tiffani. This afternoon I couldn't for the life of me come up with the name of the mechanic who always works on the car."

"Phil," D says.

"Phil, that's it. Let's get the dishes."

We do them in silence except she keeps on telling me where things go. I know where they go, I just don't put them there.

Finally I pipe up. " 'Member that first year after I was diagnosed? And you guys started reading all that stuff?"

"Take the spoon out of the bowl, Tiffani. Before you put it in the refrigerator."

"And you read how there aren't near as many cases diagnosed schizo in England as here?"

"The sugar doesn't need to be refrigerated."

"And you said to D, maybe we should move to England with her. You were standing in the kitchen by the herb pots in the Poplar Canyon house and D put his arms around you—I remember thinking it was me he should have hugged, but it was you he was comforting, and he said, no Francine, it wouldn't make any difference what name they put on it, and you said yes it might, it could because the attitude was different, the way they look at—"

"I was wrong, Tiffani," M says. "Don't put the grease down, it'll clog the drain."

It's clear I'm totally wasting my time.

I find D in the den, sitting in the dark, which is how I often sit. Maybe it's genetic. Maybe everything's in the genes. "What're you doing?" I move M's knitting and plop myself in the Barcalounger.

"Oh, just hanging out," D says. I hate it when he tries to talk like me. He looks old. He's 48 or 58, something like that. He's sitting with his palms on the arms of the orange chair that just got reupholstered so it will look good for the wedding, when a select few come back to the condo after.

I work the chair lever, sending my legs out straight. At one end of the room are louvered doors and behind them a sink with a faucet such as you might see in a dentist's office, a long skinny thing. They could just move the booze somewhere else and I could wash up there. It would help the bathroom scene.

"Listen, if I go ahead and move back in, we could go out and do stuff together. Hike on Mt. Diablo. You used to say you wished you had you a hound dog so he could go with you. It'd be like that. And we could go to the car races at Sears Point. Rafting on the Stanislaus, lots of stuff. You'd start getting your exercise you're all the time complaining about. Not getting."

"Please, Mary Alice. We've been up one side of this and down the other. A petition's only a petition. Let's not go barreling to any conclusions. You have a place you can handle and you have your Occupational Therapy."

"That's okay. I don't mind skipping O.T. for a while, I haven't been going that much anyway."

"You haven't? Why not?"

"Oh, I don't know. You get burned out. I've made more baskets than the Hopis, you know what I mean? I'd just rather be with you guys for a while." I keep working the lever of the Barcalounger. "I'll comb my hair all the time, every day. Tie it back even. Make my bed twice a week minimum, how's that? It could be neat, the two of us, like we used to. Remember how Nana used to say I was Daddy's girl? Like that time, it must of been a Saturday, I was really little and I cried when you went off for a haircut."

D has been shaking his head during my whole presentation. "Mary Alice, I want you to listen, I want you to listen to me. We'll keep doing things together from time to time, sure, but there's no use waffling. You can't live here. It doesn't work, not for any of us, neither side. We've proved that."

"Neither side? What are we, competing armies or something? I'm different now, that's what I'm trying to tell you."

He sits there shaking his head like there's a word that won't come out. He's that way sometimes. It's like trying to start the olives out of the bottle, you prod and nothing. You can't get in there.

He reaches over and turns on the ginger jar lamp, which I'd just as soon he wouldn't, it makes everything too bright, puts too much out in the open. I see he's got the down cushion from the chair tugged off for a pillow. "You're not supposed to do that," I say. "M doesn't go for it. Want me to put it back?" There was a time when we used to be in league, the two of us. " 'Member when you put the mole bomb where she planted that purple stuff, the agapanthus, and I never told?"

"Tiffani, if you'd just be all right, I'd die happy, that's all I ask, just for you to be all right. You've got to keep trying."

"If I was all right you'd go find something else to die unhappy about!" I kind of scream. "And I try more than just about anybody."

"It's all in the willpower, that's the bottom line."

"Shit," I say. "That's your bottom line."

"Give you an example. There was this fellow in Kansas City, who was dying of cancer. Done everything they could for him. They gave him weeks, Mary Alice, not months, weeks, it was metastasized all over the place. He was a dead duck, no two ways about it, but then something happened, something up here"—he taps his head—"that turned everything around. He went in for a check-up and it wasn't there, they couldn't find any evidence, he was clear." He's looking at me. I'm sweating. They must have the heat way up. I blow down the neck of my T-shirt to aerate things.

"Couldn't find a trace and they say it was all just due to his mental attitude he had, the way he was thinking. Willpower. He just wouldn't by God give in to his illness."

"You're crazier than I am," I say. "It doesn't work like that."

I pace around looking for matches, which they usually have in the Moroccan leather box. Nope. Or the cinnabar one by the magazines on the library table. *Psychology Today, New England Journal of Medicine, Science Notes.* He's got six million articles on schizophrenia, stuff underlined in red, addresses torn out. "I just wish you'd stop it. I don't want you looking at things like this any more."

"Why, Buttons?" he says, which is one of the things he used to call me—I'd get so frustrated I'd yank off the little ones when I couldn't make them work.

"Because it isn't there, what you're looking for. I'm not in any of that stuff, or maybe it's that I'm in all of it, I don't know. All I know is, it's dumb to read it."

But I can't help myself either when it's there.

Powers of abstraction are conspicuously absent in the schizophrenic.

Skits-oh-free-nya. Ever since Dr. Madsen fired off that shrapnel word, D keeps bringing home everything he can find on the topic. Brochures, books, "materials" he calls them. Enough on mental illness to boggle the mind.

I push Public Affairs Pamphlet No. 168 away. It falls off the table. D picks it up and starts looking at it. I can't stand to watch him read with his glasses on the end of his nose and his pudgy index finger tracking his place. *The schizophrenic tends toward concreteness. He or she generally interprets epigrams or maxims literally.*

In the beginning D kept throwing proverbs at me. What does it mean, a rolling stone gathers no moss? You gotta stay on the job for 30 years to get your gold watch, I said. And he got really excited. That's not bad, he said, which meant he thought it was good, first rate. That's okay, Mary Alice. Did you hear that? D said to M. That's not far off the track. They'd stand there like a congressional investigating committee firing these proverbial ballbusters at me, How about the early bird gets the worm? A stitch in time saves nine? till I'd get up and leave. It was too tiring being an overachiever.

"Hey, listen, let me move back in and we can keep doing the tests, proverbs, counting backwards, presidents' names. You can draw numbers on my hand with me blindfolded like you used to, I even know where that old blue and white bandana is, only now I'll bet you anything I'd get them right. You'd be proud of me, Schizophrenic of the Year." He's listening, not shaking his head, and I have the feeling if I could just come up with enough stuff fast enough, he might buy it. "Maybe we'll even be invited to the White House, they'll just put on an extra guard or two." A spindly little laugh burbles up in me, breaks off.

D puts a hand on my head and tears seep out, mine and his— like the tip of a glacier that would take eons to melt.

"You can't go home again, Mary Alice—"

I can interpret that one all right.

"There's a certain amount of truth in that phrase, something to be said for it."

Not much.

"You come home, it'd be all right back to the way it was, you wouldn't thank us for it—"

"I don't thank you now."

"Not in the long run."

"*Please. . . .*"

We stand there in the ginger lamp light, close enough to touch, but not touching, all this unsaid stuff pinging at me.

"No, Mary Alice," he says finally.

"The name's Tiffani," I say 99 years later. "And I couldn't live in a condo anyway. I wouldn't take it if you gave it to me! Somebody pisses upstairs and you hear it."

M is standing in the doorway. I don't know how she got there. "Try and keep your voice down, Tiffani. These walls are paper thin."

"I don't see how you can do it!" I'm not sure what I mean, live like this, I guess. I stand there sobbing, beating my fists on the paper-thin walls, ashamed for my parents. I may go to England after all, or Israel where everybody has frizzy hair.

I'm going, "There's no way anybody's ever going to make me stay here!" and M, who never listens, is trying to get me to sit down, just sit down and take it easy.

Vi The next episode in the Saga of C House goes into high gear on us a couple of days later, Sunday, right after "60 Minutes." It starts with two cats with differing points of view caterwauling or whatever. It's almost too private, you think you shouldn't listen. Then there's this high-pitched non-cat female scream. Carla and I get out there in time to see the woman from the house across the street with the pink gravel who I've never seen before despite she's about the size of a Sumo wrestler blasting Cathouse with this jet of water. A beige Siamese is watching the proceedings. Well, Cathouse totally freaks. He shoots halfway up a telephone pole, front legs splayed, hanging there wet and wild like a bat.

The woman, who is wearing black slacks and a green top with palm trees, directs another jet at Cathouse. He falls off the pole— "Got 'im!" she says—stuns himself momentarily and then takes off, a marmalade streak in the night.

"What're you doing? You bitch!" Carla yells. She doesn't even dig Cathouse under normal circumstances—he sheds on her black tuxedo jacket which picks up everything—but it's sort of territorial with her, he's a C House resident and therefore an Us.

"What-did-you-call-me?" the woman says, pronouncing every word very distinctly like she's learning to talk. "You heard her!" she says to a man who has come out on the porch. He shakes his head, he's more low keyed. "That scruffy tomcat of theirs was trying to do it with Miss Clara."

Cathouse's eyes gleam under a parked Hyundai and the woman sprays the pavement trying to get him.

By now there's a crowd gathered. Geoffrey races out with a towel that says Langley Porter, which is one of many treatment facilities in the Bay area where he's been stuck. He tries to get ahold of Cathouse to dry him.

"What's coming off here?" a man in a blue windbreaker says. "What's going on?"

"I can tell you what's not gonna go on. Miss Clara's a hundred percent pedigreed Siamese, I didn't shell out eighty dollars to stud her out with that sealpoint over in Oroville just to have her taken advantage by riffraff." She looks at all of us in a way that makes clear who the riffraff is.

Miss Clara rubs against the man's legs. "What have you got to purr about, huh?" he says. Miss Clara answers (Siamese are talkers).

"She's clearly a consenting adult," I say.

"Ha! I never heard such a con," the woman says.

Cathouse is yowling.

"That the one makes such a ruckus around three in the morning?" the windbreaker guy says.

"That's him," Bernadette next door says. "That screech of his really grates."

"I get my hands on him he'll be singing a different tune," Windbreaker says. I've seen this guy leaning against a car doing exercises. "I'm calling the pound, you better believe."

The Vespa spurts past us. "It's Geoffrey!" He's clinging to the handle bars, going like the Ewoks in the redwood forest.

"I bet anything he's after Cathouse," I say.

"Somebody stop him!" Warren yells. "He doesn't know how to brake!" By now porch lights are on all over the place, people coming out of their indrawn Sunday evening coze.

"Did y'all hear what she called me?" the woman is saying to the street at large, since the man on the porch with her didn't seem to take special exception. "The nerve! The incredible gall!" The hose is sogging up the ground in front of her. The man takes it and sets it on the petunias. You can see where he's very methodical.

Geoffrey does a complete circle of Princeton Avenue, Warren

chasing after him, flailing his arms. Geoffrey crashes into the privet hedge on the corner, dumping a sand box on the lawn and ending up teacup over tonsils on the front stoop like an evening paper.

We all dash down. Warren turns off the Vespa, picks up a piece of reflector. "We just got done putting in this hedge Sattaday," the guy on the corner says, rubbing behind his ear. A woman in a chenille robe and pink rollers comes out holding a bottle of nail polish. "All I hope is whoever owns this bike has insurance, you see my point?" the man says. Warren shifts his feet.

Geoffrey has a cut on his head with sand in it. We prop him up and he stands there like a statue, a lawn duck or something, his pupils fixed.

"You want to let him come on in and wash up?" the woman says, fanning her nails.

The man glances at Geoffrey, then us. "Doesn't look to be serious, they can just as well cart him on home," he says.

"Cathouse!" Geoffrey yells all of a sudden, maybe he thought he saw him, I don't know.

"You just watch it there, fella, this is a decent neighborhood!" the man says, hitching up his pants as though that makes it more so. People are huddled in the shadows watching silently, a tryst with the bizarre.

We walk Geoffrey home, this little knot of C Housers. Wookie's army. The shadows move, make way for us, watchful. A kid with an empty Tab bottle blows into it, an eerie foghorn sound. Geoffrey stops in his tracks—not that he has tracks to stop in, he just normally goes where he's led. "Come on, Geoffrey, it's nothing." The kid, emboldened, blows again, close to Geoffrey's ear. "Knock it off!" Carla says, "or I'll deck you." He does, thus saving himself a fat lip as Carla is into follow through. "Yah, just watch it, fella," I say over my shoulder. Warren wheels the Vespa, stopping under a street light to check the damage. We follow close together past the shadows and those bugs that sound like they're winding their alarm clocks.

We deposit Geoffrey on his bed, but he wanders around all night, pacing and gibbering (word salad, it's called), gibbering and pacing, and by morning he is howling like a banshee for Cathouse, who hasn't returned. What *is* a banshee and how does it howl? Oh who cares, it's just a figure of—

"Tiffani, snap out of it and get his ass over to Crisis," Carla says.

"Me? You want me to—" She slings his jacket at me.

"Like fast. We can't handle this scene. He's too unglued. Warren'll find the cat," she says to Geoffrey. "I want for you to go now with Tiffani, she's going to take care of you." She turns to me. "Okay, Curlylocks, you're Number One Honchette."

It's at least a 20-minute walk over the hill to Valley View Hospital where the Crisis unit is (it used to be at St. John's, but they moved it). I've been there once as a consumer, so I kind of know the ropes. Geoffrey's been there fifty million times and still doesn't. "C'mon, Geoffrey, old pal." I have a swipe at his face with the Langley Porter towel. He dodges. "Just a minute, hold it." I can't believe I'm doing this take-charge act. Usually it's me people are after—wipe your mouth, blow your nose. It's a shot in the ego being on the other side of the fence, the towel, I mean. "Okay, that's better."

"Tiffani!" Carla is yelling. "Get the lead out. NOW before shit shits." Maybe she said hits, shit hits, it kind of runs together. Anyway she gives us a healthy shove out the side door.

"Gotta find Cathouse," Geoffrey says.

"We're working on it," I say. They have this thing for each other, karmaly speaking. Cathouse sits with a mottled paw on Geoffrey's arm while he moves his chessmen around, it's like they're making their moves together. Cathouse the Chesshire cat. The right sleeve of Geoffrey's blue sweater he has on has this rectangle of rucked up thread from where Cathouse kneads his claws. He butts his head under Geoffrey's chin and bites his nose. Geoffrey told me once he gets this pain in his forehead when he holds Cathouse up close. What do you think it is? I said. Geoffrey just looked at me like I blew a head gasket or something. It's the relationship, he said. I think I know what he meant. It's knowing the body of something alive, its whims, its trust, knowing even what it can't do for you.

"Tiffani, goddam your ass, what the fuck are you still doing here?"

"Just leaving, Carla. I'm on top of it." I almost said trust me, but Carla would just have laughed sardonically or words to that effect.

This time I take Geoffrey by the hand. "We'll find Cathouse," I say. "I give you a written guarantee."

"Except in Nebraska," Geoffrey says. And for a minute I think maybe he's going to insist I write out something, which I suppose I could do if absolutely necessary, but it would involve finding a pencil.

We are at the corner. Geoffrey is mumbling to his voices. He always thinks the plagues are coming, killer bees, AIDS, the CIA. "This way," I say. Actually I'm not too sure which way, but when you're dealing with people who are confused, it's important to be decisive, which I am. I decide things all the time.

As it happens, we take the right turn and I sprint Geoffrey up to Crisis's big green door. Possibly green is supposed to look tranquil is the underlying psychological postulate. In which case having the door painted becomes a cost-cutting labor-saving device on the part of the Crisis staff who—

Geoffrey has taken off. I pursue him like Magnum P.I. It's a silent white chase past a gurney with a child in a cast, a cart with clattering trays, past open doors and pink azaleas with satin bows, past the nursery with babies in glass cribs. There's a mama in a wheelchair tapping on the glass, a crack-up infant with lots of black which-way hair like mine. Babies in glass cribs shouldn't throw bottles. I smile. The mama smiles and Geoffrey steams into Intensive Care. Yikes! You don't have a minute to yourself in this world. You stop to let your mind blink and all hell breaks loose.

I've never been in an Intensive Care before. RING BEFORE ENTERING. Forget it, not when you're chasing somebody down, when you're that person's keeper. I corner Geoffrey, panting. He's cowering beside a bed with an old man with tubes up his everything. I station myself on the other side. "C'mon now, Geoffrey. Let's not get fancy. We're in the wrong department."

"What's this? What's happening here?" a nurse says. "Who are you people? Out!" An alarm is ringing.

A man in a green smock approaches. "Look, Geoffrey," I say, "it's only a Martian (he doesn't mind them). Just stand still, it'll be okay."

"Okay, fella, everything's cool," the Martian, the doctor, I mean, says. He has a tight grip on Geoffrey's arm.

"See, what happened, I was taking him to Crisis downstairs," I say. "But he took off on me. I had to track him down. I'm in charge of him. Carla said."

"Call Security," the doctor tells the nurse. "That was quick thinking," he says to me. I smile modestly.

"I knew you'd come, Arnie," the old man murmurs, patting Geoffrey's arm.

"Whoops, let's not jiggle that I.V. of yours, Mr. Lomax," the doctor says. He adjusts an upside down bottle, keeping his hold on Geoffrey.

Two young guys in uniforms that say Valley View General on the pockets take Geoffrey by the arms and kind of skate him along through the Intensive Care doors. "Tiffani!" Geoffrey says. He looks at me with this innocent childlike expression he gets, like he's in Disneyland on a permanent pass. Which he is. "It's okay, Geoffrey, I'm here." Can you believe it—I am somebody else's support system.

One of the guys is dark, Puerto Rican maybe, with bright black shoe button eyes, and he kind of dances Geoffrey along. A West Side Story type, not uncute. He pushes the down button and I see where he's not wearing a wedding ring.

"You his girl friend or something?" he says in the elevator, which is big enough for stretchers. I see he's thinking along the same lines as me.

Geoffrey slumps down on the floor, which I wouldn't mind doing myself, this take-charge syndrome being on the strenuous side, but me kind of being Geoffrey's superior officer, that's out.

"Geoffrey's girl friend?" I say. "You gotta be kidding."

I can sense Geoffrey looking at me, trying to load me up with guilt, make me not like myself.

"Thanks," I say to the black-eyed one at the door to Crisis.

"Hey, no problem."

I thought he might say something about getting together, but I guess we were both too busy for socializing.

I march Geoffrey up to Reception and they take him into a little room where what they do is they ask you to tell them what's going on with you. If you're really in the ozone, they try and talk you down and then they call your therapist and you can go out and sit and watch television or you can go into another little room with a cot and you can just flake out, try and sleep everything off.

If you're toxic, maybe you've been off your meds or something or you're just too tired to eat or get dressed or anything like that, then you can always go to Crisis. It's open 24 hours a day. And they sell cigarettes at the counter, but only a certain number per hour. They have decaf coffee so nobody gets any more hyper than they are already and a bowl of hard-boiled eggs you can help yourself to and some shiny green apples. I tap an egg on a glass ashtray and start peeling off the little fine membrane beneath the shell, rubbing it with my thumb. They boil them too long, that's why they're kind of gray like that around the yolk. But it's free except that the taxpayer ultimately gets jabbed for it. But a dozen eggs split, I don't know, 60 million ways, it's really nothing per capita. And they have pay phones, you can call out all you want as long as you can cough up twenty centses and somebody who'll answer.

The first time you come in, you get treated really well, like the Queen of England (although I don't suppose she would ever go to Crisis, they'd send Crisis to the Palace, probably in one of those neat red buses). If the Queen of England ever did happen to stumble in—say she's on tour and everybody just keeps on asking her about

Diana till it really gets to her—they'd probably treat her like any other delusional wimp who came across the transom that week. Oh, you're Queen Elizabeth? Okiedokie, just have a seat over there between Jesus Christ and Brooke Shields, an intake worker will be with you presently.

Speaking of which, it seems a woman with a clipboard on her knee is squatted down beside me. Jeans, velour top. If it wasn't for the clipboard you wouldn't know she's staff. They don't wear white coats or anything. It's pretty democratic unless you pull any funny stuff. Then they get really hard-nosed.

"I was just having a little egg," I say, gathering up my shells.

"Okay now—Tiffany, is it?—if you'd like to fill us in with what's been going on here with Geoffrey." This is how Intervention typically begins, how it intervenes. I should really get me a clipboard. They do wonders for your image. Clipboards are associated with the super sane. "Right," I say, "with an i at the end."

She, this woman, Verna she says her name is, is sitting there waiting. It's somewhat challenging, my new role as spokesperson, it's the whole ombuds thing, which sounds Tibetan. I work a little chip of shell under my right thumb nail, which turns white, patchy white. I hold it out to inspect. "See," I squeak out, then stop. It makes me nervous to do the talking and I don't like it how she looks right at me the way she does, but then I recall that upstairs that doctor, whoever he was, said I was a quick thinker. He must be an okay thinker himself, have at least some IQ to have got through med school.

I take a deep breath and keep part of it. I tell Verna about how Geoffrey found this cat on the freeway while it was still a kitten, not pointing out my evidence is pretty hearsay.

"Was that today, Tiffani?"

"No, oh no. Like I said, it's a cat now. No, it was a while back there, I think someone said it was August. Anyway it was a kitten when he found it wandering around on the Bayshore Freeway with a life expectancy of about exactly zip. Warren was with him—you probably know Warren, he's been in a lot—he was taking Geoffrey to a Giants' game at Candlestick and Geoffrey climbed this chain link fence and dashed out there on the freeway, cars screeching on the brakes and got a hold of this kitten and buttoned him into his plaid shirt he has, the one he has on as a matter of fact. Warren said he was afraid to look. They should have given Geoffrey a medal or something, but instead Warren said these drivers were like really discourteous. They started in yelling whatza matter with you? You idiot bastard! You want to get everybody killed, you dumb fuck? things like that."

"Maybe you better tell me what happened today, all right?"

"Oh I'm leading up to that," I say firmly. "I want to lay you out an overview." I can't believe how I'm sounding. (I must have The Force. When the going gets tough, the tough get going. Lincoln said that. Or maybe it was Tom Selleck.) Verna fumbles her earlobe, I was fine till she did that. Where was I?

"I sort of forget where I was," I say. "Today's been a killer."

"Start with today. Monday. What's wrong with Geoffrey, just try and concentrate on Geoffrey's present situation."

"Okay, sure. Monday. Well, actually it's Sunday we should be looking at. But anyway. Geoffrey has this love boat thing with Cathouse, he like won't let him out of his sight. Takes him to the bathroom with him, everywhere." I stop because Crisis is wired right into the System and so on probably right up to the Surgeon General and I don't want them mentioning the cat which we aren't supposed to even have, we have enough trouble already. "You won't go mouthing off about Cathouse to Wookmook, would you?"

"No," Verna says, "everything is confidential, but let's get wicky wicky to what brings Geoffrey here today."

"Okay, sure. Say, you wouldn't happen to have an extra cigarette on you, would you?"

She ponies one up, a Merit, but that's okay. One nice thing you'll notice about people who work in Mental Health, the vast majority of them smoke. This could be for buddy buddyness with clients since mainly we are smokers. Or maybe there's some other reason, I don't know. "You don't happen to have a match, do you, Verna?"

She has a navy blue lighter. "Why don't we just keep bumping this along," she says.

"Sorry. So, okay, Cathouse sleeps on Geoffrey's bed, under the covers with him and everything like that and then today, no yesterday, Sunday—"

Verna looks relieved, that I'm getting to the point? or that I know yesterday was Sunday? Hard to say with these Crisis workers. Their minds are complicated pieces of apparatus. I wonder how Geoffrey is doing. I should have rehearsed him on the data they ask—what day is it? who's the president? (I wonder if Reagan would be upset if people didn't know.) Sometimes they even ask for the last two presidents. Or count backwards from 100 by 3's. Not presidents, of course, that'd be way too hard. "Where was I?"

"It's Sunday." Verna has written Sunday on her clipboard in capital letters and boxed it in. Lest we forget, amen.

"Yah, it's Sunday." I should at least have told Geoffrey it's Sunday, no, Monday, now it's Monday. This reporting business is really wearing me down. "Maybe we should take a break. I've got to tell Geoffrey something anyway."

"No," Verna says firmly. "You can see Geoffrey once we're finished here."

"Okay, okay. Cathouse is no longer a kitten, all right?" I pause. Things are getting delicate. "In fact it's like he's in heat or something, so he puts the moves on Miss Clara."

"Who's Miss Clara?"

"Across the street from us. The people two houses down."

"Are you telling me, Tiffani . . . ?" (They say that a lot, are you telling me . . . ? and what they mean is, if you are, I don't believe it) "That your cat—"

"It's Geoffrey's cat, I just feed him sometimes."

"Geoffrey's cat goes after this Miss Clara who lives across the street?"

"Yah and then this lady—"

"Clara?"

"No, no." (This Verna gal is not any too sharp.) "The lady turns the hose on Cathouse. Full blast. Which basically is what freaks out Geoffrey to make a long story short."

"But why does she do this, Tiffani? It's not framing up for me."

"I guess because Miss Clara is Siamese."

Verna passes a hand over her eyes. She *does* need a break. We both do.

"Let's get this straight, Tiffani. A woman across the street from Camelot House turns the hose on your cat—"

I open my mouth.

"Correction—Geoffrey's cat—who is thought to be making advances—"

"Thought to be! You should have heard how they were making out, wow!"

"Who because she is Vietnamese, am I right to assume there was a language barrier?"

"Not Vietnamese, *Siamese*. I guess you could say there was a language barrier, if that's what you wanted to say." (This Verna has really lost it.) "See, Miss Clara is a cat. I mean, that's not jive talk or like that. She's a cat cat." I try to sound patient, not condescending. I don't know how to put it any plainer.

At this point Verna thanks me for my input, it was real helpful. She sort of see-you-laters me and keeps writing. I go to check on Geoffrey. Me—checker instead of checkee. How about that! Dr. Madsen will turn cartwheels.

I run into Brad. He was on duty the one and only time I was in Crisis. He loans me a cigarette and tells me Geoffrey is in the Rainbow Room. That's where they put me that time. It was the night of Paula's engagement party which I had too much champagne at, and I started having nightmares only I was awake.

The door of the Rainbow Room is open. They let you close the doors in Crisis, you just can't go locking them. And then every hour or so they come with a flashlight and check to be sure you haven't offed yourself or anything. Geoffrey always leaves doors ajar, it's a habit with him so Cathouse can come and go.

He's lying on this cot, it's probably the same one I was on, facing the wall. I didn't face the wall though. I paced around, watched this fundamentalist sunset. They were singing a spiritual in a little white church across the street from Crisis. Black people were going in and out, and I just sat there, watching and listening. I looked over Jordan and what did I see-ee? White so bright it mocked Easter lilies, maggots, brides. Black so rich it thronged the senses, clotted the blood. A band of angels comin' after me-ee. In the state I was in everything amplified till I thought it was the Apocalypse and I couldn't stand it any more. That's when Brad came and gave me a shot and a Winston and the angels fluttered off like skittish twilight hens.

Geoffrey is looking pretty rough. They have him really strung out, it looks like, thoroughly Thorazined. I see they have a stars and stripes bandage on the cut over his eye, we should have thought of that. "You'll be back home before you know it." (This isn't too swift a way to put things to Geoffrey since everything happens before he knows it.) "And Warren's out looking for Cathouse—" He moves, starts to look around when I say Cathouse. "He's not here, Geoffrey, but Warren's gone to find him and I'll feed him, put the B-1 on him for fleas and I'll keep putting out kibble for the raccoons and everything." God, I think, what if Cathouse never shows? Geoffrey'll be a total eclipse. He'll end up on a 72-hour hold, which they can do, and then eventually they'll pack him off to Napa State Hospital. "Now pay attention, Geoffrey. When they ask you stuff, don't go saying 'except in Nebraska' if you can help it, okay?" I give him one of those friendly punches that don't hurt much. "And cooperate with the powers that be and we'll have you back to C House in nothing flat." I should really consider becoming a therapist, a para-shrink, a therapissed. You sure saved Geoffrey's bacon, Dr. Madsen'll say. Maybe.

"Good show," Brad does say as I'm walking out. "Geoffrey really needed you to bring him."

"Hey look," I say, "we're all in this together." (Shit, where'd I dig that up? Must've been M.)

"Thanks, Tiffani," Verna says.

"Oh, it's okay, my pleasure. You folks take care now." The trouble with feeling virtuous is you get sounding virtuous.

A woman, a consumer, is sitting in a chair in her nightgown, holding her knees and rocking back and forth. She has a wistful sadness about her like something's gone—a person, a dream, a mind. I think about hitting Brad up for another cigarette but don't. I have my pride, although occasionally you'd never know it. In fact if I happened to have a cigarette on me I'd probably give it to that bombed out one in the nightgown. Sometimes you have to do something to make yourself feel good about yourself.

A quick thinker, a good show-er, a bacon saver, a purveyor of cigarettes to the less fortunate, Number One Honchette. Clearly there was a need. Carla said go for it and I did. And I gave the report, kept my voice steady, didn't curl up. I really have to get me a clipboard.

By the time I bound up the steps at C House, I'm beginning to soar. Warren meets me on the porch. "Well," I say, "it was a struggle, but I got Geoffrey installed at Crisis and they all said I did good. You want to hear what Brad said to me?"

"Well at least that's out of the way," Warren says. He's really wired, nervous, unnerved.

"It was clear Geoffrey needed me, that's what Brad said. So now everything's under control."

"That's what you think. Are you sitting down?"

(Of course I'm not. I'm standing up.)

Miriam Myers called and dropped one on us, he says. They got the last of the signatures for the petition. Fifteen people signed up today after the Cathouse caper. She says it doesn't look good. She is taking it up with WHCMHC, who is taking it up with EHB, the Ecumenical Housing Board, who is taking it up with LAMDA, the Legal Aid for the Mentally Disabled Association. It's like if they wrap us in enough initials nobody will find us.

Somebody's reroofing across the street. A pot of tar keeps up its hot breathy lament. "They're trying to get us out of here by polluting the environment," Warren says. "I swear to God." It wouldn't do any good to say no, Warren, they're just sealing cracks. He has all these theories that the air we breathe is full of asbestos, fart gas, parathion, emphysemic exhalings. Sometimes I even believe him. Like right now, fear or apprehension, whatever it is, is all mixed up with the scent of tar.

Meow.

"Look, Warren, it's Cathouse!" He's back. He's climbing the steps to the side porch. He stops at the top, stretches his hind legs, flexes them as though he means to throw them away and then when that doesn't work, he settles down and begins licking them tenderly.

I scoop him up, "You stupido old thing!" I hold him out, up in the air, wiggling him the way mamas do with babies. "Now what we're going to do, we're going to call Geoffrey and tell him you're back and if they won't let me talk to him, I'll Tell Them To Tell Him, TTTTH. And you, purr, damn you."

"Tiffani," Warren says, following me in, "it's like you're not even hearing me, what I'm trying to tell you."

"Yes, I am, but I'm hearing me too." I blow in Cathouse's ear. "And you, you old woolly lecher." Somewhere a pneumatic drill stutters away, trying to split the world. I give Cathouse a shake. I giggle into his fur. I think down inside somewhere everybody wants to parent something—they say at San Quentin they'll adopt a bird, a cockroach even—to have something that knows you, that's smaller and weaker and bound to you, that you protect against the world, drizzle a little of your earthly power over. Which today showed me I have quite a bit of.

"You just don't understand," Warren says while I dial, "what's coming down."

vii

December scuds by. Everything is swelling up—Lindy, magazines with Christmas ads, the nation's personal income (but not mine), a rum pa pum pum. Two hundred Syrians are exchanged for six Israelis, which must make the Syrians feel a little funny, although glad all the same. Gloom settles on C House, a permanent tulle fog of fear. Paula is always saying the financial markets abhor uncertainty. Well, C House is very much like Wall Street—schizophrenic, manic depressive, hallucinatory, nervous, unpredictable.

Miriam Myers sends a letter to families of C House residents alerting them to the problems and asking for letters of support to be read at a Planning Commission meeting plus if possible a contribution toward legal costs, which would be gratefully appreciated and also tax deductible.

I go with M and D to a Christmas tree farm in Sonoma. It is billed as an Outing. M and D prowl around up and down the rows. Since the trees are priced vertically by the foot, M says we should look for bushy ones. "That's the old Christmas spirit," I say. I pause to study the pattern on the stumps, whorls big and complicated enough to be God's fingerprints. It strikes me if you happen to be a Douglas fir in a Christmas tree farm, you're nothing till you're chosen and then as soon as that happens, you're dead, right? This shows my then current frame of mind. I take a string of lights from the Sales Office in the trailer and put them on my head, pretending I am giving myself an EEG. M takes them off. I sit down and pick sawdust off my socks.

Christmas is at Paula and Jake's. They are Having Us Over, da da. They've been in their apartment at Raven's Crest, which is supposedly some big deal, for a month now. Plastic grass doormat with fake daisy in the corner. "Wipe your feet now." M "can't get over" what all they have done to fix the place up—tricky mirrors so you see yourself coming and going, a bookcase room divider that used to cool loaves of bread in a French bakery, kitchen curtains made out of Marimekko sheets, Polish circus posters under glass without frames.

The apartment is on a lido with a dock—they don't have a boat yet—and gulls come and peck up the breakfast crumbs from the deck. And then Jake's cats—T. Boone and Fifo—chase the birds. They're the farmers in the dell. "Hi ho the derry-o."

"What?" Jake says.

"Nothing," I say.

They're getting hitched in two weeks and wedding presents are reputed to be flooding in. M wants to see the brass service plates Ceci sent and the Imari platter from a lumber company D does business with. Paula tells her to go ahead and look in the bedroom.

Paula has recorded her need for cooking utensils at Macy's bridal registry and already she has this rack with copper pots, even one duplicate, the three-quart asparagus steamer. "What are these?" I say.

"French bistro glasses."

"No, I mean these, these mallets."

"That's what they are, mallets. For pounding stuff like chicken breasts when you want to get it real thin."

I take two and xylophone the counter.

"Mary Alice!" M and D say.

The reason why I did that, this kitchen is too still, everything in its place, nothing crawling. I could no more spend time here. . . .

The Day is a mistake from the word Go, which is a game Paula and Jake give the folks for their "empty nest." We sit around this new curved white sectional that everybody has such a fit about me getting a few cracker crumbs with guacamole on. (If I move in with Paula I will be sickle-shaped inside a week, trying to sleep on this mother.)

M and D give Paula and Jake a Portuguese/English dictionary since they're going to Brazil in the spring (plus a macho shit-brown refrigerator with a spigot on the front, which is also a wedding present).

Paula and Jake have all these little surprises for each other—a Julienne blade for the Cuisinart—you'd think they'd been married 90 years—and a key ring that beeps when you clap your hands or call it, except apparently it doesn't work, and a tea rose silk sleepshirt—"I like to see her light up," Jake says. It's all a glisten of somebody else's magic. He prods the fire, making a shower of sparks like he's Prometheus and Paula picks a piece of ash off him and he straightens her collar. Jesus! They're like two parrots picking each other over.

I get a manicure kit, thanks, a styling comb, thanks, a majolica pill box for my Mellaril, thanks a bunch, a pair of something called Foxy Sox, thanks, a 5-foot calendar you can write on, thanks, all of which strikes me as pointing out my deficiencies—yucked, up nails, hassled hair, lost pills, no sense of time.

"Don't go eating all the macadamia nuts," D says. "Leave some for other people."

I give everybody crud I cranked out at Occupational Therapy.

"A wallet!" D says. "Just what I needed."

"No you don't, I gave you one last year."

I'm not in too good of a mood, I admit it.

Everybody has champagne in silver-fluted wedding present glasses except they have gone to great pains, I am told, to provide me with something called Moussy, which is an alcoholless beer from Switzerland that nevertheless bubbles nicely like the genuine article, it is pointed out to me. (Mellaril and alcohol together are bad news. You can pass out.) Well, I suppose this is good for Switzerland's economy if nothing else. Once they've got the world saturated with

Swiss army knives and cuckoo clocks, they're up the creek. It's like what will happen to Monaco when they run out of princesses. I even say that—"What will happen to Monaco when they run out of princesses?"—but all I get is blank looks.

Fifo crawls into the Macy's bag we brought our presents in and I put a green peel-off bow on my forehead. Dead center. "Take that off," Paula says.

"Why? It's my beauty spot."

"It looks weird is why. And when you look weird, people think you *are* weird."

"Get out of there, you don't want to be in there," D says to Fifo. Fifo and I are sort of in the same category.

Later in the day I find a picture of a starving Indian woman in *Newsweek* with a beauty spot. "See there?" She doesn't see there.

Paula starts bringing out equipment—a contraption that you melt cheese on in the fireplace till it looks like somebody just ironed it, and then you take this limp cheese and you lay a trip on some plain old boiled potatoes and then you add some skiddy little onions— "Watch out for the couch"—and some midgety pickles called— "What did you say you call these gidgets?"

"Cornichons," Paula says finally. She's counting out Dansk plates.

"See if you can't help her," M says.

I dislike being delegated. Nevertheless I trudge out to the kitchen—my current energy level is very low—stepping over a rump of cellophane and tissue paper, hopping boxes, dodging T. Boone, nine lords a-leaping.

I stop to study the energy-saver refrigerator with ice water on the front and a digital gimmick that tells you if the power's been off. Paula has this *Hello My Name Is* sticker on the freezer part and she's written FRIDGE. Is a bow stuck on my forehead a dumbasser thing than *Hello My Name Is* FRIDGE stuck on the forehead, so to speak, of a refrigerator? I consider asking Paula but I don't, I'm too bushed for argument.

"Here, you can go ahead and take these in," Paula says.

"What is it? What are they?"

"Cherry tomatoes, sautéed."

"The black stuff," I mean.

"Fried parsley."

I hold up a figment. Or maybe it's a fragment. It clearly resembles pubic hair. "Um nummy."

"You don't have to have any if you don't want to."

"Is this dinner? This and that cheese thing?"

"It's called raclette, dear," M says in a Christmasy voice. "It's very Swiss."

I try a brief yodel, except I'm not too certain what a yodel is. Sometimes I'm also not sure if I want to stand out or blend in. M looks pained, so what else is new.

My yodel scares Fifo, who stands by the door. "You want out or what?" Jake says.

Fifo doesn't say.

"Would somebody just please tell me, *is it dinner?* If they would be so kind as to answer that one question."

"It's dinner," Paula says, getting hostile.

"Don't go getting hostile on me. That's all I wanted to know. I don't mind bonsai food. I can now plan accordingly."

They have a flocked tree with white lights that wink at me and some of the old ornaments from the attic. "You've got those bread dough dealies our piano teacher made."

"Yah," Paula says. "They're so much better than those scuzzy store-bought balls. . . . Mrs. Gimmel was a neat lady."

"She was always so fond of you—both of you," M says.

"That one there," I point my cheesy fork—

"Watch it!"

"That one, the boy with the blue suspenders and yellow knickers—it's mine. Mrs. Gimmel gave him to me when I finally played "The Edelweiss Glide" all the way through."

"Take it," Paula says. "If you want it. I don't care."

I do with some difficulty, a shower of needles coming with it.

"What are you going to do with it?" D says.

"Eat it," I say.

Everybody laughs so there's nothing left for me to do but start in.

"Stop that!" M says. "Look at her, what she's doing!"

They do.

"You don't know what Mrs. Gimmel put on there, you don't know what kind of preservative she put on the dough to keep it. It's got to be ten years old."

To tell the truth, it tastes somewhat worse than raclette, but I am taking little nibbles so they can save me if I go into convulsions.

"Glenn, stop her! Tell her not to, she doesn't know what she's doing!"

"Let her be," Paula says as I approach the knickers. "It's her life," Jake says. "She has choices." What a pair of prize schmucks. They both have a lot of growing up to do.

Next thing you know it's Paula's Big Day. The twelfth day of Christmas. The first 11 weren't worth shit, but maybe this will be an improvement, you never know. I try to be consistently optimistic.

Yep—today is Paula Rae Gilchrist's wedding, for which I am the official picture taker. My little sister Paula, who used to get into bed with me when she had bad dreams. What I'd do, I'd tuck the sheet around her, wrap her like they do with papooses, who are known to be secure and happy people (until unwrapped), and she'd quiet right down. I big sistered her till we were about ten and twelve and then there were a couple of years when I'd say we were neck and neck. (Paula's neck is long and "patrician" according to M.) And then the gears reversed with a screech.

She graduated from University of the Pacific. I dropped out of Foothill J.C.

She got a stat typist job at Dean Witter that everybody said would Lead to Something. (You better quit typing 8's for apostrophes, I said to her, or it'll lead to you getting fired, that's what it'll lead to.) I shelled pecans at the Contra Costa Occupational Therapy Agency. COTA. The guys all called it Kotex. The pecans which I suggested we call Nuts by Nuts—it had a snap to it—got sold to the parents unlabeled along with a recipe for something called Pecan Dreams, which so far as I know nobody ever made (or dreamed).

Now Paula has Jake and a fancy job with a squawk box and expense account lunches. I have M and D, except Paula has them too only more so. And I have squawking, but it's no big statusy thing. What I do have that she doesn't is no job and generally blotto lunches at O.T.—cold cuts, macaroni salad, and square carrots that look like bingo tokens, for example. (That was yesterday, no Friday.)

Don't get me wrong. I don't resent Paula. It's just the opposite. I feel sorry for people like her. She's a real Type A overachiever, right in line for a heart attack at any point. I read where this bride in Cincinnati keeled over at the altar just before the minister pronounced them whatever he pronounced them, dead maybe. There was a big stink because if they were married the husband collected the insurance and if not it was the family. I don't know who got the presents.

Paula won't drop dead at the altar, she doesn't do things like that, she is very organized, but if she did happen to, I wonder if I should take a picture. A photo finish, you might say. Probably not. It would be in poor taste. Maybe just one candid shot. I wish her well, I really do. What I think is, she is basically jealous of me. Schizophrenia, especially schizo-affective, is a hard act to follow, I don't care what you say, you get a lot of attention one way or another.

Here she is 22 and getting married. And I'm 24 and not getting married. Sometimes I would like to marry Dr. Madsen when he is in a good mood, but that is not infinitely realistic. I wish you weren't so old and I wasn't sick I said to him once. My heart was thumping like those cheap bongo drums people play on the beach. That would be nice, he said, but then he went on to explain how he never gets involved with his patients on a personal basis, he just tries his best to help them objectively and what I need is realistic goals. Well, no shit, you cheap bongo. Everything with him is goals goals goals, as if life was all hockey. It's a very trendy thing, the goal bit, like management by objective that D keeps telling me I should do, which I don't and which he doesn't either.

We're nothing alike, Paula and I, that's for sure. Paula is ultra structured, as opposed to yours truly, who goes on gut and raw intuition. She's a planner. I'm a feeler. In our society planners make out like bandits. Feelers get fucked over. Great, huh?

Paula is basically very vanilla. She's hyperconventional in that she can't stand to run with the herd. Take this wedding. The invitations are in calligraphy done by her friend Yoko, not the John Lennon one—it's a common name in Japanese—who would most probably have been maid of honor if it hadn't been for how to account for me, the problem of me, myself and I, the Maid of Horror. Even clever little Paula couldn't wiggle her way around that one. So no M.O.H. But I leaned over backwards—don't ask me why people think that's a good thing to do with all the lower back trouble going around—to make everything a success in her terms, witness me volunteering to be the photographer at the wedding.

So here we are, good people, January the sixth, a little black nothing square on my new calendar that has been lifted out, rounded into flowing honor-of-your-presence script. January the sixth in the year of our Lord I don't know what, nineteen hundred eighty something, this day of days that horoscopes have been combed for, menstrual cycles checked, satellite weather patterns anxiously studied.

"You're gutsy turkeys to have an outdoor shindig in January," Uncle Lester said. "Even in California." See, she's getting hitched under an oak in this lawny place in Moraga that looks as though it's part and parcel—M's phrase—of an old estate, but in reality belongs to the county who, or maybe it's which, rents it out. And then at the end when it's all over, they take off into the sunset in a fringed surrey with a liveried coachman and two fast-crapping steeds.

I pull up the shade. The sky is gray flannel but nonetheless apparently about to be continent for Paula. She usually gets what she wants. Pushy people do. Last night it rained, I'm told, on the rehearsal dinner. I wouldn't know. I wasn't there. "You're welcome to come if you want, but you have to be willing to get dressed up nicely and sit quietly through all the toasts," M said. Drinking Moussy? I said. Let's not get carried away.

So I went to bed early. But you can see from the way the dog do on the sidewalk is feathered out, melted into ochre slush, that it rained. Actually I did see the rainbow. There was a killer rainbow around four.

I decide to take a picture of the poo-poo. It will be openers in the wedding album. I have a well-developed instinct for candid shots. I can wait them out, establish a bond with the target and then just stalk till I get what I'm looking for. Although of course with the dog shit, which is basically inert, this doesn't totally pertain. You have a tendency to exhaust your subject, Mr. Eckhart, the instructor in my Creative Photography class, said. According to him a certain amount of interaction is okay, any good photographer takes something out of everybody, but you have to know when to quit. That's when I left school. I mean!

I compose the shot in my head. Let's go zoom. I change the focal length from 43 mm to 86 mm with a single one-second exposure to get the porous ethereal nature of rained-on poo poo. Voilà.

I'm taking three lenses to the wedding, the normal 50 mm and then a 28 mm for close-in work with groups and the 105 mm long lens for pulling in distant subjects. My zoom lens I got second hand and it unfortunately has a dented barrel. Good for shooting the shit, ha ha.

A week ago I checked out all the lenses by putting the Nikon on the table and focusing on two pages of newspaper taped flat against the dark wall of the dining room. I took two pictures with each lens, one at the lowest f stop and one in the middle range to see that all the horizontal and vertical lines were straight and there was no blurring. And then I took my camel's-hair brush and dusted the lenses.

I put the Nikon back in its case and I check the closet to be sure that my dress is still there. And the shoes. I try to put them on, but my feet won't go in. They must have changed sizes in the last two weeks. Or maybe it's just that I don't have on stockings. They'll get ticked with me if I have to wear my Birkenstocks, which makes me look like something out of Brueghel, rustic wedding department.

I go into the bathroom and take my meds, which M called last night to remind me to be sure and do. I go downstairs and have a cup of herbal tea—"and *please* go easy on the caffeine, you know what that does to you"—and an unripe banana, which would not concern *them* but is much more likely to zap me than coffee, in my humble opinion.

"I hate the way you eat bananas," Lindy says.

"Get fucked," I say affably. Besides, how many ways are there to eat a banana? I remove one of those strings bananas have and drop it on the floor when nobody's looking.

"It's obscene," she says.

"How do I eat thee, let me count the ways," I say, but the multifaceted nature of this comment is way above Lindy's fat head.

I start to go upstairs but Warren and Carla are standing there.

"We could probably get a rent subsidy," Warren is saying. "A Section 8. And you might be able to get your kid back even."

"No," Carla says. "Dorie's doing okay where she's at."

"Or we might could find us a place in San Pablo so you could get together with her more."

"There's some stuff cooking," Carla says. "I'll let you know later."

Cripes, what is this? Am I about to be left with Lindy and Geoffrey? And no house?

"Hi, Carla," I say. "How's Randy?" Warren turns a gratifying shit-green.

M calls again at noon. Did I remember to take my meds? Am I

dressed? Why should I be, you don't pick me up till 3:30, right? Well, am I getting ready to get dressed?

"How am I supposed to get ready to get dressed?"

"You know what I mean," M says. I don't, I say.

I tell her that I have been thinking seriously about my film inventory and we should stop off for an extra roll of Ektachrome just to be on the safe side, and also I need cigarettes. She says something like let's just see how the timing works out, which might as well be Carla talking to Warren.

Now the dress. It's sure not me, that's a cinch. Rose taupe linen with a dumb wrap-around skirt. Which way does it wrap? No, that can't be it, the ties must go inside somewhere and not separate from the skirt that way. Maybe if I know this dress is not me that means I am finding my identity. Have to review Dr. Madsen on that. I wanted to go ahead and wear my prom dress from high school, the one I never went to the prom in, I always liked that dress, but they said no, it was far and away too fussy. This is an afternoon affair, Paula wants it kept informal.

I lean my palms on my knees and do my 90-degree look in the mirror. If she'd just put her hair up, dot dot dot, Miss Beecham at Saks said. (I have wide rambunctious hair, see.) "Oh we're going to do something," M said, "very definitely." So three days ago there I am at Pizazz having an asthma attack from the hair spray, which, per Warren, destroys the ozone layer in the atmosphere. If she would just stick it out for five minutes more, Michelle said to M. Also dot dot dot. Five more minutes and I would have been dead. "There's nothing I can do," M said as I loped off down the street toward World Savings which has free coffee and sawdusty cookies in the shape of windmills, you don't have to be a customer.

I tug on these stranger-than-life pastel stockings they've bought me. You unscrew a plastic egg and there they are. White Lilac. Remember to roll them down, don't just treat them like sausage casings, M says. Does she mean she thinks my legs look like sausages? Bratwurst? They have a nice curve to them but a pukey color. I hate to sound like M and D but they don't make things like they used to. Right away left rear springs a run that shoots straight up like yucca. Big deal. I'm not the one getting married (I wouldn't consider it) so why gibber and tweet over a little missing tread. I jam on the T-strap pumps, made by someone who apparently thinks feet are shaped like arrows. So there I am, all gussied up, as they say, they being M and D.

I check the mirror. I'm one thing in the bathroom mirror and another in the one on top of my phony formica wood-grained dresser. In the bathroom I have an innocent floating-away look and humongous hair. In my room the light is softer. It's the dark dreamy eyes with shadows under them that loom up, almond shaped, sensitive. Like my last year in high school after I discovered Isak Dinesen and I started in putting kohl under my eyes to look like her, to be her. And then there's the thick black eyebrows that M used to wet with her finger and try to becalm till I got sick of being bugged and shaved them off. What happened? everybody said. They really sat up and took notice. They left, I said, but then they grew back even thicker and blacker. Plus there's the scarecrow hair, the jungle, the jumble, whatever mirror you're dealing with.

I rummage around and find one of my old kohl sticks and I make penmanship circles round my eyes till I'm in my own cave.

Mirror mirror in the hall. I move the poinsettia we spent one whole Wednesday night voting on so I can see. Did we want a wreath or a plant? A 10-inch pot? Or 12? A white one or red? It's shedding its leaves, somebody must have forgotten to water it, five somebodies. With all that democracy going, it's a fucking miracle it's there at all.

The incoming light gives a sort of smudgy effect to the kohl. There's no ultimately true mirror, there's only what I see there, what you see there, what the world sees at any given moment. For example, the mirror in the fun zone at the Napa County Fair is valid for that time and place. I am beginning to sound like Plato. Play Dough. This is what Dr. Madsen calls a clang association, which I do more than any patient he's ever had. Once he said that it really got me going, clang clang like the cable cars.

Carla wafts through the hall. "Hey, check that!" she says when she gets a load of me. (Is this a favorable comment?) She shoots a look at Warren, who is watching a rerun of "Three's Company." Once it's over he's going to go out and look for a job. Meanwhile they smile like I am the object of a private conspiracy. (Reading: it was unfavorable.)

M calls again—it's your mom—to remind me to roll down the pantyhose, not just ram them on, please. I am watching Carla who has on her denim safari jacket with nailheads in the form of heavenly bodies, Orion, the Big Dipper where there's the big dip. . . . M wants to know, am I concentrating on what she's saying, am I really hearing her? I say she said to roll the planets down, the pantyhose I mean, not just ram them on, but I have already rammed them on is what I don't say.

"And everything is all proceeding on schedule?" she says, nervous casual.

"Everything's cool," I say, but something about my tone appears to worry her. You can't worry about life forever.

I sit on the steps from 3 o'clock on with my camera gear. They finally come for me at 3:32, which it seems will not leave time enough to pick up film let alone cigarettes, which are in certain quarters considered non-essential, which is very biased.

"She's gone back to that awful black eye stuff!" M says. She's looking at me like what she sees is burned pots, smashed fenders, and cigarette holes.

"Forget it," D says. "Now's not the time to make an issue."

"Yah," I say, "just forget it. Don't I look nice? Don't you think I look nice?"

"Yes," M says too crisply. "I brought along a brush in case. Turn around, did you get anything on you from those filthy steps?"

"They're not filthy steps!" I say hotly. "It's just the cement's a little cracked, that's all."

"They're fine steps," D says, "just get in."

I check the side view mirror before I get in. The girl there is glum. She lies down on the back seat.

"You decided against Nana's little gold earrings?" M says.

"Oh them, yah," I say. "Too blah, too gold." Actually I forgot.

"Will they be okay there?"

"Sure, why wouldn't they be? Think someone's going to pike them?" I look back at the house fading in the distance.

"No," M says in a yes tone. She is holding two silver champagne glasses with lily of the valley twined around the stems.

They have this decal from University of the Pacific, U.O.P., where Paula went, on the back window. An end is loose but it won't pull off. They wouldn't think of putting on a decal from Camelot House, not that we have one. It's an idea though. We could sell them and get us new steps or something. I must be very entrepreneurial at heart.

"You've still got your tags hanging," M says. She is pointing west, in the general direction of my right armpit.

"It's okay. Get your face off my case, please."

M gives D the you-heard-her-you-handle-it look, but he's busy readjusting the side view mirror which I had to tilt to see in.

"It's not okay and I didn't bring a scissors. I knew I should bring the scissors, something told me. Glenn, do you think we should go on back and get the scissors?"

"No," D says firmly. "Definitely not."

"It would only take another five minutes," M says, but she is subsiding. She leans over the back seat and bites the little plastic thread. "There." It sticks between her teeth, a plastic T for Tiffani. She fishes it out and puts it with the tags in the ashtray, which I see is unfortunately buttless.

A few minutes later D parks the Volvo. We're in what if I do not mistake me is the Burger King parking lot.

"I wouldn't pull in here, I wouldn't pick this place," M says.

"Damn it," D says. "You want to drive the car, Francine?"

"No, but I'm warning you, I wouldn't park here."

There's a plastic burger with terrific wingspread on the roof. The mustard hasn't weathered well, it's chipping. Mustardchips, someone could make a mint. "Is this it?" I say. "Where's Paula?"

"No, family conference," D says heartily, his dark suit arm across the back of the seat.

When we were growing up, family conference meant something good, that we were going on a trip or to a movie or Stinson Beach or something. Now it makes me suspicious, maybe I'm just paranoid.

"This is Paula's day," D begins. "And I know we all want for it to be a happy one."

"So?" I say. "It's everybody's day." I mean, how possessive can you get? It's a day out of all of our lives. "Can I have a cheeseburger?"

"I told you this was the absolute wrong place to park," M says. "But you wouldn't listen."

"We want it to be something she'll look back on," D says.

"Well, she can look back on it no matter what," I say. They are beginning to really bother me.

"Yes, but you know what we mean, what we're getting at," M says.

"I don't," I say. You have to be true to your principles in this life.

M is going, "We all want for it to be specially special for Paula."

All. Part of the shadow of family they keep looking through the trees for. The family tree. I smile.

M is watching me, very earnest in her lime silk and her lace jabot—Do you think this is too much? she said to Paula when she first tried it on—and her dyed-to-match pumps and her bouncy orchid and I know it's a big serious deal for her, silly though it is.

"Okay," I say. "I'll try."

"Did you hear that, Glenn?" She reaches over the back seat and hugs me even though it somewhat mashes her orchid. I straighten the stamen or whatever it is and she tries to hug me again, but enough is enough. Basta. Basta la pasta.

Which reminds me. "I'm hungry. Do you want for my stomach to be growling at the wedding?" I say, squinting at the Burger King, so near and yet so far.

"You only get married the one time, hopefully," D says. It's like he's got a set speech he hasn't plowed through yet.

"What's the point of this discussion anyway?"

"We think it would be best," M says, picking each word carefully as though she's playing Scrabble, "if you didn't say Occupational Therapy if anybody asks you what you're doing now, especially anybody like Mrs. Aimslee."

"Like who?" (I already know who but screw them, all they want to do is crap on me.)

"Jake's mother—if you would just say you were, you know, taking some arts and crafts classes . . . okay?"

"Which is really what you're doing if the truth be known," D says.

"If the truth not be known," I say. M and D look at each other. Aimslee? I'd never given any thought to Paula's new name. Paula Aimslee? What do you know? That's who she'll be after today, Paula Rae Gilchrist Aimslee. Tiffani Aimslee sounds better, TA, like a teaching assistant, there I am clanging away. Jake is a nerd. He's really wasted. Marry a dork like him? Whatever makes them happy.

Myself I'd sooner get hitched to one of those Stanford chimps they've taught to talk sign language, Braille or Panzese or whatever you call it, I watched this program once. I think I even remember how to do *I am hungry now,* which I for sure am. I try signing *I am hungry,* I forget *now,* in the rear view mirror. They're watching me.

"One other thing," M says. She never runs out of other things. "If Auntie Beryl or anybody wants to know where you're living now, you could just say, oh, with a group of young people, friends."

"Any more terms and conditions?" I say flipping the lid of the backseat ashtray (also buttless).

"Just that we all plan to have a good time, a great time will be had by all, right, Dandy?" D hasn't called me Dandy for years. Dandelion.

It had something to do with the hair. I study myself in the rear view mirror. D puts his hand over the mirror, pretends he's merely adjusting it. They worry about me and mirrors, they think it's bad news, that I'm escaping reality or something. Well, so what? So big what? Who isn't in one way or another, name me one real-life person. People jog, snort coke, drink peppermint schnapps, make love not war, ski the Bugaboos, play Trivial Pursuit, get married. It's all to alter the reality they're in, right? Is looking in mirrors any different basically? Eat cheeseburgers when they're hungry, that's another thing they do.

I roll down the window. A man I first think is Doug Singer, Carla's case manager, but isn't, comes out of Burger King carrying two Styrofoam containers with straws sticking out the lids and a burrito in wax paper.

"Can I have a Poseidon burger? *Please!* I want it with bacon bits."

"No!" the folks both say like a Greek chorus.

"You don't understand. All I had was a banana, part of a banana. The rest was too squishy. I get worse when I don't eat regularly. If you don't believe me, go ahead and ask Dr. Madsen."

"There'll be lots to eat at the reception," M says cheerfully.

"Let's get going then," I say. I roll up the window. If it had of been Doug Singer, I would have asked him for a cigarette.

We finally come to rest in a place that says Reserved.

"This says Reserved."

"That means us," D says.

"What it is, it's saved for the official wedding party," M says. Her voice is shaky with excitement.

We slide in next to a white Cherokee van. A man with his shirt sleeves rolled up is setting out film packs and a tripod. SAY CHEESE. *Weddings, Portraiture, Restorations, Insurance, no risk sittings,* the van says in two-tone letters.

"What's he doing here?" I say. "That bozo?"

They look at each other. "Well, we felt, actually Jake thought . . ." D flubs around. "They wanted to be sure to have shots to send people back East who couldn't come."

That's about when I begin to get the big picture, the big no picture.

"Tiffani, honey," M says, "we thought it would be better if we had somebody for the hard shots, you know, the big family groups."

"So you could be in them."

"That's it, there you are. We want you in the pictures."

"Front and center."

"And then that way too you can just concentrate on the candids, you know what I mean?"

"The informal stuff you do so well."

"And it won't be such a responsibility on you."

"If anything went wrong, she means."

"And you'd be free to just enjoy."

I sling the Nikon back into the Volvo.

"Ouch!" Say Cheese says. "Good they make 'em to last." He shakes his head.

I straddle his beat-up old Rolleiflex which is sitting on the ground like a soccer ball. I nudge it with a toe. M is watching me. Ready, get set, Cheese!

"Mind if I put this up for you?" she says to Say Cheese. "We wouldn't want anything to happen to it."

"You can hum that one again," Say Cheese hums. "We don't want any disasters today." They all look at me. Or maybe I just think they all look at me.

"Like when the lady backed into the propeller," D says. "Disasseder."

That does it. "You're so gross!" I say. "He's so gross I can't stand it any more!" I appeal to them but there's no help anywhere.

Gross echoes back from the rocks and rills, the templed hills. "She's right on the edge," M whispers. Say Cheese keeps setting out his wares, like it's one of Paula's tailgate parties she was so fond of at U.O.P.

VIII

I climb back into the Volvo. I'm zapped. I need a nap. Nap. Zap. Crap. I close my eyes. My right lid starts in twitching. I can't sleep. I have indignation insomnia. I get out. I should lock the car because of the Nikon, but I don't care any more what happens to the Nikon. I compromise. I might care a little. I lock three of the doors. That way it's in the lap of the gods. God's lap, where everybody wants to curl up one time or another.

I amble over and plop down in one of the dung-colored folding chairs they've set up on the lawn, burrowing down in it as far as I can, resting my smothered toes, which are used to sandals, on the chair in front. Right away someone steps over my shins so I get up to leave. No such luck. Body sachet lassoes me. It's M's sister, Auntie Beryl, compact as a brussels sprout.

"There you are, Mary Alice. How'd you let that little sis of yours beat you to the altar, young lady, that's what I want to know." She reaches over and does something to the back of my dress. "You don't want for your label to show, hon, now do you? Saks is it? There now. You always want to look your best. What are you, two years older'n Paula?"

"More like one and a half. Just twenty months between us." Why did I bother saying that?

"Well, believe you me, it's good you take your time, be sure. In my opinion she's entirely too young, Paula is. Although I guess they grow up early these days. She won't have any thrills left I said to Francie when she let Paula go traipsing off to Mazatlan in high school. . . . I hear his family is very well off."

Auntie Beryl has lots of enlarged pores and a bowed clavicle. She is not aging well. I would have taken her at f/6, 1/250 second, focused right in on the pores, made them look like buckshot. I am smiling, smiling.

"There's that sunny smile. That's one thing I'll say for you, Mary Alice. You've got a grin a mile wide. I've got to hand it to you." She doesn't say what she's got to hand me.

M is flitting around. She repositions the punch ladle, checks the 90-cup coffee maker to be sure the little red light is coming on, spreads a cloth she got in the Philippines on a table where people can apparently put their crappy presents because one does, sweeps an oak leaf from a chair, and, thank God, hauls Auntie Beryl off to meet Mrs. Aimslee.

I gravitate toward the kitchen where some Frantics in black dresses and white aprons are chopping seaweed logs. I have one as it rolls off the assembly line. I really am hungry, nobody believes me. The Frantic who is arranging logs on a silver tray stops and looks at me. Clearly I have an impact. (What kind of impact do you really want to have? Dr. Madsen's voice says.)

"Sushi?" I say to be conversational. Nobody bothers to answer. I bow. Ah so. "Natullary nothing oldinaly fol oul ritter Paura."

"What?" the Frantic says rudely.

I have another log.

"You want to get me fired?" a different Frantic who has apparently been summoned says, fierce as a church organ.

I let the screen door to the kitchen bang shut. I put one of the champagne glasses on the bar to my lips to see if it's cold. It is. It also tastes silvery like a baby mug I once had. The bartender, who is transferring ice from a plastic sack to a cooler, hurries over. "This is a private function," he says, taking the glass from me and putting it behind the bar. He apparently thinks I'm part of the general Q public.

"Forget it," I say.

I meander along a path that says Private till I come to the old carriage house. There's a post with an iron ring where maybe they tied the horses back in the gold rush. I don't know. Now people get hitched there. Yok. I laugh.

Through the vine-switched honeysuckled window I can see figures in the filtered light. Paula. And Yoko. I move in closer. Paula is standing there in a tiny scallop of bra and a triangle of beige string bikini mapped with fading summer tan. Her underwear is so small I've seen her suds it and then squeeze the water out all with one hand and loop it over the towel rack where it starts to open up like flowers, shimmery Spandex flowers.

She puts on a camisole with spaghetti straps and the old English monogram cut out. And a half slip that matches—the monogram is to the right of the slit down by the hem. She steps into it, steadying herself with a hand on Yoko. Flesh shadows rise to the surface as she moves.

She has her arms up and Yoko lets the dress fall softly over her head. There must be a fabricky second or two there when she can't breathe, when she could even suffocate. But then her head shows up again and she shakes out her hair. The dress, I happen to know, is cream taffeta, Victoriana, M says, with a sheen to it except in the cloistered light you can't see it, you'd have to be in the know like me about the sheen. The dress has lace puttering down the front of it to form a V for victory, aimed at the crotch, and little covered buttons in back which Yoko is currently doing up.

And then the hat. Paula's had this thing about hats ever since she was a kid. We have pictures of her in M's old felt, Auntie Beryl's turban, something of Nana's called a cloche. This one is wide-brimmed, lacy, with satin streamers, none of this veiled virgin crapola. She's been making out since she was sixteen. Actually 15, it was a week before her sixteenth birthday.

Jake is on scene. In a tux, looking like a penguin. He takes Paula's hand, holds her out away from him. She stands there smiling, shining in the half light, and then they start this picking each other over thing. She straightens his boutonnière, he tilts her hat.

He's behind her, reaching in his pocket. Makes me think of a

time I went to McNear's Beach with them. She was sitting between
his knees. They were jammed like carts in a supermarket and he
took her brush out of her beach bag with the lambs on it (five white
and one black) and pushed her head down gently and started in
brushing her hair upside down, over her face, very meticulous, every
strand, till when he was through and cleaning out the brush with
his fingers, she flounced back and the hair was all fluffy. I picked
up the ball of combings before the wind took it and wound it tight
around my finger. Do me that way, I said, but Jake just laughed
and I laughed. We were all the time kidding around like that.

Jake is holding this box, a Gumps type thing, bright blue satin
with oriental embroidery. He fishes out a tiny necklace, seed pearls
it looks like. He stands there frowning, trying to get it fastened
around her neck.

They're standing close as peanut butter and jelly, she's leaning
back against him. Paula used to say I stand too close to people, it
makes them nervous. Some people don't like to be touched, Dr.
Madsen said, they have built up walls. That's Paula, I said, snapping
my fingers. But here's old Paula getting married. All of a sudden
Jake comes out the door. And then Paula. I fade into the shadows
of the cypresses, I think they're cypresses, but she sees me.

"I was just going to look for you," she says.

"Oh, I was just taking a walk. Me? You were looking for me?"

"I have something for you. Here." She hands me a little box.
Pink and gold, I. Magnin striped. *Sis* it says.

"It says Sis."

She doesn't say anything. I fumble around with the ribbon. It
won't slide. "I can't do it."

"Yes you can."

"Not without scissors or something. I don't have fingernails like
you."

"Here." She manages to get the one corner off, hands it back.
Whaddaya know. Gold hoop earrings. "Are they real gold?"
She nods.

Weird, I say. Neat. "They must have cost a bundle." And then I kind of clam up, I don't know what to say.

" 'Member the ones you lent me?" she says. "Only one fell off, I lost one for you."

She makes it sound like she did me a big favor. "That's 'cause you were wallowing around in the back seat of Ed Reisner's BMW."

"No, it was at Great America. I think it fell off on the Loggers' Run. Anyway it was Mike who had the BMW, you were always mixing them up, Ed and Mike."

She makes them sound like a tossed salad, mixed greens, which they were, sort of. I start tossing one of the earrings, catching it on the back of my hand. "And you were always getting mad. I'd say Mike called when it was Ed and you'd get really ticked."

"Yah."

"But now it doesn't matter. It was a long time ago," I say, sounding like the start of a fairy tale. Forever and a half ago that I had anything she wanted.

"You were all the time borrowing my stuff," I say. "Sometimes you didn't even bother asking."

"You would have said yes, you always did." A shadow passes over her face, her cheek twitches.

"Still . . ."

She looks sad, rebuffed, like when she was little and didn't get invited to Cindy English's slumber party. "Remember how I clobbered Cindy English with the bear flag in assembly and everybody thought it was an accident?"

She giggles, yah. I'm really surprised she remembers.

"Aren't you going to put them on?"

"Okay, sure."

"Hey, not hooked all the way inside. On the lobe, remember?"

She's such a perfectionist, you wouldn't believe.

"Listen, Paula, if you don't like me how I am, the way I do things, if you don't want me here. . . ."

She reaches over, adjusts the right one. "Too tight?"

"It's okay, I guess." My ears are burning, which they do sometimes, get feverish before the rest of me does. Her hands are cool.
It's an odd sensation. I like it when she does that, I wish she'd keep
on. "That one's loose, the other one."

She tightens it, looping my nostrils with perfume.

"Does M know about this? About you giving me these?"

"No."

"It wasn't just something you cooked up together?"

"No."

"Because it's like something you'd give a, you know, give a
bridesmaid, somebody like that." I can't stand to look at her neck,
which is so slender you're conscious of the fragile pulse thrashing
there like an upside down bug and below that the pearls some
wounded imperfect oyster was pried open for.

She's looking at me the way she did Commencement night. She
found me in the gym after practically everybody had left. *Are you
all right?* Her friends were at the door calling her. She gestured to
them to stay out, to wait. And we sat there on the bright shellacked
floor with its precise black margins. *I just wish you'd look up.* I looked
over her head, up at the empty loop you shoot baskets at if you
shoot baskets. *You're sure you're okay?*

"Yah, I'm okay." Sometimes it takes me a long time to answer,
like eight years. I run my arm across my face. "But if you'd rather
me not to come. . . ."

She's silent. One lone tear pops out of her right eye, catches a
spoke of mascara and slowly rolls its muddy obscene way down her
cheek, off her chin. I look to see if I can see where it landed. The
twin, the left tear, she catches on her knuckle that has the ring,
making a momentary bright prism.

"I want you here."

"I mean, I have plenty of stuff to do—errands like you wouldn't
believe, the laundromat and I'm out of Q-tips. And blusher. And
those little packages of Kleenex."

"You're my sister. You belong here."

"Okay, whatever you say. It's no big deal either—"

When I look up she's gone, walking quickly down the path, holding up her skirt so you can see the heels of her little white sandals getting smaller and smaller.

I should probably have given her a shower or something. I can't remember if I even said thanks for the earrings. I feel . . . I don't know what I feel.

Three rick-racked people, medieval costumes, are cooing what I believe is called madrigals. I squeeze between *Love stood amazed at sweet Beauty's pain* and *Would have said that all was but in vain,* excuse me. I guess I could have gone around.

Say Cheese is say-cheesing. The way he's framing the shots you wouldn't believe. He's going to have trees and bushes sprouting out of people's heads.

> *And let thy blissful kisses cherish*
> *Mine infant joys that else must perish*

He tries twice to get me, but I turn the other cheek, meaning I don't turn the other cheek. See, I'm proverbing right along.

I stalk back toward the folding chairs. There's lots of people now. They've begun to put things down, homesteading seats, they're very territorial. "We're saving two, this one's saved." Okay, okay. I'm pacing, trying to decide. "Just let her by," someone says.

The Emory twins are up in the oak, the big one Paula will get married under. They used to live next door to us on Poplar Canyon. I see the tree has cleats for climbing. "Mind if I come on up?" I shade my eyes.

> *Earth, heaven, fire, air the world transformed shall view.*

The twins stop rooting around and look at each other. I wish I ever had anyone to look at meaningfully. I do actually, but they don't look back meaningfully. "Whaddaya say, guys?"

Ere I prove false to faith, or strange to you.

"I dunno, I guess," Kevin says, shrugs. They must be about ten by now.

I knock some bark off by the second cleat and scuff up my right shoe, so I just kick it off with the other foot—"Timber!"—and let it be there at the base of the tree where I can get it later. "Move," I say when I get to the fork. "Just scrunch on over a little." Adam does. "That's far enough, that's okay." He recognizes the crisp voice of authority, the natural sense of command.

I give Kevin's leg a friendly poke with my toe, the way Carla did with Geoffrey. I feel better sitting in the leafy light with Kevin and Adam. They're not yet at that age where everybody's got to be just like everybody else. I wouldn't mind if I was sitting right in there between them. Actually it's better for twins to be separated, they develop faster. "Adam, tell you what, you move on down a little and that way I can get in there in the middle and see you guys don't take a header or anything." They look at each other, they're not overly bright kids. They have on matching gray pants and little shirts with button-down collars and bow ties. They are a couple of sparrows, but I don't mind. You can tell they are thinking over my deal, but then I see Mrs. Emory heading for us. She looks like her hair was done by a city planner. She probably thinks the same about mine. Different cities.

The cuckoo calls, the lamb doth bleat.

"Is that you, Mary Alice?" Mrs. Emory says, shading her eyes with her purse and looking up at us. Say Cheese starts to take a picture, but she waves him off. "Now listen—I want to see every last one of you down out of that tree so the ceremony can begin, you hear?"

There's no way we wouldn't hear. Kevin and Adam look to me to negotiate, as Lady of the Flies. I scratch my leg with the foot that doesn't currently have a shoe on (there are bugs all over the place).

The God of Love, with arrow fleet.

"So how's Erin?" I say to be conversational.

"Getting married too," Mrs. Emory says. "But not till June. She wanted in the worst way to be here today. . . ."

I wonder what the worst way is . . .

". . .but they're working her to death down there, they've got her doing promotions for all the new stores, every time The Gap opens a new one."

"So I guess you'll be having an extra room? In June, I mean."

"Mm."

"I said I guess you'll have you—"

Implanted now in every heart
By Cupid's never failing dart.

The madrigal singers stop, open a thermos, are replaced by a trumpet and viola da something. There's no applause, that's show biz.

"All right, you three, you've had your little joke. I want you down here where you belong right now, you hear? No, Mary Alice, my brother's mother-in-law's coming down from Great Falls. Leona. She's planning on staying on after the wedding."

"Gotcha," I say. "Kevin and Adam are free to leave if they want. I'm staying, I'm perfectly comfortable."

"To begin with, they can't either one of 'em move unless you do and for another your daddy asked me to tell you *please* to come on down, you aren't a monkey."

"Is that what he said, I'm not a monkey? Is that what he told you to tell me? Or is that just what you're saying?"

"Mary Alice, honey, it doesn't matter who said what."

"Since when?"

"Yes, well . . . Adam, I'm going to let you jump. Put your foot there on the other side of her and I'll catch you. Kevin, you can back around behind her. Good." She tosses my shoe up to me.

Ceci Schroeder spells her. "Tiffani!" She has her knuckles on her hips. "What can I say? I've known you and your family forever it seems like, rejoiced with them and sorrowed with them upon occasion and today's one of the happy times. Now you don't want to go and spoil it, I know you don't, Tiffani. Just you come on down where you belong. If you won't do it for them, then I want for you to do it for me, okay? As a personal favor to me."

"I might," I say carefully, "if I could come and live with you. . . ."

"Live with me did you say?" Ceci Schroeder says, fumbling the iridescent beads of her necklace. "Is that what you said?"

I nod.

"Oh. Well, I'd have to give that some thought, we'd need to think about it, but you just come on down and we'll have us a good heart to heart talk, the two of us, see what we can work out."

"No," I say. "Unacceptably vague."

Auntie Beryl is now on scene. (M must be truly desperate if she sent Auntie Beryl.) Mrs. Emory is back. They stand around the tree like a covey of Druids. They gaggle away at me. Blah blab blabber. It's just not the way to get attention, it just isn't. But I stand fast and sit tight, hold my ground (only it's a tree), and eventually they retreat.

"We tried," I hear Ceci say in the distance or maybe I just think I hear it.

Suddenly it's Here Comes the Mendelssohn. I smile. I have won. I will tell Dr. Madsen. No maybe I won't, he might nitpick. First out of the starting gate it's the minister in a black robe with flapping sleeves, followed by Jake and Mr. and Mrs. Aimslee, who is impacted with blue lace.

Everybody is turning around looking, waiting, and then looky looky looky here comes cookie, Paula in between M and D, all three of them smiling bravely, holding onto each other and right under the surface the glisten of tears, D even. Say Cheese is barreling along sniping at them.

Jake turns around—"Greet your bride"—Jake the Jerk who didn't believe I could take shots to send to the people back East. They stand there under the oak tree, the one I have homesteaded, the music swirling around them. It's now the Trumpet Voluntary, which may not have been a cliche originally but sure as shit is now. If I *was* going to come down from the tree it would be to the Trumpet Voluntary, which would be suitable for a heraldic descent if you got the timing right, cleat by cleat. But the music stops and the trumpeter shakes the spit from his instrument. The moment is past.

The winter sun shines down in spangles like a blessing, a laying on of lights, and I think I have never seen anything so vulnerable. They're my whole life struggling to be. Doesn't everybody see how beautiful they are? (Not Jake, he's a true nerd.)

D glances up once, swallows, and my tears stream down. They have rounded shoulders, that's what gets to me, the three of them, M and D and Paula, which give them a sad burdened look. I shake the limb gently. Leaves flutter down. One lands on Paula's hat. There's your shower, Paula girl.

The ceremony is in process, I think. I have to strain to hear. That comes of sitting in the cheapo seats, the bleachers. She and Jake spent two weeks writing their own vows, but they sound just like all the schmaltz I've ever heard or read except they plan to grow together and respect each other's specialness if I heard correctly. Her voice is that soft and the wind is in the wrong direction, melding high sentiment with bird song and jet stream.

The minister pronounces them husband and wife in a voice like a message on an answering machine. They kiss so long the audience laughs gently and then the recessional gathers everything in its wake and they stream down the aisle, Hurricane Paula. She was in a hurry to get to the cake, Jake says later.

The recessional is still blasting away when I back down the tree— da da the witch is dead—those might not be the exact right words but that's how I always hear it, in my mind's ear.

I brush the ants off me so they won't get on the sushi but the cateress won't take the plastic wrap off till people have started clearing the receiving line, so I have no choice but to shuffle on through, baby. I duck in by Paula, s'cuse me. I mean there's no point in exchanging unpleasantries with M and D, or pleasantries for that matter, nice to see you, glad you could make it, right?

"I thought you'd come down for the food," Paula says. She seems a little, I don't know, chilly.

"See, I've still got them on," I say, fingering my ears. I start asking her how she liked my wedding present, which is a neat toilet bowl brush which I first thought was a mixing spoon. "It's got lifetime bristles and a drip-catching well and it was chosen for the design collection of the Museum of Modern Art," I explain patiently.

"Okay, Tiffani," Paula says, passing me on to Jake.

"Hello, Bat Girl." He gives me a peck on the cheek and tugs me by the hand, moving me along carefully like Scotch tape on a roll.

"I've been through the mill," I say to a Frantic. "And I'm the sister of the bride. She said for me to go ahead and have something to eat." Turns out now they're waiting for the mothers, but they offer me a bread stick with prosciutto wrapped around it.

It's all very ritualistic. People hover around admiring Paula's ring, which is made from a square-cut emerald Jake brought back from Brazil when he went with his father to check on the gum factory they have there. (I'm wearing my white ivory-looking ring from Lindy's cracker jack box, as a joke, of course.)

Later Say Cheese says say cheese and Paula and Jake put their hands on a knife with a white 50 golden years bow and slather each other with Crisco frosting. This is a professional photographer? Please! What he should do is use soft light, which is diffuse, coming from all directions, filling in the shadows, but not him, oh no, he's using hard light which is directional, casting strong shadows. The cake's bound to look washed out. He's got far and away too much contrast going. The Nikon with its center weighted meters takes shadow areas into account, but with a Rolleiflex you're dead in the water. The guy is a total spaz.

Next event, Paula goes up on the steps of this portico deal to toss her bouquet of wildflowers. I realize I better hurry. I cut a wedge, oops, weaving through the crowd till I'm close enough to catch her eye and then I hold my arms up like a basketball player. Seconds later she drops her bouquet—giddy squeals—practically on Yoko's head. I stand there for a minute and then I pretend I was just doing exercises, jumping up and down and doing my arms over my head, one two three four. The big joke is, the real joker, Say Cheese thought she'd throw it to me too and he was focussed on me the whole time and he missed the shot. There is some justice in this shit-kicking world after all, except I think maybe Yoko's father might have snuck in there with his Leica.

The band, actually it's a mandolin, piano, and drums, cranks up. First D and Paula dance, and then Jake cuts in and he and Paula and M and D dance and gradually showoffy people like Auntie Beryl and Uncle Lester join in. He twirls her out and she does this vivacious at 65 number, hanging onto the corner of her mauve challis skirt in this sickening Medicare debutante way. She's proud of her girlish legs on which, however, age has mapped out a whole town center of varicose veins. Maybe I could live with them. I wouldn't want to, but, hey, I might not have to. All I might need to do is tell M, say I was about to ask Auntie Beryl and Uncle Lester and then—

Out of the wild blue yonder, there is Mr. Aimslee, Jake's daddy.

He leans forward. I think maybe he wants me to sniff his carnation, which I do. "I'm not sure I'm up to this," he says, "but if you can put up with an old duffer . . . you *are* Tiffani, aren't you? Sister of the bride? That's the one I'm supposed to be looking for."

He's about a hundred. Actually I don't mind older men. It's old ones give me the creeps. That little syllable *er* changes your whole point of view.

"Yah," I say. Yah to everything.

He takes my hand.

"I probably certainly wouldn't have known you two were sisters if it hadn't been pointed out to me, funny how families. . . ."

"Say, how many rooms might you have in your house where you live anyway?"

"How many rooms, did you say?"

That's as far as we get before D, who when last seen was dancing with Mrs. Aimslee, cuts in. The end of an opportunity.

"You can't have a monopoly on the pretty girls, Ed," D says, winking.

"You can probably always go back to Mrs. Aimslee," I say politely. "If you want to." It was nice of D to save me from Mr. Aimslee like that. Or maybe he was saving Mr. Aimslee, I don't know.

"Having fun, are you?" D says, foxtrotting me around in a way no fox ever trotted.

"I'll think about it," I say.

"Sure you are," he says hopefully. "You betcha."

I wonder is he going to say anything about the tree? But he's shrewd sometimes. He knows not to push me too far. It's like I have a Special Occasions pass, diplomatic immunity or something, like when you're in a foreign country, which I am in a way, if you know what I mean.

Somewhere back there the music stopped and we clap. I clap extra for the drummer, who smiled at me when I was climbing down from the tree. The way he plays the drums, you'd swear the rhythm comes up to meet the sticks, it's there waiting. "You can stop your clapping now," D says. I get round-the-clock advice, like I'm some kind of telethon.

M hands me a glass of sparkling apple cider. Everyone else gets champagne. I pour my cider on a geranium and snare a glass of bubbly from a tray going by. I deserve it. The waiter looks back. I raise my glass. After all, we finally got Paula safely married off and I don't have to worry about her any more. Let Jake the Jerk take on the burden, more power to him.

My feet have begun to kill me, the toes and also across the instep where the strap rubs. I edge my heels out and stand on them, which is some improvement. Sheez! What I put myself through for the family.

More goodies start circulating on silver trays. I plop myself on the grass with a heaped-up little white plate. There's something dark and forbidding that looks like eggplant. It also tastes dark and forbidding. It's while I'm thinking eggplant? eggplant? that I see this incredible thing at the base of the oak tree. A little skinny five-inch-long snake, one end earth brown and the other a brilliant metallic blue. Did he come out of an eggplant like a sperm from an egg? Jake and Paula, Adam and Eve and Snake, it all makes sense. A something blue crawlie. No it doesn't. How could it? Either nature has gone bananas too or I am in even worse shape than I previously thought or one good swig of Paul Masson champagne has put me in an altered state. "Look!" I say to the world at large. "Quick!" I can't help it. I want at least one ostensibly normal individual to certify yes, that is a half blue non-fictional snake you are seeing, it is not a hallucination, whomp-up, or freak out. I doubt even Dr. Madsen would know whether this one was for real if I just told him about it. I need verification.

"Found a friend?" a voice says looming over me. It's a guy in a tux, an usher. Blond. A perfect eleven on a scale of one to ten. I scramble up, pull my dress out of my butt where it's stuck and retreat a foot or two.

"It's a half blue snake?" I say pointing. "Isn't it a half blue snake?" I'm hyperventilating. I don't know, I'm a little nervous, I guess.

"I think it's a half blue lizard, which makes you half right, right?"

"Let's not quibble, Sibyl." (I don't think I should have said Sibyl that way.)

The lizard slithers under a rock as though insulted. It's like me, it doesn't want to be looked at, I guess.

"He's part blue like that to attract the female," the usher says.

It's an awkward moment, no doubt about it. Is he implying I'm the female? That lizards are attracted to me? No, he took off. Or I am attracted to lizards?

"Dance?"

I check behind me. Does he mean somebody else? He doesn't

wait for an official answer. He takes my hand, which is clammy and also a little eggplanty. I take it back temporarily and wipe it on my dress since his tux is probably rented and I wouldn't want for him to get charged extra.

It's crowded but we find us a place and kind of mark time, whatever that means. "Hey, Kurt!" one of the ushers says. "How ya doin', there, buddy?" My friend makes a circle with his thumb and forefinger.

I look back at my plate. I was planning to eat either the watercress thing or the won ton next. I just hope a Frantic doesn't come along and take everything away.

"You live around here, Mary Ann?"

"Well, not right here, no. I'm Tiffani. I used to be Mary Alice." I'm kind of twitching, which makes my earrings bob.

"Yah? I never really knew anybody who actually changed their name. Know a lotta people'd like to. . . . No, I didn't think you lived in the tree"—he must have seen me—"in the general vicinity, I meant."

"Yah, in the general vicinity, that's what I thought you probly meant. How about you?" My God, I am talking a blue streak, a blue lizard streak, socializing, exchanging good quality small talk like I'm on Joan Rivers.

"No, I'm just home for the holidays," he says. One of his co-ushers is giving him the eye. He raises his eyebrows in return. It seems like he has himself a lot of friends, which is good. "I'm Henrietta Aimslee's nephew. I go to Dartmouth," he says, returning to me.

"Oh heavy," I say, which Jake the Jerk says. I try to think if that was a good thing to say. It sounded pretty good to me, which is something to go by. You have to trust your gut.

"Depends how you go at it," he says, so it must have been an okay thing to say. You can sort of tell when what you say isn't just a net ball, when it gets volleyed back that way. It's a rhythm, you learn to swing with it. Chunk, thunk, blip, blop.

I see D eyeballing us. He and M take turns at it, it's rotational like guards at San Quentin. I hope he notices I'm dancing, dancing. Well, actually shuffling in place, I must not fantasize, Dr. Madsen says, I must get away from that. D, of course, has no way to know I am making sparkling high-grade conversation. I give him a little salute to clue him. He smiles warily.

"What are you doing?" my friend says since I had to disconnect my hand momentarily.

"Just signaling somebody," I say. "This guy I know." This is called sailing close to the wind. "It's nobody important though. Just somebody I used to have a relationship with."

"Well how 'bout that Thai place then? The Gulf of Siam?" he is saying to one of his friends.

"They use MSG over there you happen to know? 'Cause Crissie's allergic," his buddy says.

It's kind of a hard conversation to go with but then something comes to me. "Say, if you don't mind me being nosy, how come you asked me to dance?" I kind of tap him on the shoulder so he knows I'm talking to him.

"There's always Cajun. . . . Why did I ask you to dance. That's a good question. Would you believe I had a bet on with Kenny— see that turkey over there at the bar getting smashed? No, really, I just wanted to see what somebody who'd watch a wedding from a tree was like. I had you pegged for a free thinker."

"Oh very definitely. I think therefore I'm free," I say.

"Okay, but I don't think Spenger's takes reservations."

This time I really drum on him. "You want to find somewhere that's not so crowded? Not so many people?"

"If you mean the tree, I'm not a climber."

"A social climber," I say.

He kind of laughs, I'm not sure why. I like people who laugh without being sticklers about it. "I just meant some place—ground level—where we could hear ourselves think." (That doesn't make sense, but people say it, don't they?)

"Okay, if you think we can just jump ship like that."

"I don't see why not. You don't usher people out, do you?"

"You gotta point there, girl."

Yah? I ask his name. He tells me. I forget it right away. Names are not important, they're just labels somebody hangs on you. They obscure the real person, unless of course you pick your own.

"Coming, Tiffy?" whoever he is says. Tiffy? It sounds like your pet rat.

As we leave the guy at the bar—Kenny—rolls his eyes. "Hey, man, lighten up," he says. They both laugh. I like good-natured positive types. My friend gives a victory sign over my head.

That's when the comet of thought first flashes through my mind. Victory! Housing is solved. We will get married, perhaps even under the live oak, which has greater significance for us than for Paula and Jake. It is, after all, where we met. The Tree of the Half Blue Lizard, like the Street of the Wooden Clogs, only different, of course. I just knew something was going on there, the cateress will say (even though she is clearly a nerd), the way they looked at each other.

I try to remember where Dartmouth is, which is hard because I never knew to start with. Somewhere east of the Rockies. I will need a good sturdy pair of boots, possibly Carla will let me take her suede ones. They're too tight on her. She tried stretching them out. She put water in a plastic bag and then the bag in the boots, actually it was two bags, it must have been, and the boots in the freezer, but it didn't work. Also it turned out they weren't water-proof.

"Where to?" It seems like maybe he has been saying that, that he said it before. "This is your neck of the woods."

Woods with necks? From necking in the woods?

"What're you smiling about, Tiffy?"

"Just happy. Listen, there is one thing, my feet are killing me, not really killing me, but you know what I mean" (I don't want him to worry) "and if we could just stop off, I'd like to get my old sandals."

"Sure, good thinking."

This is the second time recently I have been praised for the excellence of my thought processes. It's getting monotonous.

I see we have us a jazzy little car with spoke wheels. Red. He'll teach me to drive it, every car's different. It'll be a trip because we'll be snuggled up across the bucket seats.

He is helping me in. "What kind is this anyway?"

"280Z," he says.

"I didn't mean the license number."

He looks puzzled, laughs a little. Like me.

"Jake has a Porsche," I say.

"I know," he says.

I wonder if I will have trouble learning to drive this one. "Is it a stick shift?"

"Five on the floor."

"That's what I was afraid of."

"Nothing to be afraid of, Tiffy. It's a pretty good little buggy, been across the country four times already."

I wonder if he will think it's strange if I don't help with the driving. Since I don't have a license any more, not since the accident, there could be an insurance problem, I'll explain it that way. And I'll check the map. "I'm good at reading maps," I say.

"Yah? Well, we shouldn't need a map to find your place, at least I hope not."

"Oh no, not here, I didn't mean here," I say. "Just on the open road." I could actually be ready to cut out of this hell hole in half an hour, 45 minutes at the outside.

He looks puzzled again. I am used to puzzled types, I do well with them. If we do elope, M and D will be upset at first. You have to be flexible when you have kids, M will say the way she did when Paula broke off her engagement to Wes, the oral surgeon with a condominium in Florida, and some people had already given her presents at the engagement party. What a scam! They will be relieved not to have that problem again. Wes took both of our wisdom teeth out. I mean all the wisdom teeth out of both of us. I got nothing for my three days of biting down on a mouthful of bloody gauze, looking like a chipmunk and chomping Percodan, not even the Tooth Fairy. You're too old for that stuff, D said.

"Hey, wake up, you've got to tell me which way, Miz Tiffy."

Apparently he's been asking for a while. The car behind us is honking rudely. When I drive again, I will never toot, never. "Straight ahead, where that car's going—"

"The Honda?"

It's a quiz. He's testing me. I stare at him. Next thing he'll be asking me what day it is and who's president. Maybe he's a schmuck like the rest of them. Like the people next door. Like the one who hosed Cathouse. Even though he seemed to have some potential as a human being.

"Awright, knock it off!" He gives the finger to the driver behind us. The car spurts around us, burning rubber.

"That gray one up there, just follow the gray one." (After all I can't be expected to know everything that's on the road.) "And then pretty soon you'll want to be in the left lane." I don't know why anybody would exactly *want* to be in the left lane, but that's what they say, I've heard them say it. I can't believe how great I'm actually sounding. Planning ahead like Dr. Madsen says I should, not living for the moment.

I wonder if he will insist on sex first. I hope not. That's better as a wrap-up. Otherwise it can screw the works. What a dirty mind I must have. I smile. He looks at me. "Hi," I say. He quirks an eyebrow back. "That's it up there, that house with the winter squash instead of grass."

We're there and I suddenly see a problem I haven't reckoned with, never mind all my advance planning. I can't exactly invite him in. What would Geoffrey make of somebody in a tux? What would somebody in a tux make of Geoffrey in his war surplus camouflage hat he was wearing when I left? Or Lindy? Or Carla. I don't think I want them to meet. That's instinct talking—I couldn't function without it.

". . . don't want to hold you up if you have stuff to do," he's saying.

As for Warren, he'd have an attack. He'd die of jealousy on the spot. Hey, not a bad idea. Forget it. . . . The world is such a hierarchy, people you embarrass, people who embarrass you.

". . . have to get this monkey suit back before they close . . . think maybe we should call it—"

"You just wait right here, okay?" I say.

He comes around and opens the door for me. "Thanks, 280Z," I say, delicately sidestepping the name problem. I go bounding up the steps even though I think I must have blisters on my heels by now, but I feel somehow uneasy. So I come on back down, much as the shoes are zapping me, and I ask very politely would he care to have me bring him out some juice or something? I tell him Hawaiian punch I know we have and I could maybe jar some Snappy Tom loose from Carla. But he says no, it's okay if I'll just make it snappy.

"You want some Snappy Tom after all? That's the one I'm not sure about."

"No," he says a long while later. He's not a fast talker. "We're on a different wave length. Why don't you just get your shoes."

"Enjoy," I say graciously. I'm glad he's a patient type. Dr. Madsen will be glad too (although I may never see him again). I can't stand pressure.

I find Geoffrey and I try to tell him about the half blue lizard, but he just looks at me blinking rapidly. He still has on his camouflage pants and hat but his chest is bare. It's very pale hairless skin, succinct nipples—buttons that look as if they manipulate something. You could imagine pushing one and Geoffrey slowly ascending two flights. Which reminds me, I was on my way upstairs.

I wade into my room, find one sandal, boom, like that. The second one has been piked. It's gone. I check in all the normal places, under the bed and the chair cushion, on the desk. I shovel everything out of drawers onto the floor, which is the proven best way to hunt for lost articles. Not there. It turns out to be in the john. I would have looked there early on, except that the other one was in plain view, the buckle caught on the curtain so you saw it right off.

I decide to change while I'm at it. I ram hangers together, considering options, but then I tell myself to calm down, stop hurrying. It never buys you anything. I find a cigarette in the pocket of my jumper, which must be a sign I should wear my jumper.

I sit and smoke, looking in the mirror and attempting to plan our honeymoon. Paula and Jake are going to this place on Maui with black swans and grottoes you can swim through and when you come out the other side they're there waiting for you with mai tais in coconuts, talk about tacky. It's on Kanapaali Beach. Everything in Hawaii starts with a K. I told Jake he better take lots of shark repellent so they wouldn't have to worry about losing a leg or anything, it's usually the leg they go after, though they like torso too. And other stuff. What are you blushing for? Jake said. He's all the time trying to embarrass me.

What I want for us is a small country inn. Bed and breakfast. Boysenberry muffins, wild strawberries we pick ourselves. A harpsichord in the living room. A stone fireplace, open hearth. Patchwork quilts. A Saint Bernard you step over. Maybe he only likes cities. No, everybody's got some country in 'em, a house and a stream. We'll sit by a brook with our tiny shining glasses of Irish cream such as M and D and Paula and Jake had the night they announced they were going to go legal. Except I can't have that. Mellaril and liquor's a crummy combination, as Dr. Madsen says. Unless maybe I won't take my Mellaril, not on the honeymoon.

It is, I admit, my fault that I spent time planning our honeymoon when I could have been with my beloved, getting to know him, his name and everything, or at least having a rap. Anyway when I look out the window finally I see Whatshisname—what *is* his name? he told me—talking to the man next door. To Art Ryan. At least I remember one of the names. I fly downstairs, holding my sandals. I don't even stop to put them on.

I rush past Art Ryan, wiggling a sandal in his direction, which could be taken as a wave, as an indication that we are all good neighbors, except he just stands there gaping.

"Aloha," I say breathless. (Maybe Ciao would have been better.) I just wish I wouldn't sweat buckets the way I do. I try blotting my armpits with my sandals. "I see you found yourself someone to talk to, help you pass the time."

"Yah, like an hour," he says. He laughs like I'm a punch line he's heard before, one brief little ha ha. He's looking at me funny, or I think he's looking at me funny. I slam the car door and roll up the window.

"Listen, what did he have to say anyway, that guy?" I say. "Art Ryan?" My chest is pounding.

Pause.

"Oh he says he's probably going to plant rhododendrons, give them a try, his wife's from the Pacific Northwest and she's got her heart set on rhododendrons."

"Rhododendrons," I say to show I'm tracking.

"He's not all that sure they'll make it here, but he's adding a soil amendment and he's going to give it his best shot."

"A soil amendment," I say. "Anything else? He say anything else?" I'm feeling anxious. I touch his arm, we have to be able to communicate, really communicate, if this thing is ever going to work. "Like what else did he say?"

"Not too much."

"About us, I mean? About the house?"

"He just said there had been some problems, that you all keep the neighbors hopping."

"Hopping?" I say. "What's this hopping shit?"

"Oh he was just blowing off. He thinks a couple of the people are kind of unusual, some of your roommates, but he probably doesn't know his ass from Alcatraz."

"He doesn't, you're absolutely right."

"Now let's go if we're going because I really should be getting back."

I direct us to Barney's. They have wine and beer and cappuccino if the Gaggia's not on the fritz or you can have steamed milk with orgeat and potato skins and there's some stuff Barney's wife makes when she's not back in Shawnee Mission, Kansas, or a bad mood or something. Black bottom brownies, shoo fly pie, Nanaimo bars. But mainly it's the atmosphere. There's a Franklin stove you can warm your feet on, plus a real fireplace with church pew seats on either side and booths around in back. Barney doesn't mind C House coming in there even when we're broke, but he doesn't want us occupying the seats by the fire. Tonight, of course, it's entirely different—me being a paying customer or attached to one. I just hope the pews are vacant.

Tuesdays are open mike at Barney's and the rest of the time it's usually some guitarist or pop singer, people like that. No heavy metal. They leave little flower pots on the tables for tips for the musicians. I'll explain to whoever he is, my future husband—I can't ask him any more what his name is, it's too late for that, I'll just have to wait to hear what someone calls him, one of his ex-roommates who we have over to dinner, the guy at the bar, all these friends he's got—I'll explain about the little flower pots for the musicians and we'll leave a dollar. I'll fold it lengthwise, stand it up the way Jake the Jerk did once, it has a nice style to it.

The lighting inside is dim—the shades are inverted copper colanders and there's a hundred year old coffee grinder from France they still use. The ceiling is looped with madras bedspreads. I personally helped Barney tack up the pieces of lath that make the dips in the madras. It made me really dizzy, like now, like I can really appreciate what Michelangelo went through doing the Sistine Chapel, though he wouldn't have been on Mellaril as it wasn't invented until the 50's, which is a pity as it might have done him good. Who is to say? It might have been better for him and worse for the world. If Michelangelo had been on Mellaril I'd be willing to bet you his beautiful squat angels, his Michel angels, would have deserted him, dissolved right along with the pills and the pain and he would just have sat some place like Barney's, only on a piazza, smiling blandly into his little espressos with lemon peel, which makes them Romanos, the lemon peel does. No lower back pain, no dizzy spells, no Sistine Chapel. Barney gave me a free ginger currant scone and a caffe latte that time, the madras time.

I realize we are just sitting there in the car. He, whoever he is, is running his fingers along the steering wheel. I am beginning to think of him as Dart Muth. Dartie. Dart Vader.

"Hi," I say tentatively to get things going again.

"Aren't you going to go ahead and put your shoes on? I don't know this joint, but most places won't let you in barefoot."

So that's the problem. "Oh, Barney wouldn't care, not if it was me, we're buddies." I don't quite frankly like him calling it a joint that way. "It's got a twelve hundred dollar cappuccino machine and draped madras, I helped put it up, so it looks like Persepolis or something."

"For sure," Dartie says, but doesn't look it.

I put my sandals on, grunting as I try to get the dohinkis through the hole in the strap while sitting in a small car. "Barney was hoping rich Iranians . . . could you move over a little? your butt, that's good—would start coming in, that's why he did the ceiling that way." I see he is brushing off his tux where the sole of my left sandal made a little mark. "There, I'm getting it . . . you don't have to get all the way out . . . there."

We go on in. I point things out—the tiny silver zeppelin that says Goodyear suspended from the fan, the scalloped webs on the lamps—"She cuts up her old nighties, Barney's wife does, and glues the lacy part to the shades to get that look," the crown balanced on the Libra scales, which I put on once, but she said, take it off, take it off. Okay, okay.

Two runners, sweatsuits and headbands, are sitting in the pews. "Come on," I say to Whatshisface. "We'll sit in a booth."

I finger comb the long red fringe on the lamp.

"What's the drill here? Do they come take your order or do we have to go up there?"

"You have to go up." I am pleased to see he understands I am a regular, a mentor.

He comes back with two mugs sudsing over the sides. "Hi," I say. "What's this?"

"Henry Weinhard," he says. "I guess I should have asked you what brand you wanted."

"No, it's okay. I'm a switch hitter, no brand loyalty." I start sipping, just foam at first, to show I'm regular people.

"You've got it on your chin."

I wipe it off with my cigarette package. Okay now? I ask him with my eyebrows. Nothing. I'm not sure how well this whole thing is going.

My future husband bites open a package of peanuts. He seems to have assertiveness-trained front teeth. He spreads some nuts on a cocktail napkin and then he looks at Mr. Peanut. We look at Mr. Peanut.

"Hi," I say very faintly to get things back on track.

"We've been that route," he says. He is eating more than his share of the nuts, shoveling them in.

I am sweating. I guzzle some beer. In five minutes I fling myself through the curtain of bright beads into the john where I barf up. I try to clean off my jumper with a paper towel, lots of luck. Then I get to feeling faint, light-headed. I let myself slide down onto the tile floor. A woman starts to come in, sees the mess, sees me, says Jeez! and goes out again. I wish she had stayed. I am too sick to clean things up. It's like a Turkish prison, the conditions.

I go back to the booth once I can stand up. "Hi." He wrinkles

up his nose. "We have to go home, I have to go home," I blurt
out.

"Let's go," he says. "Actually I'm due in Berkeley." He looks at
his watch, it's one of those new ones without the numbers.

"You don't think you're gunna . . . in the car or anything?"

"No."

After that we don't talk. I hook my finger in the elastic of my
pants to ease the tension on my fluttery stomach. I mean I don't
reach up under, I do it through my jumper. He rolls down the
windows and it's freezing. I close my eyes. Eventually the car stops.
"This is it, Tiffy, end of the line." He reaches across and flips up
the handle. "Thanks," I croak.

"No problem," he says, "but I'd appreciate if you didn't slam
the—" but I already have. I always forget about that, it bugs Jake
too with the Porsche.

I plunk down on my bed, the room going around. In sickness
and in health. My stomach, oh God, my stomach. I plea bargain
with the Almighty. I close my eyes. If You'll just stop all this, I
won't smoke till Thursday (whenever that is). Or as long as ye both
shall say cheese. They didn't want me taking the pictures. They
didn't want me in the pictures. What they wanted, they wanted
me there so they didn't have to account for me being not there. No,
that's not it either. I want you there, Paula said.

Seeing a wedding from a tree, it's different, you take it from the
top. When the minister said that line, as long as ye both shall live,
he glanced up in the tree. I realize now he meant Paula and me, a
joining. And there were all these creatures listening, witnessing—
birds, bugs, beetles. The blue lizard even, he must have been there
for the ceremony. Having covenanted in the presence of God and
these witnesses . . . until death do us part. I want you there. Everything keeps whirling in my head and I think how Say Cheese will
have this shot of me holding out my arms with nothing in them.
Nothing you can see.

IX
The next day or the next week, some time, the bell rings. "Get that fucking cat out of here," Carla yells at Geoffrey.

Cathouse shoots out the back door while Miriam Myers shoots in the front. Here's how it works. Geoffrey opens the door and Cathouse peers out. Carla comes along and gives him (the cat) a slight boot in the rear. By the time the jolt gets to his brain—in this sense it's like electroshock—he thinks it's his own idea and he leaves with dignity.

With Miriam Myers, it's similar but different. I let her in. She has a key, but she always rings the bell on house meeting nights, it's one of those little touches so we can pretend it's our idea she's there.

"I like your raincoat," I say.

"We've got problems, people," she says by way of answer. "Thanks, Tiffani, I got it at a garage sale."

She puts her dripping raincoat on top of the washer, which is unfortunately where we keep the dry cat/raccoon kibble and she heads into the living room heedless to the fact her path is paved with fresh vacuum tracks. She fishes a copy of the petition out of her multi-colored Guatemalan purse, which is even more multicolored because the reds have run in the rain. It starts out with generalities—quiet residential character of the area, property values, safety of the children, and similar irrelevant garbage.

"That's all sheep dip, man," Warren says, jiggling his knees.

"Let her finish," Carla snaps and as usual everybody listens, that is we listen to Carla who says to listen to Miriam Myers, who has, it seems, talked at length to all but one of the signers and she is prepared to get very specific. She cleans her reading glasses on the corner of her sweater she got in Oaxaca. It seems to be several sizes too big for her. Actually everybody's Oaxacan sweater is too big for them. (I know I have a tendency to use *actually* pretty often, it's just something I do.)

First off, Miriam Myers is saying, the people next door have come up with an ugly accusation, namely, that one of the house members is given to exposing himself. Geoffrey starts whispering into his imaginary phone. We call it his headphone.

"Given to!" Carla hoots. "It happened once, okay?"

"But it *did* happen?" Miriam Myers says.

"Shit, that's ancient history," Warren says.

"It was maybe literally true," I say, "but not figuratively."

a   "We are being attacked by Leptogurian forces," Geoffrey says urgently.

"It was all a misunderstanding," Warren says. "The people next door basically knew that. It was Thanksgiving."

"Thanksgiving!" Miriam Myers says. It is not clear whether it's the time lapse or the sacred nature of the holiday that appalls her, but she is clearly exasperated. She's wiggling her pencil with her thumb nail. "It just blows my mind how you people keep silent about major occurrences that occur." It puts her in an embarrassing light with the System, she says, her bosses. They want to know how come she doesn't know what's going on or coming off, that was how I think she puts it, and believe her me she is really good and browned off that we haven't kept her informed like we should, that we haven't seen fit to.

"What else? Anything else in their little pisspot minds? Let's have it if there is. Jesus!" Carla can play hardball too.

"Okay. Warren, they don't like your Vespa—"

"I don't care whether they—"

"They say you race the motor all hours and it's driving them cuckoo."

For some reason I laugh when I hear this. "They probably belong over here in C House. Should we vote on it?"

There's a chorus of no-ways and up-theirses.

Okay, okay, I say. Enough robust discussion as they say.

"And they don't go for the front vegetable garden—they don't feel like it's consistent with a neat manicured residential neighborhood. They even included some shots with the petition that show how the other houses have ivy or lawn or in the case of the Egnews, colored gravel in front and they feel like this is more in line with the residential character. And the lady next door, Bernadette Ryan, and the rest back this up, she's on record about how there's all the time litter around, paper from candy wrappers and cigarettes, no matter how often she picks up. Whenever a wind comes along from the east it blows everything right over there on their property."

Everybody looks at Lindy.

"And then there's noise in the middle of the night, door slamming, people coming and going."

Everybody looks at Carla.

"It's a free country," Carla says defiantly.

"It's free?" Warren says.

"What?" Carla says.

"Nothing," Warren goes.

Geoffrey continues to mutter with his hand cupped over an invisible receiver. Miriam Myers helps herself to a powdered mini doughnut from the package we have sitting there out of our entertainment fund.

"The Portellos at 831 say," she says licking a thumb, "and they're not alone, that somebody over here's feeding raccoons, such that a whole boatload of them come down Princeton every night getting into garbage cans, tipping things over and creating havoc."

"You wreak havoc," I say.

"You got it," Miriam Myers says.

"Raccoons!" Geoffrey pipes up, putting George Lucas on hold. It isn't a confession, only it is, if you know what I'm getting at.

"Shut up, Geoffrey," Carla says. "Who's the Portellos anyway?"

"You know, Carla, where Geoffrey that time . . . where the Vespa . . . they have the privet hedge."

Carla opens her mouth but only a grunt comes out.

"They seem to think," Miriam Myers goes on, "there's a cat here that causes trouble with pets in the neighborhood."

"Cat?" Warren says in a semi-amazed way. It is well to establish a certain atmosphere of vagueness—it can work to your advantage, I have often times seen it happen.

"Cat," Miriam Myers says. She's always Miriam Myers, both names, which is, I suppose because she's a cross between advocate and adversary. Miriam is the friend and Myers is the foe. "That's what it says here, C-A-T." She knows when she's being diddled. She pregnant pauses.

"And several people mentioned being bothered by a loud stereo—"

"That's her," Lindy says, pointing a banana at me, like an enormous thumb.

"And foul language, that was mentioned over and over again. That and raucous arguments."

"Weird," I say. "You know what Bernadette calls Art when he like doesn't put the garbage out? A lazy ass-sitting son of a bitch, that's a quote, we all heard her, that's how we know it's Thursday night," I say, but nobody says why yes, Tiffani, we have all heard her, you are speaking the truth. "Not only that, he wipes his car windows with a squeegee and then he wipes his nose with the same Handiwipe he uses to wipe the squeegee with."

"That's sicko," Carla says.

"Getting back to the nut of it," Miriam Myers says, "there's been a complaint one of you threatened the little Ramsey boy with bodily harm the night of the cat episode."

"Oh yah, that was Carla," I say, " 'Member, there was this kid blowing into a bottle and scaring Geoffrey—"

"Yah, Carla," Lindy says, "and you said you were going to get him. . . ."

"Deck him, that's what she said."

"I was telling it," Lindy says.

"Shit, that was nothing!" Carla says. "It's just something you say to punks."

"The point is these things happen, episodes," Miriam Myers says, "and you let them build up to where . . . accumulate like this till we have a real barn burner megillah on our hands. The tragedy is it could probably have been smoothed over by staff, headed off. But not if you don't let us know what's going on, if we don't have all the facts. That's part of our contract we made with each other, right? That WHCMHC's got to know what gives. At all times."

"Yah, okay, but it just wasn't that big of a deal," Carla says, "the Thanksgiving thing." She has her feet crossed at the ankles resting on Warren's thighs and he is holding her toes like they're a bunch of grapes. She has this neat little heart tattoo on her instep, I might get me one some day.

"It's for us to decide what's important," Miriam Myers is saying. "Even if you think it isn't, you've simply got to let me know, so I can keep the System apprised. Don't forget, I'm your ombudsperson. Anything involving C House is important to us."

"Those farthounds, all they're trying to do is hassle us," Warren says. "That's their whole mission in life."

"I make a motion we sue them," I say. "Sue the Ryans next door."

"Second," Carla says. It is a very thrilling moment. I have made a motion and Carla, Carla! has seconded it!

"Let's vote on it," I say. I'm pacing around.

Miriam Myers taps on her clipboard. "Let's not get slap-happy, people." She looks from one to the other of us. Nobody says anything. Lindy chomps on her Finn crisps. I will definitely get me a clipboard with my next SSI check. This stands for Supplemental Security Income. Basically what it is, it's severance pay the government gives you for opting out, only you don't opt. It's all pretty cut and dried—more cut than dried, I guess.

"Mrs. Ryan is on record she puts her primary emphasis on the children, their welfare. She just doesn't know what next and she says she can't stand living with this ongoing knot of fear."

"An ongoing knot?" I say. "That's one uptight chick."

"She could send the kids to computer camp," Warren says.

"Right on," Lindy says, in my opinion just to suck up to Warren.

"They're way too small, Lindy," I say.

"No, come on, what happens now?" Carla says. "We might as well have it all spelled out."

"All right. Bottom line. After talking with the people concerned, my sense is," Miriam Myers says slowly, "that if we approach this thing right with everybody's full cooperation and *if,* emphasize if, there are no more episodes, that we have a good chance to cool it and hang on to C House. If we succeed in answering these charges, correcting what needs correcting, plus if nothing else comes up, are you with me there? What we've got to do, all of us together, we've got to get back on a positive footing with the community, which is absolutely essential not only for you people but for everybody to come, all future residents of C House."

It seems we have a responsibility to posterity, to all unborn, un-diagnosed schizos and bipolars. This is a crazy idea—it belongs in a straitjacket or, as they say in Crisis, "restraints."

"The Court calendar is backed up by several months, which fortunately gives us time."

"Court?" Warren says. "Now she's saying Court."

"Time?" I say. See how practical I'm getting?

"Yes, I was coming to that. Eventually there'll be a hearing before Judge Quentin Reilly at the county level. What's at issue is whether we're violating zoning ordinances plus whether Camelot House does in fact constitute a disturbance to the peace in any way shape or form. So what we're going to have to do in the meantime, we're going to work our butts off to mend our fences—"

"Hey," I say, "I like the imagery."

Lindy looks out at the fence. She can't handle figures of speech, which may be why she's a compulsive eater. There's a lot they don't know.

". . . get everybody here as productive as possible so that we can march in there and say to the judge, Your Honor, here's what these young people are doing, this one works x hours at y job—"

"I don't want to work at the Y," Lindy says, "the woman on the desk there doesn't like me."

"How much do we get for x hours?" Warren says.

"Let's not get hung up on that for now. Hopefully minimum wage," Miriam Myers says.

"I knew it," Carla says. "There's plenty of easier ways to pull in the breadsticks."

"That's if you're laid back," Warren says. "Right, sweetheart?" Carla's foot barely misses his scrotum.

Miriam Myers pours herself some Hawaiian punch in a paper cup and goes on. "We're going to try to find mini volunteer jobs if necessary, spotted through the community, here and here and here." She puts a finger on the footlocker and Geoffrey leans closer as though a mini job is there under her finger. "That's what we're going to bear down on, do you follow me, people? And as for right now, no more feeding the raccoons, okay? And no stray cats, that's basic house rules anyway."

Warren asks to see the list of signers. He runs his finger down them. Warren has distinguished black hairs between his knuckle and the first joint.

Ryan, Bernadette, Ryan, Arthur. The Wilsons, Lionel and Rosalie. Portello, Bing and Lucille C. Ramsey, S. Edward. Egnew, Amy and Robert, Jr. . . .

I go, "Those are the ones with the cat, the Siamese."

Carlucci, Joe. Barnard, Georgina.

"Hey!" I say, "hold it, that's Barney's wife. Georgina. I don't believe it. They love me."

"Their statement," Miriam Myers says, "they state people from the House come in and order up a cup of coffee and just sit there having free refill after free refill for hours at a time till finally they have to be asked to leave."

"She does that all the time," Lindy says.

"Liar!" I say pleasantly. "Oh sure. They've practically never once asked me to leave. When have they ever asked for me to leave?"

"Last Thursday."

"Last Thursday! Don't pull last Thursday on me. That was just because they wanted to close up early. That was nothing personal at all, they were going to the Coliseum for the Warriors game, that was all there was to that."

"I talked to them this afternoon," Miriam Myers says, "and Barney's wife pointed out a sign they have that says only the one refill please, which she says she went ahead and had specially lettered because of C House. The *please* wasn't even supposed to be there. The girl who was doing it misunderstood."

"This is so off the wall! Barney doesn't even like his wife!" I shout. "When I asked him where she was he said in Shawnee Mission, Kansas, visiting her mother, she's off my back for a month, that's just exactly what he said. There was even a witness, that girl with the Yorkie who always wears pink, I bet I could get a signed statement from her even."

"Let's don't stray from the central issue, Tiffani, which is how we can increase our productivity and put the best face possible on things. I'm going to be coming up with some specific suggestions for ways C House can make itself useful to the community—they need help down at the recycling depot, I happen to know that, and it may well be when they get the program rolling to fingerprint the elementary school children, they could use some people."

"Fingerprint little kids, you hear that? Now they're fingerprinting little kids!" Warren says. "Siberia here we come."

"It's for their own protection, Warren. But the point is there are lots of avenues we'll be exploring together."

"I don't see Miss Clausen on this," Warren says. "The little old lady on the other side of us, isn't that her name?"

"No, she didn't sign. I didn't talk with her because she didn't sign. It's possible she isn't registered."

"It's also possible she likes us," I say. Everyone looks doubtful.

Unfortunately Cathouse chooses that moment to poke his way in through the loose screen in the kitchen. He rubs against Geoffrey's leg and two fleas flip from him to Miriam Myers' right ankle, bright obsidian specks. She scratches without looking down. "Now, do you people want me to take him to the Humane Society or do you do it yourselves?"

"No!" we all say except for Geoffrey, who is meowing to Cathouse. I assume he means no, but meows are funny. They're neither fish nor fowl. Also my ear isn't trained.

"We'll take care of it," Carla snaps.

"Like with the speed of light, please," Miriam Myers says grimly.

"It'll be handled," Carla says. "I told you."

Miriam Myers retrieves her raincoat from the dryer, looks briefly at the bag of kibble, and takes off.

For three minutes or so we discuss places for the neighbors to put their petition and Miriam Myers to put her mini volunteer jobs. Then Carla says, "Okay, gang, here's what we do. We don't throw Cathouse out, we throw him in. Tomorrow we get us a sand box and kitty whatever they call it and—whamo—he's an indoor cat." She's putting gold decals on her fingernails. She soaks them in a saucer of water and then slides them off the paper they're on onto her fingers—stars, moons, arrows, lightning streaks—and then lacquers over them. It's pretty neat looking. "And as for the raccoons . . ." She pauses to reposition an arrow. "With the raccoons, since we've started in to feed them, we have to keep it up, but what we'll do, we'll cut way back to where we don't keep getting more and more. Anyway it's costing too much to feed all those mothers."

The front door opens. It's Randy. Right away Carla jumps up, leaving her stuff scattered around.

"Evening," Randy says.

"I didn't hear the bell," Warren says.

"So what?" Carla says.

"I just said I didn't hear the bell," Warren shouts after them.

"She's really something," Lindy says. "So when you going to give me a ride on the Vespa, Warren?" Lindy is polishing off the Oreos and little doughnuts, talking with her mouth half full (or half empty if you want to be kind or you're a pessimist).

"Out of gas," Warren says, like it's life he's talking about.

I try putting on one of Carla's stars, but it's too soggy to stick, it's been in the water too long.

Later I'm in bed and Warren comes in. "Knock knock," he says, but he doesn't mean it, he's already there. He touches my leg, "The itsy bitsy spider goes up the water spout," he says, fingers climbing.

"That's what you think, buster," I say. "Keep your water spout to yourself. All you do is use people."

"Listen, baby, I'm user friendly."

"Oh sure. Carla's not having any so you think you can make do with me and then joke about it. Well, forget it!"

"Hey, calm down, honey chile." He adjusts the covers, tucks them in around me like he cares. Only he doesn't. "Let's talk about this, Tiffani, get it all out."

"The way to do that, go give yourself a jack job."

"Aw c'mon now, Tiffani. It's very therapeutic." He moves a hunk of hair around my eye, starts to smooth it back.

"You get outa here or I'll deck you!"

"Okay okay." He slinks off sputtering. "Assholes all over the place."

"An' you're number one!" I shout after him. "You grungy bastard!"

Score one for myself. You can't lose 'em all.

X "So things are settling down at Camelot House?" M says hopefully.

"I didn't say things were settling down, I just said if anything else didn't happen, if nothing else happens."

"Well, it's up to you people then to see—"

We are in Kramer's buying me shoes, after some back and forth on the topic of how hard I am on shoes (never mind how hard shoes are on me). The strap of my left Birkenstock has finally given way, which in turn gives way to the theory that I don't bother buckling and unbuckling, which is presumably how come the straps give out on me, tugging away like that.

The clerk is approaching with a stack of boxes tucked more or less in his oily secret armpit.

"It doesn't work like that," I say.

"How's that again?" the young man says.

"No, I was talking to her. Kramer versus Kramer," I say to include him in.

He goes, "Yah, really," as though we are now having us a sensible conversation. Or maybe it's that he's gone through that drill before, Kramer versus, this being Kramer's, if you follow me.

He extends a limp casing of footie, holding it away from him, thumb and index finger, like a leaking tea bag.

"He wants for you to put it on," M says.

I graciously extend my foot—"Other one, there we go"—keeping the arch high, very elegant. I pick a piece of what looks like mouse turd from between my toes. Maybe it is mouse turd.

What I wouldn't mind, I wouldn't mind a sandal like Carla's. "Do you have any gold mesh sandals?"

"No," M says.

Instead here comes a moccasin style wedgie with cross straps.

"How's that feel?"

It feels cold. They have it air conditioned, and M puts her sweater around my shoulders, which I like. It has the lightly perfumed scent of middle-aged ladies, the powdery silt of all those decomposing years. I bury my nose in the shoulder.

"Heel a little loose on you?"

A sweater to sweat in? I wonder if that's the derivation. I smile.

"It looks to me like it might be rubbing on her," M says. "See there what I mean?"

"She been wearing ones with a too tight of a vamp? Whip stitch'll leave a mark, it'll do that on you every time if it's too tight, I've seen it happen."

He has bright orange socks that come right at you. About my age. Most likely married or something. In his twenties somewhere. I always wonder how they fix the age of accident victims. *A white male, 20 to 25, wearing orange socks with a gun metal shoe horn in his back pocket—*

"She should try standing on them, don't you think she should at least stand up?"

"No, sure, she can go ahead and walk on 'em. Feel free."

. . . found suffocated by a pile of 7½B Hush Puppies, which apparently toppled on him somewhere between closing time and—

"So whaddaya think? How're they doin'?"

Maybe what happened, he was on a construction crew or he was a surveyor and that's how come he has the orange socks and now he just wants to go ahead and wear them out. It's plausible.

"Tiffani, he's talking to you. He wants to know does it. . . ."

"Yah, no, it's okay. I'll take 'em." I'm not a big fussy shopper like some people I could name but probably won't. Paula for one.

"How much are they?" M says, demeaning me, taking away my power of transaction, which is extremely important in a capitalistic society such as the United States of America and the republic for which it stands.

Turns out they're twenty-four ninety-five and M says I can have them all right if I will promise—make a contract—to use the buckle and no more yanking, young lady. The Yanking is a river in China.

"I don't care," I say. Whatever makes 'em happy. I am contemplating if it would be possible to walk up the shoe incline, whether or not the red corrugated grip sole would really grip. They could get Mary Lou Retton to do it, it'd be a far-out ad.

"We'll take them," M says.

"Does she want the water sealant to go with?"

"No," M says. "I doubt very much she'd ever use it." She fishes out her old gray wallet in which I happen to know is still a picture of me from when I won second prize in a sidewalk chalk painting contest on Washington's birthday many moons ago. Sometimes I take out that picture and sit there and stare at it. Knock-kneed like you wouldn't believe, no waist, tumbleweed hair. Yellow shorts with chalk stains. Red satin second-place ribbon, grin like I just won the world.

"Can I have that picture?"

"No."

"I knew you'd say that." (Actually I wouldn't want her to say yes.)

"Listen, I hate it when you treat me like I'm two," I say once we're outside. "In front of him and everything."

"Well, people treat you, they respond to you the way you come across to them."

Kittycorner across the street is Angelo's Gelato Classico, 100 percent natural ingredients. In front is a three-foot plastic banana from which the chocolate dip is chipping.

". . . if you're acting like two."

Or maybe the chocolate chip is dipping. I stop to consider and M keeps going. It's like you turn a record player off but the record keeps turning for a while till it gets the message.

"How 'bout a treat?" I say when she finally turns around to see where I am, what's happened to me.

She hesitates. She wants to do the right thing and she's always trying to figure out what that is.

"Like I'll even pay."

"You? You don't have any money." She immediately regrets this, probably hears herself being quoted to Dr. Madsen.

"Wanta bet? I've got my cigarette money."

"Young people are always broke," she says. "If you go throwing your cigarette money around, you won't have cigarettes."

Now she's trying to sound like Paul Volcker, a caring Paul Volcker. "It's okay, I want to, I really do."

"Inside or outside, ladies?" the maitre d'ess says, clutching menus to her bosom like hymnals.

"Outside please," I say, since it's my party and for once M doesn't argue. "No, inside, I mean, inside, we want to be inside."

We reverse course, squeeze past heart-shaped white metal chairs, packages on the floor, plump purses, jittery ficuses.

"Have whatever you want," I say. "We're celebrating."

"Celebrating what?"

She is very literal minded. I try to think. "My new shoes." I'm really getting into this.

"I don't want you to go spending all your spare cash on me," M says, looking pleased.

So what am I supposed to say? What would anybody out there say?—you're no more a waste than cigarettes? I mean *really*. I shrug. "No, it's okay."

She fidgets with her spoon, wipes it on her red white and green napkin, looking comically vulnerable, her you-shouldn't-have birthday look, except it's never me that remembers her birthday. It's maybe July, or June, somewhere in there. All I know is she's a Cancer, very family oriented she tells people.

"How about the Yumbria Special—spumoni and cappuccino ice on a bed of crushed amaretti slathered with raspberry syrup? No, I mean it! Or the Capri Caprice? That's probably it over there in the case, a model the way they do. It says two melt-in-your-mouth flavors in a tranquil sea of blueberry puree." God, imagine how you'd look if you drowned. I smile into space, but she doesn't dig that, so I knock it off.

Good old M. She orders a single scoop of vanilla, the cheapest thing on the menu, *vanilla!*

"Make it French vanilla," I say, "at the very least make it French." (I guess I should have said Italian.)

Myself I have the Americano (you get three flavors and anyway I'm just not that into The Foreign Experience). The Americano has two small crossed flags that if you look close say Made in Hong Kong and a dumb Nabisco fan sticking up. The water comes with a slice of lemon, which I try briefly to sink, another thing she doesn't go for.

"So. How's the French vanilla?"

"Great, it's really great." She hands me her cherry, which is loaded with red dye number whatever, but I plop it in anyway—I'm not like Warren—and make the stem into a ring.

"It was a good idea, the French vanilla, see, it's quite a bit creamier than the average," I say. "That's the thing."

"It's very refreshing, ducky."

There's somebody going around with a camera. She picks out certain tables, picture-perfect families. I wonder if she plans to stop by us. Right now she's taking a picture of one of those jovial weekend dads getting his fat little girl fatter on a sundae the size of the QE 2. I check the menu. It must be the Mount Vesuvio except I just don't see where there's a dollop of delicately roasted pine nuts.

M's done with her ice cream.

"You want some of this? Here, try it."

"No thank you, honey, I don't want to go ruining my dinner."

"I mean it. Dig around, there's nuts under the goo." I'm pretty generous that way. Besides, I'm getting full.

"No, this is just fine. Really."

"Hi, people." The one with the camera is squatted down between us, somewhat like Verna in Crisis. She's wearing black stretch pants and a fuchsia sweater with the V in back like she might possibly have got it on wrong, which I sometimes do. You can count five knobs of vertebrae—I've always been a counter, it keeps you in touch with reality. Five vertebrae (showing), there's probably more, three stud earrings (pearl, sickle, cross), two, well I guess it would have to be two stacked heel boots—I am really turned on to shoes today.

"Mind if I interrupt for just a sec?" Her hair is short and the ends make ladles on her cheeks. She parks the camera on the empty chair. Another crummy Rolleiflex. I assume she is selling souvenir photos which I quite frankly doubt I can afford at this point in time.

Turns out no need to feel anxious on that score. She is Mavis Miller from the *Chronicle,* we've maybe seen this column she has, "Sounding Off," where people, a cross section of the population, go ahead and answer a subjective question, something open ended where an opinion is called for. Like namely what? I say. Okay, she says. Today's question is: what was your favorite Saturday afternoon ever? And then we go ahead and take your picture and print it along with your answer. Either of you ladies feel like taking a shot at that one?

"Oh, I don't think we—" M starts.

"Wait," I say. I run the back of my spoon along the humps of sorbet—pistachio, strawberry, something crunch, patting it down the way little kids do. "Just what cross section are we supposed to be if we go ahead and answer?"

Mavis Miller adjusts her weight, puts her fingers down to steady herself, cocks her head. "Oh, let's say ladies out shopping."

There we go, *ladies* again. I look around. Lots of ladies, there's no denying. Too many to count even. "Okay," I say. "That's cool, let's go for it. My favorite ever?" I take my time, check everything out before I answer, panning—barber-pole candy sticks in a jar, blond girl with shoes off, espadrilles, her feet sitting on them, airing out, woman with a briefcase and long executive shins. M clears her throat—she feels threatened by long pauses. "This one, this Saturday," I say finally.

Mavis Miller doesn't start writing anything down and I think maybe it isn't Saturday or something. I look at M but you can't tell from her is it Saturday or isn't it Saturday. She's fiddling the hem of the tablecloth under her thumb nail, which she does when she's nervous, which with me she always is. "That's my answer, my final answer, this Saturday, today." (Reasonable risk taking, Dr. Madsen would call it: today feels like Saturday.)

"Okay, fair enough." Mavis Miller seems to be coming to life. "You care to expand on that?"

"Today, nineteen hundred and eighty . . ." I wish I hadn't started that.

Mavis waits.

"Nothing." I wave it away (it was gone anyway).

"Okay, you want to tell me why this is your best Saturday?"

M is really looking hard at me, concerned, scared. I expect to see her lips move the way they did when I'd be in school plays and she'd be out there mentally saying the lines, afraid I'd mess up or something.

Mavis Miller has got her clipboard on her black stretch thigh. "Because I'm here. With her," I say, jerking my thumb at M but not looking at her. "My treat," I say. I brush some Nabisco crumbs off my lap.

"Hey, I think that's neat. Mother and daughter, there you go, that's the way to fly."

I give M a sidewise glance. She's looking off into space, a soft circuitry of wrinkles, the same floaty expression she had when she read about how Meryl Streep has her mother pick out all her clothes, her mother has this wonderful taste, knows just what looks good on her. Meryl Streep sucks, I said. Right now M has that same pale distant glow as though she's looking through a store window seeing some incredible costly thing, beyond having.

"The work week's over and you feel like your mom needs to get out of the house for a while?"

M now shifts to her wary look, about to wade in, mount a rescue operation. It's a subliminal hum, a vibration you can feel, it begins in the soles of the feet, jump-starts your stomach, shoots up past the burps and blups till it's a buzz behind the temples, a certain special frequency that gets to you till you're strung out, wired, and you have to start pacing to get rid of it.

"Something like that," I say to Mavis Miller, who is getting set to take my picture, or else I would in all probability get up. M dips a corner of napkin in her water and points to her lips. I wipe off my mouth with the back of my hand. There. I sure hope I didn't blink.

Mavis Miller hands me a felt pen and a form to fill in. "She had French vanilla," I say. "Of course I don't know how much detail you want to get into."

"No problem," Mavis says.

I never thought there was a problem. Name. Okay, that was easy. Occupation? Maybe there is a slight hitch, a sort of technicality. I could say that last week at my sheltered workshop I assembled 291 canape guns some with the plunger in upside down (they go in easier that way so you can do more per hour) such that some jazzy broad's cream cheese won't pucker and she will probably shout *shit!* but not know who's to blame. Who *is* to blame? I look around. Just mainly ladies having their ices. One at the next table has fanned out a set of fabric samples, pinked on the edges. I used to think it was them that was to blame, M and D and Paula. Sometimes I still think that. But now I think more there's a ziggle of genetic lightning that creates the break. After that it's what falls in the fissure—a glance, a turning away, a misstep. If the searing, the pain is strong enough, you drift, black out. "Here," I hand Mavis back her form.

"Oops, you forgot to put in your occupation. Line three there."

I tap my spoon on the glass. The anemone of lemon breaks away from the ice cube. I look at the brass ceiling fan, four blades, I think it's four. On the opposite wall is a picture of jockeys bent into Z's, whipping their horses around a curve. The fan slows and

I see it's definitely four blades. All of a sudden my mind is clear as Crater Lake. "Let's just say I'm a Splurger."

Mavis glances at M. I guess I do too.

"Like that's my occupation," I say casually. "Splurger."

"Well, fair enough," Mavis says after a pause. "That's real original." She has been making stars on her clipboard, inking in the points. "If you want to be a woman of mystery, we won't blow your cover." I think maybe she winks at M, I'm not sure. "Let's see, how do you spell *splurger?* Is there a 'd' in there somewhere?"

I wave the question away—after all they must have dictionaries at the *Chron*—they're not that cheap, but M plods through—s-p-l- whatever, no doubt thinking how the younger generation can't spell any more, they aren't taught the basics.

"Thanks much, ladies. Have a good day now."

"Wait! When will it be in? When will they run it?"

"Probably Tuesday. It should be Tuesday. Look for it Tuesday." She holds the clip open with one hand, slides my form in. I wonder if I should maybe help, like putting your finger on a ribbon when somebody's wrapping a present, tying the bow, but I don't make a move. "Thanks now. Enjoy."

"Well," M says. "Wasn't that something."

"I think she thought I worked and everything, at a job job," I say after a while. "I guess I should have let you answer."

"No, it was fine, you handled it just fine."

"Yah? Really? You really think so? You think I handled it just fine?" My ear lobes feel hot. I try to see if they're red in the veined mirror behind the pies. "Like what would you have said?" I pause to lick the soggy edges of my Nabisco fan. "If you'd of been doing it? What Saturday? Like would it have been Paula's wedding?"

"No, don't you remember? Paula got married on a Sunday. They talked about Saturday but the Dales was already booked."

Oh.

"Anyhow, I think I'd have probably, I'd more than likely have said just about what you did, Tiffani. That this is one of the best Saturdays."

One of the . . . "In your whole life though? Think back. 'Member you're a whole bunch older than me, a lot more Saturdays, it would take a computer or a what do you call it, that thing D has, a calculator, to figure out how many."

"No, this is definitely one of the best Saturdays."

One of. That isn't what she asked though. But I guess being older than me, more Saturdays would be bound to come to mind. "See, I just happened to pick this one. I mean, there've been a lot of great Saturdays, the Monterey Aquarium. . . ." And then I kind of stall. "The Bread and Roses concert, that was pretty good. But this one, this Saturday, just leaped to mind when she asked."

She nods. At least I think she nods. She's checking her makeup, redrawing her upper lip, wiggling it around on the bottom one.

"I suppose what it is, why you'd have picked this Saturday, I guess you really dig being taken out for French vanilla? You really like it? You could have another if you want. I'll get the girl—Miss!" I wave both flags.

"No, this just hit the spot," M says. I try to picture the spot— an eager churning corner of stomach resembling tripe. "French vanilla," she says, like she's saying my lines again.

I hold the piece of lemon between my teeth—I don't want to cry or anything—chomp on it lightly, just enough to smart. I run my thumb along her arm.

"What're you doing?" M says.

"Nothing," I say.

"With that lemon in your teeth."

"Do we want anything else here?" the waitress says.

"Just the check," I say crisply.

As it turns out, I thought I had moolah, but I don't. I remember now, I spent my cigarette money Tuesday, or maybe it was Wednesday or Monday even. "Here, here's eleven cents toward the tip." I blow purse fuzz off the penny so it will look halfway decent out there.

It's all illusion anyway, who pays for what in this world. There are different ways of paying. You pay if you feel you paid, right? and for quite a while there, say the next fifteen to twenty minutes, I really feel like a splurger, whatever that is and however you spell it.

"It isn't in!" Lindy says triumphantly.

I go, "Maybe she meant the next Tuesday."

"Uh-uh, it'd be a different question."

Lindy is right for once. The next Tuesday it's What Was Your Worst Blind Date and it's all computer programmers. I keep calling the paper but Mavis Miller is "in the field." Finally this other one, Angela Linck, says maybe it was incomplete bio.

"Like if I didn't care to fill in my occupation?"

That could be it, very definitely, Angela Linck says.

Fuck! I don't go to O.T. and I skip afternoon Workshop. I put on a record—"Use It or Lose It" and put myself to bed. Maybe I should have helped Mavis Miller slide the form in under the clip. That way she would have seen I was a nice person and she would have made sure to include me. Or maybe I should just have said something like "factory worker, assembly line."

I close my eyes, drop myself into a forest of darkness, not a mellow briny murk, but a shrubby untraversable veldt to stumble in, shudder away from, run screaming out of.

"It wasn't in again," I hear Lindy saying to somebody, probably Warren, downstairs. I turn up the record, drown her out.

Xi Everything notwithstanding, by April Wookie has us pretty well plugged into the community although it never worked that we help with fingerprinting school kids because the Ryans complained, they didn't think it was suitable for us to be involved.

The way it went, Warren, who wants to be a new-wave film director, or at least a new-wave stand-up comic, finds himself standing up and stocking bins Monday nights in an auto parts store owned by the cousin of Doug Singer, who works for Mental Health. The cousin gets reimbursed by Rehab for 50 percent of Warren's salary so even if he happens to have an off night and lands the spark plugs in the fuses drawer, there's still a 49 percent margin for error in which the house still makes a profit. I realize this is rather technical. Also Warren wants Doug Singer's cousin to buy him a respirator because he claims the air at the parts place has asbestos fibers.

Geoffrey they originally volunteered to the Humane Society, putting red clips on the dog licenses that hadn't been renewed. It turned out to be a big mistake. He watched them gas 12 cats and 2 pit bulls one night after his shift. Come on, I'll show you how they do it, this guy who didn't know Geoffrey said, and Geoffrey ended up spending a week on Unit A at Valley View Hospital, Thorazined up to the eyeballs. Job-related stress, they wrote on his folder. So now they have him in Green Thumbs three hours a day, planting oleanders in freeway divider strips. He looks sad going off every morning—not every morning, but the mornings when he goes—with his Rambo lunchpail and a baseball cap he wears with the visor in the back like he's going in the other direction.

What happens is the bus, it's an old ex–school bus, comes for

Geoffrey, you hear it bleeping as it turns and then it honks and everything and he steps out on the porch and stands there blinking. You can see the sun's too bright, the traffic too fast, the choices too broad. Back in he comes and then Rhoda, the driver, has to climb out in her pink fluorescent vest, ducking her head and saying, Come on now, Geoffrey, you got to gather yourself together, wrap it all up, and then maybe he goes and maybe he doesn't. Some days the bus just sits there with its red light flashing, puzzled faces like Geoffrey's framed in the windows, until finally it takes off and Geoffrey relaxes, sits down, and eats his fishwich and tortilla chips although it's only 8 in the morning.

Lindy was supposed to be wrapping plastic cutlery in little cellophane packages for airline trays but what I heard Warren tell Carla is they caught her eating half the chocolate mousses intended for Southwest Airlines flight 605 to Phoenix and she got terminated, which she blames on the Reagan administration, like the air controllers. It seems to me the situations are not all that one on one, but who needs another argument? So Lindy got moved to Occupational Therapy. She is learning to use a word processor (although in her case a food processor would be more like it), and she goes because she is currently in love with her O.T. leader, who has her confused with somebody else and calls her Shelley.

Carla is supposed to be working with delinquent girls at a socialization center in Oakland one day a week, no doubt getting them more delinquent, but nobody asked for my opinion. I mean it's really peculiar how they'll choose somebody for a role model without giving thought to the role.

Carla's been riding out a series of depressions—her kid had a birthday and she, Carla I mean, was bummed out because she forgot to mail the card she had. It was one of those with a clock and slots for coins where the numbers would have been. What I actually think happened, she took and pocketed the nickels and dimes and then she didn't feel like she could send this card with the empty slots, so she just tore it into little bits. And then she had a fight with

Randy followed by one with Warren. People think bipolars swing from manic to depressive, but they are much more apt to bump along through a series of one or the other before the whole thing switches, much like the Dow, if you believe Paula. Although your average bipolar won't have more than one or two swings a year, unlike the Dow.

If you can't come up with a project of your own, then they find you one, which is bad news to start with. Like I had this admittedly brilliant idea that really turned me on. It came from reading the *Chronicle* waiting for my interview to show up, which don't hold your breath. What I decide to do is a scrapbook on the world, a dossier, which we might even present to Judge Quentin Reilly eventually. A sort of snapshot only it would be written down of the sane world before it blows away, was how I first put it. *Funny Peculiar,* that's the title of it. The purpose would be to give the judge some helpful perspective, a frame of reference re C House. Miriam Myers gives me a fishy eye about it right from scratch. How many hours a day did I plan to spend on this? Where would I propose to get my material from? From newspapers, I say, from the world around. And TV. I even read her my first entry. "Just listen," I say. " 'Three jolts of electricity over 14 minutes were required to kill John Louis Evans III, a convicted murderer who walked calmly to his execution in Yellow Mama, as the electric chair is familiarly nicknamed. After the first jolt Evans tensed and the electrode on his leg burst off. When he was hit with the second jolt at 8:33, a puff of smoke and burst of flames came from his left temple, but doctors said he still was not dead.' " I pause, look at Miriam Myers to see how she's taking it.

"I thought it'd be something like that," she says in this snotty little Wookie way, which is ridiculous since she probably never even heard of John Louis Evans III, though somebody must have cared about him pretty much at one time to go ahead and give him a complicated family name like that. "That's not the end," I say. " 'His lawyer then phoned the governor asking clemency on the grounds of cruel and unusual punishment, but the governor failed to intervene. In all it took three 30-second charges of 1900 volts of electricity to kill Evans.'"

"Tiffani, I just don't see where collecting gruesome titbits" (that's what she says, titbits) "is in the interest of community relations."

"Titbits?" I say. "As in itty bitty titties?" This goes way over her head. I visualize it shooting past her right ear, across her rambling dandruffy part, out the window into the ether like a kite vaporizing in the atmosphere, becoming finally an infinitesimal glint in a bright hard endless star.

So no sale. Nothing will do but I have me a new Outside Activity. I haven't been to O.T. in over a month (which is because Lindy is there) and I only chalked up 19 hours at Workshop for the month of March. Okay okay. Apparently working things through, gaining insights, thinking, reflecting, analyzing, weighing are not regarded as productive by Wookie.

So Miriam Myers says we want you to call Miss Theriot at the West Hamilton Library to see about either telling or reading stories to kids Thursday afternoons. The thought seems to be it will give free rein to my rampant imagination. So far I have not got around to it.

My big mistake is telling M. She keeps lugging over old books. *Children Around the World, The Blue Fairy, Myths from Many Lands.* You used to be such a reader, she says. You thought Christmas wasn't Christmas if you didn't get books you could bury your nose in. She waits for me to say something. It's like I'm competing with myself of fifteen years ago and the wrong me is winning. "You could read them the story of Sleeping Beauty, you used to love that, you knew it by heart."

The parents of the little princess were so delighted at her birth they held a great christening in the hall of mirrors with fairies from all the realm as godmothers.

"No."

"Why not?"

"That was a million years ago, I don't remember it even."

The table was set with golden knives and forks with tines of emerald, but alas at the great feast an evil spell was cast and the princess lapsed into a sleep of a hundred years.

"You used to love the part about the great woods opening and the thorns parting to let them pass."

It was the work of an instant, the clap of a sinister hand.

"Sleazeville," I say.

"You didn't used to think so," M says. She never knows when to quit. I'm trying to go along with Dr. Madsen and accept that M's not responsible for my current problems, but she makes this very tough to do.

Dr. Madsen keeps nibbling on me too. You should never tell a shrink anything. They won't get off your case. Why are you putting off the library project, Tiffani? This is a good way, reading to kids, to work through this fear of yours of facing an audience.

It's all a fair size drag. I tell him I'm not putting anything off, I've just been busy and also I'm organizing my materials. Actually I did go on down to the library once and look in the front door, but there was this mob scene and the kids wouldn't have listened anyway.

Ever since something untoward, you might say, happened at high school graduation, I haven't wanted eyes glued to me, leeching away at me. See, I was the salutatorian Commencement speaker. I had dashed off this dumbass upbeat thing about baby boom nuclear responsibility that Miss Grinnell put her patient non-restrictive red commas in. But then I got to thinking, hey, slow down, Tiffani, let's do something socko, come out with a lulu of a manifesto, à la Martin Luther, or maybe I mean Martin Luther King, that would knock everybody on their ears—the Board of Education, the principal, Miss Grinnell, the whole fucking PTA, everybody. So what I did, I wrote a parable. I was into Poe at this point, so it was kind of House of Ushery, Masque of the Red Deathish, strongly influenced by Isak Dinesen. I called it a Neo Gothic Tale from Alacosta High. I still remember how it began. . . .

During the whole of a dull dark and gloomy day in the month of October while all the jocks and jockettes at Alacosta High were busily taking their SAT's, doing their this-is-to-thises, a brooding and malevolent stranger from the Third World was plotting their destruction from the Straits of Madagascar. At precisely 1500 hours local time, the SS-20's were launched, pregnant with countless kilotonnage. In what was later known as the Holocosta High, the list of the dead and dying was of Jonestownian proportions. It goes on pretty much like that.

In a way what happened was Eric Noon's fault. I had him read my speech and he said it was a gas, he couldn't wait to see their faces. Of course he didn't pretend to understand all of it, the literary references and all that, but he said nobody who heard it would ever forget it and it would crack people up. It was our secret, Eric's and mine. I thought he might go ahead and ask me to the prom what with the speech and all, I even told M I thought he was going to, which was when we went shopping for the dress before they got all picked over, but then he asked Michelle Fultz instead and Michelle's twin brother Gary took Paula, even though she was a sophomore and had an incomplete in Environmental Ed.

So there I was at the mike. Miss Grinnell adjusted it for me. All these eyes are on you like you're Texas and your heart is thumping and Eric is out there grinning away at Michelle—I think he probably told her our secret—and D is sneaking up the aisle to take a picture and the mike lets out this eerie sustained howl, a warning, and I just took off without ever saying a word. Paula found me later in the gym.

Something told me not to do my parable, it might rub certain people the wrong way, which sounds sort of sexual but isn't. But I couldn't bring myself to do the other one either, the in-general-the-term-Commencement-means-beginning one that Miss Grinnell handed me a copy of just before I walked out there to face the eyes. Ever since then, I don't know, I just can't perform in public.

Don't worry, I'll get around to telling the kids their stories. Everything in its season. For now I'm busy with *Funny Peculiar, F.P.* Italy just got its forty somethingth government since World

War II. . . . The reform rabbis are arguing with the Catholic bishops about who first supported nuclear arms limitation. . . . Chinese villagers are drowning their baby girls, keeping a bucket of water by the childbirth bed. . . . Littlesun, great grandson of American Indian Chief Crazy Horse, had his bar mitzvah at the Wailing Wall in Jerusalem in full Indian regalia. Shalom! How! (that's me talking) . . . The Head Librarian at Oakland's prestigious Head Royce School was arrested after stabbing one of the teachers in a personal dispute, according to police. Paul D. Chapman, school headmaster, said both men were gentlemen.

I've also been taking some self-portraits. What I've been doing, which I seriously doubt has ever been done before, I've been photographing my dreams. Like for instance, Saturday night I have this dream where Beryl Markham is trying to push Isak Dinesen off a cliff. She is calling out to me the way she does—Tiffani! Tiffani!— and I rescue her—hang on, girl—and we sort of sail out over this peaceful valley like we're hang gliding. But Beryl Markham is there waiting for us to land.

I wake up soaked in sweat and, of course, hating Beryl Markham. So what do I do? I get up, root around in my closet till I find my old Isak Dinesen cape, and I take it and a camera and a tripod and I go out on location. I position myself at the top of the steps at the county courthouse with my arms outstretched, like in the dream, and the 10-second timer set and I get what I hope is this great shot of my dream revisualized, using daylight and my 15 mm lens. See, if I have the angle right, the steps won't even show, just this poised-for-take-off avenging angel type figure. The date of this shot is Sunday, April 13. I don't often remember dates, but I remember this one, for reasons which I will now explain.

In American History class there was this speech about Pearl Harbor Sunday, all about infamy and the hand that held the dagger stabbing his neighbor in the back with it, right? That's approximately but not exactly what happened on that Sunday in April with us.

Anyway, going back, I take my picture, my dream's picture, and after I stop off for a gelato at Freddo Alfredo's and when I come back home, I happen to see over the fence the Ryans are having themselves a barbecue. Fair enough. Innocent bit of Americana, right? Not just themselves. It seems they're expecting company. She's got him tugging chaises around out back and pouring neat manageable little ice cubes such as motels have out of a plastic bag into a bucket with tongs hooked on the side.

It's kind of lonely smelling somebody else's charcoal smoke when you're not invited. It's like not being in the club, only worse, because the smoke goes looking for you, gets in your eyes. See, what I'm doing, I'm surveying the scene through a knothole in the redwood fence. I am not in any sense spying. I am not in the employ of a foreign power. I am an unofficial observer.

People start drifting in. The one who zapped Cathouse is lugging what she says is her seven-bean salad. Will you look at that! Bernadette Ryan says, peeking under the foil. (The foil is crinkled like it's been used before, but never mind, these are difficult times.)

The Wilsons bring a corn casserole with, it looks like, circles of green pepper on top. My stomach lets out small coyote growls.

"Does it need to be heated?"

"It'd be better, otherwise the corn flakes limp up and it's got cream of mushroom soup for a binder and you know how that gets, it kind of reverts back."

"No problem. I'll stick it in with the garlic bread."

Garlic bread. . . . I go for the heel which not everyone does. Maybe I should be a hero, break bread with the enemy. But I wouldn't be welcome, that's the hard reality.

The people up on Elliott Court who are growing marijuana in with their tomatoes just bring sun-dried tomatoes. Everybody brings whatever meat they want and Art Ryan puts it on the fire—steaks mainly, wieners for the kids. It's probably a status thing, you think they'd think you were cheapo or poor or something unless you brought steaks. I'd probably break down and bring steak too if I was invited. I wonder why they say break down in that sense.

Bernadette Ryan passes around what she calls coolers in frosted glasses with sailboats on the side. "There's more ice here if anyone wants it. And goat cheese over on the stone table."

The kids train their water pistols on the barbecue. Apprentice hit men. I am peeking through a lilac trumpet vine.

Eventually Art Ryan whacks the cover of the Weber barbecue kettle with a spatula, clang clang. Gathering of the clangs. "If we could have your attention for a minute, folks. We wanted to have this get-together to keep everybody up to date on what's happened."

"Good, I'd appreciate knowing just what gives," a man I've seen out mowing says. Nice day, he even said once.

"Hon," Art Ryan says, "why don't you just go ahead and bring the folks here up to speed?"

"Well, I'll sure try," Bernadette says. She's wearing a green terry cloth deal with elastic up where her breasts take off like bladderworts and a fiord cut from the knee to the thigh that flashes white when she moves. She has one of those perfect see-me see-me designer tans that people have who don't have anything else, her minkfrugal.

"Scoot on over, Justin, so there's room for mommy." I see she's got tottery slides with cork soles. "Okay. You all know what happened at Thanksgiving?"

People murmur. Now I am really getting interested. "So I don't have to go over that nightmare again. You've all been given copies of the complaint, those of you who signed the petition, that is. And most everybody here has."

By this time I realize that this is no neighborhood Tupperware party. It's not Amway products or Shaklee they're peddling, it's stuff about us, against us. This is a terrorist organization!

"We've got a few extra copies Art ran off at his office. Anybody who wants one, see me after," Bernadette says. "I don't know how many of you know, but since the original one, we've had another episode." She nods at the cat lady.

"We sure have," Cat Lady says. "You can hum that one again.

It was just disgusting. Those weirdos with that tom of theirs. I could just a murdered them. What we had to do, we had to take and have Miss Clara aborted, don't you know, which set us back forty-five dollars, didn't it, Robbie? not counting the antibiotic pills that we had a dickens of a time getting down her. He'd have to hold her and I'd put the pill way back there the way the vet showed us and like as not—"

"Awright now, I'd like to play the devil's advocate here for a minute," the lawn mower man says. "This thing with the cat catting around, yah, I heard about that. But that could be anybody's cat, you see what I'm saying, what I'm getting at? I mean, let's face it, that tom was just doing what comes naturally if you're a tom cat."

"Now wait a minute, that's not the half of it. Did you happen to see them take off on that motorcycle of theirs after? At 90 miles an hour? Why, if a child had a happened to have been in their path—"

"They did, they crashed, you know, absolutely creamed the Portellos' privet hedge who can't be here much as they'd like to, it's his office picnic and he's on the committee."

"I grant you that one time, but that's not usual, is it?" Lawn Mower says. "What I'm saying, what I'm attempting to try to point out, I've never seen 'em do that except the one time. The way I understand it, they were out there looking for their cat that got hosed down."

"I'm here to tell you it got hosed down!" Cat Lady says.

"Also, isn't it just a scooter they have?" Lawn Mower says. "A moped?"

"Well, I don't frankly care what you choose to call it, your child gets hit by it, they're as dead as if it's one of those big bruisers, what do they call them? Harley-Davidsons?" Cat Lady says.

"Awright, I hear you, I see what you're saying, but I'm just sitting here wondering if we're maybe not all getting too cranked up here. A little excess panicky maybe."

"Lionel," Bernadette says, ruffling Justin's hair, "I appreciate your point of view, I truly do. I only wish I could agree with you, but believe me, we're a disaster waiting to happen, that's what we are. And I for one just don't think we can afford to hold still for it."

"Are we? A disaster waiting to happen I mean. Or are we just a bunch of people in a neighborhood? Some of us with more problems than others—I just want to be fair is all."

"Lionel, I don't know how much personal contact you've had with this crew next door, but these people are dangerous. We've got small children, it's much easier for you and Rosalie, not having that particular concern."

Lionel sits there studying his hands like they had something to do with him not having children. Then while Art lights some mosquito candles there's a few minutes of gabble gabble gleep gleep, all coming out to you're right, Bernadette, we can't hold still for it. (*It* being easier not to hold still for than *them*. *It* being principle, *them* being people you can throw out on their little pink asses.)

"Anything can happen, I'm sorry to say, you're just not dealing with normalcy. They're just not normal," Bernadette says.

"But that's not the same as them being violent," Lionel says.

"You can't tell what's under the surface," Cat Lady says, "you just never know. Look at the John Hinckley thing."

"She's right, they lived in a good area."

"We could be living next door to a Hinckley scene and just not know it."

"That's not my take on it," Lionel says. "These times we live in, sure, there's always that possibility of something from left field zapping you. You walk down the street and there's the possibility of some nut—"

"But you walk down *this* street and there's for sure half a dozen nuts—"

"Tooshay!" Laughter. (It's only five, but go ahead, you fiendish bastards!)

"It's the density, the concentration of wackos. I mean where we used to live in Lodi there was this family, very nice folks, weren't they Robbie?"

"I don't know who you have reference to, mama."

"Yes you do, Robbie. The Livingstons. He even ran the United Way Drive but they had this grandma, I don't know which side of the family it was, but she wasn't playing with a full deck."

"No, she was a quart low."

"But the point was they had her tucked away in a back bedroom. And nobody was ever bothered. But this, this is an entirely different story. Next thing you know, they're gonna start in calling this Crazy Canyon."

"I think we should keep our voices down, they might hear."

"Oh you don't need to worry on that score, I really don't think we need to worry. Everything just flies by them, they're on their own wave length."

"State of the Art Crazy."

"Their headlights are flooey," Cat Lady says, tapping her head.

Lionel, God bless and keep him, he goes down hard. "All right, tell me something? Have they ever actually *done* anything violent?"

"You want to wait till they do? Should we wait for the Russians to do their number, just sit on our hands and wait?"

"I'm just asking the question is all. I feel like that we ought not to be too circumstantial here. They're people like you and I, or kids of people like you and I, you know what I'm saying?"

"That's the point, Lionel, the point we're trying to make, they're just not."

"Have you heard the foul language at 3 A.M. in the morning?"

"And the doors slamming?"

"And that Vespa in the middle of the night, feeuh!"

"There's another issue," Art says. "I hesitate to bring up economics, but there's the property values side of the coin."

"Amen."

"Now I know we probably shouldn't figure that way, but I can't help it to a certain extent. I don't know how many of you happened to see the article by Sylvia Porter—"

"We sure did, I clipped it," Cat Lady says, "it's on the refrigerator under the squirrel magnet, isn't it, Robbie?"

"She does this It's Your Money column, Sylvia Porter does. Well, for the benefit of those of you who might not have seen it, she gets into how your house is your major investment of your life for most people and she takes up the impact of halfway houses on neighborhoods. See, the way we look at it, it's not just us, but someday somebody around here's going to want to sell and then with this situation next door or across the street or down the block even, you could really take a bath."

"We hear you, Art, what you're saying."

They have coffee and trifle and two kinds of pie—lemon meringue and coffee toffee and something called Food for the Gods—and conclusions summed up by a man with his thumbs hooked in his belt and his orange director's chair tipped back. "It's fair to say no one can rest easy any more. Not with that tribe there. God knows we all want to be fair, but we've gotta be fair to ourselves for a change. Fairness begins at home, is how I see it. Correct me if I'm wrong. My take is, listening to all you good people, they've got to go. That's what it adds up to. One way or another, they've got to go. This here is a neighborhood, a genuine community, and we've got to give thought to the kids, there's a lot of 'em being abused these days, it's a national epidemic, you might say."

"Stan, that's right on," Bernadette says. "We've got the signatures. We've got the court date. Let's go for it."

After that it's all just seeing to it everybody gets their right bowls back. "Here, you don't need to go washing that!" "No, it's okay, I'm just giving it a little rinse." "I had the salad servers, the wooden ones, shaped like hands, that's it, that's them."

"I thank you, lady," Stan the summarizer says, "for hosting this wing ding. If the subject matter was grim, the company more than made up."

"Shoot, we kind of felt, Art and I did, that everybody had a right to know what was going on, and you speaking up that way you did, the thanks are all the other way, that really helped clarify."

"There's strength in numbers, no doubt about it."

The party is over. It's maybe 5, 5:15. I sit there by myself for a while after everybody's gone. One of those weird summer bugs, intricate out of all proportion to its dimensions, lands on my arm and I study it. If it stays while I count to ten, we'll be all right, if it goes . . . it's gone. I guess you'd have to say it's a spring bug, not summer, it being April. The next thing you know I'll be one of those clock watcher types, you can overcorrect very easily.

Art hoses down the barbecue grill, holding it with an oven mitt in the shape of an orange fish and Bernadette gets out a large trash bag and lets the kids throw in the paper plates. They don't talk much. She says at one point, "I thought we agreed you were going to get into the raccoon thing," and he goes, "I guess I forgot," and she goes, "You always forget. Either that or you don't listen in the first place."

Art leans the barbecue grill against the side of the kettle. The last frantic underachieving rays of the sun finally find their mark, striking the wet metal. A potent blinding radiance hits me. There's no protection. I wait to be released from the ball of light that's trying to siphon away my thoughts. What happens is the phone rings next door and Bernadette yells sharply Art! *Art!* and that frees me except it leaves me with ricocheting warning lights spinning before my eyes. My knee I've been kneeling on is imprinted with a crisscross of pine needles and sword fern.

That same night when everybody's back I give my housemates a briefing, or debriefing, whatever, anyway I tell them what came down. It's 8, 8:15. I'm about to get to the two kinds of pie when I happen to look out front—holy shit! There are shadows in the garden, moving eerily in the ripening dusk, nameless nightmare figures converging. I think first it's the cypresses closing in on us and then I think no, it's the Ku Klux Klan, the Gestapo, the CIA, and then I think I must have forgotten to take my meds.

"Look!" I say. I half expect the others to say they don't see anything, there's nobody out there, but I can tell from their expressions it's not like that.

We're all there, pressed against the glass and we can make them out, various pricks and prickesses, a dozen or so, tromping all over the squash plants, some looking in the windows even. It's an Invasion of the Nerds. The people next door, Cat Lady, the jogger, Lionel—even Lionel. Some of the others from the barbecue and some I never knew were there before—an Indian woman with a sari, a pimply teen in a rainbow T-shirt, a girl in a plum-colored leotard and leg warmers, a man in a jeans suit with cowboy boots and a ten-gallon hat. Why do they call them ten gallon? Who originally saw fit to pour liquid in a hat and measure it that way? There's probably a lot of lore about it in the books about cowboys. M and D took us to Tombstone, Arizona, once. It was a drag.

Carla throws the porch light on. A dozen neighbors neighing, powered by rage, New York steaks, Miller Lite, coffee toffee pie. They come out amber in our bug light. The one with the hat puts down the Coleman lantern he's holding. He looks livid, vivid. By this time we're all of us out on the porch waiting. They're kind of hissing to each other like compatible cobras.

"You do the talking, Wynn," Cat Lady says. "You lost the most."

Wynn steps forward, all ten gallons. We see he's holding a hand gun. A Smith and Wesson? I suppose they oil them with Wesson oil. I tend to think irrelevantly when petrified, which is normal, whether you're abnormal or not.

"Put that down!" Warren yells. He picks up the cat shovel.

"Nothing to worry about," the man says. He has a red beard. He points the gun at the ground. "We just come on over, some of us neighbors. Few things we need to iron out." He looks down at the gun and kind of smiles. He looks like the sheriff in *Deliverance*.

"You heard Warren," Carla says—she can sound very authoritative. "Put that gun down or we're calling the police, I mean it."

"Maybe we should call Wookie," I whisper (Doug Singer has an emergency beeper he carries around with him after hours).

"Call the *po*-lice?" the man Wynn says. "Kind of surprises me to hear you say that. I seriously doubt you'll want to do that. And quite frankly we don't want that either. So I'll let you know along the lines of how we've been thinking. We thought depending on the outcome of our little conversation, maybe we could eliminate the basic need of calling in anybody from the outside, but we will if need be, we sure as hell will, make no goddam mistake. What we'd like to do is a few of us—no need for everybody—just a few of us, Bernadette and Amy and myself, say, to come on in and kind of have a little look around."

"What the fuck is this?" Carla says. "Some kind of weirdo social call?"

"My bed's not made," I whisper.

"Yah," Warren says, "what the fuck is this?"

"Seems like you folks have a kind of limited vocabulary," Wynn says.

"I didn't do it," Geoffrey says.

"No, I doubt you did, we're not accusing any given one."

"Neither did I," Lindy says. She's still clutching her bowl of Uncle Ben rice.

"Like I say, we're not here to accuse any one in particular but it's pretty obvious you all know what we're doing here."

"First you pull some kind of secret meeting—" Carla says.

"That's an admission right there, Wynn," Cat Lady says. "They admit they knew we were all of us out, over to Bernadette's."

"Seems like maybe you folks don't like us having a meeting, a friendly little town meeting, on a heretofore nice afternoon. Now it's one thing to get riled up and another to—"

"Sure, piss off and go on with your little meetings."

Ten Gallons raises his gun an inch, or maybe it's a notch. "I'd like to remind you there's decent young folks present here, ma'am."

Carla looks at the pimply boy. She looks at him real hard until he drops his eyes, rubs his toe on the walk like he stepped in something. His acne is oozing clear stuff like what comes out of liqueur filled chocolates.

"We've had our meeting, missus."

"So I heard."

"Who told you, a little bird?" Cat Lady says.

Oh please God in Heaven, dear Heavenly Father, don't let her say, just this once—

"Get to the point if there is one," Carla snaps.

"What do you want from us?" Warren says. He's trembling.

"Glad you asked. I'll tell you exactly what we want. We want our possessions back that were stole from out of our houses between the hours of approximately 2 and 5 this afternoon when we were all, or most of us, over to Mr. and Mrs. Ryan's place, that's all we want."

I look at the one called Lionel. "Is this true what he's saying?

" 'Fraid so. I sincerely hope none of you were involved."

"Oh we weren't," I say.

Ten Gallons goes on. "To get a hundred percent specific, I want my other gun back, the one that's twin to this. Plus my Betamax and my granddaddy's gold pocket watch with the initials WGM on the back. What do you want back, Amy? You're next up to bat."

"My sterling silver candlesticks, they were a wedding present from his cousin who's no longer with us and my Sony cassette player. And there may be more. Wynn called and we didn't have time to check all the drawers, did we Robbie? I don't know if my electroplated gold flatware is okay or not."

We are just looking at each other. This is the real world?

"I want, please, my glass bottle filled with quarters," the woman with the sari says. "The last time I counted, yes, I had 362, and I've put many more in since then, I assure you."

"Rosalie?" Wynn says.

"Well, we don't want to go accusing anyone here . . ." she looks at Lionel, "but our color TV is missing. It was an RCA. I borrowed that scribing thing the police lend you and it's got his social security number on the back, 057 dash 28 dash . . . what's the rest, Lionel?"

"Five one one eight," Lionel says.

"You better believe we won't have trouble to identify our belongings that're ours," Wynn says.

"If you got your stuff ripped off, that's tough shit," Carla says. "We don't have anything to do with it, nothing."

"So get off our property," Warren says.

"West Hamilton Mental Health property," Bernadette says. "Taxpayer property."

"You're the ones who're crazy," I say. "We've been here all day, all of us, minding our own business." (I forget for the moment about my picture taking and the gelato and how when I came in from my listening post Carla was out.) "We can even tell you what was on TV. Warren, why don't you go ahead and give them the plot of Monty Python."

Warren looks at me: "The *plot* of Monty Python?"

"I don't think that'll be necessary, but you won't mind us having a little look around, now would you?"

"Before they have a chance to fence anything," Cat Lady says.

"I'm telling you for the last time, we don't any of us have anything to do with your asshole stuff," Carla says. "Now get lost."

"If we have to wait on the police, you know how they are, they'll say we don't have us a search warrant," the jogger says. "I vote we go on in, Wynn, just let them try and stop us."

"Should we take a vote?" I say to Carla.

"Shut up," she says.

"Hold tight a sec, Wynn," Lionel says. "I think we should settle this without any rough stuff."

"We could slap a citizen's arrest on the whole kit and caboodle of them," Cat Lady says. "Why not?"

"Not so fast now, Amy. Let's just stop and review, draw a breath and see where we're at. As I get it, you folks are trying to tell us it's just a mighty odd coincidence," Ten Gallons takes up again. He has a toothpick in the corner of his mouth, like it's a relaxed occasion. "That while we're having us a neighborhood get-together which you admit you know was taking place, a meeting to discuss some common concerns, you might say, all these nine homes were burgled. You want to stand there and tell us that's not cause and effect?"

Carla walks forward slowly, tipsy with rage, right up to this guy, so close it looks as though the toothpick would scratch her. "You get out of here, shitface, just get!" She spits on his cheek.

Someone gasps (not me). He just stands there. He's holding his gun, his face gone white.

"You'll live to regret the day!" a woman beside him shouts. People start backing off. It's impossible to tell if they are afraid he will shoot or Carla will spit again. "Wynn, honey, I don't want you doing anything—"

"No, come on now, Wynn, she's right," Bernadette says, touching his arm. "She's right you can't deal with this trash, what we've got to do, we've got to turn them over to the law."

Wynn wipes his face slowly with what looks like a chamois he extracts from his pocket, never taking his eyes off Carla who doesn't move, she just stands her ground, arms folded across her chest. "You dirty little whelper," he says under his breath.

"Just don't you go blaming us for what happens from here on," Bernadette says. "You had your chance. We're going to fix your wagon but good." Wynn allows himself to be turned around and led away. He's sort of catatonic.

The tension builds all evening. Carla calls Randy, who tells her to keep all the doors locked and for once she does. It's scary to see Carla scared. Lindy hooks the back of a chair under the doorknob in her room and lines up a series of pots that would make a clatter if anyone tried to get in. "Don't take the one we need to boil water for coffee!" I yell after her. Geoffrey goes around clutching Cathouse and asking where is the wagon that is going to get fixed, where is it?

Warren paces back and forth in the kitchen, turning the knobs of the stove off and on again. He freaks over cops—he's a refugee from the drug era and he says the limpoids in his brain from PCP are cop sensitive and he gets this terrible throbbing sensation. Being as it's Sunday evening he can't take off for the U.C. medical library, which is what he does when he gets really anxious. He'll sit there for hours, soaking up symptoms and then when he finally comes home he'll say, okay, this is it. He now knows conclusively he has had a myocardial infarction. Or he has dengue fever or psittacosis. Or he needs a laryngectomy and he'll never ever be able to speak again except with one of those little boxes, so we better hear him while we can.

But this particular night we all feel vulnerable. Nobody goes out. We're conscious of where everybody is in the house. It's like we're under siege. I even help Warren move some provisions to the base-ment—a flashlight, two cans of marinara sauce with mushrooms, three cartons of Viceroys, a package of IAMS for Cathouse.

About eleven a police car pulls up across the street—"There they are, they've come!" We see them looking over at C House. We duck down so that just our eyes are over the sill in the living room— "You think they can see us?" "No." The cops go from house to house. "They're at the Cat Lady's. . . . Now they're going to the Portellos!" Lindy shouts bulletins from her room. Warren and I stay crouched in the living room. "Now it's those ones with the Hyun-dai." I suppose they're getting their circumstantial evidence. Some collective sob story to frame us with. I'm schizo-affective already, but I could easily see becoming paranoid in a big fat rush.

"I just can't believe those Old Testament faces," Warren keeps saying. Personally I can't see why New Testament faces would have been an improvement, but I guess it's a matter of personal preference.

Finally I go on upstairs and paste more stuff in my world chronicle.

Pomona, California. Police held back a crowd of 90 who were attempting to get a look at the body of a 64-year-old woman who had hanged herself from a tree on Garvey Boulevard. People were sipping pop and pointing out the body to their children.

I wonder if they were like our crowd, only larger. No, it sounds like the Pomona ones were more fun loving, less hostile. Maybe we should move to southern California, but then there's the smog—Warren would think we were being gassed.

The night is bad. I can't sleep. I don't want anything touching me, not even blankets, but then I freeze. I try reading *People* but I've had enough of people. Besides, I'm too jumpy to concentrate. Decompensated, that's the System's word. Basically what that comes out to, all the little fractures in your thoughts run together till you have this gigantic fault line and you go around with this upheaval inside you, shocks and aftershocks till it settles down again, which you think it won't ever do. Your confidence is zapped, you feel like a worm, you feel like you committed a crime you know you didn't do, except what do you really know? You don't know from nothing. You're a double negative. Tidal waves of conflicting sensations pitch you into a paralyzing void. There's too much space, the kind of infinite loneliness in which moths look for secret woolly caves and restless bald fetuses turn like clothes in a dryer and molds go down deep veining their cheeses, looking for the way out or the way in.

I go to the bathroom. There's a light coming from the refrigerator, which Lindy has open. She's gnawing on a chicken drumstick, jabbing her nose with that spiky piece of bone or whatever, that thing with meat under it that chickens have. She's wearing one of her buttons—I'M NUMBER 3, I DON'T TRY AT ALL. Later, back in bed, I hear her upchucking, which is comforting in a way—a sound like the ocean that you get used to going to sleep by.

A car backfires and I jump. Nightmares hurtle through me so fast I can't latch onto them, confront them when I wake up. I just lay there—lie there—afraid to open my eyes onto the velvet darkness. But somewhere along toward morning there's a mind-curdling scream and I go to the window in time to see Carla dash out back shrieking. She doesn't even have a sweater on, just this model coat thing she wears mornings.

Lindy and I get downstairs at the same time. "What's up?"

"Oh Christ!" Warren is saying, "I can't believe they'd do that—"

We push past him—he's standing there like he's stoned. "Oh God, don't let Geoffrey see, whatever you do, don't let Geoffrey—"

Seven, eight, nine ten raccoons. On the side porch. Shot dead.
Even the babies. They're fallen on the mama in a holocaust of dark
glued fur, their eyes open, clouded over, a look of ringed-in-black
surprise. Stiff pepper and salt fur gored by neat round bloody holes.
They're lying on the kibble, the mama with her bandit paw on the
one we called Leo because he always took the lion's share, hail to
the chief. I stand there mesmerized. What I thought was a car back-
firing, that was the shots. A plumey black-banded tail has been shot
clean off. It moves with a memory of itself, like a headless snake.
No, it's the wind.

"We'll be next," Lindy whimpers. She's jelly.

We stand there frozen in the presence of murder. That's normal
though, isn't it? At least that.

"They're psychopaths," Warren says. "That's what they are, a
bunch of psychotic crazies!"

"Don't say that Warren. We've gotta fight stigma. We don't
want anybody to think they're like us."

A piece of Mounds wrapper has attached itself to a bloody ear.
"You never pick up after you!" I scream at Lindy. "What kind of
a place do you think this is?"

"I know what kind of place," Lindy says. She sounds sad. Or-
dinarily she would have yelled back. It makes me feel insecure her
just standing there acting normal that way. It simmers me down.

"Where's Carla?" Warren says. "We need Carla."

No Carla.

"We'll never be able to go out the side door again," I say. "We
should call the cops, I think we should go ahead and call them. Get
the cops here."

"No!" Warren says. "No cops." He stands there banging his fist
on his forehead. "They'd think we did it. You want to get locked
up? Get us all locked up?"

"I didn't do it," Lindy says. "I wouldn't." She's coming back,
her old self.

I'll call M and D. They'll know what to do. No, I won't call M and D. It will be like the other time. It's our situation to deal with. "The Humane Society then. Twenty cents, somebody give me two dimes. Come on, Warren, a couple of dimes."

I call. They aren't open, but there's an emergency number. It seems they only come if an animal's been injured or, if there's a possibility of rabies, I should call the police. I can't, I say. Obviously it was a mistake to say they were dead, but who knew? Humane, my ass.

I go back to the kitchen and report to Warren. He says what he'll do, he'll dig a grave in the back if the ground's not too hard. I say I'll help him, but to get out back you have to go by the raccoons and I think I'm going to be sick. The water in the plastic bowl Geoffrey puts out for them to wash their food in is red. I close the door. My heart is rampaging like the Tuolomne River. Cathouse wants out. "Oh no you don't, you can't go out there any more." I take Cathouse and dump him on Geoffrey, who is smiling, nodding his head at yellow feathered goggly-eyed freaks on "Sesame Street." A long-necked pink thingie with an orange pom pom nose and golf tee ears gurgles earnestly.

Geoffrey sneezes, which causes Cathouse to twitch an ear. A black munchkin with a pink face and a monocle grins at us, then a ragged green woolie.

"What?" Geoffrey says suddenly. He's listening to the sound of Warren's pick out back.

"That? That's nothing," I say, and since what Geoffrey hears usually isn't there, he accepts it. I sit with him till the sound of the pick stops and you can tell he's not listening for it any more. Geoffrey frequently doesn't remember things, especially recent things. He had electroshock some time back. I think of his brain, charbroiled, sizzled, memory floating off like gray ash. "Here comes the cookie monster, Geoffrey." I think of the raccoon bodies. *Slaughterhouse Five*.

"Sesame Street" signs off. "Great Railway Journeys of the World" comes on. They're talking about something that goes from Los

Mochis to Chihuahua and took ten years to build. And then Dr. Ruth. Geoffrey and Cathouse sit there looking philosophical.

I go off and put on records, Elton John, Roberta Flack. I stand there in front of my crappy dresser with gold metal handles and I boogie back and forth to the music. When Carla comes back she will know what to do. I want to be the one to tell her about the grave in back, but it will probably be Warren, which I guess there's justice in since he did the digging.

Suddenly out of nowhere this ball of light hits the mirror, voom, like a meteor or something psychedelic. A hot bright globe of red roves the mirror and I figure it's a spin-off from the warning lights that floated in my head from the laser of light on the barbecue grill.

That's when I see there's a police car out front.

Lindy yells up the stairs, "Cops! Did you call them?"

"No, did you?"

"Are you crazy?" she says, which is a tactless question.

I turn down the stereo—could somebody have complained about that?

"Police," I say to Geoffrey, who lunges into the broom closet.

"Come on," I say to Lindy. It's up to us. Carla is out and Warren can't deal with fuzz. He'd collapse like a black lung. I will explain how we were all there at the house all day Sunday (no use getting into how I was out briefly photographing my dream, that concept demands too much of the listener, or that Carla was off with Randy). We were all right there, so we couldn't possibly have robbed anybody, that's what I will say. But speaking of crimes, if Warren doesn't have the raccoons buried, I'll take the cops around back. I'll warn Warren first so he can split. They can fill the trunk of the police car with dead raccoons, let them take the bodies to a lab somewhere, probe their tiny skittery brains with dye.

The cops are out of the car now, looking up at the house. Lindy takes my hand, which really surprises me. We stop just outside the front door. Something, some little footnote to caution tells us not to get too close. To keep our distance. It's funny if you stop to think about it, anybody being able to "keep" distance, like it's a hamster or something, especially when distance is in the public domain, it—

The cops, two of them, are coming slowly up the driveway in a hushed kind of way. Maybe ages 30 and 40. I don't like the slow walk, I don't like the hush. This could be a SWAT team, trying to look low keyed.

The really old cop looks at us, then his feet. "We didn't do it," Lindy whispers. "Shh," I say.

"Hi," he says quietly. "I'm Sergeant Moran. This is Officer Ledwith." The other one nods like he agrees he is Officer Ledwith.

We look at each other. "Good morning, sir," I say back. Lindy looks at me funny. Maybe I should just have said hi, dropping the sir, which came merely from fear, mere sheer fear. I half smile. "See, we were here all day, all of us. Sunday, I mean."

The cops look at each other, the League again. The old one scratches his head. "We have some information on Carla Janus. Did Miz Janus live here?" He hitches up his leather-creaking belt.

Did? What's this *did* bit? She and Warren were talking about getting a place but . . . Lindy looks at me. I look at Lindy. It's like we need Carla there to tell us what to do, to say whether we know her or not. I nod.

"Sure, that's Carla," Lindy says, which she wouldn't have if I hadn't nodded to get the ball rolling. "She's one of our roommates."

"She had this address on the Medicaid card that was in her pocket," the young cop says. I don't mind him.

But what could Carla have done in an hour and a half on a Monday morning—I think it's Monday—bad enough to turn out the fuzzies? Soliciting? On a Monday morning? Maybe it isn't Monday. Shoplifting? Nothing would be open. She would have been upset, and with Carla, once she's keyed up and into something, there's no stopping her. I mean if she found something open, she wouldn't swipe like a lip gloss, she'd take the whole Thrifty's cosmetics counter.

Go in and clean them out before you could say Vidal Sassoon Moisturizing Creme. I can just picture it—that's got to be what happened. I see her in one of those round God's eye mirrors. She's loading up both pockets—eyeliner, shadow, blusher, don't forget the Sandy Beige, Carla.

". . . 'Fraid what we have to say isn't good. There's been an accident," the young cop is saying. He's kind of groovy. Wavy black hair, not too slicked back or anything. (Most cops are brunettes, have you ever noticed?)

"Accident?" Lindy and I both say. I can't see if he's wearing a wedding ring. "Is she okay, Carla?" Lindy says.

He shakes his head. "I'm sorry to have to tell you, to break it to you, no—she isn't."

"What are you saying? Like what are you telling us?" My chest is all acidy.

"At 9:04 this morning Miz Janus was struck by a truck, a diesel, going south on Hamilton Drive. She was crossing, not using the intersection. She died en route to the hospital. The paramedics did everything they could. . . ."

"He tried to stop but he couldn't," the other one says. "The driver. He's real broke up about it."

Everybody looks at everybody. It takes me a minute and then it hits me and I laugh. When I laugh Lindy laughs a little too. "Hey, come on, it can't possibly . . ." I say. "If what you're saying is Carla's— She was just here. She was just here like an hour ago!" Lindy is hanging on me. I try to free up my thought processes and also my arm. All these terrible visions are pounding through my head, trucks, Carla, the diesel, the raccoons, 10 Gallon Hat, Carla being shoved into an ambulance like pizza into an oven, the shotgun, Carla shot, Carla splattered in the street.

"Did he have a gun?"

"Did who have a gun, ma'am?" The cop looks puzzled and suspicious, which they are trained at.

I pause. I have never been ma'amed before. I will tell Dr. Madsen. He will see that I am growing up, getting more mature by leaps and bounds, whatever bounds are.

"There wasn't any weapon involved, ma'am, it was a diesel," the younger cop says. "Big rig with a semi." He looks at his clipboard (I've really got to get me one of those) "near Hamilton and Walnut."

"It was an accident," the old cop says. "It was an experienced driver. Eighteen years on the road. No accidents or citations."

"What kind of truck was it?" I'm trying to sort things out, get the picture.

"It was carrying produce," the cop says, checking his clipboard again. "Tomatoes. From the San Joaquin Valley."

"Tomatoes!" Lindy is wailing.

I am not doing anything. I am just totally blitzed out.

"We need to notify the next of kin," the officer says, raising his voice to be heard. "Can you help us out, give us that information?"

"Shall we tell 'em about Randy?" Lindy whispers.

"No, that'll only piss off Warren. . . . She has a kid, but that won't help, Dorie's too little . . . and she's got a mother, I've heard her mention her mom. Wait a minute, it's Nevada, isn't it Elko, Lindy?"

"How do I know?" she shrieks. "Elko or maybe it was Ely." She's backing off. I know exactly what she's doing, she wants to be the one to tell Warren.

"You stay put," I say. It isn't fair.

Bernadette comes out on her porch. She's wearing an aqua sweatshirt, hooded, and drawstring pants. She looks at the cops with interest, glares at us.

"Carla's dead and it's your fault!" I yell at her.

The young cop looks from me to Bernadette and says, "It's a shock to her, ma'am. She's real upset at the present time. There's been an auto accident and their roommate died early this morning."

"No! You don't mean it!" Bernadette says. "The one that—Jeez!" She probably thinks this is Fate fixing our wagon.

"You did it, you're responsible!" I shout over at her. Maybe it *is* Fate fixing our wagon.

Justin is out there in his pj's, clinging to his parts like he thinks somebody's going to come along and steal them. "I'm going to forget what she just said," Bernadette says, "under the circumstances." She seems to be talking more to the cops than to me. "Take your hand out of there," she says to Justin. The little girl is clinging to her leg, and she takes a few child-hobbled steps toward the house.

That's all I remember. I don't remember going back up the steps or across the porch, but there I am back in the house squeaking at the top of my lungs, I mean like nothing is coming out, it should probably have been the bottom of my lungs—Carla's dead! It's really true, she's dead! Run over by a diesel! Still my voice is nothing, it's only my soul that's shrieking.

I remember Geoffrey. I open the door to the broom closet. "Carla's dead," I say, and shut the door again. I don't know whether he understands or believes or what—I don't even know whether I believe me. I suppose it was cruel and unusual to leave Geoffrey there with only the mops.

Warren definitely thinks we're kidding. You're both depraved, he keeps on saying. He even goes so far as to say we're jealous of Carla. We keep on telling him to go ahead and call the Highway Patrol if he doesn't believe us and still he doesn't accept it. Well, he does in a way. He says we should close up the house and leave. Then around 10, he goes in Carla's room and looks around like he expects to see her there. He stands there, picks up one of her little makeup brushes that's on the floor. It's the kind with a round sponge tip, blue-gray from the eyeliner. He stands there, holding it, running his thumb over it.

"We could go ahead and make the bed," I say. "See, she's got just the one sheet, but I could root around and get another so it'd be all nice, what do you think?"

He shakes his head no. "Not now," he whispers.

Eventually we leave him there, close the door on the unbearable silence where someone used to be.

Later in the day we do what has to be done. We call Miriam
Myers, who, I give her credit, is totally demolished, just like the
rest of us. Death is a great equalizer. If your screws are loose, they
temporarily tighten. If you're normal, you go a little wiggy.

We get Geoffrey out of the broom closet and sit him down on
the footlocker coffee table and we tell him flat out, very matter of
fact, without any gore whatsoever what's happened. Carla has been
creamed by a big rig with a semi carrying tomatoes while crossing
Hamilton Drive. She is now dead. She never knew what hit her.
(Which, if you wanted to be philosophical could be said about many
a life.) We then go on to explain that somebody, the neighbors most
likely, have shot some of the raccoons.

We had to confront the issue of the raccoons head on, tell Geoffrey,
because otherwise he'd of kept on feeding the ones that were left
and they might well get shot too. He probably will anyway, but
you have to give it a shot, which is not the best way to put it in
view of everything.

Geoffrey nods right along when we tell him about Carla, though
what he nods versus what he comprehends in his mind is anybody's
nickel. But when we get to the raccoons, he has your basic shit fit.
Also it could have been cumulative. I'm not here to say that part
of the freak out was not in memoriam of Carla. You just never know
with regards to Geoffrey.

Warren and I kind of hold Geoffrey down—he's really flying—
and eventually we take him over to Crisis in a cab. For everybody's
information, this is a free service that Yellow Cab provides for the
community it serves, but it has to be in the nature of an emergency,
you can't just be out of cigarettes or anything like that. Not that
that's not an emergency, particularly with Carla being dead.

When we get back, Lindy's in the hall waiting.

"Where were you guys? I was scared."

We close the blinds and we sit there, the three of us, drinking
coffee till we're jangled out of our minds, which we're out of anyway,

but not wanting to go to bed either. I check the old blue and white enamel coffee pot. Out again.

"Tell you what, let's just sleep in sleeping bags in the living room," I say finally, and for once we don't argue. We don't even vote. We just line up the sleeping bags by the fireplace—Warren's green mummy bag, my patchwork bed sack, Lindy's blue nylon deal—and tug sofa cushions off for pillows. There isn't any fire, but there's the three of us.

The zipper in Lindy's sleeping bag is stuck. Some of the material has raveled out and got into the teeth. "Give it to Warren, he's good with zippers," I say. He gives me a funny edgy look, but he goes over and fixes it for her.

I wouldn't even have minded making love with Warren that night (although he doesn't deserve it), but it wouldn't have been making love, it would have been making sure we were still alive. Nobody slept too much. We lay there listening to each other's breathing and waiting for whatever was going to happen next to happen next.

XII Miriam Myers is in Carla's room going through her closet, hangers tinkling, looking for something for Carla to wear to her funeral. A heavy date.

She calls me in. There's something very important she has to say to me and she really wants for me to concentrate. She pauses to inspect this neat white leather skirt of Carla's, which has a belt of bullets—they're not real, they flip right out. They're empties.

I simply mustn't go around making accusations, saying it's anybody's *fault* Carla died, Miriam Myers says.

There must be a factory somewhere makes non-bullet bullets. Most likely the people who work there go home and tell their kids they're munitions experts.

It was an accident, Miriam Myers is saying, a tragic accident. She shoves the white skirt way to the rear, I knew she'd do that.

"You don't understand the sequence," I say. "They came and massacred the raccoons, right? And that's why Carla went shooting out across the street without looking, it's your classic chain reaction."

"The raccoons, yes, Warren told me about the raccoons, but we have absolutely no way of knowing who did the shooting, Tiffani. It could have been anybody."

"Sure it could of been Chief Justice Rehnquist but we both know it wasn't. Or Deukmejian."

"The point is, the point I'm trying to make is, we can't afford to have you go around making irresponsible statements that way."

"Who told you I was? Who, who said?"

"That doesn't matter."

"Then it was Lindy, I know it was Lindy."

"The point to keep in mind, Tiffani, is it could have been anybody who shot the raccoons."

"Yah, we've been over that already, just like it could of been anybody who stole their crappy junk while they were busy plotting against us, but it sure wasn't us."

"Tiffani, concentrate! I want you to hear me out." She's wound up tight. I may have to take her to Crisis. What a gas! She'd never live it down. She'd lose her job, have to go on SSI, maybe she'd have to leave the state, go to some little town in Iowa under an assumed name. Loreen Phlup. Dagmar Yench. Jeanne Kirkpatrick.

"I wish you wouldn't just stand there grinning, Tiffani. This thing is getting so heated up, it's very very important that none of us go around making baseless accusations, things that can't be proved. This applies in spades to the residents of C House because of the commotion you people have created."

"I'm very sorry to have to say this," I nevertheless say, "but you can be a real pain in the butt." Pretty brave of me, huh?

"I realize you're feeling very anxious, Tiffani. Have you taken your meds today?" Meaning let me remind you, you jerky little schiz, that you're mentally up a gum tree and therefore incompetent to pass judgment on who is and is not a pain in the anything.

I don't answer (actually I'm not sure if I've taken my meds), and Miriam Myers continues to probe through Carla's closet for appropriate deathwear. She rejects everything that's Carla, the high-heeled brown leather and suede boots and her fallen leaf panty hose—she's got 'em in cinnamon and pewter gray. The cinnamon's still in the package even. She had her colors done by this place in Oakland and after that she quit on the blacks and went more to hot colors. It turned out she was Winter, which meant she cherished her roots but was experimental and should wear striking sophisticated colors and shapes. What about her tuxedo jacket? No wait, the royal blue safari one. This is her ultimate safari, after all. Or her boysenberry pants with the wide wrap-around metal belt that made her hips flare. When people say hips flare I think of fire, those firecracker looking gizmos they lay down on the street after accidents.

I'm going why not this? Why not that? Why not her grape Shaker knit with the dolman sleeves and the gold belt?—she wore that all the time when she went out, Randy bought it for her.

"No," Miriam Myers says. "I don't think so."

"Why? Just give me one logical reason why not." (I'm kind of acting as Carla's executor.)

"Well, for one thing it has spots, there and there." (Which I guess is two reasons why not.)

"It's got a dropped waist, she really liked that, it looked good on her. Come on, let's not be manipulative." (Oh boy, she hates that, it hits her where she lives.) "That's just coffee or something and it's on the back, right? Who's going to see the back? Nobody, just the undertaker." Does she, doesn't she? Only her undertaker knows.

"Tiffani, honey," Miriam Myers says in one of the wearier tones I have ever heard her use, "let's get one thing straight. I'm going to do the picking this time." (God, how many fatalities does she have in mind for us?)

"How come? I thought we voted on everything to do with the house, that's what you said."

She doesn't bother answering. Apparently we now have martial law. She hauls out a black challis top I've never ever seen Carla wear even before she had her colors done. It's going to make Carla look like the Bank of America building. I can see how other people might want to wear black, but the guest of honor, the hostess, should be free to—wait a minute, maybe if you added a scarf, got your color that way, you could sneak by. Carla told us once when she was in Montana she did a blow job on this guy who owned a scarf factory and the next week he went and sent her a dozen pure silk scarves. "What did you do, Carla?" Warren said in this hostile tone, "scarf it up?" She even gave me the purple one because it didn't go with anything she had. It didn't go with anything I had either, but I try to be adaptable. I fish out a scarf with vivid gold and red streaks and lay it across the black challis, loop it casually. I start in singing *I'm goin' to Montana for to blow the Houlihan.* That's not exact.

Miriam Myers waits for me to finish, which I do since I don't know the next line. "That's a maybe," she says, "the scarf." I know her maybes. She puts it to one side.

I light a cigarette. "So when's the funeral anyway?"

"Wednesday. Tiffani, you know it's against the rules to smoke in the bedrooms. It's an absolute flat out no no."

I stub out my cigarette in the man-in-the-moon ashtray that wouldn't be there if we didn't smoke in the bedrooms. "Wednesday when?"

"Some time Wednesday. Incidentally, I think it best if the people in the house didn't plan on going."

Didn't go? She's out of her gourd. Of course we're going, all of us, why wouldn't we? Okay, maybe not Geoffrey, he might still be in Crisis. "Why?" I say, really laying on the chill factor. "Of course we're going. Give me one good reason." I seem to be on a reason kick today. "You bet we're going." (Shit, we haven't gone anywhere as a group, not since the Bread and Roses concert which was early December, some time like that.)

"First off, it might be a very negative experience, it might be threatening to you. Funerals take a lot out of you, you need a lot of control, Tiffani. They can be very traumatic."

"Just what out of control thing do you think we'd do anyway, if I may ask?" Which is also something Carla said, *if I may ask.*

"I'm thinking of it from your point of view," Miriam Myers says. "It's a ceremony, just as, just like your graduation was a ceremony. You've said many times in Group that that was very hard on you. Or like your sister's wedding, these are emotional occasions. And it would be bound to be very tough on Warren too, he and Carla being so close."

That really pickles my rind, Miriam Myers talking as if she knew anything about anything. "Listen, they fought all the time, you should have heard them and anyway Warren has other women in his life," I say I hope enigmatically, but it might have been more defensively.

Miriam Myers is making an inventory of all Carla's stuff. What does she think—that we'd take it? That we took the other stuff even? Sometimes I think the West Hamilton Community Mental Health types, the Wookmooks, are double agents.

I go back to Attack Code Blue, on the squeaky wheel principle.

"If we don't come, the people in the house, who would? We're her friends, her family. Carla'd be really p.o.'d if there wasn't a good turnout, what kind of respect is that?" (If the situation was reversed, Carla'd be right in there assuring me a crowd, a quorum anyway. Thinking about my funeral, my little funeral, I get to feeling low.)

"There'll be staff present," Miriam Myers is saying. "You'll be represented."

"Represented?"

She's holding up nail polish bottles to the light, throwing the empties into the waste basket. "Doug Singer, Carla's case manager. And I'll be there and her Medicaid eligibility worker and Dee Appleby, one of the psych techs who worked with her."

"Wait a minute, let me see that, there's some left in there." Wild 'n Wet, Midas Yellow.

Miriam Myers is examining a bracelet with a magnifying glass: 10K, she writes in her notebook, 8 colored stones. Next the ankle chain, which Carla claimed was genuine amethysts, this place she got it from sent her a certificate. She was planning on sending off for amethyst everythings to match once she got the loot—ring, belt buckle, classic choker—there was this place in Dill City, Oklahoma.

I retrieve another nail polish bottle from the waste basket, which is an ex–ice cream carton. I was with her the day she picked it up out back behind Freddo's. There's still some guck left in the bottle. Mardi Gras Red. "Those people you named off, with all due respect, they're just mainly bureaucrats."

Miriam Myers looks pained, which is intentional, I mean by me.

"See, that's not the people she lived with, her peer group, the ones she brushed her teeth with." (There are other activities I don't bother going into out of respect for the dead.) I try to unscrew the Mardi Gras bottle cap. Nope. Stuck. It will take hot water.

"Tiffani, I would greatly appreciate it if you'd just go along with what's been decided, okay? And don't go making waves."

"Me making waves? Decided by who? How come we get to vote on every trivial little thing? Four-pack toilet paper, a Shell fly strip, who's on dishes, a white poinsettia, 1.5 ml trash bags, all that garbage, but then something big comes along and democracy goes out the window like Mary Poppins." I find myself being feisty, assertive, unabout to be crapped on. Maybe there's hope for me yet.

"WHCMHC is just trying to do what's best all around," Miriam Myers says. "And I've talked it over with the Housing Consortium."

I green visibly. Audibly, so you can hear me. Falling back on a consortium, that's really low, a classic System copout. It's meant to sound high level secret. Everything classified info, it would be violating confidentiality to let you consort with the consortium. There's a Housing Consortium, a Work Consortium, consortium consortiums, I don't know what all. "Just tell me one thing, does Randy get to go?"

"People who aren't in the house, who aren't part of the System, Carla's friends from the outside, they will have to decide for themselves on a case by case basis."

"But they're not even cases. . . ."

I'm wasting my time. I go to give Warren the word. He is sitting in back in this dilapidated old porch swing. He hasn't shaved—black quills of whisker have popped out—and it looks like he hasn't even washed his hands since he dug the raccoons' grave. It's like he's in a room with the shades pulled down, he's just there hibernating, turned in on himself. I'm not sure how to break it to him. It's hard to get through. He's sort of rigid, like he's operating on automatic pilot.

"Warren?" I say finally. I'm sort of mesmerized watching the movement of the swing. I climb in even though he doesn't invite me, doesn't even slow down so I can get in, which you just naturally would, put your foot out for someone. We creak gently back and forth, it's one of those with the two lattice-back seats facing each other, only I don't sit, I stand like a gondolier, brace myself with a hand on a slat which the paint is peeling off of. "Warren, are you ready for this? We don't get to go to the service. Not any of us. For Carla. Not you, not me, not anybody here."

"Who fucking says?" he says, he kind of mumbles. "I'll call Legal Aid!"

"*She* says. And we don't even get to vote on it. I asked her did Randy get to go and she said he could if he wanted, it was all up to him. Us, we get to stay home. And they're supposed to take us on outings."

"Sieg heil, this is fascism," Warren says. "Wookie über alles. She can't, she can't just operate by fiat, it's not up to her!" The whole issue is enough to catapult Warren out of his gloom. From catatonic to catapultic. That's really well expressed, I feel.

Warren gets on the phone. Hello, this is Warren Sommerfeld of Camelot House . . . like he's Chief of Staff or something, somebody it's neat to be associated with.

We call Dr. Frick, his therapist, and Ron Michaels, who is an administrative something to the Board of Supervisors and Terri Jensen, the head of Outpatient Services, all of whom claim to see our point. Then we do call Legal Aid, but they're busy conjugaling visits for prisoners and they don't give us the time of day, whatever time that is. I say "us" since we are working as a team. I write down the numbers when Warren gets them from Information. They call it Directory Assistance now, but C House has no directory to get assisted, for the reason most of the pages got ripped out by people without pencils or scruples.

"How about Mel Ziegler, the Patients' Rights Advocate? Darleen Aiello at Transitional Services? Lincoln Choy at the Coordinating Council?"

"Right on, Tiffani girl."

We go about our business quietly, no unnecessary conversation, like married people in a restaurant. We call everybody we know, or know of. When you become a so-called client of Wookmook, a full-fledged Wookie, they give you this book called *Resources Roundup*. The ones we call all say they will do what they can to lean on the good people at WHCMHC. I believe the reason for this is many people want to be thought well of by mental patients. It's important to their self-image. We're kind of a mental March of Dimes.

By five that evening we get a call back from Miriam Myers who says WHCMHC has relooked the situation and here is the revised plan, people, got a pencil? "Warren, I need a pencil. Quick. No? Okay, we'll remember."

Carla is to be cremated, but those who wish to attend a brief memorial service should be ready to leave at 2:15 Wednesday. Whoopee! That's this Wednesday, 2:15, I repeat it aloud so Warren can help keep everything straight. Butler and Butler is sending a limo for the residents of C House.

"How much is it? The limo? Can we pay next week?" I am explaining how this isn't the usual failure of money management skills while she is saying no no, it's free, it's included, the limo.

Anyone who doesn't feel up to dressing properly or who feels the strain might be too great should give themselves permission to stay home. That's the message, just as though three hours ago she hadn't been trying to shaft us, no apologies, no I'm sorrys.

"Warren, we did it, we beat the dealer! Not even the Wookmook van with the shocks missing. A limo! Pow! Power to Camelot!" I grab our Chores pad and start scribbling.

> No one admires
> Miriam Myers
> Of Mental Health
> Because she operates by stealth

"It's not all that great," I say to Warren.

"For sure," Warren says—I think he wasn't listening.

We dance around the kitchen. Warren is six feet and we knock into the hanging vegetable basket, raining zucchinis which we don't even stop to pick up. Sometimes you just have to keep your positive momentum going, Dr. Madsen says.

All of a sudden Warren sort of pushes me away. In fact he does push me away. "This is sick, man. It's like we're celebrating Carla's death or something. What's the matter with us?" He puts his head down on the drainboard, bangs it there a couple of times for emphasis.

"No, Warren," I say softly, "it's not that, it's just we accomplished something."

"Accomplished something?" He whirls on me. "You mean this jack-off doggerel of yours?" He puts my poem down in a wet spot near the sink.

"I told you it wasn't any good, I already said it wasn't all that great." My voice skates up, quivers. "You just weren't hearing me."

"Can't you feel anything? Any normal emotions? Don't you understand loss? What it means she isn't here any more?"

Tears smart. I blot my poem with a dish towel. A minute ago we were together, dancing, feeling whatever we were feeling. Happy, I think it was happy. What I can't understand is how everything can blow away so fast. It's like you're in a glider. You're soaring, way up there, and the wind quits on you and you wait for the crash.

Maybe God planned it like that. There is some Biblical evidence that God is actually schizophrenic—He sees every sparrow fall, numbers the hairs of your head and everything like that, which is very detail minded, as opposed to seeing the whole big picture. You can readily imagine how He would come out on a standard Rorschach. If scholars would busy themselves proving that God is schizophrenic it would help the whole stigma thing immeasurably. It would also explain many things about the world. He was simply having one of His spells and He was not concentrating well, that's all you'd ever have to say. I wad up my poem and heave it at the cat.

Missed.

XIII

Wednesday I go out and buy me a pair of black mourner nylons with fancy clocks in them. I paint my nails with Mardi Gras Red, leaving the moons showing, which Carla sometimes did.

I dress in front of Carla's mirror, hers being the only one that's full length. (Actually Miriam Myers says okay I can move into Carla's room, but not till after the funeral.) The stockings make me look slightly whorelike, which is perhaps a tribute to Carla. Hello there, baby, I say to whoever it is in the mirror looking at me. Wanna have a good time? Since I suppose I would really like to be Carla, minus the herpes, of course, the lady in the mirror is an idealized combination. Carliffani. Tiffarla. Naw. Sounds too phony. That's not my identity to be.

I find half a pack of True sitting beside Carla's bottle of lithium, both overlooked by Mental Miriam. Carla always had somebody to buy her cigarettes, she was hardly ever out like the rest of us slobs. She didn't have to go to the laundromat because she was lonely and wanted to bum cigarettes. Likewise with coffee. She didn't have to get her coffee in the surgery waiting room at Valley View or at World Savings even. There was always somebody to buy her cappuccino at Barney's. Or red zinger tea—one of her dudes called her Red Zinger. He'd ring her up and when I answered he'd say is the Red Zinger in tonight? Sometimes I'd pretend I didn't know what he was talking about. Huh? Who? I'd say. The reason why I did this was jealousy, since nobody ever calls me except M. I can admit this now that Carla's not around to be jealous of.

Carla Janus, lithium 300 mg. I shake out a little gray and yellow capsule. It says SKF on one side. Sex Kissing and Fucking? Couldn't be. The FDA or whatever it is wouldn't go for it. Anyway they don't know it's going to be somebody like Carla taking the stuff. Got it. Smithing, Klineing, and Frenching. Mr. Smith, I'se Klined to French you. I wriggle my hips and lips. This takes coordination, which as a matter of clinical fact most people who are severely schizo can't manage. This says something, I feel.

My next step toward reinCarlation, I take a lithium. Why not? What could be the harm? Dr. Madsen doesn't know everything. Make that two. What I'll do, I'll bop on over to Barney's and see if anybody comes up and offers to buy me one of those add-on build-your-own omelettes in return for my favors. Or a caffe mocha. Or an Unknown Jerome even.

I put the two miniature torpedoes far back on my tongue and swallow. Hey, I feel something. What? Is it the fission? A depth charge scrambling the signals? I close my eyes waiting for my serotonin level to build up, spill over into joy, Schiller's Ode to. In fact I put on one of my classical records I have—"Water Music." I've started this collection of stuff by psycho genuises—Handel, he's the best, and Salieri and Schumann. If they're schizophrenic, who needs to be sane? I play "Water Music" about 29 times till finally I fall asleep right there on Carla's bed. When I wake up the record is still revolving soundlessly and Lindy is standing there saying for my information it's two o'clock.

Two! I'm weak, thirsty, gypped. My heart is sprinting and I have the trots. If anybody ever offers you a lithium, the way people hand out lifesavers or mints, say, tell them to shove it. Well actually you should be polite, tell them you just brushed your teeth or something, but pass, definitely pass.

I guess I'm just not manic depressive, which depresses me. I don't like being a second-class nut. There's something in me that wants to be prime time, part of the aristocracy.

I sag myself downstairs to wait for Butler and Butler.

"What's the matter with you?"

"Nothing."

"You shouldn't wear those stockings," Lindy says.

"Why?" I say. "Get off my back."

"With clocks in them."

"Sure they have clocks in them. That's very in."

"Not for a funeral."

"Did you read that in Dear Abby?"

"I didn't have to. You just know it."

Lindy can grate on you after a while, like sitar music. She is wearing a black caftan. She looks like a porpoise on graduation day. Should I lay that one on her? It'd really serve her. Luckily for her, I am not vindictive, besides I'm wiped. So I just say, "Look, asshole, you don't know what's in for a funeral, I don't, nobody does, so let's just forget it, okay?" But of course I can't just forget it and all through everything I am thinking you stupid clocks! Worrying whether I should have worn them, whether people are looking at them, judging me. I tend to do that, which is really flattering your-self, since most people could care less. Or couldn't care less. Dr. Madsen says it's narcissistic. For some reason I find that word hard to pronounce, it has one too many whatevers. Nothing is simple once you let psychology in your life.

"I don't think they're coming for us. You probly got the time screwed up."

I can't go letting my emotions get nibbled by the Lindys of this world. I have to fly above the flak, cool and serene. I'm pretty sure she said two fifteen but she could have said fifteen to . . . . It's very important that they come for us since I'm Carla's chief mourner. Who else is there? When you come right down to it, Carla and Warren drove each other up the bipole with their cycles, although they could be very cliquey too. Geoffrey isn't to be reckoned with, mournerwise. He used to follow Carla around, but it wasn't that personal, he being a walking coma without the tubes up his nose. And between Lindy and Carla there was a ton of experience versus a mountain of cellulite. So I am it, right?

"You shouldn't wear that top either," Lindy says. She is slurping up blackberry yogurt, mauve milk of magnesia.

"Just exactly why not?" Now I'm really frosted, although I keep my voice steady as a cucumber.

"Because your navel shouldn't show at a funeral."

"What are you talking about? My navel doesn't show."

"But it could though, it very well could. If you lift your arms up, it will."

"Unto the hills or something? Well, I won't go lifting my arms, why should I? There's nothing to reach for. Sheez!"

"Like if you yawn or something."

"Listen," I say. "You open your fat yap one more time and I'll make a McDoubleburger out of you. Got it?" This is very true to the spirit of Carla, I just wish she could hear me. Lindy opens her mouth but nothing comes out. She licks around the top of the yogurt, watching me. She has put on one of her Voc Rehab macramé belts and she now looks like a double boiler.

I think about changing from my black top, which *is* on the short side. I left my stuff in the washer for a couple of days and Warren wanted to use it and he just went barreling ahead and plopped in everything including that top, this top, which is 100% something that shouldn't go in the dryer. In the end I just borrow Carla's black tuxedo jacket from her closet.

"Who said you could wear that?" Lindy pipes up.

"Carla," I say. Who can argue this?

Lindy, that's who. "Sure, I bet," she says.

At exactly 2:16 I am helped into the rear of the limo by a gentleman in white gloves who reminds me of the kid who played Harvey in *Harvey* when I was in J.C.—he had white gloves and also a cowlick. I only hope and pray old Bernadette is watching. If she is, it will be clear we are all of us real quality people, persons of substance for whom a limousine has been ordered up.

Warren sits beside me, sighing and holding a midget Bible that he got at Saint Anthony's Dining Room when he was living in San Francisco in one of those Tenderloin flytraps. Or maybe it's fleabags. The Bible has a narrow purple satin ribbon with a frayed end trailing from it. "Don't," he says when I touch it. He keeps bumping his knees together. Lindy is in front with the driver, which she doesn't understand is less prestigious than being in the back, properly chauffeured, and Geoffrey, who came home in the morning, is on the jump seat. He is wearing his baseball cap, team mascot.

We go directly to Oakmont Cemetery. (Lindy asks if we can please stop at Seven Eleven for cigarettes but the answer is no, it has to do with the insurance.) Why Oakmont? There have to be lots of tonier places in the East Bay. How about Berkeley? After all, Carla used to work Telegraph Avenue. Or Kensington?

We pass through a tall wrought iron gate with some flecking-off gilt. Abandon all guilt ye who. . . . Over the gate is a weird white bird with its plaster of Paris wings spread. Colomba, paloma. In Colma they have a pet cemetery.

Inside Oakmont it's old, unkempt, unmowed, un-everythinged. Cigarette wrappers scattered, plastic flowers with everlasting phony leaves and stand-up tombstones, like giants' front teeth. Not that I have ever actually seen a giant's front tooth, I don't mean that. I read once about somebody named Cadmus—or was it Camus?— who planted a field with huge dragon's teeth. It was Cadmus, Camus was somebody else. He caught the plague and got clobbered in a car accident like Carla.

We pass what looks like a mausoleum. I tap the driver on the shoulder. "Excuse me, is that where they burn the bodies?" He says no, there's another building. We pass it on the way out. He'll point to it.

We come to a stop at a little chapel that calls itself Chapel-on-the-Hill although it's really more of a hummock, but I guess Chapel-on-the-Hummock doesn't quite make it.

In the myth I had reference to an army of men spring up and fight each other until there are only five left. Like us before Carla died. Cadmus founded the City of Thebes with those five guys. I wonder for the first time who Wookmook will put in our city of Thebes. Camelot-on-Thebes.

"Come on, Tiffani, it's time to get out," Miriam Myers leans her head in. I see that everyone else has already left.

"Do you know who you're going to put—" but she's gone.

The hearse's back is open like it's one of Paula's tailgate parties she used to have. Randy is standing there greeting people, nice to see you, glad you came, shaking hands, except that Warren doesn't.

A Butler Brothers man goes up to Warren and asks would he care to join Mr. Ziegler and Mr. Forbes—he has their names on a white card—as pallbearers. Warren hesitates, looks at Randy. "Sure, I guess, okay, sure." The Butler Brothers man says how they customarily have six pallbearers, but Butler Brothers will be more than happy (what is more than happy?) to supply the additional, make up the deficit. That's a Wookmook word too, as in neurological deficit or memory deficit.

"Why not us?" Lindy is saying. She thinks she's greatly into Women's Lib.

"Well, it's not that customary," the company man says. "To use women."

"Why?" I say. I wisht it had been my idea, but I was deep in thought as per usual.

"If you ladies wish to serve in that capacity . . ." the Butler guy says, looking around, I'm not sure why. Fortunately Miriam Myers is busy signing us in in the white leather guest book during this interchange or it most probably would have got killed in committee in revenge for our managing to be there at all.

We pace around at the back of the hearse. There's a wreath of wheat on the coffin, courtesy of Wookmook. I am feeling nervous. I whisper to Lindy, who does not think ahead as I do, but lives for the moment, "Let's see how heavy it is, let's just see if we can lift it all right." We try an end. Gingerly. No problem. We're actually collaborating, yay team. Back at C House we wouldn't help each other carry in the groceries. A few grains from the wreath scatter on Carla's tuxedo jacket. That's the trouble with black, it shows every little thing.

Carla's head is borne by Randy and Mel Ziegler, the Patients'

Rights Advocate. Patients' Last Rites, I think. I smile. The Butler man looks at me suspiciously. Warren and Geoffrey are in the midriff section, which you can just tell pisses Warren off, and Lindy and I have the feet. Nation's First Women Pallbearers, maybe we'll be in the Guinness Book of Records, along with Sandra O'Connor and Sally Ride.

It's kind of a half-assed bob-tailed operation, Geoffrey who is maybe four eleven being opposite Warren, who is six feet, but we walk with dignity, trying to keep the coffin as level as possible. It's incredibly light, like carrying a dead bird. We set the casket down on the metal runners on a sign from Butler and Butler. I am careful not to be the last one to get my fingers out. "Ouch!" Lindy says.

I plan to go ahead and sit front and center as befits the Chief Mourner, but there is already a woman sitting in the first row aisle seat and Miriam Myers herds us into row two.

"Who's that?" I say.

"Carla's mother came at the last minute. From Virginia City."

Shit! This is life, somebody popping up out of left field.

The Butler man props open the coffin with a doohickey like a grand piano has. I just can't believe it, Carla in that box. She's dead and I'm alive.

The minister gets up, holding a three-by-five card. He's wearing a yellow tie with violins, which has to be at least as odd as stockings with clocks, right? He clears his throat and says, "Let us all take a moment and pray for the soul of Carlotta Ellen."

"Who?" Maybe we're at the complete wrong funeral.

"Shh," Miriam Myers says. "Carlotta Ellen is her given name," she whispers.

Really? I wonder why she changed. I'd settle for Carlotta any day. I can see how if you're like me, saddled with a dopey name like Mary Alice, where you see the parents didn't give it a moment's thought, it wasn't an important thing, you'd jump right in and change it. Tiffani . . . it has style, elegance. Mary Alice is a thick-ankles name.

I considered some others—Remora, for instance, which is the

suckerfish that lives on the dolphin, but then I didn't like the idea of having to explain it. And then I thought of Archangela (after I found out that Corelli's first name was Archangelo), but everybody went ahead and had a regular shit fit, even Dr. Madsen "deemed it inadvisable." You could call me Angie, I said. How about Archie? D said, so I gave that one up and the next day I announced I was Tiffani with an i and it was not open for discussion.

The minister is in full swing. Carlotta, he has been given to understand, had a very spir-it-ual side to her nature, a great love for the common man. Well, that's one way of putting it. I try winking at Warren, but he is stoic. Carla's mother holds up a handkerchief to protect herself against a dripping air conditioner.

I crane my neck around and I see that Doug Singer, Carla's case worker, is there and—surprise—that boy who came with the delegation of neighbors, the acne one who when Carla looked at him, dropped his eyes. You could see where she was too strong for him. Had they ever spoken? I don't know. I never thought to ask her and now it's too late. Maybe he's a spy from the neighbors, their funeral mole. I cough to get Miriam Myers' attention, tell her to keep an eye on him, but she shakes her head no. He's not more than 15, 16 tops, and he just sits there a few rows back blinking and running the zipper of his jacket up and down the track. You can see it's something personal that brought him—his first brush with sex? The death and dying movement? I don't know.

I try to figure how many dead people I have actually seen—Carla, an Egyptian pharaoh in the De Young Museum, a clerk at the Quik Stop in Albany who had a heart attack, although I didn't know at the time he was dead so maybe I shouldn't count him.

"The Lord giveth and the Lord taketh away."

I lean forward, steadying myself with a hand on Warren, to see is it really Carla they've got in there. It is and it isn't. They have virtually no make-up on her. This makes her look phony and artificial. No little circles of bright blush or watery lip gloss, no smoky lines under and around the eyes, no iridescent green shadow on the lids, and then that black challis thing. They've taken away the real Carla, like stripping the paint off a beautiful car. It's obscene. But the all-time shocker is seeing her so still. There was a quiver of hysteria in Carla, a tremor that kept her on the move—foot swinging, fingers tapping, eyes blinking as though she was trying to get the world in focus. And now I see that the life has really gone out of her, all the anger and the pain. From quick to dead, a fine finite line, no remissions.

I think of all the things Carla'll miss—a cure for cancer, the coronation of Diana, New Year's Eve 2000—my mind can't go out any farther than that. And unfiltered Camels, she'll miss them too.

"Naked came we into this world and it is certain we carry nothing from it."

He doesn't bother to say that for some there is little or nothing in between. Carla/Carlotta's mother is crying great sniffling sobs, and I think to myself, why didn't she bother coming to our fine Thanksgiving dinner instead of showing up when it doesn't do any good (thereby bumping a legitimate chief mourner). All right, maybe it wasn't such a hot dinner, things went wrong, but Carla called and invited you, you nerdy lady, I heard her. It's not more than three blocks from where the bus leaves you off, no, it's not a bad district, it's just not that far from the bus station, that's all, that's what she said to you. I will her back to crumble, her neck to fall off, her zipper to unzip. Actually she rubs her left shoulder blade so I see I am having an effect. This is magical thinking, which Dr. Madsen is not in favor of.

She stands up—if I would have started in earlier, my curse would have worked. She goes forward, I think that's the Reverend's phrase, if Mother will now come forward, that's how he says it, like it's his mother, universal Mother, a visiting dignitary to whom all honor. She puts one long-stemmed rose on the casket, fiddles with a staple, takes it out of green florist paper and lays it there.

"Baby," she says to Carla. I try again to catch Warren's eye, but he won't. Up his. If you're a mother, not that I'll ever be one, you're supposed to touch your baby and then—zzz—you're bonded forever. There's this jolt like electricity, this connection you can't let go of. Maybe Carla's mother didn't hold on long enough or it didn't take. Maybe even then there was this restless thing in Carla and she squirmed away. Or maybe there wasn't any touching, Carla's mother didn't feel like it, she didn't know she was supposed to, and now she wants to make it up.

I try to imagine Carla little, like the kids next door, sucking her thumb, pulling up her dress, looking at herself in surprise, fingering her private little clam like she's found a party favor. Figuring, always figuring, that was Paula, Carla, I mean, using, abusing, being, hoping. If I just wouldn't let myself hope, M said once to Ceci Schroeder—and then you see her slip back.

I start to cry. For Carla, for me, for us, for them. I think of all the mamas in the world holding their schizo-of-the-future babies, tickling them, beaming down at them, blowing on their stomachs, not knowing what they're incubating. I'm crying in big honking gulps like a rain forest. Everyone has their own style. Miriam Myers is looking at me. I wipe my nose on my sleeve.

They're sitting together, across the aisle from us, the Wookie brass. What makes us different from them? Well, our fingerprints may be irregular and our CAT scans and we feel every little thing— every look, insult, breeze, shadow, touch of silk—it's all blown up into this production of Sound and Light and we don't have any circuit breakers, no way to shut it off or tone it down.

But if somebody just came into this chapel and you were to say, okay, I'll give you a hundred bucks if you can spot who is us and who is them, would they be able to? I mean, we're not wearing Hello I'm Nuts badges.

Would somebody coming in from the outside be able to say who's fuses are blown? If I'm honest in the privacy of Row 2, chair 1, yah probably. Not always, but sometimes. Always with Geoffrey. Sometimes with the rest of us. Lindy walks awkwardly, sort of shambling. That's six years of Navane, day in, day out, the Navane shuffle,

which sounds like a trendy dance. And she twitches even more than
me. We both of us take stuff, Kenadrin for me, Artane for her,
which is supposed to counteract the Parkinsonian effect of the neu-
roleptics and does to a certain extent, but still we twitch. And I
laugh, beam into space M calls it. Actually everybody would laugh
if I just took the time to cue them as to what's happening—the
world out there's a gas—but it's too time consuming to explain, I
just don't have that kind of energy any more. Laugh and the world
laughs with you, they say, but it definitely isn't true. They just
look at you funny.

I've got to do something to get my act together. The trouble is
none of us really *do* do anything. We talk about it but then we sit
there and smoke and swill coffee till the caffeine charges up the
fantasies and the anxiety. I'll shape up, it's just a matter of time.
Of course Carla most likely thought she had plenty of time, all the
time in the world.

"I am the Resurrection and the Life."

Out of any given hundred schizos, a third will get functional, a
third will get worse, and a third will stay the same. But which third
are you in? That's the hot question.

They have worked out all these indicators, the System has. If your
trouble starts early, the prognosis is bad. Late teens is when most
people first bonk out, but if you get sick after age 30, you're in the
favorable outcome group. Psychotic relatives are bad, sudden onset
is good. If you fall into the well in one fell swoop, it's better than
if you inch your way down, groping, losing your grip a bit at a
time. Flattened affect is bad, paranoid symptoms are good. Some
of the things you think are bad turn out to be good.

"And behold there are last which shall be first and there are first
which shall be last."

Which was kind of what I was saying. Now where was I? I'm
always getting interrupted. Okay, as regards moi, me, on the positive
side: no wacko relatives, no hospitalizations, no blunt affect, good
rapport (usually) with therapist. On the bad side, I can't say I have

paranoid symptoms exactly, or sudden onset, or a precipitating event, all of which would be good. But toting everything up, I feel like the numbers are definitely in my favor. The odds. The odds are with the odd. Another original thought.

"Shall we pray." It sounds like it should be a question, but it isn't.

There's this saint guy, Jude the Obscure, patron of lost causes. I read in the Personals (once when I was kind of looking for a husband) that if you ask him for stuff eight days running, on the ninth day, he gives it to you. The only catch, the Personals ad said, is you have to run a little thank you ad. It's maybe some yellow journalism gimmick the Hearst papers thought up. But I just don't see how it could hurt. All you have to say at the end is just "thank you St. Jude for prayers answered" and then your initials, you can use the three-line rate.

Everybody's head except Geoffrey's is bowed. He is looking at the ceiling, which in a way makes more sense. . . . Listen, St. Jude, what I want from you, all I'm asking is just for you to shove me into the good third, that's all. It shouldn't be that tough for a specialist in hard shots. I'm not even that bad, see. It's not major like raising somebody from the dead, nothing like that. It's more like a push, a little nudge, something you could do with your left hand.

Actually I tried this once before for four days running, but then I messed up and skipped day 5 and they don't bother telling you what to do. Start over? Add day 9? Run your thank you twice? Or what?

"Dust thou art and unto dust returneth."

The mother, Mother, walks back to her place in the front row and I see her face is Carla's, sharp featured, though fossilized and she is still crying weakly.

The minister is passing out mimeographed sheets, which he'd like for us to give back at the close of the service if you will please. He produces a pitch pipe.

Our God our help in ages past, our hope for years to come.

The hymn gets to me, the ragged strain of pure hope and our voices so few and desolate. If there was one thing Carla wanted, it was people around her, never ever to be alone with the bright volatile core of herself.

Our shelter from the stormy blast and our eternal home.

And if there was one thing she couldn't stand it was silence. It drained her. She was afraid the walls would close in on her, compress her. That's why she turned down the Independent Living Program the county has with rent subsidies which Doug Singer told her she was eligible for. If she'd done it, the truck would have hit someone else.

Before we close, the minister says, he would like to provide time for those of her family and friends who wish to share memories or feelings about Carla to do so.

I certainly wisht he'd of given us warning, Jeez! I start madly trying to think of something to say, something so I won't look like a lulu head. I could say she gave me her purple scarf, her purple Montana blow-job scarf, but don't worry, I wouldn't say that. It would be inappropriate. What I actually think is sometimes your emotions are appropriate and sometimes they are inappropriate and sometimes they're just appropriate to you. Which is okay.

Miriam Myers is going on about how Carla made a substantial amount of progress in the time she was privileged to work with her. She was very realistic about her limitations and made a sincere effort to deal with them. Right out of the Wookie manual.

Carla's mother gets up and says how if time hadn't run out on Carlotta like it did, she personally for one feels sure she would have made it, her letters were that much more positive the last year and she was even beginning to talk about how some time she was going to see about getting her little girl back.

"We all just kind of looked up to her," Lindy says. "Let her decide things for us." The minister nods and Lindy gives me this superior look, which is what it's all about. But I still can't think of anything and anyway I have this thing about public speaking. Eyes flip me out.

Randy gets up. He's wearing houndstooth pants and a black velvet jacket. He takes his time, looks at everybody, very careful to establish contact. In the chapel light he has this beautiful matte finish. "We're all of us here to honor a very special lady who has touched our lives in various ways. God willing," he says in a rich soft voice you couldn't help admiring, "Carla, Carlotta," he says, looking at the mother, "and I planned to be married this summer."

"Horse shit!" Warren bellows. It's a small room and the *horse shit* seems to bounce off the walls, if you can picture it.

"Easy there, man," Randy says, calm as custard, "I realize what you're going through."

"Please, gentlemen, please!" the minister says. He's frowning and fiddling with his pitch pipe.

Miriam Myers looks straight ahead for about 10 seconds, I'd say, and then we are being swept down the aisle and out by this tailwind of the System, Miriam Myers, Mel Ziegler, Doug Singer, the triple threat combo from Wookmook, herding us, git along little dogies, git along. I am the only one has the presence of mind to leave the mimeod hymn sheet as requested. I just quietly put it on one of the empty chairs with Geoffrey's, which is all furled up.

Geoffrey stops to offer a peanut to a gibbering, possibly psychotic chipmunk. The limo man has been leaning against the hearse smoking. He tosses his cigarette into the street looking surprised and returns to his post. I bum a Marlboro from him in soft funereal tones so that it doesn't come to the attention of Wookmook officialdom.

"I knew something like this would happen," Miriam Myers says to Doug Singer as she closes the door on us. "We should never have caved in like we did. They just can't stand stress."

"Usually they're okay when they're out some place," Doug says.

I like him. I think what I'll do, I'll ask to be transferred to Doug. They can't just tell you there isn't an opening, although they give you the runaround every chance they get. Doug looks handsome standing there in the wet grass beside Miriam, his tie flapping in the breeze. Carla said Doug once made a pass at her and that he is only case managing until he gets enough loot together to buy a small vineyard in Sebastopol, where I guess he will case manage a different product. I smile, give Doug a little wave. I'd love to live in the wine country surrounded by grapes—zins, cabs and chards instead of loons, psychos and bipolars.

"He's such a mother fucker!" Warren says, which kind of intrudes on my meditation.

"He doesn't mean you," I say to the limo driver who gave me the smoke and is looking at Warren in the rear view mirror.

"Carla marry that prick?" Warren shouts. "The night before it happened . . . the night before. . . ." He doesn't go on.

"You had no call to wear Carla's jacket. Her mother probly recognized it even," Lindy says.

"*Lin*dy," I say the way Carla did. "Last warning, okay?"

"Okay okay, okay."

"Who does he think he's conning?"

"What we should do, we should have a little something at the house, a wake," Lindy says. She fishes a piece of tobacco off her tongue.

"You'd eat it all," I say.

"She'd eat shit first," Warren says, picking up from our conversation. "Before she'd tie herself up to that wimp." Maybe he said pimp, not that Randy is one, he sells fittings for solar electrical cesspools and waste heat recovery systems.

When we get back to the house I don't feel like talking any more. I put a newspaper on the dining room table and start pasting more entries in *F.P.*, my chronicle.

Religious pilgrims who flocked to the Ibarra home to see an image of the

Virgin Mary formed by a porch light reflected off the bumper of a 1975 Chevrolet became ugly and abusive when Ms. Ibarra turned off her porch light Friday night. An old lady was trampled.

Tel Aviv. (I try not to be too regional.) *A court has ordered a 16-year-old girl to stop walking around the house naked, reportedly because her 80-year-old stepfather claims she is trying to cause him to have a heart attack so she can inherit his fortune.*

That one puts me in mind of Carla, I don't know why exactly. I put *F.P.* away. My paste is all caked up anyway with these solid granules so that the articles won't lay flat. I have to remember to get new paste.

I take a bus (actually two buses) back to the cemetery, to Oakmont. I try a side door to the chapel. It's open. There are two guys— Butler and Butler?—in the little room with curtains and they are taking the metal handles off Carla's casket with a Phillips screwdriver.

They look at me, question mark.

I shrug. "I was here this afternoon and I guess I just felt like coming back," I say. I feel kind of embarrassed.

They look at each other, the League again. "Let's leave her alone," the one says to the other. He puts his screwdriver back in a slot in this green unisex apron he has on. "You want it open, miss?"

I try to think, have I backslid if I'm being called miss instead of ma'am? He is looking at me, waiting.

"What? No, it's okay, it doesn't matter." If I can reach Carla across the dreamless quiet, a little wood won't matter.

"You can let us know when you're done," the screwdriver guy says.

I sit on the floor. The place has a phony sweet insecticide smell to it. An energetic organ is pounding out sentiment somewhere in the building, probably for a twelve-hundred-dollar funeral. I wish it would stop so I could concentrate. It does.

I pluck at the carpet, roll some fuzz into a ball. I used to think people who spent the night with dead people were ghouls or voyeurs or masochists, but I see now it's not just spending time with death, it's life, the light that's gone out and left an after-image.

"I'd like to thank you for my purple scarf," I say softly. "And the nail polish. And the pack of True, the half pack. And your room, which I'm moving into tomorrow, I hope you don't mind."

I sit there very still, almost as still as Carla, except for breathing, of course. I don't flick my thumb nail or anything. I don't even smoke. I'm glad I'm the one's still alive. With chances. Time. I feel like I owe Carla something for that.

I close my eyes and really focus on her, the scent of her, the quirky emphatic way she was. I watch over her. That's part of being grown up, the vigil, taking care of somebody, of what they leave you. Taking care of yourself even. "I'm going to try," I whisper to Carla and then I tiptoe out. On my way back I even remember to get the paste, but I forgot to tell the guy with the screwdriver I was done the way he asked me to.

XIV

Carla's death temporarily overwhelmed the issue of the neighbors and the threat they posed. There was a kind of uneasy stasis on the block, a general watchfulness, everybody waiting for the hearing to come up, all of us keeping a lowish profile. Two of the younger raccoons came back, but they were wary—maybe they were even survivors of the massacre.

At one of our house meetings Miriam Myers says, "Good news, people. A guy has been arrested in Emeryville, an ex-Marine, a house painter, and he's being charged with 27 daytime burglaries including the ones around here. So we're in luck, that one's behind us."

"Well, it was never in front of us," I say, "because we didn't do it."

But something else starts bugging me. Barnard, Georgina, allegedly signed that petition, wife of Barney who gives me cigarettes. He wouldn't let her. We smoke the same brand. Actually I switched to his to make it easier for both of us. I decide to go on a reconnaissance mission.

"Hi, Trivial Pursuits," Barney says. Business as usual. He's wiping off the tits of the Gaggia with a folded mesh cloth that steams. I hold out my hands, cup them in my throw-me-a-cigarette-pal gesture. Barney shakes a Viceroy out of the pack and tosses it. Last one, he balls up the package. All's right with the world. He has more somewhere, he always does.

I get my coffee and a stirrer and the honey bear. "You care if I flake out by the fire?" I drop 60 cents into the styrofoam cup marked TIPS. Barney knows and I know, it's an unspoken thing, that I never leave tips as such. If I did I'd never be able to acquire the underlying product or service. What I do is I put my regular payment into the

TIPS cup because Barney and I are so close it would insult him if I just paid like any blotto Joe Blow.

Barney bangs the little basket with espresso grounds on the side of the counter to loosen them and flips them into the garbage. I wait for him to finish, to say *anything to eat, Tiffani.* I know, it's pure customer relations but I like for him to say it. When you figure that people say way more than they actually do, words are much more important than mere deeds, percentagewise.

This time Barney hesitates. I have to admit he hesitates. "That's really for a group there, the fireplace area," he says. "You go plunk yourself down there, spread your gear all over the place and nobody else is going to want to."

"Okay, okay, I read you. No sweat, just asking. Booths are better anyway."

"And do Uncle Barney a favor and don't slop your java on the floor this time, okay?"

I stand there looking at him. "My cup runneth over," I say.

"Yah," he says, "that's what I have reference to."

There was a period there when I was pretty religious, phrases come back to me still. I was all set to join this church group in Mendocino, but M and D had their standard model hemorrhage. They were really friendly to me, the ones in Mendocino, invited me to dinner and everything like that, said how they liked my shoes, the buttons on my sweater even. It was a sweater M made and she put on this series of hand-painted little buttons where each one had a flower that opened up more than the one below it. Some of the Mendocino people spoke in tongues, which was kind of confusing at the time. Now that I've had more experience being around word salad types, I'd probably catch on right away.

I haven't moved. I usually don't when I'm figuring things out, on the edge of a breakthrough. I also haven't spilled anything.

"So what's the good word these days, Tiffani?"

"Listen, Barney, there's something I've got to ask you. You guys didn't happen to go sign any dumb petition lately, did you?"

"What would it have had to do with?" Barney says. Obviously he didn't sign it. He's ducked down behind the counter, working with noisy coffee beans in a burlap sack.

"With us, with C House."

"Not guilty," Barney says. "Now I'm not speaking for Georgina, mind you, she could have, could be she did," he says a while later.

I have to lean over the counter with my feet off the ground to see him down there. "Why? Why would she?" I ship the questions over the counter with a little spray of spit.

"Well, I tell you. Sometimes we get some problem people in here, some people with problems, I mean who cause them, low grade ore, present company excepted. And then the regulars, they don't feel comfortable, you know what I'm saying?" Barney stands up, smooths his thinning hair.

"Georgina could have? You really think she could have?"

"It's possible."

"You think she didn't read the petition? Somebody just shoved a piece of paper at her and she—"

"I'll be up front with you, Tiffani. That woman knows what she puts her name to. No point in going round the barn on that one. But you shouldn't take it personally, Tiffani. It's just a matter of the customers want a certain kind of atmosphere. They get antsy, you're headed for Chapter 11."

End of conversation.

I sit blowing on my coffee, sending frightened little wavelets to the far shore, the opposite rim. I leave my mug sitting there on the table, half full, half empty, whatever. I don't know whether it's pointful to try to determine whether you're an optimist or a pessimist when you're a schizophrenic, I'm not too much on the sub-types.

I go out the back way, past the phone. I don't feel like seeing any more of Barney right now, it kind of depresses me the way he's losing his hair.

I go on to Cyrano's on 14th, which has a two-storey waterwheel and a tree growing through the roof. It's really quite a bit classier than Barney's anyway. I have me a second cup of coffee (actually it's the last half of my first cup). The waitress holds two Silexes breast high. "Which?" she says, like she's offering you a bosom. "Leaded or unleaded?"

"Leaded," I say, glad to have caught on. Cyrano's is definitely fast-paced, sophisticated.

I go on and have a couple more cups, which along with the Barney's scene leaves me pretty wired. I'm a coffeeholic, which I'm sure you already figured out.

To really rattle my cage, guess who's sitting at the circle bar? Bernadette and Art Ryan. They appear to be with a couple with bike clips and bright blue backpacks who I've never seen before. I'm reasonably sure they weren't in the neighborhood delegation.

They order Irish coffees all around and they sit on these tree trunk stools with their feet on the brass rail around the fire pit, their backs to me.

Bernadette is talking, it's not too hard to figure what about.

"And this policeman goes, Can you describe him to me, lady? And I go, can I describe him? You bet I can describe him. I'm kneeling by this window and he's about a couple yards away, right? Standing on one foot. For twenty-one minutes, I timed him with Art's stopwatch. And so I'm going, he has on this little black and red beanie and a green jacket with a button hanging and dirty sneakers with the laces not tied—"

"And he's got three cavities in his front bicuspid," the guy with the bike clips says and they laugh till Bernadette dabs her eyes with a cocktail napkin.

"Spoken like a dentist, Cliff, like a true molar man."

I guess he must be a dentist. I send my tongue around reviewing rough places.

"So why didn't you call the cops, you schlemiel?" the dentist says, giving Art a friendly poke. "Instead of you make the little woman do the dirty work."

"Three times I've called the cops about that crew."

"Twice," Art says. "The one time when they were making a racket and then when one of em's standing on the lawn on one foot—you didn't call about Thanksgiving."

"You're nitpicking, as per usual. Twice then. But who did the calling? I can never get him to do anything. He's afraid it'll backfire on him or something."

"No, that's not it," Art says. "She's got me out there cleaning up the snails I fed the Snarol to, see. I must of creamed 100 of the buggers. So I come in and I say, honey, what am I supposed to do with these mothers? Make garlic butter or what? And she says quick flush them down the john and don't let the kids see and then she won't let me touch her for a week because I been picking up her poisoned snails. I keep getting all these mixed signals."

"Listen to it! Him belongs with the crazies next door, him does," Bernadette says, taking hold of Art's chin and wagging it.

"Look, that wife of yours'd drive any man out of his ever-lovin' mind," Cliff says.

Everybody laughs. They're still laughing and nobody looks up when the door closes behind me. The case of the people next door versus the crazies next door. Maybe the Snarol was really meant for us, only the snails ate it first. Maybe also I'm getting paranoid. But if you have enemies out there are you paranoid to think so? Or crazy not to? Am I crazier than the world in general? If you could average everything out. If I knew the answer what good would it do me? That is something I have yet to figure out.

A limousine of creamy shouldered prom goers passes me, Waifcity. Someone holds up a bottle, waves. I am feeling very lonely. I decide to try the laundromat. We have a washer-dryer at C House, but there's a whole laundromat camaraderie. You see the same people. It's like a sorority only you don't have to go through rushing. Just washing. Well, actually you don't even have to do that if you don't want to.

There's just an old man who's there to watch TV—his is on the blink and no, he doesn't smoke. I dredge my pockets looking for stray Viceroys. I come up with a butt and some stuff I cut out of the paper for *Funny Peculiar*. "You want to hear something?"

He doesn't say. He's watching "People's Court."

I read to him anyway. *Crows are terrorizing an Israeli town, attacking residents and stealing money and jewelry from their homes. Police Chief Danny Gimche said the birds could be part of a larger conspiracy in which winged thieves are trained by human—*

"Wapner's gunna sock it to that hairdresser sure."

"You don't think it's odd that the Israeli police chief thinks—"

"Even if she is a looker."

"Listen to this. *Walter Stepetak and his new wife Moana swam toward shore after their wedding 20 feet under water off Seattle's Alki Point. The bride wore blue rubber—*"

"I knew he'd make her pay for that coat, no way he wouldn't. Just wait'll you see what she says on the way out, she's hoppin' mad."

"Hey, whaddaya know! Beryl Markham died."

"She says it's rigged just like Vegas! You hear that?"

"They've got a whole column on her. Some people will do anything for publicity."

"Win or lose they get paid off, you know that don't you? Just for bein' on the show."

Back at C House there's a package on the hall table from Butler and Butler addressed to Ms Janus and I decide to open it, thinking that it's maybe some of Carla's things. I haven't been able to figure out what happened to her water pearls, for example, or her cloisonné locket. Also since I have been thinking about Carla, it seems it is maybe an answer, a sign to me or something.

What it turns out, it's an urn containing Carla's ashes and it was probably meant for her mother, that's who the Ms Janus was, I would bet money if I had money. Along with it is a memorandum which I decide to save for my chronicle. *In the process of cremation, human remains are placed in a furnace or retort, the temperature is raised to 1450 degrees F, a little less than that used to fire fine Chinaware. Every*

*effort has been made for any gold tooth fillings and surgical pins belonging
to the deceased to be placed in the container with the cremains.*

I shake it but you can't really tell much. The aggregate weight,
the memo says, averages six pounds. Like a newborn child. It seems
you do come pretty much full circle. I put the urn carefully in the
corner of my closet, back where nobody would be likely to see it.
In the process I find a stray sock, a dime, a stretch band I'd been
looking for, and two cigarettes which I dust off. I am repaid for my
stewardship.

XV It's Sunday and it's raining when I go over to the folks. Paula and Jake are there too. It's D's birthday. Actually Tuesday is D's birthday, but Paula and Jake are getting ready for their trip to Brazil and we are celebrating early.

"Everybody in the living room," Jake says.

"What's all this?" D says, all mock birthday-boy surprise.

A humongous box.

"Guess," Paula says. She's flushed, really out there in the ozone.

"What ever?" M says.

"Open it," Jake says, "and you'll find out."

"I thought we were going to make him guess," Paula says.

"Naw, he knows it's a tie."

D is already stripping off the paper. "They're getting wider these days."

It's a stupid conversation.

"I made you a card—" I say.

"No!" D says. "Look at this, Mama—Your Personal Desktop Computer with expandable memory!"

"But I forgot it."

"You children should be spanked," M says with shining eyes.

"I'll bring it next time."

"You have no business spending your money on us old folks like that, not with the baby coming and all."

"Baby? What baby?" I say.

"This baby," Paula says, pointing to her stomach. "Didn't you know? I thought we'd mentioned it."

"That's the Standard and Poor's Stockpak software there."

"I just thought you were getting fat."

"You can track over a hundred stocks."

"That you were pigging out."

I try to visualize Paula in stirrups in the midst of an OB exam, like a car up on a rack, somebody peering at things not meant to be seen.

"You can access your info from a data base of 900 including Amex and Over the Counter markets."

"If this isn't something! I just can't believe they'd go and do this," D says, in fact he keeps saying.

"You didn't suspect? I thought sure the box would give it away."

"He told you, he thought it was a tie." Jake is rubbing his chin on her shoulder.

"The best part is it speaks English, doesn't it, Jake? You don't have to go learning a special language or anything."

I yawn. "I want to use the rest room."

"So go," D says.

"It's a bathroom," Paula says. "In a private home it's commonly referred to as the bathroom."

"This isn't a private home, it's a condo," I say. She is just trying to delay me.

"Listen," I say when I return, "I don't know about anybody else, but I'm hungry. Are we planning to eat? Or what?"

"Take it easy," Paula says, "let Daddy play with his new toy."

I stalk off to the kitchen, wading through a slush of tissue paper and skidding on an operating manual. I prowl through the freezer. Hello—it's the top tier of Paula and Jake's wedding cake, which I seem to recall is being saved for their first anniversary. I eat the wings off the doves. They have all these anniversaries they celebrate anyway so it doesn't mean all that much—anniversary of when they first met, when they became engaged, ate at the Velvet Turtle, took out the garbage, I don't know what all. When they first screwed probably. The doves look like rodents without their wings so I do them the favor of polishing them off.

D comes to get ice from the ice maker and starts yelling.

"That's your sister's wedding cake, can't you see it's being saved?"

"How can you see something's being saved? That doesn't make sense. It's not marked Save."

"Well, what do you think it's doing there?"

"The same as the cauliflower with snappy cheddar and the dim sum empress chicken balls and the Hungry Man Enchiladas with sauce verde—waiting to be eaten. Sheez!"

"Close the freezer!" D shakes his head. "She took a nip out of your wedding cake, I'm sorry to say." That makes me sound like a chihuahua or something.

Paula doesn't say anything. Her mouth scrunches a little and she looks at Jake. She has this habit of standing with her index finger on her cheek and her right elbow cradled in her left palm so she looks like a mortar and pestle.

"You're a pestle," I say.

"What?"

"Not what, when," I say. My mouth is full of frozen frosting that seems to be melting into lard.

"When what?" Paula says.

I laugh, this conversation is so funny. "The kid. When does it come out of the oven?"

"October," Paula says.

"End of," Jake says.

"Neat," I say. "So I guess I'm going to be an aunt. Since we've forgotten to mention things around here, did anybody tell you there's going to be a hearing over C House? With a judge and everything?"

"Yah, we know," Paula says. "Say, I've been meaning to ask you."

"So ask."

And she goes, "No, Daddy, I mean. I have to ask him how much does it cost to add a half bath these days?"

D looks up from his manual. It seems Paula and Jake have put a deposit down on a colonial with a greenhouse window in Lafayette. As usual no one told me. Last to know, first to go.

"All depends how far it is from the existing plumbing."

"Well, like on the average what would you say? Using Mexican tile? What would you guesstimate?"

I move M's knitting, which I see is a baby blanket, little pearly white and yellow rows of flimsy octagonals, and flop down on the davenport. "His name is Reilly, Judge Quentin Reilly."

"I'd say it'd run you a hundred a square foot, you might get away with eighty five, best case, but you're better off to figure on a hundred."

"Miriam Myers says he isn't known to be that sympathetic to mental health concerns." I want to talk about the petition, see. I want to talk about me, where I can live, never mind babies that aren't even born and Mexican tile and data bases and half baths, how about halfway houses? LISTEN TO ME!

"You think that figure'd include the bidet?"

Every fucking time you want to say something, *really* say something, there's this barrier you can't get around, a bidet or a computer or a coalition. You can't get a word in edgewise, whatever that means. I try to picture an edgewise word, upended, wedged there between the cushions of the sofa like a pencil. I smile.

I guess I must have fallen asleep. When I wake up there's this afghan over me and they're talking about me. No, correction, it's about a Tiffany lamp Paula and Jake bid on at a silent auction in Pacific Heights. They find out Tuesday if they get it or not.

I sit up, stretch in all directions, like a squid. Paula ducks. "Do you think it would be too dumb to put an oak floor in the kitchen?"

"Yah, it would be too dumb," I say.

"They're doing it a lot now," M says.

I go off to the pecky cedar den to watch pecky cedar TV. Jake is standing there drinking bourbon from one of those glasses with a Greek key design in gold. When Paula first brought him home M and D asked each other, was there possibly something strange about a young person these days who drank bourbon and not just beer and wine? Was it a sign of a larger strangeness? They have a very low threshold of deviation, or maybe I mean high, I never can remember which way it goes. Later they suspended all disbelief, the son-they-never-had jazz.

Jake looks like an ad for Calvados I once saw. I don't remember where Calvados is. What Jake should have done, he should have married me instead of Paula, who will bankrupt him with her big expensive presents.

"Can I have a swig?" (I just want to see if he'll let me drink out of his glass.)

"Here, you can have the whole thing," he says, which then fails to prove anything except that he's apparently forgotten I'm not supposed to drink.

They say Freud, who was no dummy, had an affair with his sister-in-law. "Freud—" I start to tell Jake something he probably didn't know, enlighten him, but I see he's gone.

I set the glass down. Outside the den window I see the three-penny nail M put in the soil to turn the hydrangea in the planter blue. She used to be a slow patient gardener when we—they—had the house on Poplar. She'd start stuff inside in egg cartons, seedlings with tender stalks she was always bending over, touching, propping up. Where's all that stuff you used to grow? I asked her recently. That's all gone, she said, and it seemed she meant more than just the primroses. I think about the hydrangeas out there sucking up iron like mad, not knowing one shrimpy little nail is changing it to suit somebody's ideal of perfect hydrangeaness. Derangeaness.

"When Paula first brought you home, the folks thought maybe there was something strange about you," I say, but then I remember that Jake has left.

I get out Paula and Jake's wedding album from the bookcase. Gross me out. Talk about dismal! White leather with gold banding and Our Wedding over their names, which have already started to flake off. The very first print is muddy, underexposed, D helping Paula out of the car, one tiny white satin 5½ triple A foot at a time. It's also posed, Paula having dressed at the place.

You can go straight through and find the flaws in every last one. If they'd let me do it, as per agreement, it would have been unique, a Diane Arbus type album. I wouldn't have had the brim of Mrs. Aimslee's hat in the shot of the bride and groom frosting each other, you can bet on that. Or the Newton's rings in the receiving line 5 x 7's. What those come from, they're areas of light interference that come from pressure points along the edge of the 35 mm negatives. You don't need to have them if you just take the trouble to dust the negatives with cornstarch, ordinary cornstarch, or non-offset powder like printers use. And then there's one of Yoko that Say Cheese must have taken on a Polaroid, where you get the black bar that comes from pulling the tab too soon. And the cake looks really washed out, I told you it would, even the doves, RIP. There's one with me dancing with Whoever.

I go back out in the living room where the subject is now junk bonds. "Say, listen, what was the name of the guy I'm dancing with at the wedding? The one in the picture?"

"Kurt," Paula says. Maybe she said his name was Kirk. She is doing her Dean Witter junior exec act, showing D how you take this transparency and you put it over the 13-week moving average on the tax-exempt graph and you see layers.

I snap my fingers. It comes to me that's how I think, how I can be smiling while somebody's going on about what you wouldn't smile about because for me it's all going on at once, in layers.

"Hey, you guys, I just figured out something important about how I think. It's a breakthrough."

"Not now, Mary Alice, your sister's trying to show me what to feed into the computer so I can track my Nuveen."

Kurt, Kirk, Nuveen, Navane, what's the big diff?

Dinner. They have the dumbfuck computer in the middle of the table like roses. It says Happy Birthday in little green fluorescent letters that probably give you cataracts. We are having osso buco.

"I just never thought I'd live long enough to own one of these gadgets," D says.

"It'll even do graphics," Jake says.

"It's got 16 colors," Paula says.

"It should help you track your costs," Jake the Jerk is saying.

"I don't want to talk machines," I say suddenly. "I want to talk about what happens if we get thrown out of C House." I ram my finger in the end of my osso and fish out some marrow or buco or whatever. M hands me a silver pick she got when Abercrombie & Fitch went belly up.

"We don't know yet," Paula says—she has to sit back from the table because of her blooming stomach—"how it'll all come out." I think for a minute she means the baby.

"Okay if I tell her what you're planning on doing?" D says.

"Whatever you think," Paula says. She blots the circle where the wine glass stood with her napkin.

"Your sister over here is prepared to canvass the neighborhood, go talk to the neighbors—"

"What neighbors?"

"Your neighbors, the people on the block, the ones who signed the petition that's got everybody so hot and bothered."

"I can't believe this! Talk to the neighbors? That's the stupidest one yet!"

Paula looks at Jake, at M and D. "Well, I just thought if I, you know, introduced myself, got dressed nicely and everything and explained that I'm a sibling and that my big sister Mary Alice—Tiffani—lives over there in Camelot House and if they had a minute I'd like to talk with them about something that meant a lot to us—something along those lines. . . ."

"Yah, well, how would you like me going around talking to *your* neighbors?" I say.

D mutters something about apples and oranges, Mary Alice.

"That'd sure get old Mrs. Pixley going," Jake says. "Give her something else to think about." Jake and Paula dissolve into private giggles, with M and D on the edge, smiling, taking the joke on faith. It's nothing like me laughing with nobody waiting to join in.

I point my osso pick at them. "Just you shut up! It's a phenom-enally asshole idea, okay?"

The laughing peters out. They are looking at me, all of them. M has her fork at half mast. Anxious peas roll off.

"Okay, Tiffani," Paula says. "If that's how you feel about it."

Jake looks from me to M, D, and Paula.

"It *is* how I feel about it." What I really feel is I want for them to say they're ready to take me back, take me in. There's a soft buffered place there waiting. But I see now the price is too high. The home chorus sings the same old tune. It drowns you out, keeps you there repeating the theme. I stare unblinking into their pained wary faces, the computer's pulsing green heart.

"Got it?" I say like Carla.

"Okay, Tiffani," Jake says, "we got it, we have the message."

"Well," D says. He sounds chastened. "Now that that's settled, what say we drink to Frank?" Which is what he has apparently decided to call their newly minted sea urchin fetus.

"I've had it with all of you," I say. "I'm going home." It's true, I have and I do.

The first thing I do next morning, I put on Madonna—"Papa Don't Preach"—and then I start in making a loaf of beer bread. It's easy, just three ingredients, 3 tablespoons of sugar—those aren't the three, they're just one—and a bottle of beer and 3 cups of self-rising flour. Paula makes it all the time. You put it in at 350 and it takes about 10 minutes flat, whatever flat minutes are. I'm still seething and I beat it more than necessary.

I guard it from Lindy till it's cool and then I wrap it in Saran Wrap and put on a gold ribbon bow with one of those peel-off and stick-on backs. Next I find Warren, who since Carla's death just sits and watches TV with Geoffrey through commercials for Glendale Savings, Mark Morris tires, old Randolph Scott movies, everything from "Today" to "Nightline."

"Here's the drill, Warren. We're going to visit the neighbors, let them get to know us, the real us. What we do, we start with Miss Clausen next door, who didn't sign the petition."

It takes quite a while to convince him and even longer to get him up and moving, but that's Warren. It's not that I'm afraid to go alone, it's just better, two people. I throw a cup of water on my hair to settle it down so it won't be so frizzy, pick up the bread, and we're off.

We ring but nothing happens. We're not sure if the bell worked or not. "Shall we do it again?" Warren whispers. "Wait," I say. I feel anxious there by a strange door, just the way I used to when I was supposed to go out and sell Girl Scout cookies. But nonetheless since it is my idea, my project, I am calling the shots.

Warren goes, "She sure is a long time coming."

And I go, "Listen, if she asks us in for tea, let's don't eat the bread we brought, you know what I mean? That's for her." For some reason this puts me in mind of the top tier of Paula's wedding cake, which causes me a twinge of—I don't know—a twinge of a twinge.

"She's not there," Warren is saying. "Let's split." He keeps looking around in all directions. There's this aura of insecurity. You can practically see it. Sure, why not split? I almost do.

"Wait," I say. I ring again after all the traffic has gone by. This time we listen very carefully to be sure it does ring. "She might be having her morning enema," I say. "Old people do that, it helps them pass the time."

"The time?" Warren says.

Then we hear her. "Ye-es?" she says from behind the door. She makes it two syllables. Like she-it.

"Hi," I say, "hi there."

Miss Clausen opens the door on a chain, revealing one watery eye. It looks frightened and also a little frightening, though not as bad as two eyes. "We're . . . we're the people next door," I say. I look at Warren for confirmation. He's kind of pacing. "We brought you this bread . . . here, give it to me so I can show her. . . . It's for you because we really appreciate you not signing that petition against us."

"Petition? I'm afraid I—" Miss Clausen says.

"No, see the one you didn't sign." Her skin, the visible vertical slice of it, is like speckled parchment. The eye, which is filmed over, hiding, isn't actually that difficult to look into.

"I can't hardly sign anything. The side vision's gone on the left, they may have to go in there. . . ."

"No, that's okay, it's cool."

"She means you not signing the petition," Warren says.

"I'm sorry to disappoint you, but I couldn't. My niece has to write the checks, the electric and that."

"Give her the bread and let's get out of here."

I almost forgot. "We have this beer bread for you."

"Beer did you say? I don't think I. . . ."

"Oh all the alcohol's gone, it's just bread now," I say. I am still looking into the eye, standing my ground.

"Well, how much do you want for it, dear?"

"Oh no, absolutely not, it's a gift, it's free, so if you'd just open the door. See, we can't get the bread through the crack, it rose nicely and it won't fit." She's so old she may well be beyond simple logistics.

Miss Clausen hesitates. "I promised my niece I wouldn't open the door . . . I'm expecting her any time now. . . . I'll have to close it for just a minute to get the chain off, don't you know?"

"That's perfectly okay," I say, giving her permission, as they say in Group, realizing at the same time that she may well never open up again. But a moment later she does and I am looking into two murky glazed-over eyes. You can see she is very frail. She has on bedroom slippers with fuzzy beige padding and a black button on the toe.

"That's very kind of you," Miss Clausen says, taking our bread in a palsied hand. "I'll have it with my morning lemon, my constitutional." She nods or maybe just palsies in our direction and eases the door shut.

"Well, that was our lemon for this morning," Warren says.

"No, Warren, we can't expect to be greeted like Coca-Cola in China. It was a beginning."

"She was scared shitless. She didn't want us to think she was alone, that's why she came up with that fluff about her niece coming any minute." You can see Warren melt down into one of his dark moods, depression seeping through him like silt from a black river. He collapses on this old yellow chaise pad we have on the porch and I stand over him telling him what a good thing it was we went over there to Miss Clausen's. "Like we established contact, man. . . ." Warren's sideburns remind me of tidepools, squiggly things coming up, encroaching. I've done two poems on them, one for each side. No, not really. But I *have* started two poems on Warren's sideburns. I like made a list of everything that rhymed with sideburns—wide urns, dried ferns, guide learns, fried sterns, bride yearns, Cliburns, I don't know where that came from.

"See by us going over there in person, Warren, we're not just the people next door—"

"No, we're the weirdos next door. Butt off, Tiffani, okay? Nobody wants any part of us." His arm is flung over his face, shielding him from the light, from me even. It's one of those awesome bright days when the air is juggling its allergic froth as though some giant bratty child had huffed on the world's exploding cattails and dandelion heads. I sneeze twice. Warren doesn't bother saying Gesundheit, he just waves the germs away. I don't say excuse me.

On Thursday when Warren rolls out our garbage can, there is our loaf of bread still with its gold bow in with Miss Clausen's trash—her morning lemons and iron pills bottle. Warren holds it up silently. Okay okay, I say. I have to admit it looks pathetic. There's a potato peeling adhering to one end.

"I told you," Warren says eventually.

"Here, give it to me," I say. I divvy the bread up for breakfast.

"It's still fresh. It keeps a week." I put some on to toast. "At least we tried, we gave it a shot."

"What's that got to do with anything?" Warren says. "It flubbed."

"Yah," Lindy says. "It was a dumb idea." She swivels around on the bar stool, hands under her hips like she's gathering up cellulite, hardening it the way fat people do, shards of hatred that slice into you.

"Jesus, Tiffani! You're not paying any attention again!"

Smoke is pouring out of the oven (we unfortunately don't have a toaster). "That's carcinogenic like anything," Warren says. He opens the door and stands there fanning out smoke.

"She doesn't care," Lindy says.

They are both glaring at me like I'm a stale potato chip, a death ray, a major malignancy, just because I made an effort. It was Paula's dumb idea anyway.

XVI

As the hearing gets closer, everybody gets more uptight. Wookmook judges things so precarious that Carla's place is not to be filled until after a decision is reached by Judge Reilly. That's because they think we're going to lose, Warren says, and they don't want to go moving somebody in and have to kick them out again right away along with the rest of us.

Miriam Myers keeps beating on us all to be as quote productive as possible. We each have an appointment to see Ruben Esposito, Wookie's Job Finder. I tell him I would consider being a fashion photographer and he says how about yard pick-up at Burger King? And I tell him he's not hearing me, that I feel threatened when people don't hear me. I've learned that when dealing with the System you must sound as much as possible like the System. But even then it doesn't fly.

Miriam Myers is in cahoots against me with Miss Theriot at the county library. They really work me over good on the volunteer shit till I want to tell them to pee up a drainpipe. I just don't think people who are searching for their identity should be sidetracked by busywork. But what happens is Miss Theriot finally catches up with me and I agree okay, okay, this Thursday, 4 o'clock. Can they really count on me this time? For sure. They'll have a nice poster in the kiddies' reading room. Tales from Tiffani.

On Thursday I make a beeline for the library, stopping off at Jack London Square. I walk around thinking and not thinking. That is, I'm thinking about what kind of story to tell the audience that I'll be Pied Pipering. My Life by M. A. "Tiffani" Gilchrist. *Tiff: A Life.* I probably should make some notes or something.

There was that time when I went AWOL, when I was allegedly

kidnapped. I was fourteen. I could tell them about that. Kids really dig kidnap stories.

I spent two days in the closet of a model home in the Picadilly Downs subdivision in Menlo Park. I shared the closet with an Open House sign and a wiring diagram. It was dark and sequestered and smelled of new carpet. I had a carton of Milky Ways I brought with me. I came home once I'd eaten them all. Mrs. Emory, who was pregnant with the twins at the time, picked me up when I was coming up the hill on my way back. I went in the side door. M was cutting the points off an artichoke and she let out this little scream and dropped her shears. And then we hugged and everything and Mrs. Emory said she'd leave us alone to work things out, just as if she'd known all along what was coming off, which left me really ticked.

At first they treated me like a celebrity. For about an hour. D came home early from work and we went out to Taco Bell. Then they casually dropped how they were going to have to let Sergeant Pacetti at the Orinda P.D. know I was back and D said he wanted me to level with them, they weren't going to punish me or anything like that, but wasn't that my handwriting on the ransom note? It had my big hooks on the t's. The handwriting expert said it was. What handwriting expert? I wanted to know. His name was Mr. Teague, Raymond Teague. Actually they had an argument—was it Raymond or Richard? And by evening it was all why did I do this to them? Didn't I stop to think how they would feel? What kind of position it would put them in? The phone kept ringing off the hook as they say, and M would say she's all right, yes, she's home safely, that's all I can tell you, appreciate your calling, I'll get back to you, stuff like that. I thought the *Gazette* would at least come to take my picture (M and D gave them that yucky one of me in a Scout uniform when I disappeared), but they didn't and I finally said to M, who kept hasseling me, if you were so worried sick why were you spending time cutting the points off artichokes? I remember saying that. And D said well, we had to eat, didn't we? And I said, but artichokes? With the points off? You could have had TV dinners just as well if you were glued to the phone like you said.

That's a story and a half, but I don't know if I should really tell it to the kiddies. It's more at the teen level. What if they were to say why? Why did that girl do that? The thing is, I don't know why. Maybe if I told the story one of the kids could supply the reason. Throw it open for discussion, as we say in C House meetings. Anybody have any ideas why this girl took off like she did? What do you think? Was she bad? good? lovable? I really should make notes, starting with Milky Ways, why I don't like Milky Ways any more.

Instead I try out perfume testers at Payless till I smell like Forgotten Bliss, Fallen Angel, Aegean Isles, Serenity I, Fortuna, which is also the name of a Group Home where you have to have peer passes, they don't let you out alone and they ration your cigarettes and if you don't go to Small Group, participate, they take away your mattress. Fortuna is not for me. I give another squirt. Now I am Heaven Scent.

I get to the library at 3:30, which turns out to be half an hour early. It's also half an hour late because in all honesty I thought they said to be there at three. Nobody should be enslaved to the clock, it's part of the sickness of our society. I look at my watch and try to figure now that it's summer, am I back on track or am I still an hour off?

Miss Theriot sets me to checking out books, which was not, repeat not, part of the deal. If they have a current card, it's here in the file, she says, shoving a speckled black and white cardboard box in my direction and at the same time fanning away my eclectic bouquet. Miss Theriot's glasses bob on her chest on a black elastic band like they're studying her boobs. Unusual.

"What?" Miss Theriot says. I must have said *unusual* out loud, which M says I do, not that it's important one way or the other. I hope I didn't say *boobs*.

A little boy hands me five pennies in a baggie. "You don't have to pay," I say, "that's not how libraries work." (Paula still says lyeberry, she never learned. Sometimes she even says excape. Dean Witter doesn't care, I guess.) "I'm supposed to pay my fine money." he says. "It's for *Charlotte's Web.*"

"Put it in the drawer and have him put his initials on the list there," Miss Theriot says, pushing a pad at me. You'd think this was secretarial school.

Kids are beginning to mill around in the Children's Reading Room. My favorite fingernail breaks off and I eat it for something to do. I ask Miss Theriot if she happens to have a cigarette she could lend me, but she doesn't smoke. I note that my nice poster is simply a typewritten sheet that says Story Hour, Thursday at 4, Come and bring a friend. I ask her about the Tales by Tiffani and she says that the girl who was going to do the lettering got mononucleosis. God, I thought *I* was unreliable.

One kid I notice at the first crack. She looks familiar, which is impossible since I am pretty sure I have never seen her before. Tiny, about six, with gold buds in her ear lobes as though she was born that way, dark, a mixture of something and something. She's holding a Dr. Seuss book, *The Cat in the Hat,* and a child's guide to the stars.

"Hey, you with the face on," I say (kids like for you to be clever with them). "What's your name?"

"Doriejanus," she kind of mumbles the way kids do, they think everybody knows their name.

"Janus, that's her last name, look in the j's," Miss Theriot says. "Dorie Janus."

It hits me between the eyes, zonk: Carla's kid! Has to be. I am confused in a way that although I am used to being confused is new and different. I mean Carla was the one we all looked up to and now here she is in micro format with her books pressed to her tummy looking up at me, waiting for me.

"You look like your mom, you really do."

"I know," she says. "She's gone to heaven."

Miss Theriot takes Dr. Seuss from me—it's already been stamped, I guess by me—and hands it over to Dorie. "Now this time don't you go taking out the cards, Dorie, hear? Or we're going to have to charge you. And don't go leaving it in the rain either, okay?" But Dorie's off swinging from the carousel of new fiction and biography.

"Who does she live with?" I'm really excited.

"Dorie? Oh she has a foster family. In San Pablo."

Dorie has slender pipestem legs and little white sandals and somebody's gone and put polish on her tiny tadpole toes. She's probably too young to do it herself. "How old do you have to be before you can paint your own toenails?" I ask Miss Theriot.

"This is a library, not a beauty salon," Miss Theriot says, looking at me like I'm Bugs Bunny or something. "You best get started now or the troops'll get restless."

It's pure Carla, a strain of Carla that painted those nails, I don't care what you say.

"It's already ten after, Tiffani," Miss Theriot says, looking at the octagonal clock as it bites off minutes.

I go on over and I invite Dorie to join us for Story Hour. It's showtime, folks! Like that movie with Rod Steiger or Roy Scheider, I get the two of them mixed up. No, Steiger was the rabbi in something.

I squat down so that we're eye to eye the way you're supposed to with kids. I didn't plan to. I just did it. And I realize it's more of that phony we're-all-equal jazz. I'm doing it too. The exact same way Wookmook treats C House. Condescension. Meaning everything's a con and we all descend together. Dorie keeps pumping the carousel with one foot, appearing from time to time. I put out my hand and anchor the foot.

"Don't!" she says, just like Carla.

"Just leave her be, Tiffani, she may come on over on her own," Miss Theriot says.

"Are you Tiffani?" Dorie says from the far side of the carousel.

That really revs me up. "That's me! You got it. Your mom ever happen to mention me?"

"Uh-uh."

Oh. Of course she might well not remember. Someday I'll take her to C House with me. Away from the foster home. I'll keep her in my room, Carla's room. Maybe I can even find another one of those birthday cards, stuff nickels and dimes in the slots. I might even tell her it's something her mother wanted her to have, an inheritance. She'll call me Aunt Tiffy. Or Auntie Tiff. Or Antiphony. No—nothing with phony in it. I'll be a lot closer to her than to Paula's kids. Paula's kids, they'll be given the skinny on me before they're out of diapers. I reach out to pick her up.

"No, stoppit!" she says, very spunky. She stiffens and clings to the shelf that has *Twenty-Five Years of Princess Grace*.

"You have some customers waiting for you," Miss Theriot says.

Some customers? About three. No about—three.

There's this semicircle with these incredible little oak chairs and hardly anybody except—are you ready for this?—the kids next door. Justin and what's her name? Kate? And the kid with the fine money who is blowing up his empty baggie trying to pop it. Where's all the rest of 'em gone to? Miss Theriot plants a big chair for me in front of them. Carla's little girl runs over and skids into a seat on the end. Now we are four. She has on this little broomstick skirt with rows of puckered elastic around the top.

"Is this it?" I say to Miss Theriot. "Is this all there is?" I am really hyperventilating.

"Looks like it," Miss Theriot says. "Soccer practice got moved to Thursdays and you lost some there while you were fooling around."

Looking out at them, at their faces, I'm suddenly afraid. You can't trust a mob, you don't know what they're going to do. They might laugh or they might up and walk out on you, you just don't know. It's whatever the first one does. People are like sheep, kids too, only sheep don't shoot raccoons or make people get hit by diesels.

Thinking, remembering, makes my armpits clammy and I feel

myself blushing, flushing, whatever. I just can't stand eyes looking at me that way, boring into me. That's what happened at graduation, all those eyes with shadows to hide in and the lights burrowing in on me, exposing me like I was naked.

And now these kids. Can't take their eyes off me, that's the phrase. Why can't they? It's like they know something. I'm afraid of what I'll say, afraid of what the kids next door might say in front of Dorie, something about us or the house even that would get her wondering about Carla, about me. I'm sweating all over like I do sometimes. I should have made some notes, but I didn't have time. I should join Toastmasters.

Justin shoves Kate, which causes Dorie's book to fall off the chair. They all look at me. I'm shaking with rage. "See what you went and did? You made Dorie drop her book! Don't you dare to touch her!"

"Yah," Dorie says.

Justin's chin quivers. I feel like shit. Dorie draws her knees up and pulls her skirt over them down to the ankles. "It's okay," Kate says to Justin, sounding old as Methuselah, older than me even.

"Aren't you going to tell us a story?" Dorie says. "What story are you going to tell us? We don't like that about the little engine that could." They all just sit there looking at me, Justin sniffling. A fan is drawing the thoughts out of me, wafting them away, sending them into the stacks out of reach, along with my Heaven Scent sweat. I get up very quietly while Miss Theriot is running her magic lighted wand over a book, watching the computer like it's the Star of the East. I take off. It's certainly not my fault. If there'd been 30 of them the way there was supposed to be, I wouldn't have had to deal with each pair of eyes individually that way. Of course at graduation there were hundreds. I guess what it is, I just don't do well with eyes.

"How was it?" Lindy says when I get back.

"Gangbusters."

"Yah?" She's sitting at the kitchen table with her new purse with

14 secret compartments trying to figure what to fill them with when she probably doesn't have 14 things. "How many of them were there?"

"Oh I don't know. About 50."

"Fifty? You're kidding."

"Give or take a few. I didn't have time to count, they would have got too restless on me."

She's got on Bruce Springsteen, who she thinks is singing just to her. "Born in the USA." "So what did you read 'em?" She's swaying back and forth.

"Oh different stuff, a book about Princess Grace."

"Princess Grace?"

"Of Monaco. How many Princess Graces are there, you dolt?" I seem to be shouting.

"You read little kids a book about Princess Grace of—"

"No, I was kidding, joking around. It was one of the Pooh books, *Charlotte's Web,* that's what it was. Now get off my case, okay?"

I stomp off to my room like a Hell's Angel, fully intending to take two extra Mellaril and slam myself into the sack to exterminate the afternoon. I go into the can, duck my head under the tap—the glass is gone again—swallow my pills, and glance out the open window, line of sight into a sliver of the Ryans' bedroom.

There's good old Bernadette, mother of Justin and Kate, taking off her bra. Enter Art Ryan with an erection as long as your arm, poised at the ready. Your forearm, not your whole arm. Maybe it just looks big because the room is small. Four-thirty, happy hour. Artful Art is home early. I shrug. Wait a minute. This guy's blonde and heavyset. It isn't Art. Art is small and simian. But it's somebody I've seen before. Mentally I try putting clothes on him, try to place him that way. Suit, no. Jeans? Ten gallon hat? No. Let's try a blue backpack. Got it! Cyrano's! That dude who said Art was a schlemiel . . . that wife of yours'd drive any man crazy . . . that one. There you go. He's nuzzling her breasts. He's a dentist, probably has a good bite. And then in one swift master stroke he pulls her black bikini panties down, skimming them off like you peel an avocado. Biff? No, Cliff.

I tell you, this is really something else! It all falls into place, her kids shipped off to Story Hour. It's clever. Ingenious. Original. I could holler over to tell her they better make it fast, it was a short short story. Better not. If I did, Dr. Madsen would probably say my judgment was impaired. Judgment, judge, Judge Reilly. Then is when it comes to me, what we have here is a God-given or possibly a people-given opportunity.

I dash into my room—where'd I put it? Nikon where are you? I had it when I photographed my dream. Where's the Polaroid even? No luck. No Polaroid. I am such a loser, meaning I lose everything. I try to call on the saint of missing objects, but I forget his name. Not Jude, not Judas, they wouldn't have him in there. I yell for Lindy.

"Lindy, listen, can I have your camera? Can I just borrow it, *please* just for a minute!" I'm looking under stuff, throwing everything out of drawers, off shelves onto the floor.

"It's Mom's and she says never to ever lend it to anybody, especially not anybody in the house."

(That bitch!) "She wouldn't mind if she knew it was me, Lindy. I'll give it right back, five minutes tops."

"She's afraid it'll get lost."

"How can it get lost? All I'm going to do is take it into the john with me."

"You're going to take pictures of yourself in the john? That's sick."

I think fast. "Listen, Lindy, there's a box of Turkish Delight, I've got a whole box unopened, I'll give it to you after, okay. . . ? Great!"

I dash back into the bathroom, clutching Lindy's mother's Canon, locking the door behind me. It's on 11, but the question is, how many to the roll? And what am I taking? Slides? Prints? Kodacolor? I sure hope it's color.

Now where are they? Hold it, Bernadette. I'll preserve your posterior for posterity. Have they gone into another room? I'll kill myself. I am balancing on the edge of the tub. No! They are rolling around on what looks like a down comforter on the floor. Paula and Jake have a comforter from Scandia Down. They have two different covers for it, one mattress ticking and the other a city lights pattern. Forget Paula. Forget everything. Concentrate, for once in your life, try to concentrate!

Set for distance. Stop action. Twelve. Please, dear Heavenly Father, let it have 20 in the roll. If it has 20, I promise to not smoke more than two packs of Viceroy a day. Thirteen, phew! Click. One for Arbus. The phone is ringing. Fourteen! One for Avedon.

"It's your mom, she wants to know how it went?" Lindy says through the door. "And how many kids came."

"Tell her fine, Lindy, tell her 15, Lindy, tell her I can't come to the phone right now."

"Fifteen? I thought you said—"

"Lindy, please, I'm in the bathroom."

Now where was I? I hate for my field of thought to be broken into like that, but what can you do? Fifteen for Eisenstadt. I try to remember anything I ever knew about nude photography from that air-head Eckhart's class. Never overlight nude subjects, the duller the better. That's all I can remember. At the time I didn't like thinking about nudes. . . . They are on the bed. If I shoot into the mirror I should come up with a great three-dimensional shot. Sixteen for Weegee. Seventeen, Winogrand. Eighteen, Brassai, nineteen, Metzner, twenty, Cartier-Bresson—he believed in "the decisive moment." Got it, got it! (I know, I left out Ansel Adams, but he didn't seem right on. Likewise Karsh.)

"Where's the Turkish Delight?"

I flush the john for verisimilitude. "Be right out, Lindy girl," I say sweetly. Bernadette is lying on a hefty hip, drawing doodles with her finger on Dr. Cliff, DDS's chest.

My head is in a swivet. There's something I'm forgetting to do.

Oh yah. I open the camera and plop the film in my pocket. I take one last look so I'm sure I can document everything, pale blue down comforter, reversible it looks like. His skivvies or jockeys or boxers or undies on the vanity stool with the brass back and the mock leopard seat. Make-up mirror with circle of bulbs, tortoise shell plastic jewelry case, mirror tray with gold filigree sides.

I should point out at this time and for the record that I am not in any sense a voyeur. My role is simply the photo journalist relentlessly documenting life, recording the day's events, contributing to the visual history of our era.

My work will save us at the hearing. I will be the hero.

"Here," I say to Lindy, who has been pounding on the door.

"There's no film in it."

"I'll definitely get you another roll."

"Where's the Turkish Delight?"

"Saturday. I'll have my check and I'll buy it for you Saturday."

I close my door on Lindy's outrage. Okay okay. Believe me, she doesn't need Turkish Delight, all that gluey powdered sugar mess. She's as big as a whole harem already. People like Lindy need to be saved from themselves. . . . I just wish she wouldn't kick the door that way.

I get into bed. I've had enough stress for today, thanks. Perhaps in time I will learn to live with tension. After all, what is a diamond but coal that has been subjected to pressure, right?

Hopefully by my quick thinking, justice will prevail in the case of the People Next Door vs C House, Judge Quentin Reilly presiding. An eye for an eye—"Watch it, Lindy! If that door splinters you'll have to pay for it!"—a tooth for a tooth (right, Cliff?), a screwing for a screwing. Moses would love me.

Thought before sleep: I flubbed out in the library, which depressed me. So I left early so I came home early, so I caught Bernadette's matinee performance, so I'm happy again. There is a grand plan for things in the universe, I'm convinced, a tide in the affairs of women. On that not unwell turned phrase I close my eyes. The film is in a little canister under my pillow, the fateful lightning of its terrible swift sword about to be whatever it says in the song.

I dream of Dorie and Justin and Kate sitting on their little oak chairs, Justin with a tear in his eye, watching Bernadette Ryan pranging away in the Children's Reading Room beside the case with Ojibway Arrowheads and Useful Vessels.

XVII

Two days later at 5:45 P.M. I pick up my prints at Camera Eye in Berkeley. Being Berkeley they'll print anything with no big blither or negative flak. It's a straightforward down-to-earth community.

When I first rip open the envelope I about keel over.

"It's a mountain!"

The woman behind the counter leans over. "I'll say it's a mountain. A humdinger of a mountain. That's Macchu Picchu, isn't it? I was there in April."

"Macchu Picchu!" I yelp.

"It's just a little out of focus, hon, but you don't have to pay for any you're not satisfied with."

"I assure you they weren't on Macchu Picchu, there's got to be a very serious mix-up." I check the front of the envelope, nope, Tiffani Gilchrist, all right. Okay, okay—I snap my fingers—Lindy's mother had film in the camera, that's what happened. I whip through the first group—Lindy's mom on a burro, Lindy's mom and a giant tortoise, Lindy's mom and a street fair, a mariachi, a statue of a general on horseback, an alligator farm—till I come to the heart of the matter.

Let me say flat out, those shots were not to be believed. Kodacolor, thank God. Kodacolor's gotten quite good over the years. From the standpoint of composition I can't say they represent my best work, but remember I was operating under pressure, with time constraints and a camera I was basically unfamiliar with. There's one, I admit, where I cut off the heads, but that wasn't the most important part and you can see from the others it would be the same heads, you can match it up without any real problems, it's like folding a can-

265

celled check over so you see the signature and enough of the front to prove what you've got. Well, it's not exactly the same. Well, yes it is.

I choose two prints, representative angles and positions, to have blown up to 5 x 7, the same as Paula's wedding pictures, it's a nice size for framing. "Now I don't want them grainy," I say. "You've got to guarantee me high quality reproduction."

The Camera Eye lady looks them over carefully. "Well," she says, "you're not going to get every last pubic hair, I don't want to tell you you will, I don't like for people to be disappointed, but I'd say you've got the essentials and you've got good contrast with the blurred and sharp areas."

She speaks neutrally, professionally. I like Berkeley people, I'm comfortable with them. I exhale through my mouth. "When will they be ready? How soon can I pick them up?"

"Monday, after 5:45."

"Don't go losing them on me, okay?" An artist's nightmare!

"If we do, if that was to happen which it seldom ever does, we give you a free roll of film."

"Hey, don't give me a heart attack!" I say. It comes out kind of hostile. "That won't go any good. This is like a wedding or a baptism or a funeral or something, it only happens the one time."

She looks at me oddly, which I am used to but don't expect in Berkeley. "It's hardly ever anything gets lost. Often cases it turns up again. I wouldn't worry." She writes up the order. She has round writing with even loops to it, the kind everybody I knew in high school and J.C. had except me.

"Silk finish or glossy?"

"What do you think?" I say. (You can tell she really likes me.)

"If it was me," she says, "I'd sure go with the glossy. They stand out better in an album."

If she was me, then I would be her. I would wear a peach polyester uniform and sit in a little cage all day in the Globe supermarket parking lot. People respect you if you wear a uniform, they really do. When I worked at Wendy's, those four days in '82, I'd go across the street for coffee breaks and you could see they respected you, professional courtesy, they always came around with the pot for seconds. Partly it was the *International* on the pocket, Wendy's International.

"So what do you say?"

"What?"

"Silk or glossy?"

"Silk," I say.

"It's your life," she says like Paula. "And your pictures." She has hang-ups, you can see. She's not outgoing with the public.

I stop off at the U.C. Student Union for coffee. You don't have to be a student. And an almond croissant. I look at the pictures over and over again, from a professional point of view. You have to learn from your own mistakes. If I had had a long lens, I could have gotten a smaller range in sharp detail, but then it would have thrown the background out of focus and it was important that the bedroom could be easily identified as the master bedroom next door. You have to slightly underexpose the faces and bodies if you want texture and background detail. It was a trade-off. Even Cartier-Bresson would admit that. As it was I used a wide angle to capture the scene in front and behind the subjects or screwors. I'm not apologizing. Don't forget I was working under extremely trying conditions, like wartime, standing on the ledge of the tub, trying to steady the camera. . . . (A man in a turban pauses with his tray, pretending not to look but looking all the same. I put my hands over the pictures, wait for him to leave. The important thing is not to establish eye contact with people like that.) I remember consciously attempting to make myself into a human tripod, one foot ahead of the other, breath held, elbows in. Bipod in this case. Just before I shot, I let out half my breath, otherwise you have a tendency to tremble. At this point in time, let's face it, the esthetic considerations had to play second fiddle. I had time for only one truly creative and experimental shot at slow shutter speed, I think it must have been

1/60 at f/8, which made the subjects blur so that it looks as though there are eight of them, a real orgy. Like if you see a cat crossing the road you might think it had more legs than cats are actually known to have, it's basically the same effect, except with your cat there's no orgy. Not with just one cat crossing the road. All in all, I believe we have a viable product.

I am waiting impatiently for Dr. Madsen to come and get me. I always ask Kimmie, the receptionist, when the guy who comes in before me got there so I can figure whether Dr. Madsen will be on schedule or even does he maybe spend more time with my predecessor kook than with me? The reason why shrinks are called shrinks is because the time they spend with you shrinks as you go along. Warren had this happen too. First what they do, they explain how it's a 50-minute hour so they have time to write up their notes. But then once they figure out you're bonkers, they think you won't know 50 minutes from 40 from 25, you see what I mean? That's probably why they have this counting backwards by 3's test they give. If you can't do it, they know they're safe.

The one before me has a moon-shaped scar on his cheek and he looks like he might be more interesting. I wish I had more bizarre background material—I was beaten by my case manager, screwed by my stepfather, chained to the leg of a table for 8 days, something Dr. Madsen could really dig into. It seems nowadays anybody who's anybody at all's been sexually abused as a kid, it's like getting your driver's license.

Three years ago after I'd been coming for a while, before it was decided I would go to C House, he got the whole family to come in. I was very hyper—here, I'll get you coffee, it's decaf, that's all they have, I know you don't go for decaf, you want some coffee? I think they said no, but I got it anyway because I was more or less the hostess and then he came for us, I kept on telling them he would—pretty soon he'll come out of that door there and get us. Okay, Mary Alice, just calm down now, D said.

We all sat there in a row pleading for absolution—M and D on the black leather couch, Paula in the wing chair, and me where I always am, in the Eames lounger—don't sit there! I said to Paula, that's my place. How do you people think things are going? Dr. Madsen said. What do you feel Tiffani's problems are? Well, Paula said, by her not doing her part, not ever cleaning up her messes or anything, I feel like that she doesn't even want to get better. Oh, I have to disagree with you there, Dr. Madsen said. That was when I first decided I was in love with Dr. Madsen, that I cared for him more than anyone. I wanted to climb into his lap and go to sleep, let him deal with them, he would have known how, he's used to families of nerds. I wanted him to see how they'd messed me up, but I wanted him to like them too. Instead I started in yelling at Paula since Dr. Madsen's too much of a gentleman to. His wife must be just crazy about him.

Finally he comes for me. He has on his navy blazer, charcoal gray pants, and maroon polka dot tie, good.

"Well, you look bright eyed and bushy tailed," he says.

"Yah, really." He treats me like a child too, but I don't care. I'm a little immature, I admit it, but that's reality and it's mature to accept reality, right?

Dr. Madsen gets us launched. "Seems you've been on a pretty solid uptick. Do you agree?"

"Could well be," I say cautiously. Is he trying to sneak up on me?

"Why is that happening, do you think?"

This is clearly a trick question. Does he know something? I clasp the cashew-colored envelope in my lap—code name Cashew Picchu—and smile brightly (well, I can't see it, of course, Dr. Madsen doesn't go in for mirrors in his office, but I think it's a bright smile). "You're the expert," I say smoothly. "You tell me."

He smiles back. We go through this kind of volleyball all the time. He waits. At a dollar ninety-two a minute, he can afford to. He will let a pause ride forever. I've tried it.

"I think it had to do with Carla," I say.

"Yes? You were pretty dependent on her, weren't you? You let her take the lead."

"Everybody did, it wasn't just me. But after she died, I don't know. . . ."

"You started taking some action on your own, right? Without Carla or Paula or your parents to tell you what to do."

"Yah it was their fault, they all the time—"

"Now wait. Was it?"

"No, okay. Maybe not." (I really want this session to go well, it's important to me.)

"It seems you're taking things more in stride these days and that's with all the business of the hearing coming up too."

"Yep. That's because we're going to win," I say. I'm grinning, I can't help it.

"Attagirl," Dr. Madsen says. (He's folksy scientific sometimes.) "That's the spirit."

Finally we're in sync. I look down demurely at the envelope in my lap—started taking some action on your own . . . more in stride. I think how we've had this relationship now for three plus years and how we have a contract we made that I tell him everything. This one would really impress the beejesus out of him. I know it would. For one thing he thinks I should some day go back to my photography. I showed him a sequence I took of a sunset in Banff when I was 14 and also a shot of rafters on the Stanislaus River. Captures the spirit of the occasion nicely, he said. Should I? Shouldn't I?

"Come clean, Tiffani, you look like you've got something on your mind."

Do I sometimes look as though I didn't have anything on my mind? How can he tell? Some psychos think their thoughts are broadcast to the world at large. I thank God I am not one of those. I thank God it is not feasible. In my view, private ownership of thought is the Creator's greatest gift—never mind Eternal Life— without which life near term would be unlivable.

He sits there looking at me, leaning back in his chair, waiting. What the roaring shit, let's do it! Sometimes it's best to act spontaneously, gonna let my little light shine. I could use a few Brownie points now and then. So I explain to Dr. Madsen about the pictures, starting with how I happen to be in the bathroom—I was just taking my meds and how the kids were at story hour—

Dr. Madsen wants to get something straight, he's always wanting to get things straight, sometimes it's a real drag, it interferes with the flow. How come I wasn't *at* story hour? Wasn't I *doing* the story hour? Wasn't that the arrangement?

So I have to back up and explain the part about how I just happened to leave early. I tell him wait, it gets better. (He's so impatient!) I go right to the people next door, Bernadette that is, and the pictures and Cliff and how I wasn't used to working with a Canon, but how nevertheless the results were dynamite. Dynamite! I talk kind of fast when I'm excited, what's called in the mental trade a flight of ideas, I believe. Dr. Madsen puts his hand to his temple as though he's supporting his head. It's like he's troubled.

"Tiffani," he says. "Let me get this thing clear, out of the box. You took colored pictures of this Mrs. Ryan . . . ah, having sex with some guy you'd seen her with at a restaurant?"

"Cyrano's," I say. "Over on Walnut. It's the one with the water wheel, you may have been there, they have a Merchants' Special. Here, you want to see? I just happen to have a few of the shots with me."

I spread out the pictures along Dr. Madsen's desk, moving his glass owl and a coffee mug that says "Olympiada de 1968, Ciudad Mexico." It's kind of exciting bending over his desk like a Kelly girl.

Nevertheless I go back and sit down, swinging my foot, waiting for what he'll say. For some reason I'm a little jumpy and tensed up.

He's looking at them carefully.

"See, if I'd only had my Nikon. . . ."

"Jesus Christ," he says finally.

All of a sudden I begin to have an anxiety attack, I don't know why, it's something to do with his expression he has. It begins in my stomach, a queasiness that sends runners to the tips of my fingers, to my scalp which prickles, my eyelids that twitch, my heart that hiccups, my glands that melt down the lump of uneasiness, process it into sweat. "I hope the pictures don't shock you or anything," I say. "I'm not real sure what they're doing in that one there, the third from the left." Dr. Madsen probably knows. I wish he would say, but he doesn't. "See, with these we can discredit anything Bernadette Ryan could possibly say about C House, right? . . . Don't you think?"

Dr. Madsen looks like he's ready for a stiff shot of Stellazine. "Tiffani," he says very slowly, which he does when he really wants me to get something, "I-don't-want-you-to-do-anything-with-these-pictures."

I barely breathe. In fact I don't breathe. "Why? It's the pot calling the kettle black, see." My voice yo-yo's up and down. "She's the pot and we're the kettle," I say, showing him I can deal neatly with proverbs, handle abstractions. *"Why?"*

"Because all they'd do, these pictures, is make trouble for everybody, you included. They won't solve anything. I want you to let me keep these pictures. No—better yet—I want you to put them there in the waste basket, just tear them up. The negatives too."

"No way! Whose side are you on anyway?" I am getting really agitated. I start pacing around, bookcase full of cases to door, door to bookcase full of cases. "I wouldn't have told you, but we have this contract."

I get to the desk, my side. I could probably make a quick grab for my pictures. I'd get at least some of them, although they might tear. If Dr. Madsen tried to stop me, I could bite him. Anyway I could always get more made, but they really cost. "I've been telling them at the house how everything's going to be okay, telling Warren and everybody to just simmer down, I have a secret weapon. These dealies will save C House's ass, don't you see, Dr. Madsen?" I hardly ever use his name, only in major emergencies, which he knows.

"No, Tiffani." I don't know is he saying no he doesn't see or just no, Tiffani, which it seems to me everybody is always saying, No, Tiffani, no. I get tired of the world's negativism.

I decide to spell it out for him.

"See, what I plan, I plan to let her go ahead—Bernadette—and have her say so, get up in front of the judge and carry on, rant and rave about Geoffrey standing on one foot, exposing himself, and feeding the raccoons, and Cathouse humping the Siamese, noise, candy wrappers, everything, anything her little heart desires, Warren revving up his Vespa, property values heading south, me playing my records too loud, picking their daisies (I'm sorry I mentioned that one, I don't think I ever got into it with him)—that was just the one time. All that free-floating flak. And then I'm going to stand up there very calm—you're all the time telling me to face things. I'll probably wear my gray jumper, the one you said I looked tidy when I wore it, remember? It was back in June when we were having the morning fog."

"Tiffani, I want you to sit down and I want you to listen to me. What do you think the judge would think of you for taking pictures like that?"

"What?" This is one of my life's worst moments so far. It is the same, the very same thing, as saying what do I think *he* thinks of me for taking pictures like that. He's got to first think what he thinks before he can ask what I think the judge thinks, right?

I start sobbing. "You said I was supposed to start acting independently on my own and taking . . . " I reach blindly for the Kleenex, which is green this month—"steps."

"Yes, but this is the wrong step, take it from me, Tiffani. This is *blackmail*." He says it like it's oozing pus or something. He's also sniffling. He does that. I push the Kleenex box his way, we are in this thing together. If I was married to him, I'd comfort him when things start getting to him like this.

I'm going, "Sorry, I didn't mean to make you cry too."

He goes, "No, I have allergies."

Allergies! Sheez! For three and a half years now I think he's been empathizing with me—I've even told Lindy how he cries with me and she's told Dr. Miller—and turns out it's all just mucus.

"With your permission, I'm just going to put these where they belong in the waste basket. And I want you to put the negatives there too."

"I don't have the negatives, not with me," I say. Untrue. I close my eyes. It's easier for Dr. Madsen to tell what's true and what isn't if my eyes are open, or anyway I think it is.

"Are you hearing me, Tiffani? I want you to destroy those negatives and I don't want you getting them copied or reproduced," He says. "I want you to promise, I want us to make a contract."

Turbulent silence. Shit! I squint at him.

"Okay," I say finally. "But if we all get thrown out on the street, it's your fault." (I usually don't blame him for stuff.)

"We're not going to worry about that, not at this juncture. You're a survivor. See you next week."

I don't bother saying goodbye, there's not that much between us. I sit down on the steps outside and have a cigarette. It's this redwoody building with planters and skylights that's supposed to be so warm and welcoming. I look back up at his window. Lighted. Somebody else in there getting worked over, displacing me, garbling my problems. He's not worried. . . . Well, I'm not worried either since I have no intention whatsoever of destroying my negatives. I may be schizo-affective, but I'm not a suicidal maniac. I must try and think calmly about the present situation.

For openers, I shocked Dr. Madsen. That's a terrible indictment of the medical profession, psychiatric division, which is supposed to say things like, so you just shot the Pope, hmm, well, were you upset about something? In other words, we expect unflappability like Julia Child, calm under fire like Roger Moore, although I liked

Sean Connery better. All right, you say, that's neither here nor there. And you're right, it's a side issue.

The main point is fairness. Bernadette and her bunch have no justification for getting C House closed down. All their reasons are a coverup for the real reason: the people next door don't want people next door who are different. So any little thing we do gets built up into criminality, obscenity, depravity, lethality, till it's Ity City, folks. It's an unreasoning blood hatred. No rentals to mentals! They could make a bumper strip. They want to torch us. So I say, fight fire with fire. They play dirty, I play dirty. What's more important, C House's survival or Bernadette's reputation? Like would I rather save C House than not be a blackmailer? (Actually I need to find something to be anyway.)

The world's great leaders have probably all faced issues like this. You can't always duck the tough questions. I am not a world leader, I don't pretend to be, I am not delusional, but when Truman decided to drop the bomb on Hiroshima, it was much like me deciding to lower the boom on Bernadette, which I haven't decided, but I'm keeping my options open, which is what Dr. Madsen in other situations counsels, always keep your options open, Tiffani. There is also the distinct possibility that all of us are crazy—me and Truman and Bernadette, Dr. Madsen even, Dr. Mad. I look back at his window and smile.

There's lunacy and rationality in all of us, just like there's foolishness and compassion. The world is a mix, a trail mix of nuts and Chex and dates and duds, hard kernels you work your way around or break a tooth on or swallow like pride. I have now spoken.

I take it back. In spite of everything I just said, and it's all totally logical, by the time I get home, I'm feeling pretty down. What do you think the judge would think of you, Tiffani? I go on up to my room and crap out under the covers, which I wish weren't so messed up.

I'll give you an assignment. Think of anyone you know, someone super sane even and pretend you heard he/she's in a locked facility, an L facility it's called, or a Group Home like Camelot—anyone, Bob Hope, Margaret Thatcher, Pavarotti, I don't care who you pick, and right away you begin to make it make sense in terms of little things from the past. Even Paula, I can even do it with Paula. (She used to be deathly afraid of dogs when she was little just because she was chased by a pit bull once.) What it comes out to, the human mind is infinite, a sea strewn with paper cups and orange peel and disconnected trash.

James Joyce had a daughter who was cracked. Linda? Lydia? Lucia? Maybe it was Nora. Finally he put her in this place, a sanitarium in Switzerland, but first he got a printer he knew to give her a job lettering, tried to help her learn it and everything. Like it was a sheltered workshop. When that didn't pan out, finally he went ahead and put her in this place in this little mountain town and he stayed three days not seeing her but not leaving either, waiting. For what? To see if her cries could reach him?—bore through the locked gates, skim the wilting edelweiss, hold past the willful scheming ants on the cobblestones. But between them was a river of tears wide as the Ganges. Or the Liffey.

I think of James Joyce lying on his bed the way I am, his nose in the waffle bumps of the bedspread, unable to move, the day beating down on him, pounding the poetry into meal, fragments so tiny you can't get ahold of them. No wonder *Finnegans Wake* is such a mess.

I decide to write a poem. I watched a program on volcanoes on KQED and it came to me you could do a poem on lava—red hot silent unstoppable—Mother Earth's menstrual flow. I would write my poem, but the paper is too far away and the pencil. I think about all the skittery still-born poems out of pencil reach. They disappear down a hole like clams and you're left standing there saying Hey you!

I flip over, light up a butt I find in my sneaker. You've heard stop the world I want to get off? Well, we're the ones who did, the original astronauts. The nuts, cranks, crazies, misfits, psychos, freaks, clients, consumers the System was invented for. Somewhere along the way we hopped off and we're each in a little orbit rotating with the earth. Sometimes our orbits intersect but mostly they don't. Each lives alone in a world of dark, crossing the heavens in a lonely arc. That's in "Lost in the Stars," which there was a year there when I played it all the time. I'd move the needle back before the record was quite finished till D got sick of it, hid the record. I think what he did, he put it in another cover, but I was too tired to hunt, I just didn't have that kind of energy.

I asked Dr. Madsen once what happened? What caused all this? And he just shook his head. It's an illness of the left side of the brain, he said, but nobody can say for sure how it got there. It could be the result of genetic loading or a biochemical defect or a viral infection or an excess of dopamine, which is a brain protein. It's multifactorial. Or what about what happens to you? I said. That too, it could be everything working together, or not working together. It's like war, he said, it is war in a way. You can't really say what caused it, you can just point to what happened. You can say somebody shot the archduke. I remember thinking I didn't know we were talking about the archduke, I thought we were talking about me. Sometimes even Dr. Madsen has loose associations.

I should get up and eat. I should brush my teeth, get into my pajamas if I'm going to stay in bed, clean my room, run around the block, look for a job. Dr. Madsen doesn't want me sleeping in my clothes. But Dr. Madsen has lost all credibility. Lost lost lost.

What's the matter with me? I am supposed to be this brain box. I know all these words. I help Warren do his crossword puzzles. Without me he'd be sunk. *Abulia* I gave him recently. Loss or impairment of ability to act independently. He had *a* space space *l i* space. It's true I had to use the dictionary but still. And what about *aloe, jeremiad, squamous?* Why doesn't the world see what's in me?

The good? I feel I'm talented with words and cameras. But talents are like tigers in a circus cage, either you shape them up, make them work for you or they eat you, it's that simple.

Eventually I get up and look out the window. A man is up on a ladder changing the marquee of Cinema I. *The Perils of Gwendoline in the Land of the Yik Yak* becomes *Ruthless People* and the man backs down the ladder, cradling his extra letters like a treed cat. That's my trouble, I'm in the land of the Yik Yak.

Next door new people, young ones, are moving into Miss Clausen's house with the aid of a U-Haul trailer pulled by a large truck that says Neptune's Whitewater Rafting. It has a picture of an alarmed surreal fish with a red eye leaping out of the way of a rubber dinghy. Miss Clausen was carted off to a retirement home a couple of weeks ago by her niece. I just hate to leave all my glads, don't you know? she said, looking back. (How about your beer bread, kiddo?) Watch your step now, the niece said. They really need thinning, Miss Clausen said. There's a curb there, the niece said. People often don't seem to answer each other.

I go down to watch the moving in. It's no work and free entertainment. I sit side saddle in the overstuffed chair on the porch smoking and pretending to read. They carry in one of those Japanese futon bed things. A round oak table. Paula and Jake have one too. Ferns in pots, ferns in baskets, ferns in wrought iron stands. A white rug. A butcher block deal with a back to it, unlike Paula's.

"Got it?" he says to her.

"I can't," she says. "I keep losing my grip."

"Yes you can. Go ahead and grab it from underneath."

Apparently she can. The girl has long cautiously blond hair tied back with a piece of purple yarn. He's dark with ripples of sideburn. Sort of Warren-looking except he seems to be more of a doer. He carts in endless boxes, his shoulders rounded from the strain. Must be strong as a horse.

At one point they sit down under the cherry tree and eat stuff out of little white paper buckets with metal handles that delis give you. He tips up his bucket and lets something hiding in a corner slide down his throat. They seem to be drinking those squatty bottles of natural juice, dark, possibly boysenberry-apple at a guess. "Okay, Sherrie," he says eventually. "Back to the salt mines." She groans and he pulls her up, bracing his feet against hers. They glance over. I wave on a small scale such that it could be construed as heading off a fly. She waves back! I consider offering my help but what if I got a hernia and caused them a big insurance problem. Anyway I'm too bushed.

I go inside. I think of them after everything's moved in having a glass of chablis—no, hot sake if they can find a sauce pan—and doing it on their futon. Futon sounds depraved all by itself. Where's my camera? Yecch, I hate myself all over again.

XVIII

Finally, ultimately, at last. It's October 23. The Big Day. Us vs Them. It's also the day the swallows leave Capistrano. Warren says they get it on in mid-air but nonetheless they are able to factor this fact into their flight time and take off and arrive on schedule. Is it possible I am becoming obsessed with sex?

Never mind. Now to the business at hand. We're on the third floor of the Civic Center, room 315. All surviving C Housers, plus Sheila, Howard, M (D had to bid on a construction job in Daly City, the housing industry having begun to pick up), and of course Miriam Myers and our Legal Aid rep, Sondra Huling. As many parents as possible are urged to attend to give credence to the respectable hard-working law-abiding tax-paying middle class background of the residents according to counsel.

M is wearing the bracelet Paula and Jake brought her from Brasilia, fragile threads of silver twisted into llamas with jade eyes, which I would certainly have preferred to the flea market mierda they brought me—a papier mâché piranha mask, a religious figurine, and a straw shoulder bag.

Instead of my gray jumper, I am wearing my poplin skirt and alligator-on-the-pocket shirt. The alligator is for luck—I will rise from the depths and smite them. Izod is odd and I's odd too. I brought *F.P.,* my chronicle, along just in case, but actually since the photo opportunity came up, I haven't been too good about putting in new entries. The prints, the second set, Exhibits A through F (for you know what) are in my purse, which I pat for reassurance every ten seconds. Long term I would not make a good Tiffani the little drummer girl. I am simply too jittery. Any little thing throws me off—wind, brakes screeching, somebody scratching themself. If I'm at all keyed up, like take now, everything amplifies, comes at me at once. I am a finely tuned instrument, an emotional Aeolian harp. There's a contradiction there somewhere, but fuck it, I'm too busy to concern myself.

"You look nice, dear," M says approvingly.

"So do you," I say. She looks surprised. Little does she know.

She and Sheila take up where they left off at Thanksgiving.

S: "I feel looking back on it, I feel like if I'd just of joined a church when she was growing up, but I just never was a joiner."

M: "I see what you're saying there. Me, in my case, I always thought if I just did things right—as right as I knew how—was there when she got home from school, did a stint as room mother, I even made poi—"

S: "You made poi? I did too! When they did their unit on Hawaii."

M: "Right. Of course she wouldn't touch it, Mary Alice wouldn't. She always was such a finicky eater, is to this day, but I thought everything would turn out, you know, basically all right."

S: "And their lives would be better than ours—because we knew more about child rearing than our parents did, we'd correct what was wrong, not go switching left handers to right handers and all that."

M: "The worst is you don't trust your instincts any more. You want to reach out, touch her—"

S: "I know what you mean."

M: "But they say it's supposed to be a—you know—a low-keyed thing, that they're better off without a lot of emotion coming their way."

I've had enough of their half-assed hindsight. (Come to think of it, maybe it was the poi that did us in.) I am gathering up my belongings—purse, cigarettes, lighter, purse? oh, I'm holding it, folder.

"Where are you going off to?" M says. "Shouldn't you just stay put now?"

"Outside to have a cigarette," I say. "To make my life better."

Sondra Huling from Legal Aid talks to us in the hall. Pre-game huddle, gang. Go Niners! I try to get us to put our arms on each others' shoulders, but nobody gets the point. Sondra just wants to be sure we have our side of the story down pat if the judge should ask us, direct any questions at us. And also that everybody has a goal. Judge Reilly often asks young people what their goals are, so we should remember that his bark is worse than his bite, he has kids of his own. She doesn't say whether that accounts for the bark or the bite. He's basically fair is the thing, she says. "Didn't he preside at your conservatorship hearing, Geoffrey?" "Kenneth, what's the frequency?" Geoffrey says. "Oh," Sondra says, "well okay."

Sondra wants to know how we wish to be referred to, as mental health clients? Or consumers? Or what? She has lipstick on her front tooth. "Residents," I say. "Consumers," Warren says. "No, clients," Lindy says. "People next door," Geoffrey says. Everyone looks at him as if he said something deep. Is this possible? No, it's too absurd, Geoffrey's brain being gridlocked. "Well, okay then," Sondra says, "if there isn't a definite consensus of opinion, I'll just go ahead however it comes out. Just as long as I don't say patient, right?"

She goes on to say she doesn't plan on bringing up anything about somebody shooting the raccoons and leaving them on the doorstep.

We all go, "Why? why not? Fuck that!" etsoforth.

"Shhh." She puts her finger to her lip. "Take it easy now. Easy. For one thing there's no real way to pin it on anybody, it's all circumstantial, and for another it paves the way for the other side to bring up the matter of the raccoons being there in the first place, which gets into the area of nuisance abatement, which we definitely want to stay away from. We don't want to play into their hands. The whole issue of the raccoons would be something the judge would have to weigh and you never know what goes on in their pointy little heads, you see what I'm getting at?" She pauses, frowns. "Now I don't by any chance want any of you to go repeating anything that's said out here, this is privileged, confidential, between client and counsel, okay? Just like if it was with your therapists."

"You mean what you said about not knowing what goes on in the judge's pointy little head?" I say.

Sondra looks pained. Aghast maybe is the word. "Let's not get flip," she says. "What we want to do is stick strictly to the issue, which is that no zoning laws are being broken at Camelot House and that it is, in fact, functioning like a family unit, got it?"

Nyloned secretaries with slit skirts zip by. One with black blunt cut hair holds back a red tie when she drinks from a fountain.

"Any questions, gang? Okay then. Onward and upward." She makes a victory sign. Everybody but me looks blank. I have victory in the bag. My bag.

Bernadette Ryan sits at a table beside her lawyer. She is representing the neighborhood group. The other Friendly Local Homeowner Assassins are studded through the courtroom like the Red Brigade.

It's Bernadette's big deal, you can tell. She's got on one of those suits women wear to look like men, flannel with a pin stripe and a blouse with cuff links and a bow tie and high-heeled domineering pumps and one of those Gucci striped purses that people only have so you know they have a Gucci striped purse. And the silver streaked hair.

"She looks different dressed up," Lindy says.

"She looks different dressed," I say enigmatically.

"She looks different," Lindy says. It's like we're playing some dumbass sentence-shortening game.

The Ryans' lawyer is an indefinite beige—tan suit, sandy hair, manila folders. The toes of his shoes have a pattern of punched-out holes. I wonder what failed artist now designs the dots in men's shoes, pointillism revisited.

I am unhappy to learn the lawyer's name is Marvin Abrams. I don't believe the Ryans have any right to a Jewish lawyer when we have a Gentile legal aide with lipstick on her teeth, which is equivalent in paralegal terms to egg on your face. Where is the justice? I sigh windily, sit back, clutching my purse, the contents of which will soon be admitted into evidence. I am like Reagan with my finger on the little black box.

"All rise."

The judge flows in, gown streaming. He not only doesn't have a pointy head, it's shaped like an acorn. A nut for the nuts?

"Try and not giggle that way," Miriam Myers whispers.

Mr. Abrams makes an opening statement about how he will illustrate the problem, Your Honor, with an example, namely and to wit Bernadette and Arthur Ryan, who saved for three and a half years, Arthur Ryan, a stationery and greeting card salesman, even moonlighting at a shoe store for the down payment on their dream home, which they now feel for reasons contained in the brief to the Court, is threatened by the existence of a noxious facility for the mentally ill next door. He glances over our way when he says this. A facility, the establishment of which the Ryans and their neighbors had no voice in. His clients, he must stress, Your Honor, have absolutely no prejudice whatsoever against any segment of society, but the particular individuals involved in the said facility have caused circumstances to arise resulting in anxiety and mental suffering for the Ryans and their neighbors. (Question: are the Ryans and their neighbors therefore mentally ill as a result?) The Ryans have two young children for whom they wanted the benefits of the West Hamilton school system. If Your Honor pleases, here is a picture of the family in happier days.

Sondra objects, which I could live without her doing, in view of my forthcoming pictorial presentation.

"Objection sustained," the judge murmurs, which does not bode well, as they say, whatever boding is. The judge's glasses seem to have fallen down his nose on a flume of sweat. He pushes them back up. His head may not be pointy, but his nose sure is.

It is not just the Ryan children, Mr. Abrams says, it is all young children in the elementary grades who must pass unescorted by this facility on their way to and from school. Mr. Abrams goes on to say that in the past year the Ryans have been continually harassed by a series of incidents emanating from the subject house which are also listed in the brief, including but not limited to indecent exposure in the viewing range of these impressionable young children, motorcycles of excessive loudness departing at odd hours, debris from junk food strewn on the surrounding lawns, raucous arguments, records played at unacceptable decibel levels, and generally bizarre behavior.

"Quack quack," I say, meaning like a duck and also like a quack.

"Shh," Miriam Myers says.

Abrams glances at me. I smile. (I have for you el mucho surprise, muy señor mio.) He looks away—I have the bastard on the run.

Mrs. Ryan will be happy to elaborate with dates on each and every one of these and other incidents that have plagued the neighborhood.

"Roll on Missouri!" I say. Mrs. Ryan has her legs crossed and she is swinging a foot. She makes me sick. I guess I must have said something to that effect out loud because M raises her eyebrows at me.

Mr. Abrams glides forward. His voice is mild, reasonable, oily, disgusting. "The land deed on the Ryan property, indeed on all the lots in the Stewart subdivision, carries the restriction limiting the property to single family use, R-1. Now, clearly, a halfway house, or group home, if you will, does not constitute a traditional family household within the usual definition of the word family. In similar cases the states of Maine and Ohio have upheld the concept of the primacy of the family unit in opposing treatment centers within residential neighborhoods.

"Family, as each of us understands the term, refers to marriage partners, parents, if you will, and their children, that's the standard nuclear American family, as envisioned by the Founding Fathers. Within this context responsible adults are in charge of those whose judgment is insufficiently developed to function without that guidance. Now, in the case of Camelot House, we have a group of individuals, unrelated, with no blood ties, whose behavior is seriously impaired and yet who claim to function in a community on equal terms with that community without any supervision whatso—"

"Objection!" Sondra says. "Camelot House is the most advanced of the group homes within the West Hamilton mental health system. While it's true that the other group homes in the county—Serendipity, Everyberry, Wish House II, and Fortuna—all have live-in staff, the young people at Camelot have been carefully selected and are capable to run their own affairs. But should they encounter difficulties, counseling help is available to them on a 24-hour ad hoc basis—"

"But not, clearly not, Your Honor," Mr. Abrams says, "in the sense of live-in house parents. We don't doubt that counselors are theoretically available, but if the residents do not initiate contact, then we have the kind of chaos of the unsupervised that the Ryans and their neighbors are very legitimately objecting to. There is in no sense on-premises supervision at Camelot House. Not by any stretch of the imagination. Where are your mitigations? If, for example, there is non-compliance in the taking of requisite medications on the part of these . . . mental people . . . we have a very definite threat to the community, a negative environmental impact. Additionally, the location of Camelot House near to a busy intersection makes it disadvantageous for the mentally ill with impaired concentration, one member of whom has already been killed in a tragic automobile accident. Essentially, the essence of this case, Your Honor, lies in the interpretation of the word *family,* with all the rights, responsibilities, and loving curbs that the term implies, and with the concept of compatible use in a familial neighborhood."

"This bozo ought to sell time-sharing at the North Pole," I whisper to Warren.

When Abrams sits down, Mrs. Ryan puts a hand on his arm, leans over to confide something. Watch out, Cliff old boy. "Rich man, poor man, beggarman, thief, dentist, lawyer—"

"That's enough of that, Tiffani," Miriam Myers says.

Our turn to bat. Sondra states briskly that the issue is civil rights. "Would Mr. Abrams and his clients wish to bar from their neighborhoods those who live with A Significant Other? Living trends in the 80's are changing, becoming more fluid. The courts in New York and Connecticut have allowed treatment centers in residential zones when those group homes function as quote single housekeeping units" (Sondra pantomimes the quotes with two hands and four fingers) "as is certainly the case with regards to Camelot House. In addition and more important, California courts as well as courts in New Jersey, Michigan, Minnesota, and New Hampshire have declared group homes occupied by six or less exempt from local zoning requirements. Accordingly, based on state law, WHCMHC, West Hamilton Community Mental Health Center, was not required to obtain a Special Use Permit, which was why adjoining neighbors were not noticed prior to the establishment of Camelot House.

"The group home that we are talking about here, Your Honor, has in reality a very stable population, carefully screened, whose dysfunctioning relates mainly to their own feelings of low self-esteem. They are in fact contributing members of the community."

"Contributing litter," the jogger says under his breath.

Mrs. Ryan turns and winks. Go right ahead, lady, have your fun. Comedownance is coming. I wink back, which surprises her.

"One of the current residents works in an auto parts house, another contributes time to the local library, a third participates in a sheltered workshop, and the fourth is involved in a beautification plan for the freeways. The residents are goal-orientated and vitally concerned about their relations with the larger community of which they are a part."

Sondra then reads a letter from Mr. Nelson Wodinski, our absentee landlord, who lives in McMinville, Oregon. (First I ever heard of *him*.) He states that he is well satisfied with the way in which the property is being maintained and as far as he is aware all terms and covenants in his rental agreement with West Hamilton Mental Health Services are being met.

Mr. Abrams would like to address yet another issue. It's hard to put a finger on it, but you get a gestalt for it: the economic impact of a halfway house in the area. It's a known fact that they're causal of property values to drop, stemming from houses being put up for sale or turned into rental housing. Pursuant to this, he'd like to call on Yolanda Cassidy, the listing realtor of the Clausen house.

She states under oath that the Clausen property, Mrs. Enid Clausen's home, was recently sold 10 percent below market to Ogden and Sherrie Hibbard because of the presence of a residential care facility next door. Money now having reared its ugly green head, the courtroom is suddenly very quiet.

"You felt it necessary to tell your purchasers—the Hubbards—of the presence of the facility and to explain its nature to Mr. and Mrs. Hubbard, did you, Mrs. Cassidy?" Judge Reilly says.

"The Hibbards. Oh very definitely, sir, yes, I would never not tell potential purchasers anything like that that I knew of. For one thing it's against the law to withhold information that could materially affect the value of a property, I could lose my license, but even apart from that, why I just wouldn't feel right, I couldn't do business that way, life's too short. I get most all my people on referral, you see."

"Your feeling then is that a so-called group home lowers the value of the surrounding property?"

Yolanda Cassidy wets her lips, looks over at us, scratches a speck on her skirt. "To a certain extent, I hate to say it, but yes, sir, I do."

"And that extent is 10 percent?"

'Well, that's what it sold for, 10 percent under market, that was the discount on the Clausen property, judging by the comps we have in the Stewart subdivision, yes, sir, and that's not taking into account extra amenities like the wishing-well fish pond that the Clausen house has in back or the cedar-lined closets which were customized. I'd say all things considered, 10 percent is probably a conservative figure."

Sondra then asks if it was not also true that the Clausen place had no in-place assumable financing? And wouldn't it be true that since the purchasers had to go out and obtain a new loan at a high rate of interest, paying points, et cetera, that this might have disadvantageously affected the price?

Yolanda Cassidy looks at Mr. Abrams, who is looking at a pencil. Not in this particular case, no, she really doesn't think so, because as it happens the young couple who purchased the Clausen property were in a position to make an all-cash offer if they had so desired. It seems that Sondra is rebutting her head against a stone wall. Or a wishing well.

"I take it," Sondra says, "that since the existence of Camelot House was clearly explained to the purchasers, they had no objection to its proximity?"

"They didn't seem to, no," Mrs. Cassidy says. "Oh she did say to me, she did ask once if they were, you know, violent or anything like that."

"And you were able to reassure them?"

"I told her not as far as I had any knowledge of, nothing I had ever heard."

Mr. Abrams then reminds the Court that the young couple next door have not, as yet, suffered any of the annoyances and harassment that long-term residents of the community have experienced. Moving on, he would like to direct the attention of the Court to certain very specific complaints, with reference to which the most serious is the charge that one of the residents was seen in full view of the Ryan children exposing himself on Thanksgiving Day—

Sondra then interposes a statement to the effect that the residents were in fact entertaining their families—these same families represented in this courtroom today, a rather considerable undertaking, and that on this occasion with five residents and four guests—

I punch Warren, she's got it wrong, we told her straight, but she's gone and got it bollixed up—there were five guests, M and D and Paula and Sheila and Howard.

". . .and only the one bathroom, the bases were loaded, so to speak, and one of the residents merely sought to relieve himself in the privacy of his own back yard."

Howard puts his arm around Geoffrey's shoulder. Miriam Myers got Geoffrey a navy serge suit from the Grace Cathedral Thrift Shop. It belonged to somebody in the boys' choir who the volunteer on duty told Miriam Myers had shot up over the summer. I don't know whether she meant heightwise or drugwise. Anyway Geoffrey looks really spiffy. He has a red veterans' poppy in the lapel, I don't know where that came from, and no hat, so he is virtually incognito (which nevertheless sounds like somebody who has slipped his cogs).

If the Court please, Abrams says, all righteous indignation, a functional adult in our society does not *merely* relieve himself in public on Thanksgiving or any other day of the year for that matter. It is not within the bounds of decency. It is offensive, inappropriate, abhorrent, and abnormal.

(You can well imagine how he was toilet trained. A gold star to that mama.)

Objection, Your Honor, objection! No indecent exposure whatsoever was intended or occurred, Sondra says. The incident referred to—albeit exposure—was not indecent, nor was it intentional, and therefore not a substantive offense. Further, the subsequent hullabaloo over this triviality has been a source of grave embarrassment to the resident involved and to the other residents and staff.

With respect, Mr. Abrams says, he believes the Court will find otherwise. He summons Mrs. Ryan.

At that Sheila lays aside the needlepoint lamb she is embroidering, hooking the needle in the canvas. "Don't you fret now," she says, leaning forward toward Howard. "This is all just whipping a dead horse." Which was the wrong thing to say in Geoffrey's hearing. He starts pulling his ear, which he does when he gets upset.

"If you will, Miz Ryan, I realize this is difficult for you. . . ." He is speaking in a soft consoling voice. "If you will, please, tell the Court what you observed on Thanksgiving Day afternoon."

"Well, I was there working away in the kitchen, unmolding the cranberry there in the sink. I had the mold in hot water, as hot as I could stand, and I'm there at the sink counting to 10 when I notice that Justin, that's my little boy, aged four and a half, and I see how he's looking real intently out the window. He's a little peanut, short for his age and his head just barely comes to the sill, you know, and the next thing there he is dragging one of the green kitchen chairs over and I say, Justin, honey, get down off that chair but then instead he says right out the way kids will, Mommy, he says, there's a man doing pitter patter."

"And what did you do then, Mrs. Ryan?"

"Well naturally, I dropped everything—"

"Naturally," I say. Miriam Myers gives me a System's look.

". . . left the cranberry bleeding into the sink and I ran over to where he was, to the window, and when I saw what it was, what was actually happening, well, I just told Justin very calmly to go on into the other room and call his daddy."

"Both you and Mr. Ryan witnessed this unfortunate incident then?"

"Oh very definitely."

"And how long would you say this went on for?"

"Oh I don't know exactly, I'm not real good at estimating time, five minutes maybe, a good five minutes, I'd say."

"Five minutes!" I can't help saying. "Geoffrey, you're a camel." Geoffrey looks pleased to be an anything.

"And what did you do then, Mrs. Ryan?"

"Well what we did, we went ahead and had our dinner first, just as though nothing had happened, we didn't want to ruin Thanksgiving, we had his folks and all and my brother from Chico. Art's mother just had her cataract surgery and she would have worried herself into an early grave if we'd of let on to her about anything like that going on next door, these are her only grandkids and she waited a long time for 'em. So what we did, we went ahead and put the kids down for their naps—Justin was so wound up he couldn't hardly sleep—and then Art stayed with the kids, we never leave them unattended, I don't believe in that, and I went on over there—I hated to do it, you know, on Thanksgiving and all, but I knew I had to. It was one of those things. I talked to them and made it, you know, very plain, crystal clear, that this sort of thing couldn't be permitted to go on. This is a family neighborhood from start to finish. I was just thankful for it to have been Justin, you know, instead of Kate."

"And what was the attitude when you talked with the people at Camelot House?"

"Well, I tell you, first one of *them* came to the door and it was clear, very evident I wasn't getting through, there wasn't any way. . . ."

I open my purse, check to be sure everything is there, in place.

"But then the parents, they kind of pushed the mentals. . . ." She looks at Abrams ". . . the mentally handicapped?" He nods. "The mentally handicapped inside and they were nice enough considering. I have to say in all fairness they seemed like decent people, we felt real sorry for them with this burden. They knew what I was talking about, they knew, there was no question about it." She looks over at Howard. "One of the fathers, he just said how he realized it was regrettable and most unfortunate and everything like that, being as we had little children to think about, he understood, you know, how we felt, he was a parent too, but at the same time he didn't offer to do anything to cure the situation. On a permanent basis, I mean."

Howard puts an arm around Geoffrey, it's like life is giving him an opportunity to replay a hand and this time around he's determined not to muff it, but Geoffrey wrenches away and sits on a bench at the side. I think of Justin and Kate and their butterscotch hair, the way they sometimes dance around Geoffrey when he's out front saying can't you talk? can't he talk? and I think how they're not in the same league with Dorie with her tiny red jewel toes and her bronze skin.

"And in your view, Mrs. Ryan, this wasn't simply a case of just going outside to—"

"No, sir, you could tell it was thought out, premeditated. That one had his little dinger out and he was waving it to beat the band. At anybody who'd look." Mrs. Ryan's mother-powered voice is vibrating. The courtroom buzzes sympathetically.

"That's all, Mrs. Ryan. Thank you."

Mr. Abrams summarizes: It has been alleged that this facility under discussion has a stable population. In reality it has a turnover rate of one every 8½ months. Some of the residents regress—some of them have to be sent to Crisis or moved back to lower more restrictive treatment facilities when their behavior significantly deteriorates. This phenomenon is referred to by the West Hamilton Mental Health Center staff as the Revolving Door Syndrome—"correct me if I'm wrong"—he says, looking at Miriam Myers.

"Your Honor, I leave you with one, I hope not rhetorical question: Is this troubled shifting population what we want to see planted, intrusively, in a family neighborhood where folks live cheek by jowl, year in, year out, looking out for each other's kids, picking up each other's papers, and generally caring for each other and their community?

"We strongly believe in protecting the rights of the minority. Isn't the majority entitled to protection too? Thank you."

Sondra then says, yes it is true, some of the residents do move on, some to independent living in the community, some to jobs or community service. But for those who need the support, as long as certain performance standards are met, Camelot House is actually a haven that protects the community by providing viable shelter for what might otherwise be street people. She too has one final question: "Is this hearing a pro-active process or a proscriptive one?"

Everybody looks kind of blandly puzzled.

Frankly, I don't find Sondra's final speech a real stem winder. I find myself standing. I have a tight grip on my purse with Exhibits

A through F, but my *F.P.* folder slides onto the floor. "Your Honor," I say, "there is something I want to say if it's okay."

"No!" Miriam Myers says. "Oh God!"

The judge peers down at me, ruffles the edges of some papers in front of him, glances over my head. I feel eyes boring into my back, rivet guns that tighten each vertebra so I'm rooted there.

"Very well," the judge says after an infinite pause. "If you have something you wish to add that is pertinent, the Court is pleased to hear it."

I swallow. I look at the floor. A clipping has come loose. I know that one. It's about carpenter ants that have been sent into space to see how gravity affects interpersonal relationships. I wonder if I should reach down and pick it up.

"You may identify yourself and proceed, young lady."

I turn sideways so that I'm not looking right at any of them. I hold tight to my purse, which I am not sure yet what I plan to do with.

"White asparagus," I say and I swallow again, "it turns green in the light." I clear my throat. "I'm Tiffani Gilchrist, C House resident." Warren is jiggling his knees. "And red peppers are just green peppers that have stayed in the sun—"

I look at M, which is a mistake. She's anxious, I can tell the way she keeps on licking her lips. She has her last year's Mother's Day purse on her lap, and she looks like she just missed the bus.

"Objection, Your Honor," Abrams says, "with all due respect, I submit that we should try not to stray from the issue at hand to matters horticultural—"

I freeze, studying my escape route. I could go out the door by the flag, down the corridor, burrow into the cafeteria. She does that, M would say, she panics. I could lay out the pictures first.

"Let her finish, Counsel, please, let her make her point if she has one," Judge Reilly says.

"Oh I have, Your Honor. My point is, it's the same with people.

Some just need more light and care than others and a few no matter what, they're just too fragile."

I look out at them, the eyes, the faces, some strange, some familiar, some curious, some threatening. I try and make myself hold steady. You can do it, Dr. Madsen says. What I have to do, I have to not let myself look at eyes, individuals. I have to focus out, keep the faces blurry, see the whole, not the parts, that's what the healthy ones do.

"I just want to say a little what it's like to be us. Actually everybody here in this room knows. That's because we're all of us psychotic at least a third of the time, eight hours a night." I stop to figure, be sure, is eight twenty-fourths a third? Yah, it's okay. "We all cross over in sleep. That's when you get hit with all kinds of queer fractured paranoid delusions. People chase you, do bad things to you, refuse to listen to you, frustrate you. You get into places you can't get out of. You're hungry and anxious. Things gain on you. You don't know how to handle what's happening, you don't understand. Everything's too bright or too dark, too loud, too sharp. You're afraid of what's going on in your head, you're afraid of what's out there gaining on you. Well, that's how it is with us even when we're awake.

"It's just that everyone has a right to be and to be himself—gay, born-again, schizophrenic, Vietnamese, a judge even, whatever, it's not in any way against the law." I try and think what a gay born-again schizophrenic Vietnamese judge would be like, I try to picture him (or her), which gets me off the track. My thoughts leap synapses like Chinese acrobats. Maybe Vietnamese.

I ask the judge if I can please have a sip of water, from the pitcher there. He doesn't even seem to realize there is a pitcher, but then when I point he pours some and hands it down to me. I drink it all to be polite and run my hand across my mouth. "Thanks."

"Your Honor, I'm not sure that's what I really wanted to say. Could we please just strike all that from the record?" I look over at the Court Reporter, at the silent typewriter. I want Judge Reilly to stop her, pull the plug if need be, that's very big these days, pulling the plug. I smile.

"Everything that is said in this courtroom is a matter of record," Judge Reilly says. "But you haven't said anything that will get anybody in trouble." He smiles. "At least not so far."

Not so far. . . . I guess he means for me to go on. I look at M and I speak kind of quietly. "It's like in your fairy tale where somebody's asleep, somebody innocent." I'm finally telling the story, the one M wanted me to tell the kids. "And then, see, this savior guy comes through the forest with a wand or a magic potion. A hunter from Stanford or Langley Porter or St. Elizabeth's. Somewhere like that. Maybe he was searching for something else even, a different cure, but he has the key—the drug or the laser beam. I know it will happen, I just don't know when. And then everybody'll forgive us. They were just sick, they'll say. Like diabetics. And now they're well. Someday we'll all wake up together." M has put on her dark glasses. I wish she hadn't. I want to speak to her privately, to her eyes, to the quavery skittish hope in her. "We'll walk hand in hand past the Hall of Mirrors—we won't even stop to look—and out through the great woods. We'll have clean teeth and clear heads and goals even." I look over at Miriam Myers. "Bank accounts in place of disability checks, families of our own, and nobody will look at us funny or not want us around or be afraid of us. But for now we're not doing anybody any harm, especially Geoffrey. Sure—we're not perfect, but we haven't done anything to get kicked out of our home for." I blow out some extra air that I don't need. "That's what I have to say to Mrs. Ryan at the present time." I look her in the eye, both eyes. I actually look her square in the eye! Her face is grim, unbuying. No sale.

I don't remember sitting down, I don't even remember walking back, except I think I bumped into the corner of the table where Abrams and Bernadette were sitting because that night I had a black and blue place about where that table would have been. All I know is I got back there to my seat somehow. No applause, no boos. No nothing. I made my speech, had my say. I even looked at them, endured the eyes.

M taps me on the shoulder. "I'm proud of you," she whispers. The funny thing is I was just going to turn around and ask her if she was proud of me. It was like we were in sync again.

"Thank you, young lady," the judge says, clearing his throat. I wait for his comment. It isn't that great. "The Court will recess till two. I'll meet with both counsels in my chambers at one o'clock."

I am still holding my purse like a grip on reality. Everybody starts filing out. The man—Lionel—who says he just came to observe stops to talk to M . . . should be proud, I think I hear him say. "I've heard them do it before," Miriam Myers is saying to Sondra, "a basket case in the morning and you bring them in for their conservatorship hearing and they pull it together like you wouldn't believe." Lionel shakes my hand. "Some food for thought there," the guy I've seen mowing his lawn says. Warren and Lindy go out together. I start to catch up with them. Success, noontime buzzes in my head, glasses clinking in the cafeteria, people talking out of range, like an embryonic hallucination. I wait for it to form, break out, but it doesn't.

Bernadette marches by me, stops, turns around. I smile graciously. Perhaps now she'll ask me to babysit, I could use the loot. "For your information, whatever your name is, I've never in my life heard such a pile of drivel," she says, "but you'll get yours."

I stand there smiling like an idiot. It takes a few seconds longer than it should for what she says to sink in, percolate. That's something about the illness, the Big S, sound travels slower, takes longer to get processed with all these sensations jamming things up. I focus on the receding pinstripes, which become a net, a web, a trap. "Hey, you, whatever your name is, wait up!" I catch her at the door to the outside corridor.

"Speaking of getting yours," I say—she is about to let the door slam on me—"how's your buddy Cliff?"

She holds onto the door. "Cliff?" she says. She has that expression cooks have when they're tasting something. "Cliff? Cliff who?"

"Cliff, the dentist, Cliff whatever his name is," I snap. "Four thirty-five, Thursday, September 11." Paul Newman couldn't have said it better, I firmly believe. (Or was it Wednesday? No, it was Thursday although maybe it happened Wednesday too.)

"What is this anyway?" She puts her hand on her hips. "I don't get it."

"You will."

"What are you, what are you talking about?" The challenge is back in her voice. I meet her cool gaze head on. After all I have had eyes on me, starting with Miss Clausen, and I haven't melted.

"Shall we go back inside where we can talk?" This time I hold the door, it's a good feeling.

I hand her the prints. She does one fast shuffle, sucks in her breath. She fumbles her way back to the artsy shot, the orgy where it looks like eight of everything. She lets out a squeak or a squawk or a croak, puts it on the bottom, buries it. "You dirty little tramp!"

"Madam," I say, "that is a classic case of projection, you can ask any mental health professional, don't just take it from me. Here— I can ask Miriam Myers to step back here for a—"

Bernadette gives a dismissive silent no, turns the photos face down, sinks into one of the chairs (it was the one Lindy was in and I wonder if it is still warm, she generates a lot of heat).

"I have no idea where you got these and I don't care to know," she says slowly. "It's not important."

"Fair enough," I say, although I'm a little disappointed. I wouldn't have minded being complimented on my photography, you know what I mean? The interesting use of late afternoon shadows, for instance.

"You might as well tell me, where *did* you get them? How?"

This is like conversations I'm used to. "It's just not important," I say. I consider sitting in the judge's chair, which swivels nicely, but it's up there too high. Also he might come back, say if he forgot something. "You happen to have a cigarette?"

"How about you tell me how much you want for them," she hisses. "I don't smoke."

"You're wise," I say. "A filthy habit." I am quoting somebody, I forget who. I stretch out in my chair. I am being languid.

"Let's get this debacle over with. How much?"

"For the pictures?" I say innocently. "They're actually not for sale." (It's probably just as well she doesn't smoke because I might have gone and done something really stupid for a whole carton, say.) "What I'm doing, I'm saving them, they're being saved for a photographic exhibit, a gallery opening."

"A gallery! Oh sure," she says. "Come on, what's your game? What do you want?"

It is insulting she refuses to believe that about the exhibit. I just wish I'd brought along my sunset over Kanaapali Beach shot, although it wouldn't have blended in very well. Or the white water rafting slides.

". . . tell me or aren't you?"

I am at a slight disadvantage, having tuned in late on the last interchange. I have to improvise. "It's simple," I say, "just tell Abrams you've thought it over, had a change of heart so to speak, and you've decided to cool it as regards C House."

"Shit! I couldn't do that, not even if I wanted to. They'd think I'd blown my cork. . . . I mean, I didn't mean that the way it sounded." She's looking at me edgily.

"No problem. In this business you get used to it." Pejorative expressions, I meant, but she may have thought I meant blown corks, or even x-rated pictures, no matter, people are all the time miscommunicating.

"Abrams'd never believe me." She's galloping her fingers on the arm of the chair. "What would I tell him?"

"Whatever you want," I say testily. I am just not at my most cooperative without cigarettes. "Just fix it."

"And what about the others? We're not the only ones, you know, not by a long shot. The neighbors? What am I supposed to tell them?"

I shrug continentally. "This is your Story Hour, lady."

"I don't believe this! . . . All right," she says, she's figuring, you can see the wheels going round as D says. "Suppose I try and back out of it?"

"You might want to consider saying you were influenced by the speech, my speech."

She grimaces. "That's for me to decide, that part." She picks up the pile of photos. "I want the negatives, what about the negatives?"

"Right here," I say. I hold them out, meaning out of reach, of course.

"How do I know you're not sitting there with another set? Do you swear this is it?"

"Hey, this is better than General Hospital," I say.

It is very interesting to me that she will apparently accept the solemn word of a loon. Perhaps she recognizes a fact little known except in the trade—people who are bonkers are not bonkers all the time, it's quite spotty. At times they—we—can definitely be relied on. "As it happens, this is it," I say. "It's for you to decide whether I'm telling the truth or not and what you want to do about it. And then, depending on what you decide, I have to decide do I say anything to anybody and you would then have to decide whether or not anybody is likely to believe me." She is looking confused, toxic, I have perhaps made it too complicated for her.

"Tell me one thing—does anybody else already know about this?"

I hesitate. I hadn't expected that one. *I want you to put these where they belong, in the waste basket,* Dr. Madsen's voice says. "As a matter of fact, one person does, but his lips are sealed. It's like a priest."

"A priest! Christ!"

"*Like* a priest," I say. She doesn't listen well. All of a sudden I've had enough. The game's over. I feel my energy level dropping. "You know what you have to do, Bernadette. Once the judge has ruled— satisfactorily, that is—I leave the pictures in the plain folder on the seat. You can pick them up on the way out. Unless you want me to send them over with the kids." I kind of laugh when I say that so she knows I'm not serious and I go to find Warren. He always has cigarettes.

At two o'clock Judge Reilly appears looking jovial. Good sign. He says: "I think we can wrap this thing up now on a basis that's acceptable to both parties. First, Mr. Abrams, I want to express the Court's appreciation for your client's willingness, in fact, enthusiasm in taking a flexible posture after this morning's proceedings."

I sock Warren on the shoulder. "Get this!"

"It shows what can be achieved when people of good will work together with respect for each other's point of view. Mrs. Ryan, I thank you and your co-petitioners for that. However, over and above any considerations of generosity and benevolent instinct, I want to make clear that the Court, while it appreciates and to a degree sympathizes with the anxieties of the Ryans, nevertheless has a clear and express mandate to encourage care for the mentally ill within the context of the local community whose support these afflicted citizens are vitally in need of."

The judge seems to look at me when he says this. Or possibly not. When everybody came back in, I thought they were all looking at me. The judge further states that this opinion follows from and is in line with the decision of the California Supreme Court on January 18, 1982, City of Torrance vs Transitional Living Center. This is not to say that in today's decision the residents of Canterbury House are blameless. They have not conducted themselves with the decorum and consideration we all owe to one another as neighbors, and that must change.

He pushes his glasses back, seats them on the bridge of his nose. "It is the opinion of the Court that Canterbury House does not need a Special Use Permit to continue operation. The Court would, however, like to meet with Mrs. Bernadette Ryan, Miss Marian Myers, Mr. Abrams and Miss Huling, and perhaps a representative of the resident group, the young lady who spoke to the Court, two weeks hence to see if an accommodation can be reached, certain compromises agreed to, such that the adversarial situation that has arisen in the neighborhood can be ameliorated. Possibly more conventional plantings could replace the front yard vegetable garden which some of the neighbors seem to find objectionable. Better planning re the use of toilet facilities at peak periods. Daily pickup of litter. A more tolerant and laissez-faire attitude on the part of the surrounding community. That is the sort of avenue of investigation the Court would like to see pursued by both sides. In other words, I want you folks talking to each other. Communication—that's the name of the game. Dialogue!"

Well, I think, that's one word for it.

"All rise," the bailiff says. We stand up. The judge goes out the side door.

"Hi," I say as he passes but he doesn't reply (I didn't say it very loud).

I grab up my stuff, my scrapbook. "We won!" I say, I sort of shout.

"Just barely," Miriam Myers says. "More like we squeaked by."

I *was* planning to walk out with her being as we are to serve on the same committee, which I—

"Pictures, goddam you!" Bernadette hisses.

Oh, oops, I knew there was something I was forgetting. I lay the envelope—code name Cashew Picchu—carefully on the chair and scram.

"Two cheers for the good guys!" I say in the elevator. (I don't know why I didn't say three.)

"In future let's not push our luck," Miriam Myers says.

I now know the difference between victory, which is mine and triumph, which isn't, where nothing's there nibbling away at you. "Wait!" I say, but people are already out of the elevator and off in their tight little clumps. M, Sheila, and Howard. Warren, Lindy, and Geoffrey. Sondra and Miriam (the judge thought her name was Marian) Myers.

"Going up?" a man says.

"No, I just came down."

XIX
"So, how was the meeting?" Dr. Madsen says. "I'm all ears."

Pause, meter ticking like a taxi. I am trying to figure just what and how much to come out with. There's an old saying—what people don't know won't hurt them. I'm not sure of the accuracy of this. For example, you're walking along and somebody, let's say it's me, I drop a humongous big rock on you, not that I would. But if I were to, well, it was nice doing business with you, only now you're a statistic. You never knew I did a number on you, you never knew there *was* a number, but don't tell me it didn't hurt.

Dr. Madsen writes something on the pad in front of him. I try to make it out upside down. Patients, consumers, I mean, are good at reading upside down. Reading practices are all cultural. The Jews go from right to left, the ancient Greeks switch back, right to left, and then left to right, and consumers read upside down. *Cleaners? shirts?* it says.

"I was just about to tell you," I say.

I give him a complete blow-by-blow description including as much as I can remember of my speech, which is in the neighborhood of oh 30, 40 percent, with I'd say 10 percent I-should-have-saids that came to me later. I do some expungification of irrelevant info like my talk with Mrs. Ryan, but I explain how I'm going to be on the committee, which I refer to as a consortium, to work out solutions.

When I'm done, Dr. Madsen says, "Well, Tiffani, I've got to hand it to you."

"No kidding? You think it was okay?"

"More than okay. You won, didn't you? And everything ethical and above board, no funny business."

I exhale deeply, get rid of all the carbon monoxide Warren says is poisoning us. "Like I say, Mrs. Ryan heard my speech, okay? And then there was this recess and then it seems like she had a change of heart." This is chronologically true, but possibly not causally so, if you want to split hairs (which puts me in mind of the fact I have a lot of split ends that need to get trimmed).

"Bravo, Tiffani, my hat's off to you."

He has begun to speak to me in proverbs . . . got to hand it to you . . . hat's off to you . . . like I'm some big abstractor, right along with Descartes and McNeil Lehrer. "You think it was good? From what I've told you? Really?"

"Better than good. Super."

"You're not just handing me a lot of gas? You think the speech was okay? You liked it, as much as I could remember of it? I could probably write it out for you, it wouldn't take that much time, bring it in next time."

"No, what I want you to do now is go on from here, build on that success."

He never wants for me to bring my poems in either. "You really liked the speech, huh? You're not just saying it?"

"Absolutely. You used words instead of trying to capitalize on some obscene pictures which would have done nothing except make you feel crummy about yourself. . . . Why the long face?"

I swiftly turn it into a short face. "Well, see Warren and Lindy, I don't really think they liked the speech even. They never said anything about it and when I asked 'em, 'how'd you guys like the speech? did you really like it? Warren said, 'Hey man, you could have blown us right out of the water with that stuff,' and Lindy said, 'Who okay'd you to show off—we never even voted on it.' "

"As to Warren and Lindy, you were assuming a leadership role, which they weren't, and they may well have resented what that said about their own limitations."

"Yah yah!"

"The chances are they felt threatened."

I love it. I smile like the Mona Lisa. No—Alec Guinness. Same smile.

"You had choices to make, a decision to make, and you made it."

I try to decide, did I decide? Or did it just happen like it happened? If Dr. Madsen thinks I decided, you better believe I decided.

"What I want to do now," Dr. Madsen says, looking in his blue spiral notebook, "I want to talk to you about a couple of other things. Number one—we're going to cut back on your medication, give it a try."

"Cut my meds?" I think I'm dreaming or delusional or something.

"You're on 200 milligrams of Mellaril now, we're going to try a hundred."

I sit there with my mouth open. "Beginning like when?" I finally say.

"How about tonight?"

"Tonight? Tonight. Well, okay. . . ." Then it hits me, really hits me. "Wow! You actually think I'm getting somewhere? You think I'm twice as healthy or half as sick? You think I'm improving?"

"Seems pretty clear, doesn't it? You've given some positive indications. Your overall demeanor seems more on the ball, you're tracking, responding faster—"

"Yah."

"Able to order your thoughts better."

"Right, right."

"You spoke out in a group, found you could work through this fear you've had of facing an audience. . . ."

"This is it." I want him to keep going, but he comes to a halt.

"An' I've started thinking about sex—I think about it a lot just like you wanted me to."

"Well, that's healthy, part of the pattern."

"I'll think about it more if that'll help." Shit, instead of counting sheep when I'm trying to go to sleep I could just as easily count—

"You've been taking hold ever since around the time of Carla's death, you've been developing. Once she wasn't around to make decisions, you found out you could. You're beginning to take on some responsibility. The hearing shows that."

By now I would actually like to be off the subject of the hearing. "I want to ask you something, you think Carla had to die for me to get better?"

"No. If that hadn't happened something else would have been the catalyst."

"I was just waiting to happen, like an earthquake, right?"

"That's one way of putting it."

"You think the judge decided like he did because of me? My speech?" Why do I keep going back to that?

"We can't know and it doesn't make any nevermind. The important thing is you were able to stand up there with people looking at you and by golly say what you felt was right."

Talk about being stroked—this is deep massage.

Dr. Madsen holds up two fingers, waggles them. I follow with my healthy tracking pupils. "Point number two. I want you to see about a job, a real one, start looking into the possibilities."

Job? Pride turns to panic, everything flips. What a bastard! Now I see where all the compliments were headed. I cringe. "Me? No I can't, I'm not ready, not yet. Maybe in a year or something. Next summer, how about? That'd be good, there're all these summer jobs floating around. Or a year and a half? Eighteen months, how about that for a timetable?"

"No, Tiffani, the time to try is now. Trust me. I've set up an appointment for you with Ray Pruitt at County Rehab, November 1, 3 P.M., room 114."

"Listen, I've already talked to the Job Finder, Ruben Esposito, somebody like that."

"No, this is different. Ray is hired to help with placements for people who are ready to start considering career choices, training if need be, who can be reintegrated in the work force."

He hands me a little white card. Ready to go back to work? Me? In the work force? I put the card down. "We'll start with a low-stress part-time situation and see how she goes."

"God, I don't know about this." I pick up the card, fold the corners in. I'm confused. I stammer around. "I probably just . . . yah, I mean I don't think I'd have the time, not with the consortium thing coming up and everything." Got to get out from under this job nonsense.

"Come on, Tiffani." He's watching me.

I shrug. If I'm better, I guess I can't just keep farting around any more. At least not completely. "You think. . . ?" I say. I stop.

"Yes," he says, "low pressure, part time. Definitely. For starters. I want you to be sure and keep your appointment with Ray now and I want you to check the classifieds yourself, get a feel for the marketplace, what's out there."

He waits. "You can do it."

"Okay, I'll give it a look. Now coming back, what I was going to ask, what I want to know. . . . You think I can ever be off meds? All the way? Totally?" I close my eyes, waiting for the answer.

"We'll see, Tiffani. We'll just have to wait and see. It all depends."

I want to scream, tell me, goddam you! I'm only 25, I can't flub along on *it all depends*es—what third am I in, good? bad? in between? I suppose he's just being honest. All he can offer is hope, support. No warranty, express or implied. (Except in Nebraska.) I smile.

He smiles.

I don't even stop off. I sail, float, skip, fly, dance home, passing right by two S and L's with free coffee and cookies and a bank with green and white mints.

Lindy and Geoffrey are glued to television, I think that's the phrase. The forty billionth rerun of "I Love Lucy." Lindy's shoveling in pistachios, the easy ones with cracks. The hard ones without a split she hands to Geoffrey to put back in the jar, which he tries to do without spilling Cathouse off his lap.

"Da da!" I say, beating my chest like Godzilla. "Dr. Madsen's gone and cut my meds in half!" I try to keep my voice steady, but I can't.

"So what?" Lindy says. "For God's sake, we're trying to watch something."

"I'm getting better, that's what."

"Jesus, anything would be an improvement."

"Did you hear, Geoffrey? He's gone and cut my meds, Dr. Madsen's cut me back 50 percent."

"You can have some of mine," Geoffrey says.

"You nerd!" I give his hat a tweak. He's back to wearing caps in the house and shoes without socks which leaves his sad naked ankle bones exposed.

I go looking for Warren. On the way I see that I have mail waiting for me on the hall table. A letter from Lee Iacocca forwarded from Poplar Canyon. He wants me to help him preserve the Statue of Liberty. I just may do that. I'll consider it. Funny how fast word travels once you're back on the stick.

I follow the sound of a guitar twanging away. "Listen, Warren old buddy, did you hear? I got my meds cut. Dr. Madsen cut me back from 200 to 100 milligrams, beginning right away. How about that? And Lee Iacocca wants me to help him refurbish the Statue of Liberty, it's corroded or something, all that salt air."

"They're done with all that foofaraw," Warren says.

"Yah, back in July," Lindy says. She comes in, plops down on Warren's bed, same side I was once on. "Where've you been?" she says.

There, I think but don't say. "I guess it got delayed in the mail, my letter." I feel a sudden need to change the subject. "Changing the subject," I say, "listen, Dr. Madsen says I'm supposed to start planning a career."

Warren laughs a short barking ha. "Frankly, your shrink's got his head up his ass."

"He does not! That's how much you know. Dr. Madsen says you

just feel threatened because I've begun to assume a leadership role, what with the speech and everything."

"That was a speech? About red peppers and green peppers?" Warren says. He crashes out chords on his guitar.

"Yah," Lindy says. "And white asparagus." She says it snobby, ass-*pahr*-agus. Lindy's got a carton of something frozen. "She just thinks she's better than us."

"Your so-called speech was batcrap, lady," Warren says, tenderly picking out notes.

"She thinks she's this big deal," Lindy says. She fishes out a piece of frozen French toast that she starts eating with genuine frost on it right from the carton.

"Dr. Madsen thought it was a great speech, everybody did."

"The asshole, he wasn't even there," Lindy says. On the carton she's holding is a shiny couple with a candle between them and French toast on a silver platter with a bright red jewel of jelly.

"God!" I say. "You guys are too much. It wasn't just about vegetables, my speech."

"We sat through it once, your so-called speech, okay? So why don't you go pester somebody else for a change," Warren says. He's adjusting the frets or thumbscrews or whatever you call them and listening.

"Look, what did I say? What did I do? Let's talk about it, we have to be open."

"We don't have to anything, boss lady," Warren says.

"And you can't make us," Lindy says. "She's a trip and a half, isn't she, Warren? With her cut meds and her gonna get a job and her big speeches and her asshole Statue of Liberty."

"Listen, it was me that saved the day, the house, I mean."

"Tiffani," Warren says, "do C House a favor and get lost." He starts a song, Iacocca is a joka . . . and Lindy thuds back on the bed laughing.

I go up to my room, the elation bled out of me, replaced by this gnawing rodent of anxiety. Warren and Lindy are pissed with me.

I haven't kept my contract with Dr. Madsen to tell him everything and my room is an unbelievable pile of crud. Old coffee mugs with murky stuff on the bottoms, ex–cigarette packages, candy wrappers, dirty bras, *McCalls,* a stick of Aspergum, a toothbrush I use to clean my shoes, which is never, my library card. Yikes! My library card! Some applications I picked up way back when God was a baby— Quik Stop, Kinney's shoes, International House of Pancakes. An *F.P.* clipping.

The state of Hawaii 25 years ago imported mongooses to reduce the rat population. However, the Bureau of Land Management did not stop to consider the fact that mongooses are diurnal, whereas rats are nocturnal. Thus, Hawaii now has a double extermination problem. Federal funding is being sought.

Why do they hate me? What have I personally done to them? I suppose if you're a rat and you think another rat is turning into a mongoose, that's good enough reason. Also possibly it wasn't too swift to quote Dr. Madsen. Used to be C House versus the neighbors, now it's C House versus me. Me—captain of the rescue team, photojournalist, committee woman.

I finally find the Contra Costa *Times.* Sunday. Well, that's only three days old. I open to the Help Wanted. Unfortunately they're there all right. I read the rest of the paper first right down to the bowling scores and who dieds. You need to sneak up on classifieds, get your reading skills going. Let's be honest, I just am not too crazy about the job hunt scene. It's basically degrading, plus I don't have a resumé, having never resumed anything.

I pick out seven job possibles. You have to target your opportunities and be realistic, quote unquote. Three fast foods, two shoe stores, a car wash, a clerk, shipping, only that probably takes a lot of concentration. Grunt work, all of it. I cut out the ads with my nail scissors, which produces an interesting scalloped effect. I sharpen my pencil with this dumb little plastic pencil sharpener, clear amber like Paula's glycerine soap. It bites off the point. I toss it across the room and look for another pencil. No dice. No pencil either.

I yawn, time for a break. I manage to find two cigarettes and a stray match, which I strike with my thumb nail. I flop down on the bed with my abalone ashtray on my stomach. I settle back, holding the smoke in my lungs for a while. Would I rather make pizza? Smell feet? Wash cars? Or clerk, shipping? It's complicated, all the options, never mind the part-time low-stress garbage. Dr. Madsen says I have choices, I make decisions. I decide to double up my pillow under my head. I lie there thinking and not thinking. Just letting go.

When I wake up, I see a black line of ash biting through the paper *Canadian Dollar Weakens*. It goes on to *Stanford Over Cal? The Odds,* systematically eating along the edge, a dark brown, and then black. When it gets to Foods—*Easy Amaretto Brownies*—it sends up a spit of actual flame. I watch, I really concentrate on the flame, which is bright, incandescent, with a blue tip. It seems to be coming from what fell through the hole in the abalone ashtray. It devours The World Today—*Ten Year Old Builds Model Electric Chair* (I should really clip that but I don't see the scissors any more). Flames eat along the blanket edge. I whip the bedding off, roll it in a ball. (You need to smother a fire.) Sparks land in the waste basket, which was formerly a gallon container from Thirty-One Flavors. Flavor of the month: Smoked Camelot. I begin to cough.

I consider carefully. If I have dimes, which is doubtful, and could find them, which would be unprecedented, I could call the fire department. But we're supposed to keep a low profile according to Miriam Myers and fire trucks don't. I beat the waste basket with my pillow, which promptly catches fire. I should really sue, they have an obligation to make these mothers flame retardant. I open the window. Wrong move. A gust of wind shoots flame at the curtain. Window sill paint begins to blister like the black plague. A dead fly sizzles.

"Help! Fire!" I scream. I'm not usually a screamer.

Lindy is the first one to show up. In fact she's the only one who shows up. Warren's at a Who Concert. "You maniac," she says, "look what you've gone and done!"

We both grab for the fire extinguisher in the hall, do a brief tug-o-war, end by each holding an end. We can't figure out how it works. *To operate, hold upright, pull pin*—what pin? what PIN?—*squeeze lever, direct at base of*—I let go. The smoke, it's too thick, I can't see any more, can't breathe. I stumble out into the hall. "Water!" I sob, choking.

Suddenly Lindy is spraying guck all over Christ's creation, way more than is necessary, obviously having herself a barrel of fun, like a kid with a can of Reddiwip. The flames are toning down. "That's enough, Lindy, cut it out! You're wrecking my stuff!"

The house is so full of smoke we have to go out back. My face is smudged, my hair is singed on the ends. I'm a chimney sweep, a Welsh coal miner, a charcoal calamity. I want to go back in and look for my cigarettes. "Oh no you don't!" Lindy says as though my physical presence could ignite anything. I've caused enough disaster, we could all have died, she says triumphantly.

Geoffrey stumbles out gasping—we forgot about him. We probably should give him mouth-to-mouth resuscitation, or is that only if you drown? Anyway neither of us is willing to put their mouth on Geoffrey's, who never brushes his teeth. Gradually his color starts to come back and with it the puzzled look so we know he's okay. Geoffrey is sprawled on the crab grass near the raccoon graves. I put the Wipe Your Feet Stupid mat under his head and leave him there to revive when and if he cares to, which is known in psychiatric circles as giving permission.

"Unbelievable," Lindy is saying as though there is anybody besides me to listen. "Unbefuckinglievable." (That's what Warren does, slides *fucking* in where you don't expect it. She's picked up his speech patterns. What an ass kisser!) "This chick, she's a law unto herself, I mean, she's like lethal. . . ."

"Sorry," I say. I find a couple of spent matches there in the grass which I arrange in a T for Tiffani.

"Sorry!" she says a long time later like it's a new word arisen from the ashes, something she was waiting for.

"See, it was that abalone shell. It had holes. We shouldn't use them for ashtrays."

"That's right, blame it on the fish."

Eventually she gets up and goes back in. I wait a while, long enough for dignity, before I trail along.

I am shivering. "Hey, Lindy girl," I say (better to unruffle her feathers), "could we like shut some windows? It's cold."

"You want us to asphyxiate? Is that what you want?"

"Look, haven't you ever heard the word accident? These things happen every day of the week, otherwise we wouldn't have fire departments or fire extinguishers. They were invented for your ordinary run-of-the-mill individual who has an occasional minor conflagration."

Lindy doesn't deal well with simple truths. It's a function of her illness. She slams the door to her room. I'm concerned for her, being freaked out like that. Now she'll eat everything in sight. Well, it's her life. Nothing I can do. Maybe I should go out and get her the Turkish Delight, it would be a nice gesture, smooth things over. But I don't have the energy.

My room is a new low in disgustingness. A new high. Even the blankets have this slippery foam goop. I should start cleaning up. I don't.

The house has an ominous stillness to it. There's a sliver of fear in me, hard to pinpoint, like an itch. Eventually—minutes, hours, years later—I hear people talking in low secret CIA tones, the way M and D close the bedroom door in the middle of the day and you know they're in there talking about you, they're too old to be doing anything else.

I open the door cautiously but I can't make out anything. I close it. I open it again.

People come trooping up the stairs. Miriam Myers (where did she come from?) is at the door of my room, trailed by Warren, Lindy, and Geoffrey.

"We've come to talk to you," Lindy says, huffing. "To tell you something," she says, looking at Miriam Myers.

"Oh hi, Miriam," I say, "did she tell you how Dr. Madsen cut my meds?"

"She knows, it doesn't make any difference," Lindy says.

"Tiffani—" Miriam Myers says. She sighs, looking at the mess, one hand on an official looking hip.

"Okay, okay, I'll get to it. I'll clean it up, give me a break, okay? It looks worse than it is." For some reason I feel like I should just keep talking. "It's still pretty cold, maybe we should like think about turning the heat on for a while, you know, turn the thermostat up to 75, say. Just for a little bit, till it warms up." And then I can't think of anything more. I'm drained.

"Aren't you going to tell her?" Lindy says.

"The group," Miriam Myers says, "has voted unanimously that you have to leave."

Miriam Myers is wearing her gray Minnetonka moccasins. Leave? Me? They have red and white and green beads in the shape of a tepee. Me who saved the day for us, for them? Me? I stare at them, at their familiar unfamiliar faces. Vision blurs and they elide, the bland buttressed face of democracy in action. Your poor, your tempest tossed, your huddled masses Iacocca wanted my help with.

"Okay," I say about ten hours later. "Sure. That's fine with me."

"You've been smoking in the bedroom again, which is strictly against the rules. Today just underscores the problem. You've been told time and time again."

What time is time again? I look at my watch. Apparently it's 3:20 if daylight saving hasn't got in there.

Everybody smokes in their rooms, Miriam Myers, and you know it, I could easily have said. Just because it was me that happened to get a little fire started. Everybody smokes just like nobody gets out of the house every day from 9 to 3 the way they're supposed to to do something productive, that's a rule too.

"We just get through the hurdle of the hearing by the skin of our teeth, and now this."

They are all looking at me like I'm This. Unanimous. Lindy, Warren, Geoffrey, Miriam Myers. Six unblinking eyes, two blinking rapidly, Geoffrey's. Stare stare stare blink. On the blink. I start to smile, don't.

What is this, a Salem witch trial? Their faces are hard, set solid, except Geoffrey, who is along for the ride. "What is this, a Salem witch trial?" I say. Maybe I even said it before.

"No," Miriam Myers says, "nothing like that, but you're a danger to the house and the neighborhood and yourself. You're an unacceptable risk. You've had fair warning. I'm sorry to have to say it, but that's it."

"Yah, that's it," Lindy says.

"All right," I say finally, speaking in a measured tone. "It's now the 31st, isn't it the 31st? Halloween? I'll be out by Thanksgiving" (couldn't do that number again anyway).

"No, you have to go *now*," Lindy says. "Doesn't she, Miriam?"

"Yes, it's been decided, Tiffani," Miriam Myers says. "We think it best for all concerned that you leave at once, that's the will of the group. I'll be getting in touch with your family in the next twenty-four hours. For tonight you can call Emergency Housing."

"I wouldn't be able to sleep right," Lindy says, "not if she was here." She's running her fat thumb along the stitching of my straw purse they brought me from Rio.

"Cut that out!" I yell at her. She does.

"I'm writing the EH number down for you here," Miriam Myers says. "Occasionally they can even book a client into Serendipity House on an ad hoc basis." She holds out a pink While You Were Out piece of paper. When I don't take it, she puts it on the desk under the iron which isn't supposed to be in the individual rooms.

I start gathering up my stuff, pitching it into a mound in the center of my rug, trying to hit the biggest burn hole, ignoring them all. Tampax, Christ of the Andes, bull's-eye. Earphones. Paula's wedding napkins. I come to Warren's book of double crostics which he can't do, he'll never be able to get even one without me, and I skitter it across the floor at him. Library books—date due, Aug. 18, yikes. Plastic bag of dimes, whaddaya know? The Macchu Picchu pictures, the real Macchu Picchu—I hurl them at Lindy—"For your mom so she can see how she looks on a burro. She can send me the money for the prints." Where? Send it where?

"We were unanimous," Lindy says. "Everybody."

"Get outta here."

One at a time they leave. I don't look up. I also don't have a suitcase. The folks took back their dumb brown one so they could go to Zihuatenejo in April. It might have been March. I find a macramé belt I made in O.T., put it on. My Transit Card. A key to something, but what?

Warren reappears with one of the plastic trash bags from the kitchen. (Good I voted for the large size.)

"Listen, I'm sorry," he says. He tries to put a hand on my shoulder, but I duck, leaving his hand in space along with the rest of him. "Don't you touch me!" You voted, one, two, three, out goes she. "Just don't bother coming on to me," I say. "You wimp. Carla knew you were one too."

I throw my clothes in helter skelter, some with the hangers still attached. I take the Polaroid, which was under my patchwork bed sack, Carla in her urn, my *F.P.* folder. I can't find the Nikon. I make my way downstairs, lopsided, blinded by tears. Into the kitchen, where I clean my shelf out in one swat.

Cathouse is by the front door. "Come on Shithouse," I say softly so only he can hear. That's in case he doesn't come. "Come on, fatso." He looks out, cautious, switching his stupid tail. We'll take care of each other. Cat, I am willing you to come with me. It will serve Geoffrey right. But he tucks his paws under him, pretends he doesn't have feet to come with. "You're so fucked up," I say. He closes his eyes, immune to insult, above the storm. I let the bag drag over his ears on the way out. I should have used his right name, the one he was used to.

I plunk down on the curb, rummage through my trash bag for smokes. My hand gets black from my face. My hair seems to have exploded with the heat.

Now what? I have to think out how I feel, but this is really chasing your own tail because if you are thinking out how you feel, how can you feel? I guess Siamese twins could do it, but they're an

exception. Anyway what I *think* I feel is a lot of things kluged together. Anger, shame, some I-blew-it-againness, all the stuff you'd
expect. And I won't say relief, no, not relief, but maybe a sense of
inevitability. It's time for me to get my ass in gear. At least try.
Some people walk out of things, I get thrown out. Well, there are
different operating styles. I'm more like Iacocca in that regard. I
didn't kiss Miriam Myers' Minnetonkas or beg that sack of guts
Lindy to forgive me. I have my pride, which for quite a while there
I didn't have. And, hey, let's not kid ourselves, groveling plain
wouldn't have worked. I am maybe becoming a tad realistic. And
realistically my current problem is I'm sitting on the curb smoking
and the son of man (that's me) hath nowhere to lay her sooty little
head this nippy Halloween.

There's an elderly couple at the bus stop across the street sitting
on a green bench. The man takes off the woman's glasses, puts them
on the seat, and squeezes drops into her eyes from a little plastic
bottle he has in his pocket. She keeps her head back for a few seconds
so they won't fall out. The drops, not the eyes. He pockets the little
bottle, looks at his watch. They have obviously been through this
particular routine many times.

Who will put drops in me when I am old? Who? Who will care?
For a moment I bother to hate that couple across the street. I put
all my energy, which is about a billionth of an erg, into bad vibing
them. The pain that passeth understanding be with you now and
forever more. Instead the Number 20 chugs right up and they totter
on not knowing hate waves are coming at them from across the
street. All I have over them is years. Years for what? Years with
whom? I pick up a stray dragon's tooth from the sidewalk and put
it in my mouth without thinking.

Gotta have a plan, man. A man a plan a canal Panama. I seem
not to know if I'm coming or going. I'm a living palindrome.

Okay, let's try Barney's. I wipe olive green snot from my nose
before I go in so I will be kempt. Once Barney even held a Kleenex
for me. Blow, he said. I liked that. I tried sniffling noticeably a

few times subsequently but he never did it again. I told Dr. Madsen about him holding the Kleenex. I don't know why he did that, I said. Neither do I, Dr. Madsen said.

Maybe Barney will let me sleep in the kitchen if I bus the tables for him. Barney's not there though. Just Georgina, his wife, the she-wolf who signed the petition. People in a booth are singing Happy Birthday, dear Me-*lin*-da.

"Well, you look like you lost your last friend."

I never had a first one, I think but don't say.

"Barney around?"

"You don't see him, do you? He's too big to miss."

She starts grinding coffee beans, which drowns out all communication, not that any was present to start with.

" 'Kay if I have me a cup of java?" I say when the little beans quit hopping around.

"Okay if you have the sixty cents."

I exhale. "Thursday I'll have my check."

"Well, this is Tuesday."

"If it's Tuesday, it must be Barney's," I say jovially.

"I'm kind of busy, Tiff-knee," she says, "so if you'll excuse me . . ." Dot dot dot.

A dollop of balloons—pastels, plus one silver one that resembles a canteen, float over the top of the Happy Birthday booth. One pops and the birthday people go "aaaaah." Birthday girl Melinda has punk hair, a paved pink strip on top and checkerboard on the cropped sides, and a rhinestone in her right nostril. Georgina doesn't seem to object to her. I guess in her view there's customers and there's paying customers. Piss on her fine distinctions.

Georgina turns to put an almond croissant in the microwave and I take a handful of change from the TIPS mug. On beyond blackmail. New game—TipRip. Probably akin to defrauding an innkeeper, which Carla used to get picked up for, but this is a crisis.

I go call Crisis from the Shell Station. (I wouldn't think of calling EH or anything else Miriam Myers suggested.) What I'm hoping,

I am hoping that Brad will answer. He knows me and according to Warren he is often on nox, which is Wooky for night shift. Fat chance. If fat chance means no way, shouldn't slim chance mean for sure? It doesn't though. The world just pretends to be logical. I realize someone has been saying Crisis Center, Crisis Center for a while. It isn't Brad.

I tell my sad story. Crisis is sympathetic, but they cannot keep people unless they are a danger to themselves or others or too gravely disabled to feed and clothe themselves and you, Tiffani, happily don't fall into either category. Am I the one who is happy I don't fall into those categories or is Crisis? Or is *happily* just one of those miscellaneous expletives that should be deleted? Crisis says what I should do, I should call Emergency Housing and ask for Mary Jamison, she's the person to talk to. I start to explain why I can't possibly call Emergency Housing, but to no avail. I'm beginning to think avail is one of those things there's never any of.

Well okay, finally I go ahead and call EH. I think I was really trying to call another number, but as long as they answer, I ask for Mary Jamison. It's her day off. I have reached Karin Nichols, perhaps she can be of help. Perhaps. I give her the skinny on my plight. She is real sorry—that's really rough but really all their beds that the county has contracted for in both Serendipity and Progresso Lodge are currently full, mainly with battered women, it must be the full moon. Call back tomorrow if I still have a problem. They have a high turnover, she assures me. (They say you can't go home again, but obviously you can if you don't mind another walloping.)

Speaking of going home again, I line up my remaining dimes on the ledge in the Shell station phone booth. Okay. I don't want to do it, but finally I have no choice. It's beginning to get cold and I left my sweater in my room, my ex room, Carla's ex room. C House has a high turnover too. Maybe there's something the matter with that room. I ring up the folks. D answers on the first jingle.

"Hi, it's me. You must of been right there."

"You better believe it," he says.

"Can I speak to M?"

No I can't speak to her. She's gone to the hospital with Paula. He was hoping I was the hospital calling. Paula's water broke right after Ted Koppel and they expect the baby before morning, she's got everybody on pins and needles, the whole town's rooting for her. The next time I call I should ask for Grandpa.

"Listen, I need to come on over, okay?"

No, not okay, not now. There's too much going on. He says I sound like I have a sniffle. He'll let me know the minute it comes and then if I don't have a sniffle. . . . "I don't mind being a grandfather, but who wants to go to bed with a grandmother?" he says.

"That's so gross," I say. "You might try rooting for me some year or other—"

"I've got to cut out on you, Tiffani, there's some goblins at the door."

I hang up. Maybe he does first. I don't know. What I do know is it's 5:10 and half dark and not funny and my father's a prick. I cry a little thinking about my line—you might try rooting for me. I say it different ways. You might try rooting for *me*. You might *try* rooting for me. It's got a fair amount of tragic dignity to it.

Back to business. How now, brown cow? I call Dr. Madsen. I get the medical exchange. Tiffani? I call often enough that they know my voice. Dr. Madsen's not on call this evening. Dr. Miller is subbing. Dr. Miller! That's Lindy's shrink. "Dr. Miller has crappy patients," I say. Medical exchange is quiet, digesting this information, maybe even putting it on his card. Dr. Miller will call me back, medical exchange says eventually. He can't, nobody can, I don't have a phone. Pause. Well, then, give us a number where you can be reached. I don't have a number! Medical exchange refuses to understand. And I wouldn't talk to Dr. Miller anyway (unless it was to set him straight about Lindy). I realize I am beginning to sound whiny, desperate, tearful. What I need is to talk to Dr. Madsen. Tomorrow morning 8:30 he'll be in his office. I slam down the receiver. A lot of good that does me, 8:30 tomorrow or slamming down the phone for all of that. There's a cloud layer over Mt. Diablo.

I call my case manager, Mort Duggan. He's left already or not at his desk or never was there, I forget what they said. Call tomorrow. I call back and ask for Doug Singer—I wish I'd thought to get transferred to him and saved myself 20 cents—but he's in Sacramento to lobby against AB1855, which would fund the counties with block grants.

For some reason those dimes come back, maybe because God knew I didn't reach my party, never mind Ma Bell or Pac Tel or whatever the hell.

After some thought I use my gift-of-God dimes to call the Suicide Prevention hotline. I succinctly explain my problem at some length. Am I thinking of committing suicide? the voice on the other end interrupts. Her name is Ruth, she says. No, definitely not. I just told you all the places I've been calling. That's great, Ruth says, but I sense I've just skidded off the lethality scale and she is no longer really interested in my case. I know the system, I know it cold. I just want everybody to understand that, I've been around.

I should call Emergency Housing, Ruth says. She will give me the number, I should hang on for a sec. I already have, I told you, I tell her. She gives me the number anyway, they're very good over there. Here it is, she says, gotta pencil? No, I say, that's part of the problem.

I hang up. I'm out of gas. Also dimes. I have networked and there was no net. The last dimes didn't come back. God seems to have given up on me. Maybe He noticed I didn't keep my promise to not smoke more than two packs a day if He did whatever it was I wanted Him to, I forget just what at the moment. I was smoking filters though and that should be worth something to Him if the shepherd cares for His flock. I recheck the coin return to see if He is persuaded by the argument. Nope. Have it Your way. I am now an atheist.

The street lights come on. Maybe I can just stay in the phone booth. People in glass houses sleep standing up. I don't care, I'm not proud.

A man is tapping on the glass. He is interested in me. I smile. It's destiny. No, it's the phone. He is holding an envelope with numbers on it. Through? He's probably a hit man. This is ridiculous. I could be mugged, molested, stabbed, strangled, raped, robbed, anythinged. Or maybe nobody'd bother. That thought really depresses me. I start sobbing.

I walk down our street, their street. The night is turning into Dungeons and Dragons. People in costumes are going into Miss Clausen's house, I mean the new young couple's house, the Hibbards.

I go up to C House's back door, it just kind of happens.

Lindy comes flying.

"You can't come in."

"I'm not, I just want my sweater."

"You wait on the porch. I'll get it."

"Well, see, I need other stuff too, I think I forgot my toothbrush."

"Tough. You can't come in. We forgot to get your key."

"I don't know where it is."

"It's her and she doesn't know where her key is," Lindy says to someone in the house who doesn't bother to come forward, Warren it has to be. "You can't come in, you don't belong here any more." She closes the door and I hear her bolt it. Bolting me out into the world?

I sit in the old overstuffed davenport on the side porch. It's so overstuffed that the stuffing is coming out. I smoke a cigarette, thinking, inhaling. You don't belong here any more, you can't come in. . . . We don't want you. It's unanimous. You're out.

For smoking in my room? True, but not the real reason. Necessary but not sufficient, the trigger but not the bullet. The fact is Lindy's right, I don't belong there any more. Life has butted me in the butt, but the butt was ready. It's kind of mystical. I blow a smoke ring.

It's also stressful. I'm wiped, bone weary as M would say. Right now she's at the hospital with Paula in the Alternative Birthing Center. Patting Paula-who-can-do-no-wrong's hand. Putting cool washcloths on her forehead. While I'm now officially a street person. Tears sting my eyes. They let you play tapes at the Birthing Center during labor. You choose music like for a wedding. Paula's having Pachelbel's "Canon." Either that or "Exsultate Iubilate." With Pachelbel what I think is you'd get grand sonorous contractions and with the other thing a lot of sharp coloratura stabs. The personality of the kid you'd have'd be totally different, but Paula never stops to think things through.

Going back to me for a change. I feel centuries old, as though all the world's failure and fatigue is wrapped up in me. Pain and confusion have run through me so long there's no clear track for reason. My sweater hits the porch, tossed from an upstairs window by an unseen hand. It lands where the raccoons died. I decide to leave it there. It was partly a ploy anyway, the sweater, to see if I could get them to the bargaining table.

Fierce fluorescent masks skim by, jaywalking trick or treaters, UNICEF cups—or maybe it's Muscular Dystrophy—jangling. Flashlight parents in the shadows, watching, checking apples for razor blades, Hershey bars for cyanide, keeping a vigil. But there's nobody for me, nobody.

"Trick or treat!" a two-foot Superman says.

"Get lost," I say. "You're not Superman, you're just a squirrelly little punk, take a hike," but he's racing on—"Wait for me!" Not even reality darkens his spirit.

Well, speaking of reality and all that jazz, there's no point in me sitting here waiting for Godot or the Butler Brothers limo. If Lindy dies, which I hope is soon, or Warren or Geoffrey or Miriam Myers, I'd dance at the funeral. The ritual dance of fire, ha ha. I pick up my bag, head off toward I'm not sure where.

People in costumes are piling out of cars, going into the Hibbards. A dude in what looks like a shirt of Monopoly money fits a pair of stilts under his armpits and clunks past me.

"Hey, Bag Lady, trick or treat," he says, breathing gin and tonicly.

The woman with him inspects me briefly. She has on a long gold satin dress. "I like your get-up," she says. "Like how'd you ever get your hair to do that way?"

"It was easy," I say grimly.

"I'm the Deficit," the guy says, "that's why I'm way up here, and she's the Gold Bug, get it?"

They are going up the steps. They turn and wait for me. We are going up the steps. I remember the fan-shaped trellis. The door is ajar. The Deficit pokes it open with a stilt. I'm swept in, stunned by the sudden light and a dillion decibels of Donna Summer.

The party is wall-to-wall people including a giant tube of Crest toothpaste, a belly dancer with a ripe cherry tomato taped to her navel, a chick with a black satin flapper dress and glass beads, Dracula, a can-can girl, a shower stall, a gorilla, a skeleton with a space helmet and NASA on its chest, four hirsute legs in a horse suit, two witches, assorted pumpkin heads, and an orange rabbit. It seems to be a real cross section of the population, which can still happen in a democracy such as ours.

There's a wicker bar with a keg of beer and a steaming punch bowl and a big buffet on the round oak table, which having leaves in it is no longer round.

I fill an orange paper plate with guacamole, rare roast beef, an onion roll, frittata—what's this? red pepper dip with endive, Paula does that too—and enough Brie to constipate the whole cast of "Dynasty." I reject something called glüg in favor of a diet Coke and wait patiently for the skeleton to move on so I can reach the chocolate decadence.

He puts an arm around me, the NASA sign knocking one of the frittata squares off my plate. Good I took two. "Hello my little bagette, have we not met somewhere in the distant reaches of the universe?" Bourbon fumes are coming from the grille of his visor.

"Possibly at Barney's—" I start to say.

Rabbit plops a licorice jelly bean in my mouth. He has two-foot plush-lined ears. "Anybody know how the market did today?"

"Yah," I say. "They sold a lot of cheese."

Toothpaste laughs. "They sold a lotta shit too, believe me. The high tech stuff took a real bath." He's fixing himself steak tartar on pumpernickel, building very carefully, bread, meat, capers, lemon, onion. He pauses to look me over, jabs me in the ribs. "L'il ol' bag lady, haven't I seen you shufflin' round the Tenderloin?"

People who are in hearshot laugh, so I do too, but I don't just knock myself out. I hold my plate in one hand, and tug my bag along with the other one.

"You've done it so authentic," a girl in a T-shirt that says Mothers' Cookies says respectfully. "The hair especially. Don't you love the hair! Is it a wig or what? Did they do it at Shamlocks?"

"No, I did it myself." My face is burning. At least with the smudge nobody can see. It's hot as Billy-be-damned, as D would say.

"Fantastic! But how do you ever get it back to normal?"

I think for a while. It's one of those questions that sound simple but there's a lot of assumptions buried in.

"I'll work out something."

"No way," Rabbit says, loud and sloshed. "Once a bag lady, always a bag lady. She's gonna haul that act around day and night from now till Miami comes back to the Super Bowl, and that's fuckin' never."

I look to Mothers' Cookies to defend me, but she is being nuzzled by Crest. "C'mon, baby, you're supposed to squeeze me, don't you know what you do with a tube of toothpaste?"

Ogden Hibbard, Oggie, the host, is wearing a Neptune suit (I guess it goes with the whitewater rafting truck). He starts blowing on a conch shell. It makes a melancholy sound like it's from the sad sorrowing soul of the world, all full fathom five of it. "Awright, all you Favorite Fantasies, it's time for our awards ceremony. We've got a nice little prize here, a bottle of Pouilly Fuisse—did I get it right, honey? Pooyee Fweesay? Sherrie's the French major around here—for the best costume. Entries will be judged on originality, sincerity, and aptness of thought, how's that? We'll entertain nominations from the floor."

"Over here, we've got it right here," Crest says, pointing at me, just as I am contending with a ropey piece of roast beef.

"The ba-a-a-g lady!" Rabbit says. He chants it like he's imitating a sheep. B-a-a-a-g. "Now I ask you is this original or is it original?"

There's a whole bunch of cheering, loud enough for them to hear at C House even, except of course they wouldn't know it had anything to do with me. "All in favor!" Oh God, they're going to vote! But turns out it's not even a question. I have it! Are you listening, O Camelot?

They all crowd around me. They're taking pictures, kissing me, toasting. I'm as popular as Brooke Shields. I'm loved, honored, cherished—accepted!—by the people next door and their buddies, all Rabbit's friends and relations. "Heads," Oggie says. He reaches in, in to the inner circle, hands me the wine. I'll give it to Paula and Jake for their anniversary. It's better than stale wedding cake.

"Congrats," Oggie says. "That costume is something else."

"To the Bag Lady! Long may she rave!" the skeleton says.

Suddenly I begin to get the drift, the message. I'm being venerated as the evening's Chief Impostor. They think I'm just a normal, someone like them, masquerading as a freak, an untouchable they'd detour around the solar system to avoid.

"No!" I suddenly scream. "This is crazy!"

I grab up my bag, dash out of the room.

"What the fuck's with her?" somebody says. "Belted down a few too many? Oh well."

I find the john, shut the door, lock it. My heart's flip flopping. I look at myself, my face, my hair, my eyes, in the mirror rimmed with shells. Christ! I start washing up with some black soap shaped like a mint. Face, neck, hands, arms. I scrub till my skin turns red in spots and little clay-colored bits slough off.

I pick up a brush, genuine boar's head bristles, made in England. But it won't go through my jungle of hair. I'm crying in frustration, shit shit shit. I hold my head under the tap as best I can, glop on some shampoo from a bottle that looks like it should hold vinegar but says it's avocado. I squint my eyes against the soap.

I find a razor in the medicine cabinet and I whittle off tangles of hair till it's short and docile and kind of curls up. Razors really work with curly hair. Wet it looks dark, black almost. The hair that fell on the floor makes a variety of marks, which I pause to consider. Is it a code? A message to me? Someone knocks timidly, tries the door, goes away. All I see is apostrophes and carets, that's all I can make out, no message.

I rummage in my bag, come up with my gray jumper. No. The pocket's coming loose. My senior no-prom dress, the one I never wore? M insisted we get one, in case, before they were all picked over. I've always loved that dress. Silky Qiana. Claret to magenta depending on the light. Wine obi belt, off the shoulders, full graceful skirt. We got it in the spring. Before the Fall. I smile. M gasped at the price. She's only young once, Miss Beecham at Saks said. But in a way I never was. In another way I always was. It's sinfully expensive, M said to D. Our eyes were bright and shining and all he said was he wanted to see it on. They sat there side by pudgy side on the old davenport with pencils and pennies under the cushions, smiling, proud of what they had produced—turn around— while I twirled and bowed and conjured futures.

It still fits. Four hooks and eyes. I remember now, the side placket, don't yank, Miss Beecham said. You have to treat these new materials with respect.

Next—teeth. I have a choice, a blue brush or a pink one. The blue one's probably his. I use it. I've never used a man's toothbrush. It's very sexual.

I blot my lips dry on a finger towel with an orange pumpkin. I check the lip gloss in the Lucite holder. Percussion red, too bright. Ruby Grenadine—I slash it on my hand. Not quite. Frosted Nightshade. That's it.

Then blusher, a little color. And some eye shadow. She's got a dozen tubes, more than Carla even. What I need is an accent, something that doesn't barricade the eyes, that visibilizes them. Cappuccino Brown. Well all right!

The woman in the mirror is one I've never seen before. Someone you might wonder about, want to get to know even. Whimsical, patrician, a princess? The eyes really come out at you, and the full eyebrows, the classy portrait shoulders. The hair is beginning to fluff as it dries. Give it time, it's all a question of time.

From the john window there's C House, which I'm seeing like I'm my own next door neighbor. Silent now, settled into its tattered glooms, full of people named Warren and Lindy and Geoffrey. Who are they? Names from another country passed through a thousand thousand light years ago on my journey to wherever.

They're there and I'm here, with the people next door. The thought that crosses my mind is one of my life's scariest. If I am now one of the people next door, do I really want C House there? Maybe that's your basic paranoia or maybe all of a sudden I'm thinking normal. Whichever way it is, you don't win any points with yourself. It's like there's a streak of Bernadette Ryan in me. But then there's a streak of me in her. Right? Wrong? I don't know.

I put the bath mat on the edge of the tub and sit down. I empty my bag, take out my pills, nail scissors, Carla's urn, my *F.P.* chronicle, the Polaroid. And the card, Ray Pruitt, County Rehab. Dump it? Keep it? Keep it. I jam the rest of the stuff back into the trash bag, which is a deep dull army green, and shove it into the clothes hamper on top of Oggie's shirts. God, I never want to see another bag—ever. Whenever ever is.

Carla, I apologize for what I'm going to do, but I can't be your disciple any more. You were you and I've got to be me and hope the world doesn't run me over too.

I pry open the urn with the edge of a tortoise shell shoehorn, lift the oak toilet seat, which has a nice smooth grain to it, I might get me one someday. Shit, forget the frigging toilet seat. Concentrate! Dump! The ash floats. The cremains. A few piece of bone collide and sink with a little clicking adios.

Listen, Carla, I know this isn't exactly getting scattered at sea, but they've got good water pressure and you should make it to San Pablo Bay with a little luck, okay? And I promise when I get my act together, I'll find Dorie. We'll go to the zoo, the new primate center, we'll do things. I'll pay her library fines—if I have any loot.

I flush twice, not everything goes down the first time. I think about Paula's water breaking and the kid she's having, a wet shrimpy thing they'll expect me to aunt. Tyrannized by genes, born with everything it'll ever have. Paula's neck? Jake's broad shoulders? My neighborliness? Maybe even my nuttiness—the black pearl. But no matter what happens, how it turns out, there'll be some valid moments.

I get up, bracing myself with the hand rail that must have been installed for Miss Clausen, open the door a crack. Ready? I say to the haughty scared girl-woman.

Music assaults me—"Daydream Believer," the Monkees—bright swirling light, laughter. Are they laughing at me? No. They don't even know I'm there. They're laughing because they're drunk, stoned, young, happy, normal jerks at a party. Which is okay.

The belly dancer is boogeying or bellying on the oak table, which they've cleared. (I wish I'd got around to the duck salad and the tabbouleh—it was on the other side.) Mothers' Cookies is out cold on the futon, an arm dangling, which people step over. Crest is cresting in the corner with a lady pumpkin.

I'm at the head of the stairs, ready to be presented to society, storm the barricades. Or quit before I start, make a dash for it, sneak out the back way.

Too late.

Rabbit looks up. "You know—there's people here I haven't even seen before. Who's *that?*"

I wait for somebody to tell me, to say, but nobody does. "Mary Alice," I say softly.

"Well, get your ass on down here, Mary Alice, and join the party."

He tries to make it sound easy, but it's a long way to where it's at. Through the great woods. I feel dizzy. Stop the world, I want to get on. Or do I? "Whatza matter, beautiful? We too far out for you?" Oggie says. We'll have to see, we'll just have to wait and see. It all depends.